The
Things
We
Left
Unsaid

Emma Kennedy is a bestselling author, TV writer, actress and presenter. She has written nine books including her bestselling memoirs, *The Tent the Bucket and Me* and *I Left My Tent in San Francisco*. She wrote the Wilma Tenderfoot series for children and has also adapted *The Tent the Bucket and Me* for the BBC, renamed *The Kennedys*. *The Things We Left Unsaid* is Emma's debut adult novel.

As an actress Emma has appeared in many award-winning comedies including *Goodness Gracious Me*, *People Like Us* and *Miranda*. Emma won *Celebrity Masterchef* in 2012 and is a Guinness World Record holder.

Emma lives in Surrey with her wife and their dogs, and is hard at work on her next novel. You can follow her on Twitter @EmmaKennedy.

Praise for The Things We Left Unsaid

'A gorgeous, rich treat.' Jane Fallon

'Warm, intriguing, brimming with tenderness... A joyous book.' Ruth Jones

'This book is incredibly special... I cared so deeply for all of the characters.' Gaby Roslin

'Involving and emotional.' Janet Ellis

Emma Kennedy

The Things We Left *Unsaid*

arrow books

1 3 5 7 9 10 8 6 4 2

Arrow Books
20 Vauxhall Bridge Road
London SW1V 2SA

Arrow Books is part of the Penguin Random House group of companies
whose addresses can be found at global.penguinrandomhouse.com

Penguin
Random House
UK

First published by Century in 2019
First published in paperback by Arrow Books in 2020

www.penguin.co.uk

A CIP catalogue record for this book is available from the British Library

ISBN 9781787463288

Typeset in 10.32 pt/13.38 pt Palatino LT Std
by Integra Software Services Pvt. Ltd, Pondicherry

Printed and bound in Great Britain by Clays Ltd, Elcograf S.p.A.

Penguin Random House is committed to a
sustainable future for our business, our readers
and our planet. This book is made from Forest
Stewardship Council® certified paper.

For Aunty Ann and Uncle John

PART ONE

'Nothing is ever really lost to us,
as long as we remember it.'

L. M. Montgomery

Chapter One

Then

September 1964

Eleanor was packing. She had a ticket for the 9.42 to Paddington and she couldn't be late.

'Do you think you'll have sexual intercourse?' Agnes was lying belly down on the bed, behind Eleanor's suitcase. Her arms were stretched out above her head, her face pressed into the eiderdown. She said the words as if she'd only just learned them.

'Don't be coarse, Agnes.' Eleanor turned and looked at a pile of jumpers. She wasn't sure how many to take.

'I'm not being coarse. I'm thinking about all the things that might ruin you, like being mauled by a bear or being crushed by falling masonry or having sexual intercourse.'

Eleanor frowned. 'You have the most vivid imagination of anyone I know. Mauled by a bear?'

'Exit, chased by bear. That's Shakespeare. So, you know, you *might*,' said Agnes, turning her face sideways 'Do you think by the time you come back I'll be as tall as this bed?'

Eleanor glanced down at her little sister, stretched out to her limits. 'Only if you grow at least two feet in the next nine weeks, which is unlikely.'

Agnes gave a small huff and pushed herself up. 'It's so frustrating. As soon as I'm as tall as you I can wear all your clothes.'

'No, you cannot. And when I'm not here, don't try.' Eleanor picked up a heap of socks from a washing basket and began to sort them into pairs.

Agnes dangled her legs off the edge of the bed and peered into Eleanor's suitcase. 'Are you sure you're taking enough? You're going to be gone for ages.'

'I don't know. But I've only got one suitcase. And I've got to fit books in as well. I'll take two of everything. Except for socks and knickers. I'll take seven pairs of those.'

'Are you going to miss me?' Agnes looked up, hopeful.

'Not in the least.'

Agnes's face fell. 'That's disappointing. I think I shall miss you terribly.'

'You're not supposed to tell me that. Sisters are supposed to roll through life quietly resenting each other.' Eleanor pressed a powder-blue jumper down into the suitcase.

Agnes pushed herself off the bed and wandered over to the bookshelves in the corner of the room. 'Can I have your encyclopedia?' she asked, fingering the spine.

'You can borrow it. Pass me those books on the top shelf. The Sylvia Plath, the John Fowles, *To Kill a Mockingbird* and' – she peered towards the shelves, then glanced back into her suitcase – 'anything else that's thin.'

Agnes gathered up the books carefully and carried them back to the bed. 'I think you will miss me,' she said, sitting down and swinging her legs. 'I think you're going to get to London and wish I was there. Unless you're planning sexual intercourse, in which case you won't.'

Eleanor frowned. 'You're obsessed, Agnes. You're only thirteen. You're supposed to be riding around on a bike, pretending it's a pony. Besides, I haven't even got a boyfriend. I rather think that comes first, don't you?'

'Eleanor!' a voice shouted up from downstairs. It was their mother. 'Are you packed?'

'Almost!' Eleanor threw the socks into the side of the suitcase and squished them down.

'It's so strange you're leaving,' said Agnes, screwing her nose up. 'It's almost as if I don't quite believe it. You know Daddy cried?'

'He did not,' said Eleanor, placing the books on top of the packed clothes. 'You're making that up.'

'I am not. I saw him getting into his car and his face was entirely wet. You're his favourite, you know. He'll be furious he's left with me.'

'Nonsense,' replied Eleanor, pressing down on the suitcase. 'He hasn't got a favourite. In fact, I'm not entirely sure he likes either of us. Not really. Here, lend a hand. Press down on that side so I can get this shut.'

'I think I'll only have one child.' Agnes pushed her full weight down on to the top of the suitcase. 'That way there can be no confusion as to who I like the best. How many children do you think you'll have?'

'Heaps of them,' replied Eleanor. 'All running around. At least five. Press down harder. I can't get this done up.'

'Don't be ridiculous.' Agnes pushed again. 'If you have five you won't remember their names. You might lose one in a department store and not notice for days.'

'It's no good. You're going to have to sit on it. I'll put it on the floor.'

Agnes leaned back and Eleanor picked up the suitcase with both arms. 'Right,' she said, placing it down, 'you sit on it.'

Agnes scrambled off the bed and sat, as heavily as she could, on the suitcase. Eleanor got down on her knees and pulled at the leather buckle. 'Almost,' she said, straining. 'Sit a bit harder.'

Agnes bore down.

'Got it.' Eleanor leaned back and blew out. 'You can get off now.'

Agnes stood and Eleanor picked up the suitcase and rested it buckle side up. She glanced at her watch. 'Just in time too. Shall we say goodbye now?' She looked at her sister.

'No, thank you,' said Agnes, clasping her hands behind her back. 'I'd rather not.'

Eleanor shook her head. 'What a peculiar child you are, Ag. I shall miss your oddness. I'll give you that.'

'I am not odd. I am interesting. And I can definitely borrow your encyclopedia?' She glanced over towards it.

Eleanor nodded. 'Yes. You can read it whenever you want.'

'Eleanor!' Another call came up the stairs. 'We're going to be late!'

'Coming!'

'I'm not going to cry,' said Agnes, sticking her chin out.

'Neither am I,' said Eleanor, dragging her suitcase out to the landing.

Agnes stood listening as her sister thumped the suitcase down the stairs. Her mother was muttering something, agitated and tense. She looked around her sister's room. It was slightly bigger than her own and had a bed that didn't creak every time you turned over.

'I'm not going to cry,' she said again, as if willing herself to believe it. 'I'm not.'

Downstairs the front door slammed shut and she could hear Eleanor dragging her suitcase up the front path. She went to the window and looked out. Her mother was getting into the car. She was frowning, the way she did when she was on the verge of feeling frantic.

'Oh no,' Agnes suddenly said. 'The beret I made for her!' She ran from the room and dashed into her own.

Eleanor cast a glance back up to her bedroom window. There was no sign of Agnes. Despite all her bravado, she felt a short pang of regret. She'd never been away from home, not even for a night. This was the house she had been born in, the pretty white cottage that sat on the hill and looked out over wide horizons. The world had always been there, right in front of her eyes, and yet here she was, standing still, unsure, a little frightened and longing for her sister to reappear.

'Eleanor,' called her mother again. 'Get a move on.'

She put a hand on the garden gate. It was time to leave.

Chapter Two

Now

Rachel stood, bag in hand, facing the single bed rammed into the corner of the room: the old iron bedstead that creaked every time you breathed, the mattress that sucked you into an inexplicable hole like a thin, narrow coffin, the springs that felt as if they might bruise your kidneys.

She let the bag slip from her hand to the floor. She'd bring the boxes up later; for now, she needed a moment, away from her mother, away from any set of eyes that might catch hers. Here she was, back in her old room, and there wasn't a single thing she could do about it.

The bed was made up, as it always was, the lighthouse for whenever she needed to come home. Her mother had never got round to upgrading it to a double. Rachel had always considered that a deliberate rudeness; now it felt prophetic. She let her hand drift across the crumpled cotton of the duvet and the faint scent of something clean and clinical drifted upwards.

She looked around. Bright yellow wallpaper, imprinted with tiny daisy chains, a charcoal sketch of Rachel as a child, drawn by her mother one autumn morning when they still got on. Rachel stared at it and thought about how life chips away at you: the disappointments, the bad decisions, the small, brooding resentments that take hold in the gaps. She had no solid memory of when it began to turn sour, still less of whether either of them really cared. They had been through so much of late, it was hard to remember if they got on or not. They were two women bound by a birth, and Eleanor had no other children to fall back on. Here was another thing her mother could be disappointed in. Add it to the list.

To the left of the portrait was a rickety bookcase that relied on a battered encyclopaedia for a leg. It was crammed with Rachel's old books: vintage children's stories that took her back to big chairs and roaring fires. A desk sat in front of the large sash window that always stuck on the way up, and on it were a pencil pot waiting in vain, a pair of cashmere socks that were still in their shop wrapping, a packet of royal baby playing cards, a small rosewood Buddha, a silver tankard she'd won at school for a painting competition and a crumpled, over-loved teddy, her beloved Mr Tumnus. He was leaning against a photo frame and, as she picked him up for a reassuring cuddle, she saw it: the smiling photo of Claude, the man who was now supposed to be her husband. Without a second thought she picked up the frame and tossed it into a wicker bin.

She noticed her old bedside table: thick oak legs and a round top that Rachel had once spent a day covering in pictures cut from magazines. There was a word for it in crafting circles. *Découpage.* The art of taking disparate things and making something new. She'd removed the varnish, sanded it down and spent hours cutting pictures from her mother's art-and-design magazines before gluing them on. Her father, Charlie, had come in and opened all her windows, letting out the scent of acrylic sealant. 'Do you want me to carry that outside for you?' he had asked, nodding towards the table. 'Air in here's like a glue factory.' She couldn't remember how she'd answered but she had a visceral memory of how she had felt: the sudden blind outrage at a parental intrusion. She'd sent him packing, backing out of the room, hands held up in defeat. 'Only trying to help,' he had said.

Rachel lifted another framed picture from the table and stared into it: black and white, taken when she was five, perhaps six. She had a mass of blonde wayward curls, a sea breeze blowing it back from her ears. She was sitting with Charlie on a rock at the edge of a cliff, Cornwall maybe, the perfect chilly image of an English summer. She had a curious expression, her eyes slightly narrowed, and she was looking off, following the direction of her father's pointed finger, one arm extended, his other arm cradling her back, keeping her safe. His corduroys, a little flared (but not enough to be fashionable), billowed out as if his ankles were flagpoles, but the one detail she loved most were his shoes. For some reason that summer, her father wore a pair of blue-and-white bowling shoes. They were entirely out of character, as too was the beard he was sporting. It was a summer of rebellion. He'd stopped shaving, as if for a dare, curious to see what would manifest itself on his chin. She ran a finger over his face.

This was her favourite picture of him.

Downstairs, a door opened. Someone had arrived, again, the third that day, to 'see how Rachel was'.

Rachel froze, listening for her mother's hushed voice. Over the last two days it had been as if Rachel had died: sombre calls from relatives, deliveries of endless boxes of cupcakes as if they were somehow imbued with the power of healing. Note to self: they're not. But Rachel hadn't died.

She'd moved back to live with her mother because she had to. She was the ghost of her former self.

Rachel let a long sigh heave itself out, put the framed picture back down on the table and turned towards the door. Soft footsteps were padding up the stairs. Rachel felt the knot in her stomach tighten another twist. Here we go again.

Two gentle raps and the door opened towards her. A head appeared, soft blue eyes hooded in an expression of empathy.

'Hello, Agnes,' said Rachel, seeing her aunt. Her mouth mustered a weak smile. She felt her shoulders relax. Agnes, she could cope with.

'My poor darling.'

Agnes approached, arms extended, and drew Rachel to her. Rachel stared over Agnes's shoulder towards a small chest of drawers against the wall, her eyes blank and lifeless.

'I can't tell you how furious I am. Boiling,' she said, pulling back and holding her by the shoulders. 'That man is an utter shit.'

Rachel let out an involuntary laugh.

'Do you know, I'm glad,' Agnes continued. 'I am. I'm glad that pond scum of a man hasn't married you. You might not think it now. I don't expect you to. But if he's capable of doing that, you're better off out of it.'

Agnes let her hands fall from Rachel's shoulders. She was younger than Rachel's mother, Eleanor, by five years, an unexpected bonus for her grandparents, who had thought all chance of having another child was gone. She was in her mid-sixties, a light, bouncing presence, wicked, mischievous, blunt. She wasn't as attractive as her elder sister: Eleanor had been blessed with high cheekbones and a heart-shaped jawline; Agnes was more solid, full of the sort of enthusiasm that's required when someone needs a personality to get on. She'd aged well.

'Have you spoken to him?' Agnes moved to the edge of the bed and sat down, her hands falling into her lap. The ancient springs groaned.

Rachel shook her head and leaned back against the wall, folding her arms. 'Not a word. Not a single word. It's like he's vanished. I wouldn't put it past him to be on our honeymoon in Turks and Caicos.'

'He wouldn't dare, surely?'

'All bets are off, Agnes. I didn't think he was capable of doing this and look where we are ...'

'I'd happily give him a piece of my mind. I'm tempted to set up shop here, just in case he turns up. Chase him off with a spade. No. A rake. More prongs.' She stopped and tilted her head as she looked up at Rachel. 'Has he given you any indication why he did it? Anything?'

Rachel gave a shrug and Agnes's eyes widened, her eyebrows raised in a look of utter incomprehension.

'No. Tom just had one text telling him he wasn't coming. That's it. That's all we've got.'

'How extraordinary. How awful. How ... *cowardly.*' She spat the word out. 'How *dare* he? Well ... I'm sorry,' she said, her voice softening. 'I really am. I think you're handling this with enormous dignity. You've been incredible. I'd have been face down in a ditch. Or permanently drunk.'

Rachel stared at her shoes. She hadn't cried yet, a small puzzling detail of the shambles thus far. She'd arrived at the venue, her cousin Johnny, Agnes's son, ready to walk her up the aisle, when Claude's best man, Tom, a thick-necked City sort, had stopped them. He was on his mobile, top lip sweating, a look of panic and failure in his eyes. 'I don't know how to tell you this,' he had muttered, and the rest was a blur.

She had stood, her bouquet limp against her thigh, while Johnny gesticulated and threw his arms in the air. Tom looked embarrassed. This wasn't what he'd signed up for. He was supposed to hand over the rings, give a speech and cop off with a bridesmaid. It had taken him six weeks to prepare that slideshow. He was fuming. Yet here he was, standing behind a Corinthian column at a minor stately home, hiding, because his best friend from university had bottled it.

The news had rippled forward like slow-moving lava. Rachel was glad she hadn't seen it: the looks of shock, the gasps, the sideways glances between couples quietly totting up what it had cost them to be there. This wasn't how it was supposed to work out. This wasn't the deal. What a waste of everyone's time.

Outside on the steps, the photographer had packed away her camera as discreetly as possible while the woman Rachel had picked the canapés with all those months ago click-clacked across the marble floor as fast as she could to tell the kitchen to stop cooking. People began to swarm around Rachel. Someone sat her down, no recollection who, but they wore a fragrance, a rather heady, sickly sweet floral assault, that Rachel knew she never wanted to smell again.

She'd looked up at one point to see Johnny prodding Tom in the chest, his face hot and red. Eleanor, her mother, stood with her fingers knitted so tight they were turning white, her mouth snapped shut in a tiny ball as she worked out what was the best thing to do. Behind her, Claude's mother had fainted. What were his parents going to say to her? She'd only met them once. Was everyone going to eat the food they'd paid for? Have a drink? Who was going to take the cake? What was she supposed to *do*?

Outside, sitting on the gravel, was the vintage silver Jaguar with red leather seats – the getaway car to the rest of their lives. Rachel stared at it, a stone statue, watching the chaos unfold around her. People kept asking her if she was all right, but she had nothing to say. She had fallen down a well; the sun had gone in for ever. Her mother had stood by her side in silence, Rachel feeling the weight of everything unsaid: the pressure to be good enough, successful, liked. It was yet another thing she had mucked up.

Agnes pressed down into the collapsing mattress with her hands. 'God,' she said as the springs twanged, 'this hasn't got any better. I can't believe this is still the bed I slept in.' Glancing sideways at the bedside table, she nodded towards the picture of Charlie. 'Can you imagine what he would have done? I'm almost glad he isn't here to see it. It would have killed him.' She caught herself and grimaced. 'Sorry. Stupid thing to say.'

'I think he was more furious there was a chance he'd miss my wedding than he was about being ill,' Rachel said, her voice quiet. 'Sort of glad, really. Turns out he missed nothing.' She pushed herself away from the wall and moved over to the chest, pulling the top drawer open.

Agnes draped her hand around the bedpost and watched Rachel as she started to take out old T-shirts and stack them into the crook of her arm. 'I'm sorry I couldn't put you up. The builders won't be finished for another month. Such bad timing. Do you think you'll be all right? Here, I mean? With Eleanor? I know you two haven't always ... well ...' Her voice tailed off.

'I'll be fine. It would have been easier, though, if Charlie was here rather than her,' Rachel said, her voice flat. She stopped and turned to face Agnes, a look of guilt creeping across her face. 'Is that wicked?'

Agnes shook her head, 'No ... I understand.'

She pulled out another T-shirt. 'Johnny's very lucky. To have you.'

'You've got me too,' Agnes said. 'Don't forget that.'

Rachel twisted her mouth sideways, her arms now full of old clothes. Agnes pushed herself up from the bed. 'Can I help you with that?' she offered. 'Here, give those to me. I'll put them in your mother's room. There's space in the big wardrobe where ...' She stopped before she said the words.

Rachel turned to look out of the window. 'Does it get better?'

Agnes grabbed the moment. 'Of course it does. You're young. You're fantastic. Someone will come along who deserves you. You'll look back and think you had a lucky escape.'

Rachel blinked and turned towards her aunt, her face lifeless. 'No. I mean when your father dies. Do you get used to it?'

Agnes looked at her niece: the dirty-blonde curls tucked behind her ears, the pleading brown eyes, the freckles on top of her nose and cheeks. She was still that little girl dancing on the beach, running with the balloon, poking down into a pond with a stick. 'No,' said Agnes, 'if I'm being honest, not really. But you do get better at holding on to the good stuff.'

Rachel gave a nod. 'Someone sent me a card, before the funeral. It had a quote – a snippet from a poem, I think. It was about how if we knew when people were going to die we'd take them for a drink and tell them how much we liked them.'

Agnes made a small noise of appreciation.

'And it stuck with me. I loved Charlie with every bone in my body. But I really liked him. It's funny, isn't it? Your parents are just your parents. They're there and you're over here, and you rattle along doing the family thing and it's taken for granted you all love each other. But to like some-one? That's different. That's a choice. And I never told him how much I liked him.' Her voice caught in her throat. Her head fell a little and she chewed at her bottom lip, fighting the urge to cry.

Agnes reached out her hand and placed it on Rachel's forearm. 'He liked you too.'

Rachel looked up, her eyes pained and doubtful. 'Did he, though?'

'Of course he did.'

Rachel's hand went to her mouth, as if to catch the sorrow that wanted to vomit out of her.

'What's wrong with me? Why did he stand me up, Agnes?' Her eyes filled with tears.

'There's nothing wrong with you. Come here.' Agnes got up and pulled Rachel to her and, with the childhood clothes squashed between them, her niece sobbing on to her shoulder, she stayed there until she could feel the tears on her skin.

Chapter Three

Then

'Eleanor!' Agnes shoved up the sash window of her bedroom, giving it the extra push it needed at the point where it always stuck, and leaned out. 'I forgot to give you this!'

She waved the soft pink beret she had made for her, a going-away present.

Eleanor turned and stared up at her sister. She gave a small smile. She knew she'd say goodbye. 'Hurry up and bring it down! I'm going to be late for the train!'

Agnes disappeared from the window as if she'd been sucked back by an unknown force, and moments later clattered out the front door. She was panting.

'Here you are,' she said, holding the beret out. 'I made it specially. It took for ever.

Agnes threw her arms around her sister's waist. 'I know I said I wasn't going to cry but I probably am.'

There was a toot from the car. 'Hurry up, Eleanor. Say goodbye, Agnes. I don't want to be late.' Their mother, a rather dour woman, frowned from the front seat.

'Got to go,' said Eleanor, rubbing her sister's back. 'Try to be good.'

'Don't forget to write!' called out Agnes, pressing up against the gate as it banged shut behind her sister. She wiped at her eyes.

'I won't!'

Eleanor opened the back door of her mother's blue Morris Minor and threw her suitcase inside. Pink beret still in hand, she shut the door and got into the front passenger seat.

'We're only just going to make it,' said her mother, shoving the gearstick into first and pulling away. 'I knew this would happen.'

'Goodbye! Goodbye!' called Agnes, waving furiously.

'Bye!' shouted Eleanor, waving the beret out of the window. 'Silly thing,' she added, as they turned the corner and the house slipped from sight. 'Still. Sweet of her to make me this ...' She fingered the beret and pulled it on to her head. 'How does it look?'

'Fine,' said her mother, still frowning. 'I suppose I should ask you if you really want to be doing this. There's a perfectly good art school in Oxford. You could stay at home.'

'I'm supposed to be leaving home, Mother. That's the entire point. Besides, London is far more exciting. And further away.'

'Agnes does have a point,' said Eleanor's mother, choosing to ignore her. 'Chelsea is all very well, but it's a bit "fast" for my liking so I don't want you going to any of those crazy hang-outs. Marjory says all sorts go on. Promise me, Eleanor.'

'I promise ...' Eleanor pulled the beret from her head, looked out of the window, thought for a moment, then turned back. 'What sort of crazy hang-outs?'

'Never you mind,' answered her mother, straining past Eleanor to check if anything was coming.

'Agnes told me Daddy cried. Is that true?'

'I doubt it,' Eleanor's mother said, now staring at the road ahead.

'I wonder if he did. I think I'd have liked to see it,' said Eleanor, turning to look at her mother. 'Are you planning on crying?'

'I haven't got time to cry. I've got to get you on to the train.'

'I don't think I've ever seen him cry. I don't think I've ever seen him express any emotion at all.' Eleanor let out a small sigh. 'I did think he looked a little odd at breakfast. I thought it was indigestion.'

'If your father is upset, he'll just go and sit at the bottom of the garden for a few hours and he'll be fine. Have you got the address Marjory gave you?'

'Yes, it's in my pocket.'

'Good. And you know how to get there? From the train station?'

'Number 46 bus.'

'And Marjory will meet you there and give you the key to the flat. You should pick up some flowers for her, to say thank you. There'll be a stall at Paddington. Don't forget, will you?'

'No. I won't.'

'Marjory says there's a nice chap at the flats, floor below. Writer or something. Can't remember all the details. But he's a few years older than you. A Steady Eddie, she said.'

Eleanor curled her lip.

'Don't sniff,' Eleanor's mother warned. 'There's nothing wrong with Steady Eddies. Boring they may be, but when you're in a bind they're all you need. Anyway, Marjory's asked him to keep an eye on you.'

'I don't need to be spied on, Mother.'

'It's not spying. It's a sensible young man looking out for my daughter. And that's the end of the conversation. Is anything coming?'

Eleanor turned her head to the left and cast a glance down the road. 'No.'

She let her chin fall into her hand and closed her eyes as the wind from the open window pushed back her hair. She was excited to be leaving, excited to be finally heading for London, but the thought of a sensible man informing on her to her mother was rather putting the brakes on.

'What's he expected to do? File reports or something?' she said, with a scowl.

'Don't be impertinent,' said her mother, waving on a pedestrian at a pelican crossing. 'If you don't do anything stupid I suspect your paths will never have to cross.' She shot her daughter a sharp look. 'Marjory says he's very nice. It's very kind of her to be looking out for you.'

'Looking out for me or looking out for you?'

'All right, that'll do, Eleanor,' snapped her mother. 'You'll understand when you have children of your own. You will thank Marjory and you will be polite to whatever his name is. And that is that.'

Eleanor sat in silence. There was no point fighting. She'd be free of all this soon enough and as for the Steady Eddie, well, she'd be giving him the slip sharpish.

'Goodness,' said Eleanor's mother, as they ran on to the platform. 'A minute to spare! Don't mind me, get on! Guard! Hold that door!'

Eleanor leaped up into the open doorway just as the guard went to close it behind her. He stood back and blew his whistle and Eleanor came forward and leaned from the window.

'Don't forget to write,' her mother said, walking along as the train started to move. 'And don't forget the flowers for Marjory. And don't forget to eat. If you need anything or get into a fix, then call. And soon as you arrive, get milk. You always need milk.'

'Don't fuss. I'll be fine,' said Eleanor, itching to be gone.

'Did I give you that five-pound note from your father?'

'Yes.'

'Well, don't lose it ...' Eleanor's mother was now moving at a brisk trot but the train was picking up speed. As it quickened, she realised she was beaten and came to a stop. She raised her arm to wave. 'Well, goodbye, my darling! Goodbye! And *please*, Eleanor, be *careful!*'

'I will. Goodbye!' Eleanor waved. 'Goodbye!'

Eleanor stared back towards her mother until the platform disappeared. She took a deep breath. This was it. She'd done it. Breaking into a broad smile, she turned from the door into the carriage and found a rack for her suitcase.

'Is that seat taken?' she asked, pointing to an empty seat next to a matronly woman with a bag of knitting.

'No, go ahead.'

Eleanor squeezed past. 'Thank you,' she said, with a smile. As she sat, she stared out at the Buckinghamshire countryside, impatient for the oaks and beech trees and gorse bushes to be replaced by rooftops and the cramped squeeze of the city. She thought about her mother and felt a pang of guilt that she found her so irritating. Why was it so impossible to tolerate her kindness? 'Hang on,' she mumbled to herself, *had* she remembered the address? She reached into her pocket and pulled out the piece of folded paper. There, she thought, triumphant, the address of the flat in Belsize Park. Of course she'd remembered it. All the same, she found herself fingering the envelope with the five-pound note in her other pocket.

Marjory was thrilled with the flowers. 'Oh! You shouldn't have!' she said, hand clutching at her chest in mock protestation. 'Really. I should give them back to you. Brighten the place up. Put on a welcome and all that. No, no. You keep them.'

'But they're for you,' said Eleanor, with a frown. 'Besides, I can't imagine what my mother would say if she found out I'd bought you flowers and kept them.'

'Honestly,' said Marjory, handing them back to her, 'I have a wretched lunch at twelve. As lovely as they are, they won't thank me after being stuck in a cloakroom for three hours. We can put them in a vase when we get upstairs. And I won't tell your mother a thing.' She winked.

Eleanor smiled. 'Well, all right. You've twisted my arm. I do love lupins. They're so ... noble.'

'This has worked out rather well, hasn't it?' Marjory beamed. She was attractive, the same age as her mother, early forties, but with an edge of glamour her mother lacked. They'd been to school together, hence the connection, but Marjory was a lady of leisure, a tennis-on-Wednesdays, hairdresser-every-Friday type. She was immaculate, trim, poised, a poster girl for sophistication. 'You know, you're doing me a huge favour,' she said. 'We're off to New York for a year – did your mother tell you? Dickie's been posted – and it's all terribly exciting but I would have sat worrying about the flat, you know how things niggle, but here you are to save the day!'

'It's you saving the day, Marjory,' said Eleanor, trying to be charming. 'I'm very grateful.' She flashed her best smile.

Marjory squeezed Eleanor's upper arm. 'Don't mention it. We're helping each other. Let's leave it at that. So, shall we? Let's get down to business.' She opened the small black handbag hanging from her wrist. 'This key's the one that gets you into the building,' she said, pulling it out and holding it up. 'Would you like to try?' She held it out and beamed.

'Thank you,' said Eleanor, taking it.

'That's the keyhole,' said Marjory, pointing towards it.

'Yes ...' Suitcase and flowers in one hand, key in the other, Eleanor slid the key in.

'That's it. In she goes. And turn it to the right ... in the direction of the Underground, that's how I always remember!' She gave a tinkling laugh.

Eleanor felt the door yield and pushed it open with her shoulder.

'Well done!' Marjory was brisk and efficient. 'And in we go. So here's the hall,' she added, ushering Eleanor inside. 'As you can see – post cubbies all there ...' She wafted her hand to her left. 'Lift or stairs? Let's do lift.'

She trotted towards the 1930s cage lift at the back of the hall and pulled the grille door open. 'Have you used one of these before?' she asked, walking into the walnut-lined compartment.

'Actually, no,' said Eleanor. 'Never like this—'

'Fine,' said Marjory, interrupting her. 'So you come in and you have to shut the door before you hit the button. Slide it across until it's locked into place. And then ... floor 3 ...' She paused as she pushed an old ceramic button. 'And hey presto. We're off.'

The lift clunked into action and Eleanor, conscious of the confined space, shoved herself into a corner and lifted her suitcase into her arms, holding the flowers rather awkwardly in front of it.

'That looks heavy,' said Marjory, nodding towards the suitcase. 'I imagine you'll be delighted to put it down.'

'I'm rather regretting packing the books.'

'Oh, you can't be without books,' said Marjory, resting her fingers on the top of her handbag and staring at the lift door as it rattled upwards. 'Not far now.'

There was a small tinny ping. As the lift shuddered to a stop, Marjory leaned forward.

'So wait for the click ...' She tilted her head and held a finger in the air. 'There it is, and slide the door open.' She heaved the door sideways, stepped out into the hallway and turned, waiting for Eleanor to join her. 'Now you must make sure you shut this door again. If you don't, nobody will be able to use the lift. You'll be frightfully unpopular.'

Eleanor nodded, then looked down the corridor: the cream walls looked rather tired and a purple carpet, trodden down at every doorway, gave off the whiff of an institution, the smell of boiled mince and cabbage. 'This is all getting a lick of paint in the summer,' said Marjory as she slammed the lift door shut. 'You go first. That way. Number 12.' She gestured off down the corridor.

Eleanor walked, suitcase still held to her chest, checking off the doors. She'd felt so excited, leaving Brill, but now, walking softly ahead of Marjory, a feeling of anxiety hit her. It was her first time away from her family and the home that had been theirs for generations. She knew where she was in Brill. She knew what was expected. In London, there was a danger of getting lost.

'And here we are,' said Marjory, trotting behind her. 'You've still got those keys, yes?'

'Umm, yes,' said Eleanor, uncertainly. She put down her suitcase, laid the flowers on top and reached into her pocket. She gave an awkward smile. 'Found them. Phew.'

Marjory shot her an indulgent smile. 'Wouldn't do to lose them on day one, would it?' She gave another insubstantial laugh. 'Now, the second key on the fob – that's the one you need for this door. Let me warn you – it can be a bit sticky – so when you turn it, give it a little shove.'

Eleanor did as she was told. 'That's it,' said Marjory, with a cursory glance at her watch. 'Give it a shove.'

Eleanor opened the door and Marjory, picking up the flowers, handed them to Eleanor. 'You take those. I'll take your suitcase. Goodness,' she added, as she grasped the handle. 'That *is* heavy. Bedroom's off to the left. I'll pop it in here. Sitting room's to the right.'

Eleanor stepped inside and made her way towards the sitting room, flowers in hand. It was light and spacious, tastefully decorated. As she stood there, wondering where she might find a vase, Marjory appeared behind her.

'And here we are! All in. Pretty straightforward. I won't give you the grand tour. If you have any problems, just ring for the caretaker. His number's by the telephone. Super.' She looked again at her watch. 'Such a shame I've got this damn lunch. I'm going to have to dash.' She pulled an expression of exaggerated regret. 'Oh, and I'm not sure if your mother mentioned it, but I've asked a thoroughly nice chap to look out for you. He lives downstairs. You'll like him. Very up-and-coming. His name's Charlie.'

'Yes, she did say—'

'Super. Well. That's me. You'll find a vase in the top cupboard in the kitchen,' she said, pointing towards the flowers. 'Lupins are so wonderful. Goodness. I really am going to have to fly.' She leaned forward to give Eleanor a kiss on the cheek. 'Where is it you're going again?' she said, trying to remember.

'Chelsea Art School.'

'Chelsea! That's it! Very prestigious. Well done you.' She walked back towards the front door.

'I feel very lucky to have got in. My father rather thought I wouldn't. Actually, neither of my parents thought I would get in. My mother kept telling me to go to secretarial college.'

'I suspect luck had nothing to do with it.' Marjory opened the door and looked back. 'And don't be too hard on your parents. It's our job to manage expectations. Well, goodbye, Eleanor. I'll tell your mother you're in. Good luck, and make the most of it. Goodbye!' Marjory shot her one last encouraging look and then disappeared, closing the door behind her.

Eleanor stood, listening to the soft thump of Marjory's shoes marching away on the corridor carpet. She let out a sigh and felt her shoulders lower and her cheeks relax. She looked around. 'Goodness,' she said out loud, taking in her new home.

The apartment faced north, towards Hampstead, but from the window she could see into other apartments. Opposite, there was a woman kneading some dough; to her left, an elderly man reading a book; and then down to her right, she saw a young man, sensible haircut, round spectacles, knitted tank top, cigarette in mouth, sitting at a typewriter. 'I wonder if that's my spy,' she mumbled to herself, staring down at him. 'He looks sufficiently square.' He glanced up, catching her eye.

'Oh no!' She pulled back from the window, feeling a sharp flush of embarrassment, and busied herself with the vase she'd found. Filling it from the tap, she dropped the lupins into the water, carried the vase back to the sitting room and placed it in the centre of the small round table.

She stood there, hands on hips, and then, curiosity getting the better of her, she went back to the window and peered out. He was still staring up.

'Oh!' she squealed, leaping back again. 'Don't do that again. You're not in Brill any more, Eleanor.'

And with that, she grabbed her beret and her purse and headed out to find milk.

Chapter Four

Now

'I'm just popping out to get milk,' Eleanor shouted up the stairs. 'Do you want anything?' She waited, her head tilted, to catch a reply. 'Rachel!' she shouted again. 'Do you want anything?'

Rachel blinked and called back, 'No,' her voice flat and listless. She was curled into a ball, another attempt to catch up on the sleep that no longer came at night.

'No, *thank you*,' shouted back Eleanor, shaking her head. She turned away, muttering under her breath, grabbed her bag and left.

Rachel heard the sharp slam of the front door, rolled on to her back and stared up at the ceiling. Her relationship with her father had been straightforward, fun, a comfort, but with her mother, there was always a sense of something unsaid that felt complicated and compromised. While Charlie was alive they had managed to muddle along, but now, with him gone, they were raw with grief and disappointment, and they had nothing to scratch up against except each other.

She had still heard nothing from Claude. Two weeks. Not a peep. There was no sign of him on social media; none of their mutual friends knew where he was; he had simply slipped away. It was probably for the best. The thought of facing anyone she knew was more than she could bear.

Tom, Claude's best man, had posted her the wedding rings in a Jiffy bag by Special Delivery, with a note that just said, 'Sorry.' They sat together in a little white leather pouch on her bedside table: two platinum bands, with a ring of gold running through the middle. As they grew old together, the jeweller had told them, the gold would darken. It was a neat, sentimental gesture. So much for that.

She thought back to when Claude had taken her away for a long weekend to Harris, in the Outer Hebrides. He was wealthy: a lucky inheritance from an obscure, childless relative, he'd told her. He made the effort, in those early days, to treat her, to take her to nice places. He wanted her to have experiences, he said. It was very easy to fall in love with him.

He'd rented an S-shaped house that looked out over a two-mile stretch of white sand and turquoise sea. The house was almost ridiculously beautiful and the weather had been perfect.

'Can you believe this?' was Claude's constant refrain, and she couldn't. They were entwined in a feeling of enormous luck.

They had been for a walk, following the famous Coffin Road from the barren rocks of the east to the fertile lands of the west. It had been another hot day and, after an hour of steady uphill climbing, they had stopped to drink water and share an energy bar. 'What are those flowers?' Rachel had asked, pointing at some odd, wispy white blooms that looked like ballerina tutus.

'Bog cotton,' Claude had told her. 'It's everywhere.'

Rachel had always marvelled at Claude's never-ending capacity to teach her things. It was why she liked him. They'd met at a dinner party in Shepherd's Bush and had bonded over the comics of Michael Kupperman. Neither of them had ever met anyone else who had heard of him, and they had laughed easily and freely. He was attractive too, with the wiry physicality of a long-distance runner: his face lean and chiselled, aquamarine eyes with long eyelashes, the backstop for a boyish charm he was happy to play on. He seemed fun. That's what Rachel liked about him. He was different and interesting and odd and she had told him about Brill and her mad, famous mother and he'd asked her if she'd like to see his gallery and that was that. Six months later and here they were on the Isle of Harris.

It hadn't shocked her, how quickly their lives had intertwined. She had been restless and afloat, her painting career failing to take off, and he had offered her a job working in the gallery and a home, with him, in the flat upstairs. It had felt effortless and obvious and had allowed her to quietly relegate the career she hadn't had the confidence to pursue. He had been her get-out clause, her fort, her excuse.

They had ended the walk at Losgaintir beach, an enormous stretch of white sand that looked over towards Taransay. Claude had brought an old tablecloth for a pound, an emergency purchase from a charity shop, and had stretched it out, rocks at each corner, for them to lie on. He was on his back, eyes closed, top off, and she had lain next to him, watching him doze. The sky was clear blue apart from two oddly shaped wispy clouds that, in an act of perfect symmetry, looked like bog cotton. It was so hot. Rachel had pushed herself up and wandered down to the shoreline. She wanted to dip her toes into the sea but, despite the weather, the water was so cold it made her bones hurt. She had turned back, and as she walked she found a long length of kelp, about four foot long. She picked it up and danced with it, twirling it around her head, her arm outstretched, her face towards the sun. There was something about that moment that would stay with her for ever: a feeling of extraordinary freedom and release.

She saw Claude was sitting up, smiling at her, and she had smiled back, letting the kelp slip from her fingers. She walked back towards him. He took her hand and looked up at her. 'Will you marry me?' he asked.

And she said yes.

Rachel blinked and put the rings back into the pouch.

Downstairs, the front door opened and she heard Eleanor bumping about in the hallway: a bag being thrown down, the rustle of a coat being hung on a hook by the door. Normally, she'd hear her walking towards the kitchen, but to Rachel's dismay she heard her mother's heavy footsteps coming up the stairs. She could practically hear the reluctance. Rachel had never really confided in her. That had always been Charlie's job. He was the quiet listener, the one with whom all worries could be shared. Rachel dreaded these moments with her mother. She didn't have the strength to be silently judged. She wasn't sure she ever had.

'Oh God,' she mumbled, and turned over so her back was towards the door.

'Rachel,' Eleanor said, coming in. 'Rachel, can you look at me, please?'

Rachel rolled over and stared at her mother with a look of deadened disdain. Eleanor's face was speckled with paint, her hair tied up into a colourful bandana, her features still fine and striking after all the years. 'What?'

Eleanor's hands went to her hips and her lips tightened into an irritated ball. 'I just don't know what to do with you,' Eleanor began. 'You've been up here for days. It's not healthy. I wish you'd come down. I know you're waiting for the pain to stop, but still ... it's like when your father died.' Her gaze softened.

'The pain hasn't stopped about that either,' said Rachel, her voice low and quiet, disarmed by the sudden honesty.

'No. It hasn't,' said Eleanor, turning to look out of the window. 'Look, I've got a quiche from the farm shop. Do you want some for supper?' She was trying not to look strained.

'I don't like quiche, Eleanor,' replied Rachel. 'I never have.'

Eleanor stood for a moment, then: 'Well, you could go and pick some tomatoes from the garden. Get a handful of basil from the pots? There's cheese in the fridge ...' Her voice trailed off. She turned back towards the landing. 'Please don't call me Eleanor. I don't like it.'

There was a short silence. Eleanor looked down at the floor.

'My husband is dead, Rachel.' Her voice was quiet but firm. 'We buried him six weeks ago. He wasn't just your father. I'm trying to help you. Try and remember that.'

Rachel felt the tension in her shoulders give a little. She pushed herself up on to her elbows and looked over at her mother. She seemed hunched, burdened, tired. Something in Rachel softened a little. 'Sorry,' she said, trying to be better. 'I'm just ...' Rachel stopped. She didn't have the words to articulate what she was. 'I don't know. I don't know what I am.'

'Look,' said Eleanor, sensing a brief breakthrough, 'I need those tomatoes picking in any event. It'll do you good to get out of this room. Please, Rachel. We don't have to do this. I wish we didn't do this.'

Rachel nodded and slowly swung her legs off the bed.

Eleanor turned to look at her. 'It's a shame, isn't it,' she began, 'that we don't seem to be able to help each other?'

Rachel went to answer, but her mother's candidness had caught her off guard. She wasn't used to Eleanor being so emotionally open. There was something about her that was different, like a woman carrying a heavy load with the end in sight. She looked into Eleanor's eyes and saw something pleading that she didn't recognise or fully understand. Rachel looked away: she wasn't ready for this yet, and besides, she didn't feel able to offer up anything useful.

'Well,' added Eleanor, patting the frame of the doorway. 'I'm going to have a bath.'

Rachel stood for a moment, then followed Eleanor out of the room, glancing down the corridor as she disappeared into the bathroom. It was difficult. Years of being the only child, the expectations that were impossible to live up to: career, family, the art of growing up, Rachel had fallen short at every hurdle. The emotional distance, the constant sense that her mother was missing something, trying to hold something down, a sense of loss that took Eleanor away to a private place to which neither she nor Charlie were ever invited. It was hard not to feel resentful, when her mother was so very successful, even harder as the only profession Rachel might have had a shot at was the same as hers. Harder still if you're simply not good enough to make it work on your own terms. Eleanor had experienced it all, and now Rachel was relegated to being the seagull chasing the fishing boat. Her mother still had the ability to make Rachel feel small and disappointing. Eleanor was right. They hadn't managed to find a way to help each other.

Rachel trudged down the stairs, her feet bare, and padded across the hall and through into the kitchen. The radio was on, *The Archers*, and she was reminded of her father, sitting with his feet up on the Aga, paper in hand, listening rapt as Helen was found not guilty of attempting to murder her husband. He'd punched the air and phoned Agnes. She switched it off.

She had avoided Brill in those first few weeks after Charlie had died. Everywhere was an echo of him: the armchair in the sitting room, the barometer he would tap every morning. She hadn't had the strength to cope. As she made her way to the back of the house and her mother's studio, she was reminded, in tiny cuts, of everything she had lost: a father, a fiancé, a future. And all in less than two months.

Eleanor's studio was the largest room in the house, south facing, and was bathed in sunlight. It had never felt anything other than entirely normal to have a famous mother. It was all Rachel had ever known, but her mother's bright light had cast a long and deep shadow. How do you live your life when all your ambitions pale in comparison? How do you impress someone you can never match up to? Rachel thought about her father, standing at her mother's side at every exhibition, every auction, quietly being ignored, his name constantly forgotten. He never complained. 'Your mother has a great gift,' he used to tell her. 'A lot of people rely on her.' It was his gentle way of trying to explain why Eleanor couldn't be at sports day, the school concert, pick her up from parties, be a mum like all her friends' mums. She had no other sibling to ask for advice, share the burden, figure it out with. There was a distance between them that Rachel had never been able to breach.

Rachel stood and looked around. She loved the smell of the studio, that deep, metallic scent of oils, the empty canvases that promised the world, the brushes soaking in turps. The door at the far end opened out into the garden and, as she walked towards it, she stopped for a moment to look at the painting Eleanor was working on. It was a portrait of a young man: very early stages, the outline of a face and a pair of arresting blue eyes. Eleanor always began with the eyes. 'They're the soul of the painting,' she would say. Rachel stood, looking at it. She didn't recognise him, but something about it made her feel sad.

The house had a wonderful view. It was a chocolate-box cottage, white walls, red roof, smothered in roses and a rather grand wisteria. It was as English as bowler hats and bulldogs, the perfect place, an idyll. They'd lived in Brill for as long as Rachel could remember – when Rachel's grandmother died, Eleanor couldn't bear to part with it so she sold a painting and bought Agnes's share and here they still were. It was the only home Rachel had ever known and, like her mother, she was attached to it, like ivy to a tree.

Rachel made her way across the lawn, her toes pressing down into what was left of the grass. They were in the grip of a heatwave, and the once lush lawn was now brown and in distress. The tomato plants stood tall in a raised bed to the side. She began to pick, dropping the tomatoes into the bottom of her T-shirt, a perfect mindless task. Her mind wandered back to Claude, as it always did these days. She thought about other women who'd been stood up at the altar, and the image of Miss Havisham popped into her head. 'Oh God,' she mumbled.

'What?' said a voice from behind a cistus to her left.

Rachel, startled, turned and sent the tomatoes she'd picked scattering across the lawn. 'Damn!' She bent down to gather them up and, as she did, she saw the silhouette of someone standing against the sun. She peered up, eyes narrowed, and a man with dirty-blonde hair, green eyes and muddy hands, in an olive polo shirt, came into view. She had no idea who he was.

'Sorry,' she said, frowning, 'are you looking for someone?'

'No,' he said, shaking his head. 'Do you need a hand?' He bent down to pick up a tomato.

'No, thank you,' she said, briskly.

'Don't worry,' he said, reading her face, 'I'm meant to be here. I do the garden.'

'Right,' she said, standing again and dropping the last of the tomatoes back into her T-shirt.

'Here, do you want this one?' He held out the tomato he'd picked up.

'It's fine. You have it.' She went to walk back to the house.

'I'm sorry about what happened,' she heard him say. She stopped and turned to look at him. 'With your fiancé, I mean,' he added.

Rachel felt a hot surge of embarrassment. Not again. She was sick of it. Every time the phone rang, every time someone came to the door, and now this, someone she didn't even know. How dare her mother go around telling anyone and everyone? She stared at him and her mouth fell open to reply but she was too stunned. Lacking the strength to tell him to mind his own business, she blinked, closed her mouth and walked towards the house. She'd have this out with the person she really wanted to argue with.

Chapter Five

Then

Eleanor approached the Manresa Road campus of the Chelsea School of Art with delicate steps. The building was new that year, a modernistic rectangle that seemed to float on pillars, and Eleanor, wide-eyed and awestruck, couldn't help but feel overwhelmed.

Not knowing quite what to do, she followed the red arrows to a large temporary table that had been erected in a hurry by a woman who was clearly running late. 'Sorry, what's your name?' she asked, not looking up.

'Eleanor Ledbury.'

'Course?'

'Painting.'

There was a shuffle of papers. 'I'm at sixes and sevens,' the woman muttered. 'Normally I ... ah, there you are.' She put a blue tick next to Eleanor's name and handed her a piece of card.

'Fill in your details on that,' she said, still not looking up. 'And put it in the box at the end.'

37

Eleanor shuffled to her right and looked around for something to fill out the card. There was a pot of pencils sitting on a desk beyond the immediate circle of the entrance and, picking up her blue hessian bag, she wandered over to it. She pulled a pencil out from the pot and stared at it. Was she allowed to use it? she wondered. Desks in institutions tend to belong to people. It was her first day; she didn't want someone accusing her of stealing. She looked around. Nobody was paying her a blind bit of notice. Nobody, apart from one young man leaning against a pillar who was staring at Eleanor with a puzzled frown.

Eleanor blinked. Was he actually staring at her or was there someone behind her? She looked over her shoulder. No, he was staring at her. She looked back at him, drawn towards his gaze. He tipped his head to one side and screwed his eyes into narrow slits. He was really looking at her, almost as if she were an exhibit. He seemed worse for wear. His shirt was undone, half hanging out from the top of his trousers, and he seemed to have only one shoe. His blonde hair was standing on end and he had a significant bruise under one eye that seemed to be darkening with every second. Eleanor drank him in. He was utterly beautiful.

Disconcerted by the intensity of his gaze, Eleanor turned away and leaned against the desk to fill in her card. Behind her she could hear protests and she glanced back to see two other young men pick the staring boy up, their shoulders under his armpits. They were dragging him off towards what looked like the gentlemen's toilets. 'He needs to throw up,' one of them shouted, back towards a small group of men and women, all sporting sunglasses, who had drifted into the atrium.

Goodness.

Eleanor turned back to her registration card, her heart beating a little faster. The encounter had unnerved her and she thought of her stern mother and what she might make of this.

'I've done it,' she said, catching the eye of the lady at the registration table. The woman gave a cursory nod and pointed to the cardboard box at the corner.

Eleanor dropped the card into the box and wondered what she should do next. She had some papers she should sit and look at, work out where she had to go. She reached into her bag and turned away from the table.

'What's the longest word you know?'

She looked up, startled. The staring boy was back and standing in front of her, peering, inquisitive. He was sizing her up.

'Umm, I'm not sure.'

'Mine is *proditomania*. It's a noun. It means an irrational belief that everyone around you is a traitor. I don't think I know a longer word than that.'

She could smell the vomit on his breath. 'What happened to your eye?'

'I was punched by a sailor in Sloane Square.' He said it as if this were a normal occurrence.

'*Fedifragous*,' she said, the word popping into her mind. 'It means to break a promise.'

His eyes lit up and his face broke into a broad smile. 'That's very good. In fact it's tremendous. Hello,' he said, holding out his hand. 'I'm Jake.'

'I'm Eleanor.' She took his hand in hers and they shook.

'I'm not quite at my best,' he said, looking down at himself, 'and I seem to have lost a shoe.'

'I can see that.'

'Well.' He smiled again and there was a moment of silence.

Eleanor looked at him. He wasn't remotely embarrassed. That was the most startling thing about him. He was like a treasure washed up on a shore, a sudden find, a keepsake.

'I was rather hoping for an influx of excessively beautiful people,' he said, tucking his shirt back into his trousers. 'I'm glad they started with you.'

Eleanor didn't know what to say or think. Nobody had ever spoken to her like this.

'You seem to be precisely what is required. Fresh blood and all that. Does my eye look romantic?' He presented it to her for inspection.

'I'm not sure,' she said. 'It looks sore.'

'Yes,' he said, with some regret. 'I think it might be. I'm still too drunk to tell. I can't even remember why he punched me.'

Eleanor could feel a small smile curling into shape. He noticed and smiled back.

'Haven't you been to bed?' she asked.

'No,' he said, matter-of-factly. 'I think it was someone's birthday.' Another puzzled look drifted across his face as he tried to remember. 'We ended up at the Ad Lib. Have you been?'

Eleanor shook her head.

'I shall have to take you. It's a private club, but when you're pretty they don't seem to care.'

'I've never been to a private club.'

'Oh,' exclaimed Jake, his eyes widening. 'How thrilling.'

One of the boys who had helped Jake to the toilet appeared behind them. He had dark hair and was tall, pale and tired looking. 'Come on, Jake,' he said. 'Let's go home. I must apologise for my friend,' he added, towards Eleanor. 'He has a drinking problem of improbable dimensions.'

'This man is a liar,' said Jake, letting himself be dragged away. 'I shall take you to Soho and show you all the delicious delights.'

Eleanor watched him go.

'Don't forget me, Eleanor!' he called out.

'Don't worry,' said the woman at the registration desk, 'not everyone here is quite as wild.'

But Eleanor couldn't bring herself to feel relieved.

Chapter Six

Now

'How dare you,' Rachel said, pushing the bathroom door open.

Eleanor stared up from the bath. She was lying back, her hair splaying around her shoulders in the water. 'What's the matter now?' she asked, her voice flat and weary.

'I have just met a man in the garden who seems to know every last thing about me.' She was furious. 'He told me he was sorry about what happened. How does he know what happened? You must have told him. I don't even know who he is.'

'Are you talking about Caspar?'

'I don't know. The bloke who does the garden.' She was flustered.

Eleanor pushed herself up, her breasts rising above the water. She was not embarrassed to be seen naked. If anything, it made her feel more dominant. 'Rachel,' she began, with a sigh, 'I'd hardly call it "every last thing". The reason Caspar knows about what happened was because I asked him to find the flowers for your bouquet. He asked if you had liked them.

I wasn't betraying you. I was simply being polite. You did like his flowers, but one thing led to another and out it came. There's no subterfuge here. People are entitled to be kind.'

Rachel paused, her righteous anger sideswiped to the floor. Her eyes were filled with anger and confusion. Her mother looked back at her, the way she used to when Rachel needed to have an argument.

'Why are you really angry, Rachel?' she asked. 'We may as well have this out. Pass me that towel.'

'I don't know what you're talking about,' Rachel mumbled, tossing a large white towel on a chair towards the bathtub. Eleanor caught it with one hand and pushed herself up with the other.

It had been a long time since Rachel had seen her mother naked and she couldn't help snatching a glimpse at the new contours and ridges, the skin that had lost its shape, the scars of childbirth, the pale grey pubes that momentarily startled. Rachel looked away. It felt intrusive. She was on the back foot.

Eleanor stepped out of the tub and stood on a small rectangular bathmat, rubbing herself down with the towel without a scrap of awkwardness. 'It was not my fault Charlie died, Rachel,' she said. She tossed the damp towel over towards the laundry basket and walked past Rachel to the clothes that were on the chair beside her. 'Why are you so angry with me?'

Rachel chewed at her lip. 'I don't know. I feel furious. All the time. I find myself trying to think of reasons to argue with you. It makes no sense. I want to blame you. I don't know why. Because you're here. Because you gave him your cold.' Her voice was barely a whisper, her fists tight by her sides. 'He couldn't fight it off.'

'Your father died of cancer. Not from my cold.' Eleanor sat and pulled on a pair of white pants.

'I wanted him to walk me up the aisle.'

'I know you did.' Eleanor stood and pulled a thin smock top over her head. She looked at her daughter. 'There are things I want to say to you, Rachel. Things we need to talk about, but I can't do it now. We have to get through this first. Everything is on hold. We're getting nowhere. Perhaps we should see a therapist? Together? Or you could go on your own?'

Rachel's eyes pricked with tears. 'I don't want to,' she said, wiping them away. 'I don't think it's necessary.'

'Really? Thinking I set out to give Charlie a cold isn't rational, Rachel.' She bent down and retrieved a pair of blue linen shorts. 'I know you miss him. So do I. I don't know what else to say to you. Charlie died of cancer. Claude did what he did. We're both under enormous strain. I think feeling angry is par for the course.'

Rachel stared down at the floor.

Eleanor buttoned her shorts. 'You must try and move forward. The lying about all day, the not leaving the house, the staring at the ceiling. It's not healthy. I'm worried about you. And I understand. Believe me. I understand your rage, your pain. I feel angry too.'

Rachel's face screwed itself into a knot. 'Don't be kind to me.' She shook her head. 'Don't. I can't cope with it. I don't know what to do. I'm not sure you do understand, not really.'

'Rachel, I do understand.' Eleanor's voice was conciliatory. 'What Claude did was unforgivable. Grief, we can deal with. But humiliation, that's a different sort of hurt.'

Rachel reached for a piece of toilet roll and blew her nose into it. 'I can't imagine you ever having to deal with humiliation.'

Eleanor folded her arms, her voice soft and quiet. 'There are lots of things you don't know about me, Rachel.' She moved towards her, a hand outstretched.

'No, don't. Please.' Rachel pushed herself back against the wall. 'I don't want to cry again.'

'You're not the only one who's hurting.'

Rachel stared at her mother. It had only been six weeks since Charlie had died. Rachel had been driving when Eleanor had called. She remembered nothing other than being told to pull over. The rest was a blur. Somehow she had turned around and driven back and they had stood, holding each other, numb and shocked.

They'd expected that moment for over a year, from the moment they all sat together in a small room at the Royal Marsden and a man with kind eyes had told them that was that. Eleanor had spent a day on the telephone, telling everyone in one go so she would never have to say it again. She had made Charlie write down last requests, unfulfilled dreams, things he'd never done but always meant to. Eleanor had torn those lists into strips, folded them and put them in a hat, and every day she'd made him draw one; she would go to the ends of the earth to honour them.

What was Rachel doing? She didn't need to stand in her parents' bathroom – the place Eleanor had washed Charlie and cared for him – and insult her mother by telling her she'd brought about his end.

'I'm sorry,' she whispered. She stared down at her toes.

There was a short silence.

'What did you want to talk to me about?' She cleared her throat and looked up.

Something flitted across Eleanor's face, a moment that wasn't ready to be revealed. She blinked. 'Not now. I'm going to make something to eat,' she said, moving back to the tub to pull up the plug. 'Why don't you come and help me?'

'I'm really not hungry.' Rachel had her hands crossed over her chest, her back hunched, as if she wanted to fold in on herself and disappear.

The room was filled with the dark gurgle of water running away. Neither of them knew quite what to do.

'I'm sorry if I've upset you,' Eleanor relented. 'I didn't mean to.'

Rachel chewed at her lip.

'Well,' Eleanor said, sensing the flare-up was at its end, 'I'll be downstairs.'

Rachel remained glued to the wall, her cheeks wet. She waited for her mother's footfalls to drift away before pushing herself upright and looking at herself in the mirror. She looked awful, thin to the point of illness. She had spent months going to the gym, watching what she ate and giving up booze for a dress she would never be photographed in and now she was half the size, with no effort. The Misery Diet. It didn't suit her.

She didn't want to fight with her mother, she knew that, but she didn't know how to stop it. She'd been Claude's fiancée. Charlie's little girl. She needed to remember who she was, now that she was alone. She needed to be Rachel again.

Downstairs, she heard the gentle ramble of Radio 4. There was a comfort to it, the pressing of a reset button, the promise of a quiet evening. Rachel went to the sink and splashed some cold water over her hot and itching eyes. Her pain felt so complicated. She didn't know where her grief for Claude began and that for Charlie ended. Of course it wasn't her mother's fault.

She wiped her face on a hand towel and went out to go back towards her room, but when she got to the stairs she stopped. She should go down, join her mother in the kitchen and chop tomatoes without making a fuss. Nothing would have to be said. It would be a quiet gesture, one that would not go unnoticed.

She laid her hand on the banister and forced herself downwards.

Eleanor was peering into the fridge, one hand on her hip, examining the state of a cucumber. 'Bit vintage,' she said to herself, placing it behind her on a butcher's block in the middle of the kitchen. She pulled out a packet of peas still in their pods. 'Forgot I had these. Do you want to shell them?' She took a white tin bowl from a shelf and handed it to her daughter. 'There you go. Sit outside if you like. It's a lovely evening.'

Rachel was about to reply when the door opened behind them.

'All done,' said Caspar, running a hand through his hair.

Rachel turned her back. She didn't want to look at him.

'Thank you, Caspar,' said Eleanor, smiling. 'Do you need a cup of tea or . . .'

Rachel stiffened.

'No, no,' said Caspar, holding a hand up. 'I'm all good.' He stopped and shot a glance towards Rachel. 'Sorry if I misspoke,' he said, his voice low and contrite. 'I didn't mean to upset you.'

Rachel closed her eyes tight and gripped the bowl. She didn't want to cry again.

Eleanor put a hand on Caspar's arm and manoeuvred him out of the door. 'She's very upset,' she said, quietly. 'Don't worry. She'll be fine.'

Rachel wiped at her eyes and began to shell the peas.

Chapter Seven

Then

Eleanor was seated at the heavy teak table that overlooked the window in the sitting room. She had found some writing paper, good quality too, and an ink pen that felt comfortable in her hand. It slid across the paper like silk. She liked it. She was halfway through a letter to Agnes, as promised. She'd had three from her little sister, all rammed with local nonsense, school gossip that meant next to nothing and a few moans about their parents that demanded total secrecy.

Don't worry about the jug, Eleanor wrote. *If you're lucky, Mother won't notice it's missing before Christmas. She'll think she put it in the harvest festival box and think no more about it.*

Eleanor stopped and took a quick peek out of the window. She hadn't seen the man with the round spectacles again but his typewriter was still there, empty ashtray next to it. Perhaps he was away? This must be what it feels like to be a spy.

As to your question about chums, I haven't really made any yet. There are a few girls in my painting class, but everyone seems a bit shy.

Eleanor turned the paper over. Should she write on the back or start a new piece of paper? No. She'd write on the back.

I did meet one boy. His name was Jake. I've only seen him once, on the day I arrived. He was wild and rather exotic and had a black eye. Mother wouldn't like him at all. I think you would. As for the other chap, the dreaded Charlie, I still haven't met him. Phew! I have the advantage though. I can sit in my flat and spy down on his. At least I think it's his.

She underlined *think* three times.

He's disappeared entirely, which is probably a good thing all round.

She took a bite out of the toast on the plate next to her. It was buttery and salty and delicious.

I think I shall like it here. I am enjoying the course. We had a life drawing class yesterday, which you would have hated, because the model was entirely nude. Don't tell Mother. She'll make me come home immediately. I do feel very grown up living here. Write back, won't you? Love Eleanor. PS I do miss you but let's pretend I didn't say that.

As she sat back and looked at what she'd written, her mind drifted off to that beautiful boy with the tousled hair and the dangerous look in his eye. She'd managed to ascertain that he was in the year above her and was, by all accounts, quite notorious.

She finished her toast and licked her fingers before folding the letter in half and sliding it into an envelope. She could go to the post office on Haverstock Hill and buy a stamp on her way to college. She cleaned her teeth, tied her hair up into a high ponytail, gave herself a small, *that'll do* once-over, and grabbed her pink beret. Slinging her blue hessian bag across her chest, she picked up the letter to Agnes and left.

She still hadn't quite got the knack of the sliding grille door on the lifts, and as she descended to the hall she found herself struggling again with the latch.

'Can I help you with that?'

She looked up. It was the man with the round spectacles. He had a paper and a box of eggs tucked under one arm.

'Thank you but I think I've' – she managed to heave the door open – 'got it.'

She stepped out and gave him an awkward smile. He didn't look awful close up. In fact he looked rather kind, like the sort of person who'd end up becoming a vicar: brown hair, cut short, warm hazel eyes and the open expression of someone with nothing to hide. He was wearing a cream checked shirt tucked into soft beige corduroy trousers, a navy-blue tank top, and he definitely had two shoes: brown brogues, polished.

He held out his hand. 'Charlie Allen. I live on the second floor.'

'Eleanor Ledbury. I live on the third.' They shook. His hand was large and soft.

'Marjory's flat? She told me to look out for you.'

'Yes. I know.' Eleanor wasn't sure how to present herself. Her natural instinct was to be polite, but this was her mother's spy. She didn't want this agent of maternal forces worming his way into her everyday life. She was going to have to pretend to be unfriendly. Put him off. That would do it.

Charlie glanced at the envelope in her hand. 'Ah,' he said, pointing with a finger. 'You need a stamp. The post office on Haverstock Hill is closed. They've had a burst pipe. You'll have to walk up to Hampstead.'

'Oh,' said Eleanor, blinking.

'I can take you there if you like.' He began to move back towards the door.

'But you were just coming in.' She shot a glance towards the eggs and pointed at them. 'Breakfast and whatnots.'

Charlie looked down at the eggs cradled in his arm. 'I don't think they'll go off,' he said, smiling, as he pushed the door and held it open for her. 'And it's a lovely morning. I really don't mind at all.'

This was the last thing Eleanor wanted. He had caught her on the hop.

Everything she said, she was convinced, would be re-layed back to her mother. She hesitated. 'I'm sure I can find it on my own. I can always ask, if I get in a muddle.'

'Really,' he said again, 'I don't mind.' He shot her a confident smile. She stared at him. He did seem very nice but she mustn't fall for it. This is how tricksters do it, she thought: inveigle their way in, make themselves useful. Next thing, she'd be relying on him for everything and every last hiccup would be reported back to Brill post-haste.

'It's not far,' he said, raising his eyebrows.

'All right,' she said, trying to conceal her reluctance. 'But I don't want to be late for college. Do you promise it's not far?'

'I promise.'

She gave him a thin smile and followed him out to the pavement. They turned and began the climb to Hampstead. Eleanor wasn't used to the company of men, other than her father and a few younger boys in the village, and she had never felt confident as a starter of conversations. She'd have to say something, she thought. This was probably a ghastly test, set by her wretched mother.

'I like your shoes,' she said suddenly. She regretted it instantly.

Charlie looked a little surprised. 'These old things? Don't look too closely. Right one's got a hole in the bottom. I need a trip to the cobbler's.'

Eleanor felt panicked, on edge. She now had nothing further to say.

'How are you finding it? London, that is?' Charlie looked down at her.

Eleanor kept her eyes fixed on the pavement ahead. 'Fine. I think.' A police car went past, the siren puncturing the air. 'Noisier than Brill.' She shot him a nervous smile.

'Ah, Brill. I've never been. Buckinghamshire, yes? Isn't it famous for a windmill or something?'

Eleanor nodded. 'Yes. The Brill Windmill.'

'I love windmills.' His voice was light, untroubled.

'Why?' Eleanor shot a glance sideways. 'Why do you love windmills?'

'*Don Quixote* is my favourite novel,' he replied. 'Tilting at windmills and all that.'

She frowned. 'I'm not sure I know what that means.'

'Fighting imaginary enemies ...' A small smile moved across his lips.

Eleanor bristled. She wondered if that was directed at her. She felt self-conscious and uncomfortable. All the same, she didn't want him to walk her to the post office and then ring her mother and tell her she was on edge and rude. Perhaps she needed to tackle this head-on.

'Look here,' she said, stopping. 'You're not to report back to my mother. I know you've been told to. But I'm asking you not to.'

Charlie looked down at her, his gaze a mixture of bemusement and indulgence. 'But I've spent a month learning Morse code.' He was teasing her.

Eleanor chewed her lip and walked a little faster while she thought of what to do next. Charlie kept pace.

'You're at the Chelsea School of Art, yes?'

Eleanor nodded. She felt annoyed with herself for being so gauche.

'Did you know, Dirk Bogarde studied there?'

'The actor?' Eleanor asked.

'Yes. Before the war.'

Eleanor didn't reply. She could feel her cheeks reddening. She shook her head again. Why could she think of nothing to say? It wasn't difficult. She picked up the pace. Perhaps it was better to get this over with as quickly as possible. She began walking as fast as she could, but her sandals, which were new, were rubbing the backs of her heels.

'His father was the art editor at *The Times*, where I work.'

'You work at *The Times*?' She sounded surprised, then checked herself. 'Sorry. I didn't mean to sound … incredulous. Of course you work at *The Times*. I didn't mean …' She ran out of steam. 'To cause offence.' She screwed her eyes tight shut. This was a disaster.

'None taken. Don't worry. I'm nothing fancy. I'm only junior. I'm currently allowed to cover cats up trees and girls who need stamps …' He glanced down at her, his eyes twinkling.

Eleanor gave a laugh, despite herself. 'I hardly think you'll get a column out of *me*,' she blustered. 'I'm exceedingly dull. All the more reason for you not to tell my mother anything.' She looked at him for a response but none came. 'Sorry. I shouldn't bang on about that. I think I might be paranoid.'

Eleanor winced. The backs of her heels were stinging and she stopped, momentarily, to adjust. As she pulled at the back of one of her sandals with a finger, she saw a small circle of blood seeping into her sock.

'New shoes?' asked Charlie.

Eleanor looked towards him. 'Do you notice everything? Perhaps I'm right to be paranoid?'

'I do actually,' he said, amused. 'Look. The post office is only five minutes away. You sit here on this bench and I'll take your letter up for you.'

Eleanor held the letter tighter to her chest. 'I'm not sure that's—'

'Or I can bring a stamp back down to you? Would you prefer that?'

They stared at each other in a strange, one-sided stand-off that neither of them properly understood. Eleanor looked again at the back of her sandals. Her heels really were hurting. She had some plasters in her bag – her mother had always taught her to go nowhere without them – and she did need to sit and sort herself out. 'All right,' she said, handing him the envelope. 'You can take it.'

'I won't be long,' he said, and she sat down, watching him as he went.

She reached into her bag and pulled out the box of plasters, fixed one to the back of each heel and stood. She glanced up the hill towards the post office. She felt awkward and panicked. She knew it was wrong, but she didn't want to be here when he came back.

She picked up her bag and ran back towards the Underground.

Chapter Eight

Now

'I didn't make them,' said Agnes, gesturing to the Tupperware box of scones on the bench next to her. 'It was my neighbour. She's a godsend. But she always gives me far too many. My new cooker won't be coming for eight weeks. I've been living on one-pot suppers. I've got one of those single-ring halogen hob things to see me through. It's quite good ... but eight weeks!' She stopped and noticed Rachel's slumped look. 'First-world problem. I'll stop moaning on. Thank God it's just me in the house though. There's an upside to being divorced after all!' She gave a light tinkling laugh.

They were sitting on the terrace in the garden under a large umbrella. It felt as if it hadn't rained for months, and the air was thick and oppressive. Agnes was balancing delicately on the edge of a wooden bench, one hand extended so that her fingertips were on the armrest. Rachel was lying in a zero-gravity chair, her legs raised, her arms splayed to the sides. It was as if she didn't even want the responsibility for her own weight. Despite the drought, the lavender in Eleanor's garden was flourishing, and Rachel watched as bees and butterflies dipped in and out like they were swimming in an ocean. One of Eleanor's neighbours had beehives. Lavender honey. How delicious.

The heat wasn't helping. It left Rachel feeling lethargic and ill. She was finding it hard to motivate herself. Every morning was a new affront. It was all she could manage to put clothes on. Even that was proving a struggle. She'd worn the same battered green shorts and blue polo shirt for five days in a row. It was her uniform for unhappiness. It was easier than having to make decisions.

Agnes was holding a small fan a few inches from her face. It was battery charged, so required no effort. It had a turquoise handle and a rubber grip that could be slipped about the wrist. It looked like an enormous sex toy. She shut her eyes and let the air flow across her face. 'I don't think it's rained here since April,' she mumbled. 'I'm amazed anything is still alive.'

Rachel squinted out into the blazing heat and the scorched earth beyond.

'Have you made your mind up?' Agnes said, opening one eye in Rachel's direction. 'About work, I mean?'

Rachel, still watching the bees, gave a shrug. 'I'm not going back to the gallery, if that's what you're asking. Can you imagine?'

Agnes grimaced. 'No,' she replied. 'I can't. But you can't let him ruin your career as well as your ...' She stopped herself. She didn't need to say that out loud. She shot an anxious glance sideways. Rachel hadn't flinched.

'I'm not sure working in Claude's gallery was a career. Not really. I think it was the easy thing to do.'

'But have you thought about ...'

'Actually,' said Rachel, interrupting, 'would you mind if we didn't talk about it? I'm not sure I'm in the mood.'

'Would you like a go on my fan?' Agnes held it out. Something to change the subject.

Rachel shook her head. 'No, thank you,' she said.

'I'm hopeless in the heat,' said Agnes, putting the fan back in front of her face. 'I don't know what I'd do without this. I'd probably end up killing someone. Heat makes me furious. Completely unreasonable.' She fell silent for a moment and turned her face slowly from left to right in the cool blasts of air. 'Perhaps you could find some curating work? At a museum? Or the university?'

Rachel said nothing.

'Or start painting again? You had a gift for it. It's going to waste.'

'We've already got one painter in the family, remember?' Rachel's voice was muted.

Agnes peered in Rachel's direction, worried she was pushing too hard. 'Sorry.' She put her fan down. 'These scones are going to ruin in the heat. Shall I get some plates?' she asked, to nobody. 'I should get plates. And the clotted cream. I put that in the fridge. Eleanor will have strawberry jam ...' She stood and waited for a sign of encouragement.

Rachel looked across the garden. Her mother, in a wide-brimmed hat, was trying to rescue her herb garden. She'd been filling a watering can from the dregs of a water butt and pouring carefully, at the roots, so the leaves wouldn't scorch. A trio of bird feeders hung just beyond her and a charm of goldfinches were swooping in and out, their little red faces looking like they had been burned in the afternoon sun.

'Well,' said Agnes, behind her. 'I'll get those plates.' She disappeared inside. 'Eleanor!' she called after a few minutes, as she re-emerged on to the terrace with the missing items. 'Scones!'

Eleanor cast an uninterested look over her shoulder and went back to what she was doing.

'Eleanor!' Agnes called out again. She curved her fingers across the top of her forehead and looked over at the herb garden. 'Do you think she heard me?'

'She heard you.'

'Oh well,' said Agnes, her mood still breezy. 'We don't need to wait.'

She pulled out a wire garden chair and sat down heavily. 'Everything's such an effort in this heat, isn't it?' She stretched out an arm for the Tupperware box but it was just out of reach. She scraped her chair backwards and got up again, with a theatrical roll of her eyes, picked up the scones and sat back down. 'Honestly,' she said, 'it's too much. Scone?'

'No, thank you,' said Rachel, watching passively as Agnes peeled back the lid of the Tupperware box. It made a satisfying slurp and a waft of just-made scones drifted towards her.

'You sure?' Agnes asked, raising her eyebrows in mild astonishment. 'They're fresh.' She took one, placed it on the plate in front of her and cut it neatly in two. 'I was thinking,' she said, reaching for the clotted cream. 'I wonder if it might be helpful to write Claude a letter.' She dug her knife greedily into the crust and smeared a thick wedge of cream on to her scone. She made small involuntary noises of pleasure, not unlike a cat.

'I haven't had any contact with Claude. I'm not sure I want to start.'

'No,' Agnes said, licking a finger voraciously, 'I don't mean a letter to send. I mean a letter to vent.' She held her knife in the air and pulled the jam towards her. 'A letter for your benefit. Write whatever you can't say to him. All of it. Splurge it out. Then don't send it. Burn it! Stick pins into it! It might help. Eleanor and I used to do it when we were younger. We wrote endless letters that were entirely for our own benefit. Every little grudge, every dark secret. Write it down, never send it. It's incredibly cathartic. You have no idea how it takes the weight off.' She dropped a dollop of red jam on to her scone. It looked like blood on the back of a sock.

Rachel didn't reply. The thought of seeing his name written down made her feel ill.

Eleanor walked slowly across the lawn and up on to the terrace. She dropped her hat on to the table and ran the back of her hand across her forehead. 'Did you make those?'

'No. Neighbour. Do you want one?'

'Not sure. It's too hot to eat.' She pulled out a chair and turned it so she was facing away from them. Kicking off her shoes, she spread her toes wide on the red brick floor of the terrace. She let out a sigh.

'You look pale, Eleanor,' said Agnes, her mouth full of scone and cream and jam. 'Are you feeling light-headed again?'

'It's just this infernal heat,' she replied, her voice drifting off across the garden.

'I had an idea,' said Agnes, pushing on. 'For Rachel. She could write Claude a letter. Get it all out of her system.' She picked out another scone from the Tupperware box. 'Do you remember when we used to do that? Every time we had a problem we couldn't solve: write a letter! Never send it.'

Eleanor said nothing.

'And another thing,' continued Agnes, cutting open her second scone. 'Why don't you keep an eye out for something at the university? Something for Rachel? There might be a job going at the Ruskin?'

'I doubt Rachel would like to go from working with the man who jilted her to working with her mother.' She stared off into the distance.

'Are you all right? You seem somewhere else entirely.'

'Do be quiet, Agnes.' Eleanor's voice was tired.

There was a short impasse. Eleanor rose, with some effort, to her feet. 'I think I'll go for a lie-down. I need a rest before I start painting again.'

Rachel watched her go, her body drifting like wood on water.

Agnes leaned over and put her sticky fingertips on Rachel's forearm. 'She's not herself. She's taken everything very hard,' she whispered.

'We all have,' said Rachel, then, sitting up, 'Pass me a scone.'

Chapter Nine

Then

Eleanor stared down at her fingers. They were covered in blue paint and she was rubbing at them with a wet rag. She looked around the sink for a bottle of turpentine: nothing, just a bar of dirty soap that wouldn't do. Perhaps there was some in the adjacent studio?

Using her elbows to open the door, she walked across the corridor and peered into the room opposite. It was the studio used by the second-year painting students, a large white space with enormous windows. It was filled with easels and, as far as Eleanor could tell, everyone had left for the day. Leaning down on the door handle, she wandered in.

She weaved her way through the canvases, still rubbing at her fingers, the smell of fresh paint in her nostrils. She paused at a canvas to look. A naked woman lying on a bed, her arm across her face as if she'd just committed an act of shame. Eleanor blinked. In her class, they weren't allowed to paint their own compositions yet. It was all still life and learning how to use oils.

'What do you think of this?'

She jumped and made an involuntary noise. Jake was standing back, his finger resting on his cheek. He had been hidden behind an ostentatiously large canvas and had a streak of red paint running through the front of his hair. He didn't have a black eye and he was wearing two shoes. He was questioning her as if they had known each other for years.

Eleanor's stomach flipped. She'd thought about him every day since she'd met him two weeks ago. Of course he was in the second-year painting studio. Why had she not thought to look for him here before now? She drank in his face to see if he was as beautiful as she'd remembered. He was.

She walked over to his canvas.

It was a self-portrait. He was sitting back, in a high armchair, looking off into the distance. It had a certain charm.

'I think you've made yourself look rather serious,' said Eleanor, tilting her head to one side.

'Aren't all great artists supposed to be serious?' he asked, turning to look at her.

'Do you think you're a great artist?'

He smiled. 'What do you think?'

'I think you look too serious.'

He narrowed his eyes as if trying to retrieve a memory. 'We've met, haven't we? Wait!' He held up a finger and closed his eyes tight shut. 'Fedifragous. Do I have that right?' He popped his eyes open and leaned towards her, expectant.

'Yes,' she said, smiling, 'you do.' Inside her chest, a small flock of birds took off.

'I never forget a long word. I live for them. What did it mean again?'

'Someone who breaks promises.'

'That's right. Remind me of your name. I'm afraid I can't remember that.'

The birds landed. 'It's Eleanor,' she said. 'My name is Eleanor.'

'Yes,' he looked at her properly now. 'Eleanor. I'm Jake.'

'I know.' She regretted saying so, instantly. Hesitating, she added, 'Only because someone mentioned you.'

'Oh, so you were talking about me? How delicious.' He tapped the end of her nose with a finger. 'You're a terrible liar. You need to work on that.'

Eleanor felt her cheeks burn.

'Why are you in here?' Jake turned away and put down his palette. 'Have you come to check out the competition or are you trying to steal ideas?'

'No. I'm looking for a bottle of turps. I have blue paint all over my fingers.' She held them up.

Jake took her hands in his and held them up to look at. His fingers felt smooth, silky, as they cradled the back of hers. His skin was tanned, unusual when they'd had such a poor summer. 'It looks like you're dying,' he told her, as he peered at the blue fingertips. 'Can't have that, can we?' His eyes smiled at her. 'I shall have to save you. Come with me.'

He slid her hand into his and led her carefully through the canvases. 'I feel like Orpheus,' he whispered, 'leading you out of the Underworld.'

'That story didn't end well,' said Eleanor.

'Don't worry,' he said, 'I won't look back.'

Eleanor glanced down at her hand in his. She felt a comfort she had never experienced, a feeling of being precisely where she should be. This felt uncomplicated. It felt right. It made her greedy. She wanted to know everything about him.

'Why are you so tanned?' she asked, as he led her towards a sink in the corner of the room.

'I've been in Greece. Karpathos. You won't have heard of it. It took three days to get there by boat from Rhodes. I think I was the only person there who didn't come from the island. They'd never seen anyone with blonde hair. Can you even imagine? I was like an exotic creature to them – something sent from the Gods. I had five proposals of marriage. But I didn't want to be a squid fisherman for the rest of my life. All that nasty ink.' He scrunched his nose up.

'How did you end up there?'

'Long story. Hold your fingers over the sink.' He reached up and pulled a bottle smothered in paint-stained fingerprints from the shelf above him.

She did as she was told and watched as he poured the turps over her hands. He had long eyelashes, she noticed, and he didn't need to shave. She could have insisted she do it herself. She was perfectly capable. Yet there was something intoxicating about having him do it for her. 'Rub your fingers together. Fast as you can.'

He smiled at her, as you would an animal that had grasped a command at first attempt. 'That's it,' he said, pouring a little more. 'Now put your hands under the tap.' He turned the water on and Eleanor wrung her hands together until the last of the blue was gone.

'There,' he said, looking at her fingertips again. 'You're alive again. Now we can go out.'

'I'm not sure you've asked me if I'm free,' Eleanor said, reaching for a hand towel. She curled her lip into a small smile.

She imagined him kissing her, there and then, leaning into her, his tongue reaching for hers. She longed for it. She'd only been kissed once before: by the man who ran the Brill Windmill. It had been his birthday and he was 'full of sauce' as her mother would have said. He'd grabbed her and kissed her on the lips, his breath all Scotch and ginger. She hadn't liked it. It was wetter than she'd imagined. Eleanor's gaze lingered on Jake's lips. They were full and inviting. She had never been kissed properly. She wanted that to change.

'I must warn you,' he said, grabbing a caramel suede jacket and throwing it on, 'that I have an almost endless capacity for unpredictability.'

'How do I know if that's true?'

'You don't. But it's only fair to warn you.' He flashed her a dazzling smile. 'So are you free to go out?'

'I'm free to go out.' She threw the hand towel back towards the sink and followed him towards the door.

Chapter Ten

Now

Rachel's phone rang. It was Johnny, her cousin, Agnes's son. They had grown up together, both only children, her almost-sibling.

She held the phone up to her ear. 'Hey.'

'How you doing, Squirt?'

'Currently very hot. I don't know how you cope with it all the time.' Johnny had married an old-money Italian aristocrat and lived in a large villa outside Siena. Rachel wasn't entirely fond of Francesca, his wife. She was high maintenance with film-star looks: haughty, lazy, entitled.

'Air con. That's how. Go and sit in your car and turn it on.'

'I love that you think I have a car with air con.'

'You're not still in that old Mini, are you?'

'Yes, I am still in that old Mini.'

'Well. That was your first mistake.'

Johnny was one of the few people she was comfortable talking to since that day. He never asked her about it.

'What are you doing?'

'Eating an ice cream.'

'I hate you. What flavour?'

'Actually, it's a mango sorbet. I'm lying to you.'

'Why are you eating mango sorbet for breakfast? What time is it where you are?'

'Eleven something? It's not breakfast.'

Rachel sat up, swung her legs round and picked up her watch: 10.24.

'How's Francesca?'

'That's why I'm calling. She's pregnant. I thought I'd tell you first.'

Rachel let out a small gasp, as if all the love left inside her was punched out. 'Oh, Johnny ... how long?'

'Twelve weeks. So, safe to let the cat out of the bag.'

'How do you feel?' Rachel's hand gripped the edge of the mattress, her knuckles whitening.

'Terrified. Thrilled. Like I want to eat mango sorbet.'

'Does Agnes know?'

'No, you're the first person I've told. I'll call her later. Don't say anything, will you? And don't mention it to Eleanor. She might tell her.'

'No chance of that, I'm avoiding her at all costs.'

'You know you can come and stay with us any time you want?'

'I know but ...' Rachel's voice trailed off. She wasn't ready to venture beyond her safety pit and, besides, it was all too hot. 'Maybe I'll come in September, when it's not so ... crazy.'

'All right, Squirt. So, there it is. You're going to be an aunt. Sort of.'

'And you're going to be a father ...' Her eyes drifted across to the photo of Charlie. 'I'm happy for you, Johnny. Really, I am. Give my love to Fran? How is she?'

'She hates getting fat. And she's been quite sick. Although I think she's secretly pleased about the being sick because it means not getting quite so fat.'

Rachel wiggled her chipped and forgotten toes. She really did need to find some nail polish remover. 'You're such a snitch, J.'

'I know. I learned from the best. I have to scoot. Don't say anything, remember?'

'I won't.'

Rachel let the phone slip from her hand on to the bed. She sat for a while, suspended in thought. It had been her plan, post-wedding, to get pregnant as soon as possible. Another thing on hold. Another thing sent crashing back to square one.

Pushing herself up from the bed, she reached over the desk in front of the window and pulled at the edge of the curtain. She was wearing nothing other than a pair of pants, a trail of sweat working down her torso. The room needed more air. She pulled back the curtain and reached forward to shove up the sticky window. Pushing hard, the window put up its usual fight but with a grunt she managed to shift it slowly upwards.

Down in the garden, she heard a metallic, clanking noise. She looked down to see Caspar staring up at her. She was topless with her arms in the air.

There are moments in life when time seems to stop and, as they both stood, frozen in mutual horror, Rachel thought of her mother standing naked in front of her the previous day, unbothered, defiant, her boldness leaving Rachel feeling subservient. For Eleanor, nakedness was strength, but Rachel felt nothing but embarrassment. Caspar looked away, quickly, bending down to pick up the spade he had dropped. Rachel pulled back from the window and stood, staring at it. She turned and looked at herself in the mirror. She had once had fulsome breasts, proud and pleased to see you, but she had lost so much weight over the past year it was as if someone had let the air out. She could see her ribs poking out and, as she stood, looking at this new unfamiliar body, she felt ashamed.

What had she been thinking? She had been desperate to lose weight for a man who hadn't shown up and then, to compound his control over her, she'd lost more. There was that cruel expression: 'She lost all the weight and she's still ugly.' That was how she felt. She was embarrassed that Caspar had seen her, not because she was naked, but because she was like *this*.

She turned back to a chair in the corner of the room and picked up the T-shirt and shorts she had worn the previous day. There was something in the shorts pocket. She put her hand in and pulled it out, a dried-up plum stone. Jesus, she thought, throwing it into the bin, this wasn't right. She used to have standards.

Perhaps she should write Claude that letter?

Pulling out the wooden chair from under the desk, she sat down and slid the pad of paper towards her. She flipped it open and stared at the blank page, then reached towards the pot of pens and chose a black rollerball, sleek in the hand and smooth on the paper.

Dear Claude, she wrote.

She stopped and ripped out the piece of paper, screwed it into a ball and tossed it to one side.

Again.

Claude

There was so much she wanted to say to him and yet, pen poised, she suddenly had nothing. It wasn't writing she needed to get out of her system, it was shouting.

FUCK YOU. FUCK YOU. FUCK YOU. She underlined the last *YOU* with a furious scribble.

She sat back, tore the page out, screwed it up and started again.

Claude, Agnes told me to write to you. She thought it might be cathartic. I have no idea where you are. I have no idea why you did it. Your lack of kindness has been breathtaking. I can only imagine how little you thought of me, how tiny your regard.

She stopped and looked up. A swallow was sitting on the telephone line beyond the garden. Charlie always used to point them out. 'Look,' he would say, his voice eager and urgent, 'a swallow!' and she would follow the end of his finger up and watch in wonder as they swooped and dived, little summer spitfires. Memories. They're all we have to bind us.

Perhaps there is something wrong with you? Do you have an illness? Are you dying? Were you trying to spare me a secret pain? When did you decide you were going to do it? A minute before? An hour? A day? A week? A month? Perhaps you wanted to tell me before Charlie died and you couldn't? For future reference, if your fiancée's father dies and you think, fuck it, I'm not that into her, just tell her there and then. You could have told me when my forehead was on the back of his cold hand. You could have told me the worst news in the world in that moment and it wouldn't have touched me. But waiting until the day? No, Claude. No.

She paused. The noise of a distant lawnmower was rumbling quietly through the window. 'Someone's still got grass?' she muttered to herself, frowning. She lifted her chin and shut her eyes. It was the sound of summer holidays, lying in a hammock, swinging, using an old bamboo stick to push yourself off, the smell of just-cut grass filling the air. Simple summers. Simple pleasures. She opened her eyes.

I wonder if you're wondering how I am? Well. I'm sitting in my old bedroom, the one back at Mum's. It's less than ideal. My mother is getting on my nerves and her gardener has just seen my tits. I look awful. I smell. I don't know who I am. Who do you think you are? I haven't got a clue. I don't know what else to say to you.

She stared down at the letter.

Rachel, she signed off finally.

She stared again, the pen floating above the paper.

PS: Johnny is having a baby.

PPS: I miss my dad.

She sat hard into the back of the chair, her hands falling into her lap.

What would Charlie have said to her? What would he have told her to do? He wouldn't have let her sit moping with old plum stones in her pockets. Every moment she spent doing nothing was another second stolen from her by Claude. Charlie wouldn't have stood for it and neither should she. Johnny was moving forward with his life. And so should she.

She pushed back from the table and stood up. She was going to leave the house. She was going to go back to Oxford, the place that had been theirs. She was going to sit in the Queen's Lane Coffee House and order a BLT and a latte, and then she would walk into a beautiful bookshop and take her time and buy a bag full of books and feel normal again. She was going to reclaim her own life.

She opened the chest of drawers and, with a flourish, pulled out a pair of red three-quarter-length trousers and a loose, light, flowery smock top. There was an urgency to her as she changed, a snake sloughing off dead skin at the speed of light. She ran a hand through her hair. She was tanned from sitting in the sun. A little mascara. That would do. She slung a battered brown-leather pouch bag across her chest, stuffed her wallet into it and slipped her feet into a pair of already tied Converse trainers. She opened the bedroom door and clattered down the stairs.

'Rachel!' Eleanor had heard her.

'I'm going out!' Rachel shouted back. She stood in the hallway and looked at every available surface. Where had she left the key to her car three weeks ago?

'Where are you going?' Eleanor appeared in the hall doorway, behind her.

Rachel lifted up a pile of magazines and some unopened post sitting on a side table. 'I'm just popping into Oxford.'

'Can you wait till later? There's something I want to talk to you about.'

'Not really. Have you seen the key to the Mini?' She rifled through a box of random flotsam with her fingers.

'I think I moved it. I think it's in the blue box in the kitchen.' Eleanor held her hand to her forehead. She looked troubled, heavy with thought.

'Right.' Rachel pushed past her into the kitchen. Eleanor turned round to watch her forage for the key.

'Rachel,' said Eleanor again, her voice rising a little. 'I would like to talk to you. It's important.'

Rachel saw the key and grabbed it. 'Found it. Just tell me quickly,' she said, moving back past Eleanor into the hallway. She didn't want to lose momentum. If she didn't act on this impulse it might disappear as quickly as it had arrived.

'I ... can't.' Eleanor faltered. 'There isn't a short version. It's the thing I've been waiting to talk to you about. Something I should have spoken to you about years ago but ... there was Charlie and ...'

Rachel stopped and looked at her mother. She seemed out of sorts, not her normal cool and aloof self. Something was rattling her. 'Can it wait till this evening?' she said, her hand on the front door. 'I've suddenly got an urge to go out. And you were rather keen for me to do that ... so ...'

'Well,' Eleanor began. She seemed a little lost, confused, deflated, as if she'd built herself up for something that was now not going to happen. 'All right,' she said, her voice resigned and weary. 'Go to Oxford. We'll do it later.'

She looked at her daughter and Rachel noticed it was not a look of irritation or disdain. It was one of profound sadness. Without another word, Eleanor turned back towards the kitchen and slipped away.

Rachel opened the door and left.

Chapter Eleven

Then

Jake was in full swing: garrulous, beaming, iridescent. He had taken Eleanor's hand and hailed a taxi, ushered her into it and ordered the driver to take them to the Ad Lib club at 7 Leicester Place.

It felt so good to be going out, exciting to be here, with him! Eleanor could barely believe it.

'Can you afford this?' Eleanor asked, keeping an eye on the meter.

Jake shrugged it off. 'Of course I can afford this.'

'Have you sold a painting?' She looked innocent, inquisitive.

Jake let out a roar of laughter. 'No, I have not sold a painting. I just can. Besides, it's vulgar to discuss income. We're having fun, aren't we?'

Eleanor nodded. It was impossible not to feel delicious and wicked. She stared out of the window at the boutiques, the Chelsea women in Mary Quant minis, their eyes like dark pools, their hair in dancing bobs.

'People don't look like this in Brill,' she mumbled, then, turning to explain, 'that's the village I'm from.'

'Don't tell me anything about yourself,' Jake said, holding a hand up to stop her. 'I don't care where you've come from, or who your father is, or if your mother once waved a flag at the Queen. All I want to know is everything, and I mean *everything*, from here forwards. Deal?' He offered her his hand.

Eleanor stared into his dancing eyes and took his hand. Her previous life in Brill had been safe and predictable. There was something seductive about starting anew. 'Deal.'

It was an ugly building, anonymous, the perfect fit for the pop stars, actors and fashion designers who wanted to have fun, unnoticed and unbothered, but all the same, it still came as something of a shock that a club so notorious as the Ad Lib was housed in such a forgettable shell.

'Ignore the concrete,' Jake said, waving over at the building as they got out of the cab. 'Trust me, your life is about to become a little bit more fabulous. How much, cabbie?'

Eleanor stood and stared upwards. Surely this was a joke? It looked like an office building for insurers or people who sold pencils. It was impossible to comprehend that somewhere up there, on the fourth floor, the movers and shakers of the happening scene were merrily doing whatever it was they had to do.

'Are you sure they're going to let us in?' Eleanor asked, as Jake appeared at her side.

'Of course they are!' he replied, with faux outrage. 'We're artists, aren't we? EVERYBODY loves artists. We're so de rigueur. Besides, I know the doorman. He adores me. Come on.' His enthusiasm was outrageous.

He skipped up the short three steps to a stuccoed door and, winking at Eleanor, rapped three times. A little wooden panel behind a metal grille slid to one side.

'Billy!' Jake exclaimed, on seeing a pair of grey rheumy eyes peer out. 'I've got a pal with me. Soon-to-be-famous artist. Do you mind?' He flashed his charming smile.

There was a loud click and the door opened. 'Evening, Jake,' said the doorman, 'here till the milk comes?'

'Probably,' Jake replied, scrunching his nose up. 'This is Eleanor. She's devoid of inhibition.'

Eleanor felt a small surge of anxiety. It was hardly the case that she lacked inhibitions. If anything, she felt smothered with them. She looked at the doorman and managed a weak smile. He was wearing a navy suit, white shirt and blue tie. His hair was slicked back. He looked like a gangster. He didn't respond. Instead he sat back on a tall wooden stool and pointed off towards the lift a few feet up the corridor.

'Can't believe there isn't a queue,' said Jake. 'It's like Moses and the Red Sea. All for you, Eleanor.' He took both her hands and spun her round as he dragged her towards the lift. 'Isn't she beautiful, Billy?' he called out as he pressed the button inset into the wall.

'Very pretty,' said Billy, tapping a cigarette out from a packet on a shelf next to him.

'You're like Peter Pan,' she said, as the lift doors opened and she walked inside. 'I feel like we're off to a dodgy never-never land.'

'We shall have to keep our eye out for pirates and crocodiles,' he said, pressing the button for the fourth floor. 'I've always fancied myself as a Lost Boy.'

There was a ping and the lift came to a stop. Jake shot her a mischievous look. 'Ready for your grand entrance?'

Eleanor felt a knot tie itself in her stomach. She wasn't sure she was.

They walked out into a short, wood-panelled corridor at the end of which was a silver door. It was startling, the stuff of fairytales, thought Eleanor. She could feel her heart beating a little faster but it wasn't excitement, it was nerves. She wasn't at all sure that she was remotely interesting. She wasn't at all sure she fitted in, and she didn't want to be found out.

"'In Xanadu did Kubla Khan a stately pleasure dome decree,'" said Jake, his hand on the door. 'Shall we?'

Eleanor nodded and Jake pushed open the door to reveal a dark, pulsing mass beyond. The heat of bodies rushed over her in a wave, the slightly sour smell of excess, and as she walked into the thick beat of an R&B band playing on a raised platform at the back, her eyes darted greedily from left to right. The walls were a gaudy swirl of colours, peppered with glass mosaics. The room had a sensuous gloom, the little light there was dancing off the squares of glass on the walls so that the people huddled in corners appeared dappled like flowers on a forest floor. Everywhere she looked she caught glimpses of people she recognised, the bright young things of the London scene, all capering towards their own skyline. Fame, Eleanor thought, was as fleeting as the light bouncing off the walls. She was captivated.

'Do you know these people?' She tried not to sound overwhelmed.

'Of course,' said Jake. 'Think of it as a rather small garden pond. If you're all frogs with only a few places to go, you're going to keep bumping into each other. And besides, artists are like rock stars at the moment. It's so easy. You have no idea.'

A girl with shoulder-length hair sashayed past her, high cheekbones, a lime-green minidress with a bold white stripe across its hem. She was wearing matching white-and-green winkle-picker slingbacks. Eleanor was wearing her cut-off cotton trousers with a loose blue blouse tucked into the waistband. There was paint on one sleeve. 'I'm not sure I'm quite dressed the part,' she shouted across the din to Jake, who was pushing his way forward.

'Don't worry,' he shouted back. 'You look incredibly authentic. You're an artist, remember? You're going to make quite the first impression. John!' He waved over to someone sitting in a far corner. A young man, cigarette stuck to his bottom lip, looked up and raised a pointing finger. It was the only invitation Jake needed.

Grabbing Eleanor's hand, he pulled her to him and shouted into her ear, 'John Farson. Photographer. Knows everybody. He's the second-worst person I know. Let's go.'

As they approached, Eleanor could see John Farson wasn't quite the young ingénue he had seemed from a distance. He was sitting in a red velvet booth, leaning back, his eyes lazy and louche. He was wearing a black leather jacket and a shirt, open to the top of his chest. His arms were spread out on the back of the banquette, his legs splayed wide. He was confident, sexy, and had the aura of a large carnivorous animal casually waiting for his next prey. Beside him was a woman, a tarnished beauty, who was laying into him with a ferocity Eleanor wasn't used to.

'You're a bastard!' she yelled.

'I know,' he replied, as if accepting the inevitability of the assertion.

'Your soul is like a burned-out grate.'

'Ah,' he said, glancing up at Jake and leaning forward to shake his hand. 'The cavalry has arrived. Jake, do you know Hen?' He gestured towards the woman at his side.

'Everyone knows Hen,' said Jake, with a glorious smile.

She looked up at him, her eyes blazing. 'Do you know what he's done?' she asked, casting an accusatory look in John's direction. 'He took pictures of me, naked. Research, he said, for God knows what. I don't give it another thought. And then I come in to be met with loud cheers from that table over there.' She pointed to a rowdy group of young men who didn't quite look local.

'Sailors,' explained John, draining his glass.

Eleanor turned and looked at them. They were young, giddy, entirely drunk.

'And the reason they were cheering was because John has sold them prints of my nudes for ten shillings a pop. It's an absolute disgrace.'

'It is,' nodded John. 'I should have given them to them for nothing.'

Jake gave a loud guffaw and Eleanor, too shocked to say anything, stood staring awkwardly.

'God, John,' said Hen, reaching into her handbag for a compact and her lipstick. 'I'm surprised you haven't choked on your own venom.' She reapplied her lipstick. 'Is someone going to buy me a drink, or what?'

'Oh dear,' said Jake with a sly smile. 'It would appear we are entangled in trivial matters. You sit there, Eleanor. I'll get the drinks. Buck up, you two. It's our duty to impress our new friend. This is Eleanor,' he announced to the table. 'She's only just met me and yet she's here. I think you'll agree, that's excessively brave.'

Eleanor sat and stared into the eyes that were now boring into her. She felt the way she had on that first day at college when Jake had stood peering at her. It made her feel uncomfortable.

'Do you smoke?' asked John, offering her his packet.

'No, thank you,' said Eleanor, shaking her head.

'Is that paint on your sleeve?' asked Hen, folding away her compact.

'Yes. I'm at Chelsea. I've arrived straight from college. I didn't expect to come here. It was rather spur of the moment.'

'Mmm,' mumbled Hen, putting her lipstick away. 'Get used to that.'

'Is it true? What Jake said?' asked John, studying her closely. 'That you're brave?'

'I'm not sure,' said Eleanor, not wanting to betray herself. 'I don't know if I feel brave.'

'I rather like brave people,' said John, taking the last drag of his cigarette, 'mostly because I'm a terrible coward.'

'Yes,' agreed Hen, 'you are.'

'Hen has slept with pretty much everyone in this room,' said John, with casual indifference.

'I haven't slept with you,' replied Hen, with cool disdain, 'I've got *some* taste.'

John leaned forward and mock-whispered to Eleanor, 'Pay no attention to Hen. She doesn't care about the pictures really. She likes sailors. Don't you, Hen?'

'Yes, I do.'

'Tell her why.'

'Because they always have to leave in the morning.' Hen, who, up till that moment, had been frowning, burst into a loud laugh. John laughed along with her.

Eleanor was puzzled. Moments ago they'd been at each other's throats.

'Where's that beautiful boy with the drinks?' Hen asked, trying to drain dregs that no longer existed from her glass. 'Are you two lovers?'

'No,' protested Eleanor, slightly shocked. 'We've only just met.'

'Probably for the best,' said Hen, with a thin smile.

'Oysters!' yelled Jake, appearing back at the table. 'I have ordered champagne and oysters!' He threw himself on to the banquette next to John and grinned at Eleanor. He was in his element, a bird of paradise, back in the canopy to which he belonged. He was followed by two waiters: one with an ice bucket and a champagne bottle, the other holding a large oval silver platter on his shoulder.

Hen clapped her hands in delight. 'Oh goody,' she squealed. 'Aphrodisiacs. Precisely what's required.'

'I always forget you've got money,' said John, tapping out another cigarette. 'The joys of an enormous trust fund.'

'Oh, this isn't for you,' said Jake, with a twinkle. 'But you're very welcome to watch us enjoy it.' He shot a wink at Eleanor, who felt her cheeks redden at the gesture. She was starting to understand the dynamic. Everyone was ghastly to each other, as if they didn't care, when in fact it was very clear they all cared enormously.

'You can only be awful to people you like,' said Hen, noticing Eleanor's expression. 'Remember that.'

The waiter lowered the vast and opulent platter smothered with opened shells, lemon wedges and a little hill of crushed ice. Eleanor had never seen the like. She'd once had a glass of brown shrimp at a cousin's wedding, but oysters!

'Tuck in, tuck in!' said Jake, waving his hand generously.

Hen didn't need asking twice. She picked up a shell and took a small silver fork from a tiny pot at the platter's centre. Eleanor watched as she slid the fork under the oyster and squeezed lemon on to the bulbous surface.

'I love to see them wince,' Hen said, her eyes narrowing in wicked delight. Lifting the shell to her lips, she threw the oyster into her mouth and tossed her head back. 'Scrummy,' she said, licking her lips. 'Shall I pour the champagne?'

'Ignore her,' said Jake. 'Squeeze of lemon, Tabasco if you like a little heat, don't chew, down in one.' He threw back his own, shook his head and let out a delighted gasp of intense satisfaction.

'I'm not sure I want one.'

'I thought you were supposed to be brave?' asked Hen, with a pout.

'Perhaps you think we're trying to corrupt you?' said John, staring at her.

'You can't corrupt the incorruptible,' replied Eleanor, picking up her champagne. 'I knew someone once, a friend of my mother's. She ordered two hundred and ten oysters for her daughter's twenty-first birthday but she didn't realise you had to keep them completely cold and alive until the moment you ate them.'

'Oh no,' said Hen, her face lighting up at the thought of a terrible failure, 'I can see where this is going.'

'I think she poisoned every person there.'

John leaned in, his eyes wide and eager. 'Did anyone die?'

'I don't think so, no.'

'Ah,' said John, leaning back again. 'A story without the proper punchline.' He lit a match and held it to his cigarette.

'You're so morbid, John,' said Jake. 'What shall we drink to? Eleanor? Our new muse?'

He was a flatterer, unapologetic, romantic, treacherous. He was a cliff edge about to crumble. She could see all this and yet she was unable to do anything but career towards him like a burning rock hurtling towards the earth. She had never been to a place like this, never been around people like them, never felt more alive than she did now. And it was all because of him.

Hen stood up and raised her glass. 'To our new muse!' she cried, lifting her glass into the air.

Jake stood too and hoisted his glass aloft. 'I love meeting someone new, don't you?' he said, smiling at John. 'It's so ... intoxicating.'

John said nothing, picked a strand of tobacco from the end of his tongue and tipped his glass towards Eleanor. 'Welcome to the madness,' he said, and downed his drink in one.

Chapter Twelve

Now

Rachel was sitting at a table next to a window in the Queen's Lane Coffee House, a book of Japanese myths open in front of her. She had always loved fairytales. There was something refreshing about the clean lines between right and wrong, the lack of ambiguity. You knew where you were.

She stirred her cappuccino and licked the spoon until all the chocolate had gone. Outside, tourists were wandering about, heads turned towards distant spires, staring down at maps, taking group selfies with phones at the end of sticks. What a funny breed we are, thought Rachel: trying to create memories, to cement them, to hold on to fleeting moments for ever. She wondered who she was in her own story. Was she the heroine? The baddy? Was she to blame for what had happened with Claude? Who was Eleanor?

'Wicked Witch,' Rachel mumbled, her chin resting on her upturned palm.

What did Eleanor want to talk to her about? Rachel wondered. Now she was out of the house her mind felt clearer than it had in weeks. Her mother had seemed out of sorts, quite unlike herself. Perhaps it was about Charlie's will? Maybe Eleanor was thinking of selling Brill? Rachel had always thought the only way Eleanor would leave that house was in a wooden box. All the same, it was meant for a large family ... and maybe ... Rachel felt some annoyance then. If Eleanor was moving, Rachel would have to move too. Where would she go? To Siena, to stay with Johnny? Her nose scrunched up at the thought of weeks on end with Francesca. She'd be even worse now she was pregnant.

'Are you finished?'

Rachel looked up. 'Sorry?' she said. Standing above her was the young waitress, well presented, fresh-faced.

'With the plate? Are you finished?'

Rachel stared down at the empty things in front of her. 'Yes. I'm finished.'

The waitress took her plate. 'Do you want another coffee?'

'Umm, no,' she replied, picking the spoon up from the table and putting it back on the saucer. 'I'll just get the bill, please.'

She leaned into the back of her chair and closed her book. Was she finished? No, she wasn't finished, despite Claude's best efforts.

She felt a surge of rage. She'd managed to keep a lid on her anger, but now, back in Oxford, the city they had lived and worked in together, she felt annoyed at having given up everything she had built for herself and he had ... well ... she didn't know. She stood, unhooked her bag from the back of her chair and slung it over her shoulder and across her chest. She picked up her bag of new books, walked over to the counter and paid. She knew what she needed to do.

The Three Choughs Art Gallery was in a small side street off St Giles, the road that headed towards Jericho. She hadn't been back since that terrible evening: driven there by her stony-faced mother, she had let herself in, half hoping she would find him there. Eleanor had sat outside in the car, staring dead ahead while Rachel silently removed her wedding dress, packed a bag and left. She hadn't been back since.

She wasn't quite sure how she felt, returning to the place they had worked and lived together for five years She wondered if her wedding dress was where she had left it, draped accusingly over the back of a chair. If anything she felt a little unhinged, verging on hysterical.

She edged slowly up the road, like a cat prowling for prey, her eyes fixed on the black awning of the gallery. If he was back, it would be open. She'd given up trying to contact Claude ages ago. Now here she was, on their street, staring at their gallery, and if the door was open, he would be inside. There was a Range Rover parked illegally opposite the gallery, not enough to be directly in front of it, but just enough to allow Rachel to see in from behind it. The gallery's door was open. She felt a tight knot in her stomach. He was there. Just inside the door, she could see a woman, smart, attractive, mid thirties. She was looking up at a Harland Miller that Claude had acquired, a Giclée print of a Penguin book cover, a deep olive green with five coloured horizontal stripes across the top. *Five Ring Circus*, it was called: *It's All Fun and Games Till Someone Loses an Eye*. How prescient, thought Rachel.

It was strange to stand there, hovering behind a black Range Rover, looking in at her old life: the happy memories, the late-night suppers, the bottles of wine, the sex. She hadn't imagined it would come to this. There was something vaguely ridiculous about it. 'What am I doing?' she whispered to herself.

And then she saw him.

Rachel could hear the blood pumping in her ears. There he was, his back to her, standing next to the woman looking up at the Harland Miller painting. She knew what he would be doing: talking about the power of the artist, the bold design, the nostalgia captured so contemporaneously, the intellectual commentary, the *investment*. She didn't blink, her eyes boring into him. He was wearing a cream linen suit, the one Rachel had bought him for the wedding.

She felt stunned, frozen. He turned, smiling down at the woman by his side. He was tanned and looked relaxed, his eyes bright and engaged. He put his hand on the middle of the woman's back, leaned in and whispered something. She roared with laughter and he laughed too. She could barely bring herself to think it.

He was happy.

The bastard was happy.

'What am I doing?' Rachel mumbled. She turned and caught a glimpse of herself reflected in the shop window behind her. Her hair was scraped back into a ponytail, her fringe sticking to her forehead in the heat. The little mascara she was wearing had bled down under her eyes and the floral smock top she'd pulled on that morning in a moment of triumphant dynamism had, on closer inspection, got a large oily stain over the left breast. She looked mental.

She glanced back. Look at him. He's in a £3,000 suit that Rachel used the last of her savings to pay for. He's sufficiently content to be able to charm strangers. 'Oh my God,' Rachel muttered. 'I hate him.'

She had to get out of here. Where was her car key? She needed to leave. She reached into her bag, her eyes still fixed on Claude. He was moving the woman on to a sculpture of a hare set on a plinth that sat in the front window. They turned and were now facing out. Rachel instinctively ducked down but, as she did, the key in her hand fell loose, bounced off the edge of the pavement and slipped down between the holes of a grate.

'Oh, for fuck's sake,' Rachel complained, kneeling down to look. The grate was shallow and she could see the key, but as she reached down with her fingers she couldn't quite grasp it. This was the last thing she needed. She bobbed back up, peering again towards the gallery's front window. He was still there, his arm now around the woman's shoulder. She stared back at the grate. Could she lift it? Was it loose? She put her fingertips under the slit nearest to its edge and tried to pull upwards. No, that wasn't going to work. Think. What did she have in her bag that might be useful? She was crouched, her back against the Range Rover, her thighs beginning to burn from the effort of staying out of sight. She stared down into her bag.

'Fuck this,' said Rachel, grabbing some chewing gum, a biro and a paperclip.

She tossed three pieces of gum into her mouth and chewed ferociously, then stuck the ball of gum on the end of the battered biro. Holding the biro in her mouth, she undid the paperclip to its full length, turned one end up so it made a hook, took the biro from her mouth and pressed the long end of the paperclip through the chewing gum so it was sitting inside the barrel of the biro. Getting down on to her hands and knees, Rachel thrust her homemade hook down through the grate. 'Come on,' she muttered, as she tried to catch the end of the paperclip in the ring of her car key. To her surprise, she managed to do it on the first attempt and, angling it so she could lift the key, she reached in with her fingers and pulled it out.

Claude stood in the doorway of the gallery and waved off the woman.

Rachel was already gone.

Back in Brill, Rachel pulled into the car park of the village pub, the Pheasant, and put her forehead on the steering wheel. She had cried all the way back from Oxford and hated herself for it. She glanced at her watch. It was just past three. Caspar's green van was still in her mother's driveway. If she remembered rightly, he'd be gone by four. She reached into the side of her car door and pulled out a mass of tissues, found one that wasn't entirely gross, and blew her nose. She needed a drink.

'I'll have a glass of the Gavi, please,' she said, trying to avoid looking at the barman directly. Her voice was low and joyless, and part of her felt ashamed of wanting to drown her sorrows. This felt like a slippery slope. All the same ...

'Medium or large?' asked the barman, turning to take a glass from a shelf behind him.

'Large. Actually, sorry. Make that two.'

She didn't want to sit in the bar. It was still trilling with the aftermath of jolly summer-holiday lunches. Besides, the place was still haunted with memories of Charlie: him handing her a bottle of Coke with a straw, leaning against the bar with an illicit packet of pork scratchings, sitting together by the fire, waiting for the Sunday lunches with the enormous Yorkshire puddings. She wanted to be somewhere where she didn't have to remember and nobody could look at her. She wasn't convinced the crying had stopped. She took her drinks out to the beer garden at the back. It was so hot that people were choosing to sit in the shade, but there was one table, out in the blazing sun, that was empty. She slid on to the bench under it and stared out. She felt like a burnt-out car.

Behind her she heard a soft 'wow', and she glanced back to see a young woman, twenty at the most, standing next to a young man the same age. It was a scene that played itself out regularly: people came here on first dates, the windmill being the perfect secret to reveal. Look at what I've found. Look at the place I know about. It's our secret place now. It's everyone's secret place.

Rachel thought about her first proper date with Claude. He'd invited her to Oxford for the day and she'd travelled up excitedly from London, keen to get away from the dirt and the thick, hot air. He'd taken her punting, laid on an expensive hamper. She had been touched by the effort. He'd worn a white panama hat with a black ribbon above its brow and a crisp white shirt, sleeves rolled up to the elbows. His faded blue cotton three-quarter-length trousers were fastened with a battered brown leather belt that was a little too long. His ankles were chiselled, his feet brown and long. She had sat, staring up at him, as the water from the punt pole trickled down his arm, and had wondered whether he was going for a modern Mr Darcy or was trying to look like someone in a Graham Greene novel. All the same, she had fancied him rotten.

He had talked lucidly on a range of topics, skimming easily from one to another. He was engaging and attentive. He made her feel interesting. At one point, they had punted around a bend in the river, only to see two middle-aged men on their knees on the bank, violently wanking each other off. It was shocking. Claude had done nothing more than raise an eyebrow and shrug. 'Needs must,' he said, and punted on. He was unfazed, in control, charming. She had sex with him that afternoon.

Rachel sighed and pushed the empty glass to one side, then pulled the second towards her. Shutting her eyes, she lifted the glass to her mouth and began to gulp it down, stopping to breath heavily through her nose. She had never been able to chug down drinks. This was an effort. Second glass dispatched, she pushed herself up and reached for her purse. She'd get two more before the alcohol kicked in.

Several drinks later and she looked down at her phone. Bloody hell. It was seven o'clock. She'd been there four hours. Caspar would be gone now and she was sufficiently fucked that her mother would let her go straight to bed. She could put off being told about Charlie's will or selling the house or whatever it was Eleanor wanted to tell her until the morning. She pushed herself up. She'd leave the car and walk back through the hollyhocks and the buddleia and the late summer roses, the heat of the day still lingering, and remember that life is a wonderful thing even if you are dragged through it.

As she walked through the front door, the house was silent. The radio wasn't on and she stood for a moment, wondering if she should call out and announce her return.

Where was her mother?

Rachel walked through to the kitchen. Her mind wandered and she looked around the room, taking everything in lazily. Her eyes rested on a small rectangular tin that was sitting at the end of the table, an old toffee box by the looks of it. Next to it lay a knitting pattern with four tiny ladybird buttons scattered on top. Rachel pulled it towards her. The pattern was for a baby's cardigan. Agnes must have told Eleanor about Johnny. She picked up one of the ladybird buttons and frowned. She recognised it. These had been her buttons, from a little jacket she used to love wearing.

Rachel reached across the table for the toffee tin and peered inside. It was full of buttons, each one a memory, each one a tug back to the past: a button from Johnny's first school blazer, a large brown button from a jumper Charlie used to wear, jolts back to places and moments. She rifled through with her fingers, pulling out buttons and holding them in the palm of her hand: the button from Rachel's first snowman, a button that had once been the eye of a much-loved teddy, a button from a coat that Eleanor had bought Rachel for her tenth birthday. There were little birthday gift cards, hand-drawn pictures, a few letters still in their envelopes, some old photographs. It was a treasure trove of memories. Rachel stared down. All this time, Eleanor had been quietly keeping these trinkets of love. Rachel felt disarmed.

There was something else: a little, tightly wrapped piece of cotton. Rachel picked it out from the box and began to unwrap it. A beautiful handmade button fell into Rachel's palm. It was a bright sea blue with a coat of arms painted on it. Rachel had never seen it before. The cotton had some embroidery on it. She flattened it out and read, *My love, my love*. What was this button and who had it come from?

Rachel pushed herself up from the table and wandered into the studio. Where was her mother?

The studio door was open. She walked across the room, turning the button over in her hand, and stumbled a little down the steps into the garden.

'Eleanor!' she called out. Nothing.

She padded across the hot red bricks of the terrace, wincing a little at the heat on the soles of her feet.

She came to an abrupt stop as she saw her. Eleanor was lying face down among the lupins, her legs splayed, one arm folded under her. Rachel felt an urgent, piercing panic. She wasn't moving.

'Eleanor,' she shouted, as she ran towards her. She fell to her knees and took her by the shoulders. 'Eleanor, wake up!'

She turned her mother over. Her lips were blue, her face an awful grey, her eyes staring.

Rachel gasped, with the sharp, certain shock that her mother was dead. There was nothing to be done but despair. She clawed at Eleanor's dust covered shirt. 'No,' she cried, pulling her to her. 'No. No. No!'

She called out, choking desperately, 'Help me! Help!' but nobody was there to hear.

PART TWO

*'Let us not burden our rememberances with
a heaviness that's gone.'*

William Shakespeare

Chapter Thirteen

Now

'Her heart just stopped.' Agnes sat, her hand on Rachel's forearm, her voice soft and warm and kind. 'There was nothing you could have done. Not even if you'd been there when it happened.'

Rachel pulled at the front of her dress. She'd bought it in a hurry: a black wrap-around she'd found in a sale. It was on a rack with a gaudy plastic sign: 'SUMMER'S A BALL!' it yelled, with little firework explosions and popping champagne bottles. She hadn't bothered to try it on and, with all the weight she'd lost, she wasn't quite filling out the top. She hadn't worn black for Charlie's funeral, it had felt like an affront, but now, with this sudden, unexpected death, it was all she wanted to be in.

'I wasn't nice to her,' said Rachel, staring down into her lap. 'At all.'

'If we knew the precise moment when everyone was going to die, we'd be doing nothing but apologising,' said Agnes, with a sigh. 'I should have taken her to the doctor, but you know what she was like. Headstrong. No. I have to take some sort of comfort from the fact she died in the garden she loved, with no fuss. If she had to go, that's how she would have chosen it. We can hold on to that. And Charlie will be pleased to see her again ...' She gave Rachel's hand a squeeze then reached into the pocket of her jacket for a tissue. 'Oh dear,' she added, wiping her eyes. 'That's me off again.'

They were sitting in the front pew of All Saints, the parish church in Brill that, across generations, had seen all their triumphs and disasters. Rachel had chosen not to ride in those long black saloons so associated with death. Instead, she had insisted they all walk. Eleanor would be the only one to arrive by car. Her coffin had been delivered to the house that morning, and Rachel, Agnes and Johnny had stood staring at it in the studio. It was nice to have her back. They'd chosen a wicker coffin: it looked more like a glorious summer hamper than the usual miserable boxes, and they'd gone out into the garden and picked Eleanor's favourite flowers to weave into it. By the time the undertakers came back, Eleanor's coffin was a burst of colour and fragrance. It would be like planting a spring bulb.

The weaving of the flowers had been cathartic. It had allowed them to sit and tell stories, catch up on each other's news and gossip. At one point, Agnes started telling a story about the woman she paid to zap her 'old lady whiskers'. She'd been trying to book an appointment for months, but the woman hadn't replied to any of her calls. 'I wondered if she'd died,' said Agnes. 'Turns out she was in prison.'

They had all gasped and stopped what they were doing. 'What for?' asked Johnny.

'She was running a brothel,' said Agnes, her eyes wide. 'Can you imagine? I was having my whiskers plucked in a brothel!'

They had all laughed and Rachel had found her hand resting on the side of Eleanor's coffin, the way you'd put a comforting hand on someone at a dinner party to let them know you hadn't forgotten they were still there.

Eleanor's death had left Rachel devastated, not only because it had been so unexpected but because of how deeply she was affected by it. She had been unaware of how much she loved her mother and it had come as a shock. What a terrible way to find out. She had replayed that last conversation with Eleanor a million times: the way her mother had stood staring at her, the insistence that she had something important to say. She had seen something in that moment that she had never seen in her mother before: anxiety, doubt, vulnerability. Her mother had been burdened with something, but what that burden had been, Rachel had no idea. She was plagued by it.

Yet it went beyond words unspoken. With Charlie, the illness took the brunt of Rachel's anger: there was time to process what he meant, where his footsteps in her life were. Eleanor's death felt different: it was complicated, gnarled, messy. Rachel was yet to process her memories. She didn't know which shelf to put her mother on. It wasn't just a conversation they hadn't managed to have, it was their entire relationship. It was unfinished business and it was hard not to feel consumed with regret.

Johnny had read the eulogy, a potted history of a life in seven minutes, and yet Rachel was struck by how little she really knew. She knew the facts. She knew about the awards, the recognition, the work. She knew Eleanor, the mother, the person to whom all things deferred, the distant presence, the artist, but as to who she *was*, Rachel was at a loss. We spend so much time with our parents, Rachel thought, it's a shame we don't get to know them.

The church was packed, another surprise. Who knew her mother was this popular? The pews were full, as were the side naves. 'Have you seen how many people are here?' whispered Agnes, as they stood to sing a hymn. 'There are even people standing at the back.'

Rachel glanced over her shoulder towards the rear of the church. There were men in smart overcoats, women in hats, all of them in black. A rather lovely light was pouring in through a stained-glass window and, as she was looking back, she realised with some horror that standing by the door, framed and illuminated by the delightful smoky beam, was Claude.

Rachel turned back, her voice catching in her throat as she tried to sing. Her mind emptied. She grabbed Johnny's arm. 'Claude's here,' she mumbled.

'What?'

'At the back. By the door. Lit up like an evil cherub.'

Johnny strained to see. 'What the ...' He turned back. 'I can't punch him until Eleanor's in the ground.'

'No,' said Rachel. 'I don't want you to punch him.'

'Punch who?' said Agnes, noticing something was afoot.

'Claude is at the back of the church,' muttered Johnny, with some urgency.

Agnes turned to look. 'My God. He's got a nerve. Are you going to punch him?'

'Please,' said Rachel, holding her hand up. 'Nobody is punching anyone.'

Rachel's mind was racing. She stared down at the hymn book but the words were swimming. She had to regain her composure. She was not going to allow him to take this from her.

'*O still small voice of calm*,' she sang. '*O still small voice of calm*.'

They all sat, Johnny throwing another dark look back towards the rear of the church.

'Just concentrate on Eleanor,' Rachel whispered, gripping his forearm. 'It doesn't matter. Forget him.'

She could sense Johnny's anger. He'd had less time to obsess about what Claude had done. This was a grab of the collar to drag him back to that day, that moment. She relaxed her grip but left her hand resting on his, calm and reassuring. It was OK. This was not going to bother them.

But it was bothering her.

She closed her eyes tight, took a deep breath and opened them again as if there were a magic reboot that could reset her mind, but however hard she fixed her gaze on her mother's coffin, she could feel his presence. Was he looking at her? What was she going to say to him? The vicar, who she had lost all track of, was now waiting for the pall-bearers to raise Eleanor up. 'I won't leave your side,' whispered Agnes, leaning in. 'I won't let him anywhere near you.'

This wasn't right. Eleanor was about to be carried for her last journey and they were all preoccupied with that sham of a man hanging around the back of the church, unwanted, unwelcome. Eleanor had never warmed to him. It had been another bone of contention. If anything, it had been more annoying that her mother had been right, again. Quite why he was here was anyone's guess. Rachel's breathing felt shallow and uneven. His presence had knocked her for six.

They stood. The coffin went up on to good men's shoulders and began the slow procession towards the door. Johnny took Rachel's hand and gripped it tight. How awful that this was the aisle he would end up walking her down. Head bowed, she looked at nobody. Her mind was a mess: it felt frantic, muddy. She stared at the stone slabs beneath her feet. *What was she going to say to him?*

She felt Johnny's grip lighten and the warmth of the summer sun pouring in through the open door. She steeled herself. If there was one thing she could do for her mother, it was this. She would hold her head up and she would look at him and she would stand tall and strong and undiminished. She took a breath and looked up.

But there was no sign of him.

'Must have bottled it,' muttered Johnny. 'Good thing too.'

Rachel walked on behind her mother. His disappearance left her shattered.

Rachel watched as the vicar, solemn and serious, committed her mother to the ground. She took her handful of earth when invited to do so, and stared down at the coffin. Death is not the final humiliation, she thought, this is: you're stuck in a hole and your relatives all take it in turn to throw mud at you. She didn't want to be here any more.

She stood back and scanned the cemetery. Only close family had come to the graveside. Everyone else was lingering back at the church entrance, waiting for the flag to go down for the rush to the pub. *She's dead! Now let's eat chicken wings and get pissed.*

'Francesca's feeling a bit pukey,' said Johnny, his hand touching the middle of Rachel's back. 'I think she should go back to the house for a lie-down.'

'It never lasts long,' Francesca said, pulling a small pot from her bag. 'Do you mind?'

'Of course not,' said Rachel, watching her unscrew the lid and fish out a sliver of pickled ginger with her finger. 'Does that help?'

'Ginger?' replied Francesca, popping it into her mouth. 'It's an absolute godsend. I'll go now. Before the ... don't want to interrupt the ...' She gestured off to the dark clump of mourners ahead of them.

Johnny placed a hand on her shoulder and kissed her cheek. 'Thanks so much for being here,' he said, a gratefulness that was received by Francesca as if she really had made the most enormous sacrifice. She blew a kiss into the air towards Rachel and Agnes and tottered off on her Italian high heels.

'Horrid to feel sick,' said Agnes, with an empathetic sigh, 'Roger!' she said, switching gear as a man with an ample moustache approached. 'How kind of you to come.'

Rachel watched Francesca trotting back to the house and wondered how it was that her cousin had found himself in a position whereby he felt lucky that his wife had showed up at his aunt's funeral. Was that it, then? Did they all shuffle off to the pub and check their phones and relegate Eleanor to the land of legends?

And had Claude really gone? She peered through the crowd of waiting acquaintances. She wanted him to see her and be consumed with regret.

'Rachel.'

She turned round, her eyes squinting in the sun. It was Caspar. He had put a suit on but his hair was still a rumpled mess and his fingernails ingrained with mud. 'I wanted to say how sorry I am about Eleanor. She was a lovely lady. I hope you're bearing up.'

She stared up into his face and found herself noting that he looked sadder than she did. She almost felt jealous. Here was someone with an uncomplicated relationship with her mother, who understood what he thought and felt about her.

'Thank you, Caspar,' she said, and held out her hand to shake his. It felt rough and honest. She wondered whether she should bring up the embarrassment of the last time they'd seen each other. No, perhaps not. 'It's very kind of you to come.'

He gave a small nod and looked as if he wanted to say something too, but instead he gestured towards the hole in the distance. 'I thought the coffin looked special,' he said. 'That was a lovely thing to do.'

Rachel nodded. 'We were spoiled for choice. You've looked after the garden very well.'

As they stood there, their eyes not quite meeting, an air of awkwardness threatened to settle. 'This is my cousin, Johnny,' Rachel said, by way of an escape.

'Hello,' said Caspar, shaking his hand. 'Sorry about your aunt.'

'Thank you,' said Johnny. 'How did you know her?'

'He does the garden,' interjected Rachel, folding her arms and pressing her lips together. She wanted to look for Claude, see if he was still there.

'I imagine it's been quite the challenge. In the hot weather.'

'Not too bad. There's lots of drought-resistant stuff. Lavender and the like. I didn't bother with the grass. That always comes back.'

Johnny nodded, but it was clear they all wanted to move on.

'Well,' said Caspar, sensing the mood. 'I'll leave you to it. It was a lovely service.' He gave another small nod and walked away, running a hand through that mess of hair. Rachel watched him go.

'He's seen my tits,' she said, looking evenly at Johnny.

'What?'

'Not like that. By accident. It was borderline horrific.'

'Hang on,' said Johnny, staring at her. 'How does someone see your tits by accident?'

'I'll tell you later,' she said, weaving her arm through his. 'I'm not sure I'm quite in the mood for the pub yet. I think I need to settle.' She looked up, at the people milling towards the road. Agnes was in full swing, herding people out and away from the church.

Johnny glanced at his watch. 'I think there's a wedding here in half an hour.'

As the crowd shifted, like a flock of starlings, Rachel saw him. Claude was standing on his own by the yew tree at the front of the church.

'He's still here,' she murmured. 'Claude.'

'Where?' said Johnny, pulling his arm free. His body tensed, his face hardening.

Rachel put her hand out to pull him back. 'Actually, Johnny, I think I want to do this on my own. Please don't do anything. Go to the pub.'

Johnny's face was urgent and protective. 'I don't know if I want to leave you on your own with him.'

'I appreciate what you're doing, but please. I have to.' She looked at him, her eyes resolute and resigned.

Johnny pulled her to him and held her. 'Come and get me if you need me. Deal?'

'Deal.'

There are moments in people's lives that should be played in slow motion, and as Rachel walked through the gravestones and across the grass towards the yew tree, she felt the weight of her suspended life. A strange calm had descended, all idle chatter blocked out. People were offering her their condolences as she passed, but she drifted through them, her focus entirely on the man in the navy suit standing under the tree.

'Hello, Claude,' she said, coming to a stop in front of him.

'Hello, Rachel.'

She looked at him properly. He was very tanned. He'd clearly been abroad. He'd had a haircut. His hair was swept back with some sort of wax. He's started using grooming products, she thought. That's new. He was wearing a salmon-pink shirt she hadn't seen before, entirely unsuitable for a funeral, and a navy tie with a Windsor knot. His jacket was buttoned up. The trousers were tapered at the ankle and he had on a pair of suede brogues that would be ruined if it suddenly decided to rain. She glanced up at the sky. No chance of that.

She stood, her arms by her side, scanning his face. This was the man she had loved – still loved, probably. This was the man responsible for one of the single greatest hurts of her life. This was the man who had been her biggest disappointment and she wanted him to say something.

'You look good,' he said, his eyes drifting down her body. How predictable.

'I've lost a lot of weight,' she said, her voice neutral and calm. 'I don't care for it.'

'I didn't wear black,' he said, holding out an arm to show off his suit. 'Eleanor never liked it so —'

'I wore black.'

'Sorry,' he said, letting his arm drift back down. 'I didn't mean to —'

'Call off the wedding?' She stared at him.

Claude's jaw tightened a little, enough for her to notice.

'What are you doing here, Claude? Did you think you'd be a comfort? Do you think Eleanor wanted you here?' She tilted her head to look at him.

'I shouldn't have come. This was clearly a mistake.' He went to move but Rachel held her hand up and pressed it into his chest.

'No, you don't get to run away again.' Her eyes were firm. 'I want you to see what you did,' she said, her fingers gripping his shirt, 'what you have done to me. Look at me.' She stood back and pulled at the looseness of her dress. 'This is hanging off me. I don't want to eat. I sleep all day. I lie awake at night. I cried at a cashier in Sainsbury's last week because he offered to help me with the packing. I can no longer tolerate kindness. Is this what you wanted? When you decided not to turn up?'

'I don't think this is the ...' Claude looked over her shoulder towards the road. He wanted to get away.

Rachel leaned in. 'I want you to explain to me why you did it. Why, Claude?'

She stood back, her eyes blazing.

'I can't make this better for you, Rachel,' he said, 'I'm sorry. I'm sorry about your mother.'

Putting his head down, he paced away from her.

'No, Claude,' she shouted after him. 'Don't you dare ...'

She watched as his walk became a run and he disappeared from view. She stared, numb and dumbfounded: he'd done it again.

Chapter Fourteen

'You should have let Johnny punch him,' said Agnes, handing Rachel a toilet roll.

She tore off two sheets and blew her nose. They were standing in the ladies' toilet at the Pheasant, Rachel's back up against a sink. Agnes stood, hands on hips, and looked furious. Rachel turned, threw the used tissue into the bin and stared at herself in the mirror.

'I look a state,' she said, rubbing at the mascara on her cheeks with her finger.

'You look fine. You're supposed to have puffy eyes. You just buried your mother. Even if that's not what you're crying about.' She lay a hand on Rachel's shoulder. 'You've had too much to cry about lately. Come on. Let me get you a drink.'

'I think I'm going to go back to the house,' said Rachel, turning round. 'Do you mind?'

'Of course not,' said Agnes. 'Johnny's popped back to see Francesca. Talk to him, won't you? We're all here for you. You're not alone.'

'I feel terrible.' Rachel's arms drifted around her torso, gripping herself for comfort.

'Of course you do. It's natural.'

'No,' said Rachel. 'I feel terrible because I'm not crying for Eleanor. I'm crying for myself. That's the truth of the matter. I've made bad choices and I'm blaming other people. I didn't make time for my mother when she asked for it. And now there's nothing I can do to turn that around. The last time I saw her she wanted to talk to me and I couldn't leave the house quick enough. And then I stayed away, deliberately. And if I hadn't, well … we might not be here. And now all I'm left with is a deep feeling of shame. No, worse than that. I'm embarrassed. It's so lazy to be cross with your mother. And cross about what? She was my mother. And now she's dead. And I didn't expect to feel like … this. I don't know who she was. I don't know who I am any more.'

Rachel heaved a deep sigh and looked up at her aunt. 'God, sorry, I'm venting. I'm so selfish. You've known her longer than I have.' She held out her hand and took Agnes's.

'Do you know,' said Agnes, her face lightening. 'I spent for ever thinking I was wary of her, resented her, but I adored her. I really did. Glamorous, beautiful big sister, and all that talent. I should have hated her, but I didn't. I pretended to, but actually I longed for her to like me. I hope she did. I think she did. I was no competition. The "plain girl", that was me. Plodding along. I was happier than her, though.'

Rachel frowned. 'She wasn't happy? Why?'

'I'm not sure. She had an air of regret, don't you think?'

Rachel pondered. 'Yes, now you mention it. That's exactly what she had. As if she was missing something.'

Agnes nodded. 'Yes. She was missing something.'

The door into the toilets opened and a rotund woman with a fleshy face came in. Agnes turned. 'Ah, Muriel, don't mind us, we're not in a queue.'

Rachel straightened and pushed herself away from the sink. 'I think I'll go back to the house. See Johnny. You'll come back later, won't you?'

'Of course I will.'

Rachel squeezed her hand and left.

The house was filled with the smell of sweet peas. There were little pots of them everywhere. Who had done this? She bent down to a cluster gathered in a glass tumbler and breathed them in: that heady sweetness that was so delicious. She stood and, hearing a noise in the kitchen, wandered towards it.

'Brace yourself, Johnny,' she said, as she approached the door. 'It could not have been worse ...' She stopped, her hand resting on the door frame.

Caspar was standing at the sink, filling a glass with water. He looked towards her. 'I hope you don't mind,' he said, putting the glass down on the table. 'I thought I'd cut the sweet peas and put them round the house for you. She always loved them.'

'No, not at all,' said Rachel, somewhat mollified, 'thank you.'

She stood and watched as he filled the glass with another handful. 'That's the last of them,' he said, with a smile. 'I was going to ...' He looked at her. 'Sorry, do you want to ...' He held it out.

'The table's fine,' she said, mustering a polite smile, 'it's very kind of you.'

He placed the glass down and gave a short nod. 'Well, then.'

They both stood, the awkwardness returning.

'Have you seen my cousin, Johnny?' Rachel looked past him to the open door beyond. 'Is he ...?'

'In the studio?' asked Caspar. 'No, I haven't seen him.'

'Right.'

'Look,' said Caspar, his head tilting, 'I'm not sure this is the right time to bring this up, but ...'

Rachel felt herself stiffen.

'Would you like me to carry on? With the garden, I mean?'

'Oh, I ...' Rachel felt a small wave of relief course through her. 'Sure. It's once a week, right? Of course.'

Caspar smiled and nodded. 'Great. OK. Thank you. Sorry to ask, but —'

'Not a problem.' She watched as he wiped his hands on a tea cloth.

'You don't need to do anything about the ... I just come and get on with it.'

'Right.'

'OK then,' he said. 'I really liked your mum.' He gave Rachel a look she couldn't quite place at first; she found it so difficult to recognise gentleness. But before she could respond, he was gone.

She looked at the little jar of sweet peas on the table and wondered if she was already regretting telling him he could keep his job.

'Johnny!' she called up the stairs over her shoulder. 'Are you up there?'

She pulled off her shoes. She hated wearing heels; they always made the balls of her feet burn. She hadn't eaten since last night and, feeling a pang of hunger, she reached for a large purple plum sitting in a bowl next to the fridge. She bit into it, the ripeness of it catching her by surprise. The juice trickled down her chin and she grabbed a piece of kitchen roll. As she wiped, she caught sight of the button box. She'd forgotten about it since coming home drunk from the pub the other night. She had a vague recollection of having found something important in it, but she couldn't quite remember what. She pulled it out again and went to sit at the table.

'How did it go? What did he say? Has he gone?' Johnny walked in, jacket off, sleeves rolled to his elbows. Seeing his cousin eating a plum, he grabbed one.

'Be careful,' she warned, 'they're super juicy.'

He bit and the plum spurted open splattering his shirt with spots of purple. 'Damn,' he said, pulling at his shirt to assess the mess.

'I did warn you. Don't wipe it. There'll be some of that magic stain remover somewhere.'

As she opened the intricately decorated box and peered in, all the memories from the night she found Eleanor flooded back. 'Have you seen this?' she asked, gesturing towards it. 'So many treasures. Eleanor kept them. There's all sorts in here. Old jewellery, letters ...'

Johnny threw his plum stone into the sink and, tap running, tried to rinse out the juice stains before they set in. 'What happened with Claude?'

'He didn't tell me why he'd called off the wedding, and then he ran away. He seems to be using wax in his hair. I'm not sure what that signifies.'

Johnny turned and stared at her. 'He ran away?'

Rachel nodded. 'Look, this one was off your old school blazer.' She held it up. 'I was looking through this right before I found her. There was something ...' She rooted around and found the little wrap of embroidered cotton. 'Here,' she added, pulling it out. 'Look at that. Do you know where that came from?'

Johnny turned the tap off and stood frowning at her. 'Squirt, never mind about the button, are you OK?'

Her eyes remained fixed on the tiny hand-painted coat of arms. 'I don't know.' Her voice was no more than a whisper. She felt tired and drained, as if she had to hold on to little tethering memories to stop her life from crumbling. 'Do you think I was awful to her? To Eleanor?'

Johnny sat down at the table and took her hand. 'No, I don't. What's all this about? Why don't you want to tell me about Claude?'

'She wanted to talk to me about something. That day. She asked to speak to me and I couldn't wait to get away from her. I could see she was upset and I was glad ...' She stopped, her face settling into a stark picture of regret. 'I have to find out. What she wanted. I feel like everything is on hold until I do.' She paused and looked into her cousin's eyes. 'Let's not mention Claude again, Johnny. I think I'm done with that.' Rachel looked down at the button in her hand and they sat in silence, the tap dripping behind them.

'I have to find out what she needed to tell me,' Rachel said eventually, wiping at her eye. 'I think I really need to do that.'

Johnny cupped her hand with both of his. She looked broken.

Chapter Fifteen

Rachel was on her knees in her mother's studio, sorting through things that would have to be kept, chucked or taken to a charity shop. A week on since they'd buried Eleanor, Rachel had made herself a promise: the summer would be hers and when the leaves changed colour she would think about getting a job. She was in a lucky position: she had the house to live in, rent free, and she had received the contents of Eleanor's savings account, which were considerable. It was more than enough. Rachel had options. There was no immediate need to get back to work. If she wanted to devote her time to finding out more about her mother, she could.

'Why don't you start painting again?' asked Agnes, tying her hair up into a blue bandana. 'You were always so good at it.'

'Not good enough,' replied Rachel.

'Nonsense,' replied Agnes, finishing the knot. 'Eleanor always said you had talent. It's going to waste. Look at all these paints, these canvases. We can't get rid of them. You could use them. She'd love it if you took up the reins.'

Rachel sat back on her heels and tossed another pile of dried-up pens into an open bin bag by her side. 'I don't know,' she said. 'I'm not in the right headspace and, besides, I'm *really* not good enough.'

'I always thought you should be exhibiting. And then Claude came along and you went to work in that wretched gallery. And that was that.' She eyed her niece, waiting for a response.

'I'm not sure that had anything to do with Claude. I rather think that was my own insecurities.' Rachel cast a glance up but chose to change the subject. 'Thanks for helping to do this, by the way. I was dreading it.' Rachel peered into another opened drawer. There was a heap of letters. She pulled them out and started to go through them.

'I feel like I've been clearing this house out for decades,' said Agnes, with a sigh. 'Had to do it when your grandfather died, then your grandmother.'

'Then Charlie. It shocked me a bit. How quick Eleanor wanted his stuff out.' Rachel picked up an envelope with smart handwriting and pulled out a card.

I find myself back in London. Don't ask. Might you care to …

She put it to one side and turned her attention to a handful of old bills and bank statements. 'I don't need to keep this junk, do I?'

Agnes shook her head. 'Clear-outs are always depressing *and* cathartic, if that makes sense? It's so difficult. Everything's a memory.'

'And we throw them away.' Rachel tossed the papers into the bin bag.

'Making room for new ones. I'm glad we're doing this, Rachel. I think it'll be good for you. Take your mind off things. Help you process everything. Look at Caspar. He's the poster boy for picking yourself up and moving on.'

Rachel frowned. 'What do you mean?'

'Do you not know?' Agnes perched on the edge of the old oak table that sat to one side of the studio, her fingers idly rifling through a tall pile of papers. 'It was quite awful. His girlfriend was killed on her bike. Run over by a lorry on Oxford High Street. He saw it too. He was with her.'

'Oh God. That's horrific. When?'

'Few years ago, I think. Charlie knew the girl's father, heard Caspar was in a terrible state. I think he had a breakdown over it. She'd been chasing, to keep up with him and overtook him, and then it happened. Charlie offered him the job here. He was a lovely man, your father.'

Rachel stared up at her aunt. She felt her chest deflate. 'He asked me if he could carry on,' she said, 'and I said yes. And then I wished I hadn't. And now I feel terrible.'

'Why on earth would you wish that? He does a wonderful job.'

'I know he does. I don't know. Awkwardness. Vanity. Not wanting someone you don't know around you. I think I took an irrational dislike to him. I think I've been a little unkind.'

'Kindness costs you nothing,' said Agnes, 'Charlie always used to say that. It's a good maxim to live by.'

'I seem to be making terrible decisions,' said Rachel, pushing herself up from the floor. 'I wish I could stop doing it.'

'You will,' said Agnes. 'Ah!' She gave out a short, delighted laugh. '*Brief Lives*! I'd forgotten about this.' She held up an old, battered book and stroked the cover. 'Lovely memories of reading that.' She smiled.

'How do you manage to be so ... uncomplicated?' Rachel tilted her head.

'I'm not sure if that's a compliment or an insult.' Agnes walked over to a wooden cupboard. 'Pleasures are everywhere, Rachel. The trick is to find them.' She opened the cupboard and peered in. 'What do you want to do with these?' She pulled out a dusty blue notebook and opened it. 'Diaries. Lots of them too.' She held one out for Rachel to take.

'Eleanor wrote diaries?'

'Heaps of them, by the looks of it.'

'I don't know how I feel about reading her diaries,' said Rachel, flicking through the one in her hand. 'I'm slightly afraid of doing it. I might have to shore up some courage first.'

'If you don't want people to discover your secrets, don't keep a diary,' said Agnes, reaching up and pulling a great pile down. 'That said, nobody writes things down any more. How is anyone expected to remember anything?' She stacked them up on the oak table and turned her attentions to a wooden crate that was filled with all sorts of small useless things like a faded postcard of a saint, a stapler that no longer worked and a lavender-filled rabbit that had lost its odour long ago. 'I made this,' she said, holding it up by its ear. 'Lavender from the garden, too. It's so difficult to know what to do with all this stuff. But you have to let go of memories, don't you? Or your brain would be like treacle. What do you think? Keep? Chuck? Charity?'

'Keep the rabbit,' said Rachel. 'You keep it. It'll remind you of her.'

'Yes,' said Agnes, holding the rabbit to her chest, 'I think I will. It's funny. Sometimes I forget I grew up here. It's shocking how time drifts on, isn't it? Do you think you'll stay? In this house?'

'I don't know yet. Not sure I want to now it's only me. It was only ever supposed to be temporary.' Rachel stared down at her mother's diary. The handwriting wasn't as she recognised: it was juvenile, neat, unfussy *Mother took me to Oxford again today and walked me, quite deliberately, past the art school. It's as if she doesn't know that I know what she's up to.* She snapped it shut. She didn't have time to stand here reading and, besides, it felt odd and wrong.

Rachel glanced over at her mother's stool. Her cardigan was draped across it, left as it had been on the day she died. She picked it up and instinctively lifted it to her face to breathe it in. The faint scent of her mother's hand cream still lingered: Oil of Olay, the soft, gentle smell of books at bedtime, being picked up from the train station, crying into her neck. There was a tub of it in the bathroom cabinet. Rachel made a mental note to keep it.

The cardigan was a light blue cashmere, something she would sling about her shoulders on a summer evening, and the buttons were creamy pearls, one of which was loose. Rachel wound the wayward thread around the button's base and put it back down on the stool. 'Did you see the button box?' Rachel asked. 'The one on the kitchen table? It looks like a very fancy toffee tin.'

'No,' said Agnes. 'I don't think I have.' She'd found a shoebox of loose felt-tip pens and was testing them all on a pad of paper. The ones that were no good were being thrown into a bin. 'What's in it? Very fancy toffees, I hope.'

'It's full of all sorts. You should see it. Letters. Rings. Buttons. Little photos. It's rather touching. All Eleanor's special memories. I haven't sat down and looked at it all properly. I don't recognise half of it. There was one button that stood out though. Really beautiful. Hang on,' said Rachel, heading for the kitchen.

There was something about this button that kept drawing her back and she couldn't understand why. Perhaps it was because it was the most beautiful, the most ornate? Perhaps it was because it was wrapped preciously in the white cotton that was so thin it was like a shroud? The tantalising and enigmatic *My love, my love* stared up at her, begging to be explained. There was a story to this button and Rachel wanted to know it.

'Here,' she said, holding it out on her palm towards Agnes. 'Look at that.'

'Goodness,' she said, taking it between her thumb and forefinger. 'That is beautiful. Is it hand-painted?'

'I think so.'

'God, my eyesight is absolutely shocking. I'm one prescription away from a magnifying glass, I swear. Is that a coat of arms?' She pointed with the tip of her fingernail.

Rachel peered down. 'Yes. I don't recognise it. Do you?'

'No. Maybe it's a prop from a play? Amateur dramatics. That sort of thing?'

'Did Eleanor do amateur dramatics?'

'Don't be ridiculous.'

'Charlie?'

Agnes laughed out loud. 'Charlie could barely do charades at Christmas! It's not something of Johnny's?'

'No. Asked him. He'd never seen it before.'

'Well,' said Agnes. 'Looks like you have a mystery on your hands.' She smiled and handed the button back. 'Mind you, my memory is shot to pieces. It's a miracle if I can remember what happened last week, let alone years ago.'

'It's probably nothing. Besides, the house is rammed with things I don't recognise.' Rachel re-wrapped the button and began to walk back to the kitchen but stopped and turned back. 'Eleanor wanted to tell me something. On the day she died. I still can't stop thinking about it. She didn't mention anything to you, did she?'

Agnes shook her head. 'No, nothing at all.'

Rachel shrugged it off. 'Doesn't matter.'

She carried on into the kitchen and put the button back into the box, carefully and gently, then stood and stared down at it. She had lied to Agnes. It mattered hugely to her that her mother had wanted to tell her something. It was consuming her.

Chapter Sixteen

'Right!' announced Johnny, clapping his hands together. 'That's the last of the bags. We're done. We're out of here.'

'You'll let me know when you're home, won't you?' Rachel pushed herself up from the old daybed in the corner of the studio. She'd been lying looking at her mother's unfinished pictures. Eleanor always had three or four paintings on the go at any given time. It stopped her getting bored or obsessed.

Johnny leaned in and, gripping her upper arm, kissed her on the cheek. 'Take care of yourself, Squirt,' he said, his eyes soft and concerned.

'Come on,' said Rachel, weaving her arm through his. 'I'll walk you to the car.'

Francesca was sitting in the passenger seat, touching up her lipstick in the mirror underneath the sun visor. She had large expensive sunglasses on and her hair was tied back and tucked into a red cap. Rachel stood on the porch steps and waved down to her. 'Bye, Francesca,' she said, managing a smile. 'I hope everything goes OK with the pregnancy.'

'Thank you, darling,' she replied, still applying her lipstick. 'We'll call you when it's out.' She tapped Johnny on his forearm. 'When is it booked for?'

'December 20th. Just in time for Christmas.'

'December 20th. Just in time for Christmas,' Francesca repeated, as if she'd remembered it on her own, then added, 'Nanny starts five minutes later, right? Ha ha ha!' She threw her head back and laughed.

Rachel laughed along to be polite and then hated herself for it. She watched as they drove away, compelled to keep waving and shouting 'Goodbye! Goodbye!' but as soon as the car turned the corner, Rachel's smile and arm fell. She stood and looked up at the sky, which was clear and blue and endless. It was already too hot for the clothes she was wearing. She would change into a pair of shorts and a T-shirt. That would give her something to do. So that was that. Her mother was buried. Her cousin had left. What next?

She wandered back into the hallway. It was so quiet. A clock was ticking thickly in the kitchen, but other than that there was nothing. Rachel felt alarmed by the stillness of the place. She'd never lived anywhere on her own before.

It was an odd feeling. She could do what she liked. She had nobody to answer to. She wasn't required to explain a single thing. Every decision she made would be for her own benefit. She could wear what she wanted. She could watch a film before lunch, drink wine in the afternoon, buy microwave meals from Marks & Spencer, eat on her lap in front of American reality TV shows. She could decide what she was going to do with the rest of her life. She should be feeling an enormous sense of release, of freedom, of possibilities, but she didn't. She felt the exact opposite. She felt hemmed in, restricted, shackled. Her world had shrunk down to nothing and all she could fixate on was the one conversation she hadn't had. 'One thing at a time,' she mumbled.

She stood there, her arms by her side, the loneliest kind of lonely, surprised to feel herself crying.

'Maybe I should get a dog,' she said, wiping her cheek with her hand.

She pulled out a thin cotton T-shirt from a pile on her bedroom floor and slid it over her head. Outside, through the open window across the hall, she heard a car pull up on to the driveway. She frowned and wandered out to the top of the stairs, waiting for a knock at the door or for something to be slipped through the letterbox, but nothing came.

Behind her, back through the bedroom window, she heard the shed door in the garden open. It was Caspar. She went over to the window and glanced out over the garden. He was removing some long bamboo canes from the shed.

She didn't know what to do with herself. Perhaps she could try painting again? Something straightforward. A still life. She could paint a few of her mother's memories? She turned from the window and made her way down to the studio.

Retrieving the old toffee tin from the kitchen, Rachel opened it and fingered the things inside, looking for something suitable. She didn't want to paint a photograph and she didn't fancy tackling the jewellery. Perhaps she'd try that button? The beautiful one that was so intriguing. She picked it out and unwrapped it for the third time. There was a wooden plinth against the wall and she dragged it over so it sat next to the easel. She drew up her mother's stool and arranged the button on top of its embroidered shroud until it was just how she wanted. Taking a pencil, she made a faint outline on the canvas and stopped.

She wasn't ready. She didn't want to pick up her mother's paints, her brushes. She didn't want to squeeze oils on to her mother's palette. She didn't want to sit on her mother's stool and paint a stolen memory. She didn't know what that memory was. She didn't understand the button's story. The need to feel connected to her mother's past was overwhelming. It took her by surprise. Those little treasures, hoarded by her mother, had rather undone her. She felt more connected to Eleanor than she had for years. She heaved a sigh. 'God,' she whispered. 'It's not just what she wanted to tell me. It's everything about her. I need to know everything.'

Taking her phone from her pocket, Rachel took a picture of the button and walked back to the kitchen. Her laptop was sitting on the table and, opening it, she googled 'heraldry website'. Finding one, she clicked on Contacts and sent an email to someone called Barbara, photo attached.

It was just a button with a coat of arms on it, Rachel thought. Perhaps it wasn't so mysterious after all. But it was a start. And that was something.

She sat back in her chair, her arms hanging by her sides. Her dynamic start to the day seemed to have fizzled to nothing.

Rachel wondered if she should sit in the garden for a while, but Caspar was there and ... she checked herself, remembering what Agnes had told her. Kindness costs you nothing. No, it didn't. She would pull herself together and ask him if he wanted a cup of tea.

He was out by the roses, secateurs in hand, deadheading.

'Hello,' Rachel said, walking barefoot across the scorched lawn towards him. 'Dad loved roses.'

Caspar looked up. 'He did. He put this one in. Planted it for your mum.'

'Did he?' Rachel frowned. Why didn't she know that? 'What else did he do?'

'In the garden?'

Rachel nodded and dug her hands into the pockets of her shorts.

Caspar stopped what he was doing and looked around. 'He put that little bee house in.' He pointed to a small black hive hanging on a wooden lattice. 'It's for leaf-cutter bees. Go and have a look. It's lovely.'

Rachel followed his finger and walked towards the wall to look at it. She'd never seen it before. It looked like a little Swiss chalet with holes instead of windows. Each hole was filled with either a leaf or a rose petal. Caspar was right. It had a certain beauty. 'Gosh,' she said, peering down at it. 'I never knew.'

'Every hole that's filled has got a little leaf-cutter bee growing in it. Look round the garden,' Caspar said, inclining his head behind him. 'You'll see chunks bitten out of leaves all over. That's the bees.'

Rachel stood and walked towards a group of fruit trees: semicircular shapes were bitten into the leaves. How had she never noticed this before? Why had Charlie not shared it with her?

Rachel turned and stared down at her toes, brown with dust and covered in bits of grass that had turned to hay. The ground was hard beneath her feet. It was giving up nothing. 'He never showed this to me,' she said, her voice quiet. 'But then, why would he?'

Caspar watched her, his face careful and considered.

'I'm not sure what to do with myself,' Rachel said, suddenly. 'I'm at a loss. So I thought I would come and ask you if you wanted a cup of tea.' She surprised herself with her own honesty.

'It's a bit hot for a cup of tea,' said Caspar, still watching her. 'But I'd love a glass of water.'

'Yes,' said Rachel. 'I can do that.' She walked back towards the studio. 'Would you like some ice?'

'Yes, please.'

Rachel walked on. She could do ice.

Chapter Seventeen

Then

'I could have you arrested. Really. I should call the police and have you carted off. This is the most monstrous torture.'

'Shut up, Jake,' said Eleanor, brush in hand. 'And stop moving.'

They had become inseparable. The past four weeks had been a blur of parties, dancing and endless hours of talking. Eleanor had never felt so interested in another human being, never felt that someone else was so intensely interested in her. It had been a month of outrageous bonding that had catapulted Eleanor into a glittering stratosphere.

'Couldn't you wait until I was drunk and paint me while I sleep it off? That would be far more cordial. That's what Bacon does. He gets people roaring, takes them home, then paints through the night. It's why his paintings are so visceral.'

'I don't want to be visceral.'

Jake pushed himself up from the armchair. 'It's no good,' he declared, heading for the record player in the corner of the room, 'this won't do. I'm refusing. I'm on strike. Down with you! History shall write of this day! An uprising of righteous fury! People shall erect statues in my honour!'

'Not if you can't keep still for five minutes they won't.' Eleanor gave a small, indulgent sigh and watched as Jake fingered through a long line of vinyl records on the shelf. 'Are you really not going to sit down?'

'No,' he replied, his back to her. 'I'm really not going to sit down. What shall we dance to? Ray Charles? Or Charlie Mingus?' He held the two albums up: one bright red, Ray Charles leaning to the left, head back, singing, the other with a woman draped against a large jukebox, her skirt lifted provocatively up to mid thigh.

'*Modern Sounds*,' said Eleanor, putting down her palette. 'The Ray Charles one.' She pulled off her headscarf and watched him slide the record from the sleeve and put it on the turntable. She knew when she was beaten.

The needle touched the record, there was the crackle of vinyl, and then, '*Yep!*': trumpets, syncopated drumbeats, female backing singers and Jake. He was like a firework.

'*Bye-bye, love!*' he sang along, twisting on the balls of his feet. '*Bye-bye, happiness! Hello, loneliness! I think I'm gonna cry!*' He was clicking his fingers and grinning, his blonde hair flopping over his eyes as he bounced around the room. 'Come on!' he yelled towards her, but Eleanor shook her head. She wasn't sure she liked dancing: it was too brash, too animalistic. Besides, she liked watching him.

Jake danced over to her, his body curled into a cat-like pose. He held out his hands and took hers, his top teeth hooked over his bottom lip, coquettish and daring her on. His shirt was open – she had wanted to paint him that way – and his still-tanned torso looked smooth and muscular. She wanted to put her hands on him, to let her fingers trail slowly over his body, but as she was trying to protest he pulled her off the stool and swung her round. She loved that he made her feel this way. It was so effortless, so natural, so light. They had become extensions of each other: Eleanor had a new home and it was him.

'That's more like it!' he yelled, grinning. *'Bye-bye, sweet caress! I think I'm going to die!'*

'I can't imagine you ever dying,' shouted Eleanor, as he spun her round.

'I never want to be old,' he yelled back. 'Being old will be wasted on me. I hope I die young and beautiful and everyone is devastated and rips their clothes and wails.'

'That's incredibly selfish.'

'How so?' He grinned. 'Death is totally life-enhancing. Prolific national mourning is something to aspire to, don't you think? To be so adored ...'

'Most people only need to be adored by one person,' Eleanor replied.

'Hmm,' said Jake, tilting his head, 'well, I adore you. So you can die happy.'

The music changed: a surge of strings and a slower, more romantic song began to fill the room.

You give your hand to me,
And then you say hello,
And I can hardly speak,
My heart is beating so ...

Eleanor, slowing to the more laconic pace, leaned into Jake's body.

And anyone can tell
You think you know me well ...

She rested her hand on the top of his chest, her eyes unblinking, looking into his. He smiled down at her.

But you don't know me ...

She closed her eyes, and pushed herself closer. If she lifted his head towards his, he might kiss her, she thought. Or perhaps she might kiss him.

No, you don't know me ...

'No,' he said, suddenly. 'Can't have this.' Jake pulled away to walk towards the record player and Eleanor, now abandoned, felt her arms falling to her sides. She watched as Jake lifted the needle from the record. 'I can't bear the sad ones,' he said. 'Why do people need to be so maudlin?'

She blinked, aware of her heartbeat gently slowing.

He glanced over his shoulder towards her. 'Do I infuriate you?'

'I think you rather wish you did,' said Eleanor, narrowing her eyes. 'I shan't give you the satisfaction. What do you think about that?'

'Infuriating,' he replied with a sly grin. 'Look at the day!' He stood with his hands on his hips and looked out of the window into the blazing blue sky. 'It's beautiful. Shall we sack this all off? Have a picnic or something?'

'We haven't got a picnic.'

Jake pulled a face. 'I know we haven't got a picnic. That's the point. We need to get a picnic. And eat the picnic. And drink the picnic. And lie in the sun and discuss matters of great importance.'

'Like what?'

'I haven't decided yet,' he said, turning to take her hand. 'Let's make our minds up on the way.' He dragged her towards the door. 'We could just talk about you for hours on end?'

Eleanor smiled. 'I rather think we can have me covered in five minutes. I'm not that interesting.'

'To me you are.' He walked towards the door.

Eleanor didn't follow him. It was unnerving, all this attention. He made her feel significant. There was something mildly terrifying about that. She called after him, 'Why do you do this?'

He stopped and looked back over his shoulder. 'Do what?'

'Make such a fuss of me?'

'I like having you around.'

'But why?'

Jake narrowed his eyes and wagged a finger at her. 'You're jumping the gun. We haven't got where we're going yet. Come on. We're wasting the day.'

'You still haven't told me where we are going.'

'Surprise,' he said, with a grin. 'I'll tell you when we get there.'

Eleanor gave in, again. He was a riptide sucking her away from the shore.

They travelled from Chelsea to Hampstead on a double-decker bus. Jake had insisted on sitting on the top deck at the front – 'There's no finer way to travel' – then spent the entire journey pointing out pedestrians who were dressed appallingly. Her sides ached from laughing. They jumped off at a bus stop halfway up a very leafy avenue and walked arm in arm until Jake came to a stop in front of a rather impressive house. It was quite extraordinary: four-storey Georgian, bricks the colour of summer and large sash windows that let the light pour in. A blue plaque on the front wall proudly proclaimed John Constable had once lived there. 'That's not *the* John Constable, is it?' Eleanor asked, pointing up at it.

'No, it's John Constable the painter and decorator. Of course it is, you clot,' said Jake, opening the arched front door. 'Come on. Don't worry. I've got the place to myself. Ma and Pa won't be back before Christmas.'

'Where are they?'

'Lake Como. They always beg me to come, but I can't bear spaghetti.'

Eleanor laughed and followed him into a light, high-ceilinged hallway. It opened out into a long corridor, and she followed him down to a blue door that led into the kitchen. It was quite splendid. The polished wooden floorboards were a worn-in russet, and the light from the enormous window on its south wall bounced off them, creating a golden glow.

Jake already had his nose in the fridge.

'What shall we have? Cheese? There's a ham in here. I think we've got some bread. Ah. This is what we need!' He held out a bottle of champagne for her to take. 'Glasses are up there ...' His hand wafted off towards a cupboard behind her.

Eleanor turned round and reached up, bottle in hand, and pulled out two glass tumblers, pinching them between her fingers. She held them up for approval. 'Will these do? They're not terribly posh ...'

'Who cares about posh?' said Jake, sliding the ham from the fridge. 'Bigger the glass, all the more for me. Right. Let's go.'

He took her up, through the house, passing paintings, sculptures and just-ajar doors with enticing glimpses into sitting rooms, a library, bedrooms, all of it tastefully decorated and opulent. Eleanor had never asked Jake about his family, but it was clear they had that relaxed, old-money wealth that provided freedom and indulgence. It came as no surprise: he didn't have a care in the world; his entire sense of urgency was devoted to averting boredom.

They went through a door that led to a roof terrace. She'd never been on one before, and the notion of a small garden on top of a building struck her as delightful. There was a round table, over which Jake draped a tablecloth

– 'Let's not be pigs' – and a pair of striped deckchairs. They sat.

'So. Let's turn our attention to you, shall we? Do you hope you'll be a very great artist?' he asked, as the deep pop of the champagne cork sounded inside his fist.

'I'm not sure I've given that any thought,' said Eleanor, holding the glasses for him to fill. 'I know I can paint.'

'I know I can paint, too,' he said, leaning back and turning his face up to the sun. 'But it's not about that, is it? It's whether you have anything to say. Sometimes it bothers me I might end up a painter of people's children or pets. I don't think I could bear it. I would feel entirely unconscious.'

'Even unconscious you'd be more interesting than anyone else I know,' said Eleanor, closing her eyes.

'Do you mean that?' asked Jake, turning to look at her.

Eleanor turned her head towards him, her eyes squinting in the trembling heat. 'I do mean it, yes. I've never met anyone like you. I feel . . .' She thought for a moment, wanting to say precisely what she meant. 'I feel as if I'm on my own. When I'm with you. Does that make sense?'

'Not in the least.' He cupped his chin in his hands and stared at her, smiling.

She smiled back. 'You're just after compliments now, Jake,' she said, flicking his fringe, 'don't think I don't know.'

'What if I am? I think I deserve them, don't you?'

'You put me at ease. That's what I mean. I'm not sure anyone's ever managed to do that. You like me for who I am.' Eleanor paused. Her friendship with Jake was constantly surprising her. It felt unusual, unique.

'But do you like me?'

Eleanor frowned. His face was serious and vulnerable. 'Of course I like you. What a peculiar question.'

'I'm not entirely sure I am likeable. My parents don't seem to like me at all. And as for friends, it's always difficult to know if they like me or my money.'

Eleanor sat up straight. 'Jake, you're very likeable. Even if you are maddening. I'm not sure my parents like me much either. So we have that in common. It never occurs to me to think about whether you're rich or not. We could be sitting on an old cardboard box in an alley for all I care. I just like you.'

He gave a soft, thoughtful smile. 'I always think if you like someone very much, it's because they like you too. I don't think I've ever been fond of someone who loathed me. Apart from my father. Have you?'

Eleanor paused to think. She wanted to tell him she loved him, to be as confident and assured as he believed her to be. But she couldn't. 'There was a boy when I was ten. His name was Donald Harwood. He had freckles and was very good at throwing balls. He couldn't bear me.'

'Donald Harwood was an idiot. What's happened to him?'

'I think he works in a bank.'

'Well, there you are,' said Jake, throwing his hand into the air. 'He's given up on life entirely.'

Eleanor laughed.

'I wonder if I do have anything to say?' Jake raised his arm over his head and let his legs spread wide in front of him. His mood was languid and liquid. He was like mercury dancing. 'I met a writer once, a friend of my mother's. He told me it took him forty years to work out what he wanted to say and then he wrote one great book. I'm not sure I'm that patient. It's so easy to be a pale imitation of everyone else, but to be yourself, that's the trick. If you're not going to be great, what's the point?'

'You're being very serious today,' said Eleanor, leaning back and lifting her hand to her forehead to shield her eyes from the sun. 'Not like you at all.'

'The thought of being dull terrifies me.'

There was a pause. Eleanor frowned. 'The notion of you being dull is ridiculous.'

'Really?' He sounded as if he wasn't entirely sure of what he was saying. 'I sometimes feel like a terrible fraud.'

Eleanor watched him. She'd never seen him like this.

'You never judge me,' he said, his hand reaching for hers. 'I can relax with you. All the same, I can't imagine you'd like me if I let you see *all* the craters.'

'Of course I would.'

'The thing is, Eleanor,' he said, 'I am entirely inauthentic. I'm a mirage. I am not who I was born to be.'

'What's got into you? You're talking rubbish.'

'Am I?' said Jake, his left foot sweeping softly back and forth across the black asphalt.

Eleanor was unsure of what Jake was getting at and found herself trying to lighten the mood. 'Maybe you should have gone to work in a bank with Donald Harwood?'

Jake turned and grinned. 'I *hate* Donald Harwood.' He said it with relish. 'Seriously. I *loathe* him. I never want to meet him. How dare he not like you when you liked him.'

'Oh, it's worse than that. I didn't like him,' said Eleanor, laughing, 'I loved him.'

'Love is awful.' Jake ran a curl of his hair through his fingers. 'Unrequited love is delicious, of course. Very masochistic. Good for artistic aspirations. But I'm not sure any serious artist should ever really be in love and be loved back. No, far better to be unhappy. We need torture and misery and sleepless nights and the constant threat of Victorian illnesses.'

Eleanor frowned. 'What Victorian illnesses?'

'Oh, you know, consumption, rickets, an infernal dropsy.' He laughed.

'Are you really unhappy?' Eleanor said, turning to look at him.

He chose to ignore her this time. 'You should move in. To here, I mean,' he said, leaning forward and refilling his glass. 'We could have a decadent term and pretend we've eloped.'

'You can't pretend you've eloped when you're still in the same place,' said Eleanor. 'Don't be silly.' She turned her face away from him. She was still thinking about what he'd said. 'Did you mean that? That love is awful?'

'To be avoided at all costs.'

She stared at him carefully. 'Have you been in love?'

'No,' he said, his voice flat and lifeless. He pouted his lips and stared at a pigeon sitting on the edge of the roof. It was limping and looked ratty and wretched. He picked up the champagne cork and lobbed it at it. 'Bloody pigeons,' he said. 'Can't bear the things.'

He pushed himself up from the deckchair. 'Let's start a society!' he declared, throwing away the moment. 'One where only you and I are members. It should be entirely secret, of course. I shall be the Grand Poobah. And you shall be Lady High Everything Else. We shall meet at four o'clock every day with the sole purpose of getting very, very drunk. We must have ceremonial robes for important occasions. What shall we call ourselves?'

Eleanor couldn't keep up. His mind fluttered like light.

Jake looked down at her, his face held in suspension. There was something unattainable, impossible, about him, almost as if he didn't really exist.

'I think you rather like changing the subject,' said Eleanor, looking up at him. 'So you never have to dwell on anything too serious.'

'When you keep moving,' he said, his voice flattening, 'it's harder to be pinned down.' He took her hand in his. 'I don't believe you, by the way, about your parents not liking you.'

Eleanor gave a snort. 'Parents are such odd creatures. Everyone goes on about how much they want children and then they have them and they couldn't care less.

Jake looked away. 'I barely know my parents. They're virtual strangers whom I occasionally spend Christmas with. I wish I didn't mind. But I think I do.' He mustered a small, sad smile. 'When you don't fit in, you have to make your own family, don't you?'

'Yes,' said Eleanor, squeezing his hand a little. 'I suppose so.'

'This won't do,' he said, sticking his chin out. 'We are supposed to be having fun.'

'We don't have to be laughing all the time, Jake. It's all right to feel sad.'

'No,' he said, shaking his head. 'It's not. Sadness is an awful storm. You have to run away before it ruins you. Besides, I've found you now. That's all that matters.' He stopped and looked back at her. 'You'll never hate me, will you? Promise. Please?'

He looked down at her and she was struck by his sudden need of something tangible, a hand hold he could hang from.

She went to open her mouth.

'JAKE!' A man's voice sounded from the street, before she could answer. 'OPEN THE BLOODY DOOR!'

Frowning, he walked to the roof edge and looked down. 'It's John and Hen,' he said. 'HOW DID YOU KNOW I WAS UP HERE?'

'CHAMPAGNE CORK!' came the voice back.

'I'LL COME DOWN!'

He turned to her. 'Well. There goes our desert island.'

Eleanor watched him walk away and listened as his footfalls tripped down through the house. He was humming as he went, as if the rare moment of seriousness had never happened. He doesn't want to be serious, Eleanor thought, it's why he hates love so much, and she took another sip of her champagne, trying to ignore the feeling of dread and excitement gnawing in the pit of her stomach.

Chapter Eighteen

A woman was crawling on her hands and knees across the floor of Jake's house, fingering through ashtrays in the pitch dark. She was trying to find a discarded cigarette. Eleanor watched her. She was barefoot, dressed in a pair of striped Capri trousers with a tailored short-sleeved blouse tucked into the bright red waistband. Her hair, a rich chestnut brown, hung down to her shoulders, the ends turned up in outrageous curls. She looked expensive.

More people had turned up.

Eleanor had no idea what time it was – and how long before dawn would break. She was lying on a chaise longue in the sitting room, which was now filled with the detritus of the Soho and Chelsea club scenes, people who had made their way to Jake's house to see in the dawn. A rather striking poet was sitting in the far corner of the room, surrounded by various hangers-on. Somewhere there was a famous actor, Eleanor couldn't remember his name, an author of a book that everyone was reading and a sprinkling of up-and-coming artists, some of whom Eleanor admired.

Eleanor pushed herself up and dropped her feet to the floor. She wasn't sure if she was still drunk, but she must have passed out at some point and now she was here, sitting on a chaise longue. The air in the room was thick with the smell of stale cigarettes, booze and sweat. A few hours ago there had been dancing, but by the looks of it the impromptu party had run out of steam.

'The muse awakes,' said Hen, pouring some wine into a glass and handing it to her. 'Here, have this. You'll get a second wind.'

'I'm not sure I should,' said Eleanor, running a hand through her hair. 'Where's Jake?' She looked around the room for him.

'I think he got into a fight,' said Hen, putting the glass down at Eleanor's feet. 'Last time I saw him, his nose was bleeding.' She took a delicate sip from her own glass. Her lips were tinged with the dark purple slash of red wine, and her forehead was moist with sweat.

'Bleeding?' Eleanor said, frowning. 'I need to find him.' She went to stand but Hen put a hand on her arm.

'I wouldn't if I were you,' she said. ' "Wild birds aren't meant to be kept in cages." '

She reached into her pocket and pulled out a crumpled packet of cigarettes. 'Want one?' she said, offering them to Eleanor.

Eleanor shook her head. 'No, I don't . . .' She glanced over to the woman on all fours.

'She was on the cover of *Vogue* last month,' said Hen, holding her lighter to the cigarette that was now balanced on her bottom lip. 'How the mighty have fallen.'

'Are you going to offer her one?'

'No.' She took a long, deep drag. 'You're very sensible not smoking. I rather admire it. It's so hard to avoid.'

Eleanor looked at her and blinked. 'What did you mean? The thing about wild birds?'

Hen blew out a long, thin stream of smoke and picked a slither of tobacco from the end of her tongue. Her teeth were stained and her tongue was the colour of an aubergine. 'Nobody will ever tame Jake,' she said. 'You're not the first person to try.'

'I'm not trying to ...'

'But you're in love with him. It's obvious.' Hen took another drag. 'And I don't say that to be unkind.'

Eleanor didn't reply. Her eyes drifted back to the woman on the floor. She had crawled over to the nest of hangers-on in the far corner of the room. Someone had given her a cigarette and she was sitting holding it like a toddler holds a ball.

'I was like you once,' said Hen, stretching her back against the side of the chaise longue. 'I remember what it was like, being the new face in town. You only get one chance with that. Blow it at your peril. This is all fun though, isn't it? Being here, getting drunk, watching bright young things spin their plates.' She took another drag from her cigarette.

'Did you? Blow it, I mean?' Eleanor reached down for the glass that was sitting on the floor. She sniffed it and took a sip.

Hen let her head fall back on to the chaise longue. 'Of course I did. Look at me. I'm a joke. I'm *the* joke. I'm the girl who lies naked for artists. I'm the girl who has given everything away. And to think I was taught by nuns.'

'Were you?'

'Sent away to a convent. Hated every second. Awful place. Thought I would never be warm again. Got myself expelled. Not very sensible.' She took another drag of her cigarette.

'You were expelled?'

Hen's face lit up. 'And in style, too. I'm just that girl who turns up in the hope of a party. Nobody takes me seriously.'

'I do.'

'No,' said Hen, with a soft smile. 'You don't. Ugh,' she said, dropping her cigarette into her glass of half-finished wine. 'Ignore me. I'm being maudlin. Time for me to go.'

She pushed herself up from the floor and stood defiant, shoulders back, her chest thrust forward. 'Right,' she announced to the room. 'Which one of you is going to fuck me?'

Eleanor made her way through the house to the kitchen, stepping over bodies, picking up discarded bottles and placing them on chests of drawers as she went. She was thirsty and wanted water, and when she reached the sink she turned on the tap and leaned down to drink from it.

'Had a good night?'

She stopped and ran a hand across her mouth. John was leaning against the door frame. He had a tumbler in one hand and a bottle of Jack Daniel's in the other.

'Have you seen Jake?' she asked. There was something about John that made her a little nervous. She wanted to be near Jake, to recharge her energy, to feel safe. She looked away, leaned back down towards the tap. The water was cold and refreshing.

'Not lately,' he replied, putting the bottle down and walking to the fridge. 'Is there any ice in here? I want some ice.'

Eleanor turned the tap off and watched him as he opened the fridge door and peered in. There was something very attractive about him: he had the quiet confidence of a man who can persuade people to perform for a camera, and Eleanor found herself wondering what he looked like naked. He was wearing a black leather jacket over a shirt covered in the small stories of a long evening: a smudge of something greasy, a few dots of red wine. He found a tray in an ice compartment at the top of the fridge and turned to bash it down on the table in the middle of the room. Ice scattered across the wooden top.

'Want one?' he asked, pouring the Jack Daniel's over two ice cubes he'd dropped into the tumbler.

Eleanor shook her head. 'No. I need water. I'm thirsty.' She reached up to a shelf and took a large glass. She held it under the tap and filled it.

'So am I.' John raised his glass towards her. 'Bottoms up.' He dispatched the drink in one go.

'Are you an alcoholic?'

John smiled. 'That's a bit bold, isn't it?'

'Well, it is the end of the party. People are supposed to say things they shouldn't, aren't they?'

'Probably,' John replied, pouring another drink. 'It's a sad game.' He stood back and leaned against the work surface, crossed his legs and stared at her. 'You're a very pretty girl. You haven't got a fella, have you?'

'No.' Eleanor felt the cold of the water on her lips.

'Have you ever been kissed? Properly?'

Eleanor shook her head. 'If you mean by someone I enjoyed kissing, then no, I haven't.'

John's gaze felt unnerving, masculine. 'Maybe I should take your picture.' He tilted his head. Still looking at her, he fingered an ice cube from his drink and sucked at it. 'Would you like that?'

'I'm not sure.'

'You know Jake is like this with everyone? You're just the new one.'

'That doesn't feel kind.' Eleanor returned his unblinking stare. 'Or necessary. It makes me wonder why you would tell me that.'

He popped the ice cube he was sucking into his mouth, swirled it round and took it out again. 'Maybe I'm trying to put you off him. You can't blame a man for playing dirty. It's what we do.' He dropped the ice cube back into his glass and stretched himself out in front of her, open and receptive. 'Are you a virgin?'

'Yes,' Eleanor answered, her voice barely above a whisper.

'Would you like not to be?'

Eleanor hesitated. His sexual confidence unnerved her. 'I'm not sure you deserve to know that.'

A smile flirted across his lips. 'You're right.'

They stood staring at each other.

'I think I might kiss you,' said John, breaking the silence. 'How do you feel about that?'

'I don't know.' Her mind flew to wherever Jake might be and she looked towards the door, hoping he might walk in and take John's place.

'You don't have to. Might be good practice, that's all.' He gave a charming shrug.

Eleanor looked at him. This was the new world she found herself in, where inhibitions were frowned upon and everything was meant to be free and easy and uncomplicated. She hesitated, then: 'All right,' she said, deciding to embrace her boldness. 'I feel fine about it.'

John pushed himself away from the work surface and walked towards her. He smelled of smoke and whiskey and Eleanor was reminded of the other time she'd been kissed by a man. That had felt desperate, grubby, distasteful. This felt different. He pulled her into him, his broad hands across the small of her back. He looked down at her. Eleanor wondered whether she should close her eyes. No. She wanted to watch. His eyes closed and she felt his lips on hers. She could feel the roughness of his stubble against her cheek and chin. She watched him as his tongue pressed into her mouth, touching hers. She wondered whether she should put her arms around his neck but was wary of the intimacy of such a gesture. John moved down to Eleanor's neck and, as he kissed her just below her ear, she let out a gasp. She was amazed by the sensation. She felt reckless.

'What are you doing?'

Jake stood in the doorway of the kitchen. He had blood on his shirt and his nose looked sore and red.

John pulled away and retrieved his glass of Jack Daniel's. 'I was kissing Eleanor,' he said, 'it was rather pleasant.'

'Did you like him kissing you?' Jake stared at Eleanor. He looked affronted, but Eleanor couldn't really tell whether he was angry or hurt or jealous or pretending. He was clearly very drunk.

'Yes,' she said, her voice quiet and restrained. 'I did.' She cleared her throat and stood back against the sink. The excitement she had felt fizzled away and now, staring at Jake in the doorway, she felt anxious, all her boldness gone.

'How fortunate. Have you got anything to drink? I've got nothing to drink.'

John passed him the bottle of Jack Daniel's. 'Have that. I'm going to walk home.' He downed his glass and placed it carefully on the kitchen table. 'Thanks for the kiss,' he added, looking at Eleanor. He placed a hand on Jake's shoulder and left. Eleanor listened to him walk the length of the corridor. The front door opened and shut and she said nothing.

Jake unscrewed the top from the bottle of Jack Daniel's and drank from it.

'Who did you fight with?' Eleanor asked.

'I'm not sure,' he said, not looking at her. 'I think it was someone who's written a terrible play.'

'Does it hurt?' She pointed to his nose.

'Yes.'

Eleanor took a clean dishcloth that was hanging on a hook behind the taps and laid it on the kitchen table. She placed a handful of ice cubes into it and gathered the corners to tie a knot. 'Here,' she said, holding it out to him. 'Put that on it.'

Jake took the cloth and sat on the cushioned window seat at the far end of the kitchen. Leaning into the corner, he slumped down, his head resting against the wall. He placed the ice pack on his nose and breathed out, the way a dog does when it settles.

'Did you really like kissing him?'

'He kisses everyone, doesn't he? Are you jealous?'

'Do you want me to be jealous?'

'I think I do. Yes.'

'Then I'm jealous. Is the sun up?' he asked, closing his eyes.

Eleanor moved towards the window and pulled back the heavy velvet curtains. She looked out and saw the golden glow of light breaking over the treetops. 'Yes. The sky is beautiful. You should see it.'

She moved towards him and lay next to him, curling herself into his body. His arm moved across her. 'Do you still like me the most?' His voice was mumbling, drifting away. Eleanor slid her hand into his, the adrenaline of the moment with John subsiding.

'Of course I do.'

'You must never hate me, Eleanor. Never. You have to promise.' His face flattened itself into her back.

Eleanor stared out across the kitchen. She wasn't sure why Jake was feeling so vulnerable. Perhaps he really was jealous after all.

'I love you, Jake,' she whispered.

But he was already asleep.

Chapter Nineteen

Now

'My goodness!' said Agnes, with some delight. 'I made this!' She waved a faded pink beret in Rachel's direction. 'It was her going-away present. Before she went to Chelsea. I was so jealous of her. And furious at being left behind. How lovely that she kept it.' She dusted the top of the beret with the flat of her hand. They'd been at it for three days, clearing, chucking and keeping; Agnes would arrive each morning and they'd work together till lunch.

Rachel paid her little attention. She had become more frantic of late, more desperate. She had upended boxes, tipped out the contents of filing cabinets and large Manila envelopes. She had pored over the diaries they had found, but there was nothing of significance. She was no nearer to finding out exactly what her mother had meant to tell her. It was a resolution she desperately craved.

Agnes watched her as she pulled out another drawer and tipped the contents on to the floor. 'Rachel,' she said gently, 'why don't you take a break? I could make us a cup of tea. We should sit in the garden. It's lovely out.'

'I just need to go through this.' Rachel's voice was clipped, distant.

Agnes put a hand on her shoulder. 'Rachel, please. I'm starting to worry about you.'

'Starting?' Rachel snorted. 'I thought worry was the only emotion I inspire these days.'

'Please. It'll all still be there when you come back.'

Rachel glanced up at her aunt: her kind eyes, the good heart, the quiet strength. She was right. Rachel pushed herself up from her knees.

'It's fine. This one's just old pens and theatre programmes.' She gestured at the contents on the floor. 'I'm starting to think my mother was more sentimental than I ever gave her credit for,' she said, trying not to sound embarrassed. 'Either that or she was a secret hoarder.' She ran a hand through her hair. She felt raw and ragged.

'Is this still about what Eleanor wanted to tell you?' Agnes spoke quietly and carefully.

'No,' said Rachel, shaking her head, then, letting her head fall, 'I'm just ...' She lifted her eyes to her aunt's. There was no point keeping up any pretence. She let out a sigh. 'OK, yes it is. I keep thinking about what you said about how you used to write letters when you had something important to say to someone.'

Agnes's eyes narrowed. 'Yes, I remember.'

'And I've fixated on it. Wondering if Eleanor wrote a letter to ... me.'

'And now you're looking for it?'

'Yes, I am.'

'Hmm.' Agnes thought for a moment, turning the soft pink beret slowly in her hands. 'You know, she might not have written you a letter. It might have been nothing important at all. It might have been a chat about getting a new car or thinking about a new exhibition or a problem with the boiler or a million other boring details.'

'I don't think so,' said Rachel, shaking her head. 'It wasn't just what she was asking, it was the way she asked. It was something important. I know it was.'

'It's possible you might never find out what it was, Rachel.' Agnes took her hand. 'At some point, you have to stop punishing yourself for things that are beyond your control.'

Rachel stared into Agnes's eyes. 'I don't know if I can.'

There was a short silence. 'Come on,' said Agnes. 'I'll make us some tea.'

'Do you remember that button? The hand-painted one?' Rachel was sitting at the kitchen table, watching Agnes fill the kettle. 'I emailed a heraldry website but they didn't recognise it. I thought I might paint it. The button, I mean. I think it will help me feel closer to Eleanor.'

Agnes turned, her face a vision of pleasant surprise. 'I think that's a very good idea. You should be painting again. Good. That's really good.' She turned off the tap and carried the kettle over to the power point.

'I wouldn't say I've started. I've thought about it. That's progress, I suppose.'

'You know, you're much better than you give yourself credit for.' Agnes pulled a small Tupperware box out from a cloth bag on the kitchen table. 'I wish you believed that. Eleanor thought you had enormous talent. Biscuit? They're nothing fancy. Chocolate chip.' She held the tub out.

'You're just saying that to be kind, Agnes,' said Rachel, taking one. 'I'm no Eleanor Ledbury, that's for sure.' She bit into the biscuit. It crumbled easily.

'No, you're not Eleanor Ledbury,' said Agnes, agreeing. 'You're Rachel Allen.' She took a bite out of her own biscuit and fixed Rachel with a knowing stare. Behind them, the kettle came to a boil.

'It's funny,' Rachel said, resting her face in her upturned hand. 'I always thought Eleanor didn't rate me.'

'Now that *is* nonsense,' said Agnes, turning to deal with the boiled kettle.

'I wonder if I'd feel differently if they'd had more children. Do you wish you'd had more?'

'Absolutely not. Once was enough, thank you very much.' She reached up for the teabags. Have you decided what you're going to do with the cottage?' Agnes stirred the teapot with a spoon.

'Sort of.' Rachel stretched her hands out in front of her and splayed her fingers on the tabletop. 'I'm starting to think I might stay here. But it's such a big house. Feels a bit selfish. Maybe I'll make my mind up at the end of the summer. If Johnny lived nearer, I'd persuade him to take it. It's perfect for a family.'

'I hope you do stay,' said Agnes, letting the teapot sit. 'We've all grown up here. So many memories.'

'Yes,' said Rachel, then, thinking: 'I wonder if that's the problem. This is Eleanor's house. Her space. It always will be. Perhaps I should leave her to haunt it in peace?' Rachel took another bite of her biscuit. 'I had a strange experience, the night she died. Did I tell you about it?'

Agnes shook her head. 'No, you didn't. Do you want a teacup or a mug?'

'Mug, please.' Rachel picked at a crumb that had fallen on to the table with the end of her finger. 'It was the strangest thing. I slept in her bed that night. Don't really know why. And I woke up at one point and felt as if Eleanor was in bed, behind me, and was holding me. It sounds nonsense but I feel absolutely certain it happened.'

'I believe you.' Agnes passed Rachel the mug of tea, poured some milk into her own and sat down heavily. 'Goodness, it's lovely to be sitting down. We've been at it all day.' She picked up a biscuit and broke it in two.

Rachel stared out of the open window. A family of starlings were sitting on the phone lines, chattering and clicking. 'I can't let it go, Agnes.' She shook her head. 'All the questions I should have asked her when I had the chance. All the stories, the adventures, the upsets, the scandals. All gone.' She gave a sigh. 'And that stupid button. It's nothing really and yet I don't know its story. It's all driving me mad. Are you absolutely sure that it's nothing to do with Charlie? I can't think who else it would be.'

'Well,' said Agnes, taking a sip of tea, 'I can't be certain, no, but your father was a plain white button man. He thought duffle toggles were suspicious. And as for him being able to embroider, no. I'm as sure as I can be. It's not Charlie. She may have made it herself. It is hand-painted after all.'

'But the embroidery. She never sewed. I don't know. There are letters too. From way back. When she was at college, I think. Did she have a boyfriend?' Rachel turned and looked at Agnes. 'Before Charlie?'

Agnes frowned. 'I can't recall any boyfriends before Charlie. That's how it was in those days. You married the first person who seemed as if they'd do. Thank God I didn't. If I had, I'd be visiting the clink every Sunday. My first boyfriend went to jail for fraud. He was selling people plots in Highgate cemetery.'

Rachel laughed. 'Stop it.'

'It's true. Absolutely ruthless. Let me think ... I did visit her once, but I can't remember anyone else being ... no, I just recall being wide-eyed. I've got a vivid memory of women in basques and enormous feathers eating bacon sandwiches in a café. We went to Soho and they all came in from the Windmill. Sitting around, eating bacon butties. It was wonderful. Couldn't take my eyes off them. She wrote me lots of letters though. I've still got them. You're very welcome to have them.'

'Yes, thank you.'

Agnes sat back and watched Rachel as she looked out at the starlings. 'You know, it might just be a lovely button. Not everything has a story attached.'

'I know,' said Rachel, her voice low and quiet. 'I just need to understand who my mother was. I need to know who I've come from.'

Agnes reached across the table for her niece's hand. 'Would you like me to help you? I can help you look.'

Rachel glanced up, her eyes tired and lifeless. 'Yes. I'd like that. I'd like that a lot.'

Agnes took another biscuit. This time, she didn't bother breaking it.

Chapter Twenty

Then

'What is it?' Eleanor stared down at the beautifully wrapped parcel Jake had placed in her upturned hands.

'Open it and see.'

'Why are you giving me a present? It's not my birthday.' She smiled up at him.

'So? Presents for no reason are the ones that count. Anybody can give you a birthday present. Besides, it's almost end of term and I shall have to go to Italy and I won't see you for weeks.'

'Don't,' said Eleanor, shaking her head. 'I shan't be able to bear it. Don't mention it again. I'm going to pretend it's not for ages.'

'End of term is in two weeks. You clearly haven't been paying attention.'

'No. Not listening. Stop it.' She slid her finger under the silky red ribbon and eased it off. 'What fancy wrapping paper,' she said. It was black with a peacock feather design.

'I got it in Biba,' he said, throwing himself into an arm-chair in front of her. 'Everyone just goes in there to stare. I thought I ought to buy something.'

They were in the common room at Chelsea. There was a faint smell of clay and paint, and coloured fingerprints were everywhere.

'God,' said Jake, reaching for a scarf, 'it's freezing in here. I know artists are supposed to suffer, but honestly.'

She opened the wrapping carefully so as not to tear the paper. 'That big radiator in the corner is on. I saw someone sitting on it earlier.'

Jake glanced over at the large cast-iron radiator on the back wall. 'Who designed this room? Why would you put a radiator there? All the heat is going straight out of the window. It's making me furious. Open your present a little quicker. That'll take my mind off it.'

Jake had been in a funny mood of late: a bit distant, more self-absorbed than usual. He'd been spending a lot of time in Soho, late nights, provoking arguments. Eleanor had put it down to stress and the widespread preoccupation with end-of-term exhibitions. She had said nothing, partly because she was besotted but partly because she didn't quite know how to vocalise her concern. This was who he was.

'What could it be?' She felt giddy, the warm thrill of knowing someone thinks you're special. She felt courted, indulged, spoiled. She lifted the just-released paper and peered under it. There was a purple velvet bag with a smart gold trim tied down at the top like an envelope. She slid it out. There was something in it. 'What is it?' She looked at Jake.

'I'm not telling you. You'll have to find out.' He looked around. 'Christ, I'm still absolutely freezing. Has anyone left a coat?' He leaped up from his chair and went over to a couple of battered sofas behind them. 'Thank God. It's hideous,' he said, pulling on a green duffle coat, 'but it'll do. Don't tell anybody you saw me in this. Smells of wet feathers.' He sniffed at the collar.

'How would you know what wet feathers smell of?' Eleanor gently undid the delicate braided hoop. 'Oh, it's a book,' she added, looking inside.

'It's not just any book. It's my favourite book.' Jake leaped back into his armchair and tucked his legs up into the duffle coat.

She let the book fall into her palm. It was midnight blue, almost black, with an engraving of writhing figures at its centre. *'The Prophet,'* she said, looking at the title. 'Kahlil Gibran. This looks rather serious.'

'Open it. I've written inside.'

She smiled, gently turned the cover and read. *For Eleanor. Love knows not its own depth until the hour of separation.* Her chest filled. 'Oh, Jake,' she said, not quite knowing how to contain her delight, 'it's beautiful.'

'Normally I wouldn't be so sentimental, but I'm going away. I thought you'd enjoy the *drama*.'

She stared at the inscription. She didn't know what to do. Nobody had ever been so effusive, so romantic with her, and yet here they were, ostensibly still just friends. There was something about Jake that unnerved her. She had seen him give gifts before, to other people he wasn't sure liked him. It was a defence mechanism, a shoring up of the barricades.

'I'm making you something as well. But I haven't quite finished it.'

'You don't have to give me presents to get me to like you,' she said, looking back at him. He was curled into himself, trying to keep warm. 'I like you already.'

'I know that,' he replied, then said nothing further and shifted in his seat.

He turned his attentions to a broken toggle on the duffel coat he was wearing.

Eleanor flicked through the book, but her mind was fixed on precisely what she should do next. She wanted to force the matter, to tell him she loved him, to call herself his girlfriend, to take him home to Brill. She wanted to relax.

'Jake, I ...'

Behind them, the door into the common room swung open and a group of five students clattered in. They were laughing and animated, and Jake's attention immediately shot towards them.

'Are you wearing my duffle coat?' said one of them, bearded, in a chunky blue rollneck.

Jake thrust his chin out. 'I am. I'm unbearably cold. Do you mind?' He stood up and gave a twirl. 'Do you think it suits me?'

'Not in the least,' said the young man, a student from Jake's year. 'You're not planning on wandering off with it, are you?'

'Hardly,' said Jake, enjoying the attention. 'I'm not planning on going on a demonstration.'

The bearded man smiled and shook his head. 'Fancy a tea?' He pulled down some mugs from a shelf that sat above a rather ancient-looking kettle. 'By the way, they're going round the studios upstairs, seeing where everyone's got to with their exhibition pieces. They're sorting out wall spots too. If you want a good one, you need to grab it'

Jake gave a small sigh. 'Oh well, fun's over,' he said, taking off the coat and handing it back. He glanced back at Eleanor. 'Read that book. You'll like it.' And with that, he was gone.

Eleanor stood, the chatter of the other students lightly filling the room. She had a problem. Jake wasn't taking this seriously. He was slipping away and it was beginning to feel as if there was nothing Eleanor could do about it.

Chapter Twenty-one

Eleanor stood on the main concourse of Waterloo station, looking up at the board. Agnes would be arriving on the 11.20. It was cold, London was still in the grip of a sharp freeze, and Eleanor was wearing a large pair of sunglasses she'd borrowed from Hen, her hair bundled up into the pink beret Agnes had made her. She thought it would be a nice gesture, a throwback to the old Eleanor her little sister would recognise. She was conscious of having shifted. She was no longer the little girl from Brill.

She had bought an apple from an Italian man with a fruit stall on the concourse and was enjoying it. It was juicy and crisp. Around her, there was the usual bustle: elderly couples with suitcases, housewives arriving for a day out, a group of schoolchildren in uniform standing in pairs. She tried to empty her mind of everything to do with Jake. Instead, she thought about what Agnes might like to do. A trip to the zoo? The King's Road? Harrods?

'Eleanor?'

She turned and her heart sank. Her mouth was full of apple and she raised a hand to cover her mouth. 'Sorry, I ...' She swallowed. 'Charlie. Hello.'

'I recognised the hat. Wasn't sure with the glasses.' He stared at her, delighted to see her. 'What are you doing here? Off somewhere fun?'

Eleanor blinked. She was debating whether to apologise for having run out on him the last time they'd met, almost two months ago. 'I'm waiting for my sister. She's coming up for the day.'

'Lovely!' His face was open and friendly. If he'd harboured any resentment about their last encounter, it wasn't on display. She wouldn't mention it. Yes. That was best.

'You look very smart,' she said, noting what he was wearing. He was dressed in a dark grey tailcoat suit and waistcoat, set off with a turquoise tie.

'Wedding,' he said, clearly thrilled with the compliment. 'Just outside Woking. Not mine, I should add.'

'How nice,' said Eleanor, taking another bite of her apple.

'It's my best friend from university. I'm the best man. Hence the togs.' He grimaced.

'I hope you've got the rings safe?'

Charlie patted the top of his jacket. 'Glued in,' he said. 'I must have checked a hundred times.'

'Quite the responsibility,' said Eleanor, swallowing again. 'Sorry,' she said, nodding towards the core in her hand, 'I didn't have any breakfast. I'll just ... put this in the bin.' She walked away, racking her brains as to what to say next. She glanced up at the large round clock that hung over the concourse. She still had ten minutes to wait. This was going to be torture.

'When's your train?' she asked, turning back.

'Quarter of an hour. I'm in good time.'

Her heart sank further. She nodded, pressed her lips together and folded her arms. They stood side by side, looking over at the platforms.

'I'm glad I bumped into you,' he said, breaking the awkward silence. 'I rather think we got off on the wrong foot.' He stared at her, waiting for a response.

'Really?' said Eleanor, feigning surprise. 'I'm not sure that's ...' She stopped. He was looking at her with kind eyes. He was being sincere. She knew she needed to apologise. 'You're right. We did. No, that's not right. *I* did. I was entirely rude. I'm sorry I abandoned you at the post office. I shouldn't have done it. I think I lumped you in with the enemy. Snooping mother at home and all that. I panicked. I thought you'd been sent to spy on me.'

'Well, that bit is technically true,' said Charlie, straight-faced and serious. 'I had been sent to spy on you. I have to send back daily dispatches. It's all very hush-hush but the pay is rotten.' He smiled.

Eleanor's mouth skewed sideways. She knew when she was having her leg pulled. 'Sorry,' she said. 'I think I was being paranoid. Can we start again?'

'Yes,' he said, smiling. 'I'd like that.'

Eleanor looked at Charlie with fresh eyes. Since her encounter in the kitchen with John she felt, how could she describe it – different? She had found herself staring at men, on buses, in shops, sitting in parks, and imagining herself lying with them, their lips pressed into her neck. That moment in the kitchen with John kept replaying itself in her mind: the strange, delicious tingle, the thread that kept pulling her back. Perhaps she should go to John's studio and have her picture taken? She wasn't sure she had the courage for it.

'You really do look very nice,' said Eleanor. 'But you've nicked yourself shaving. Did you know?'

Charlie frowned. 'Oh hell,' he said, 'where? I haven't got blood on my collar, have I?'

'Here.' Eleanor reached into her bag and pulled out a compact. 'Use that. It's just there.' She pointed towards the cut with her index finger. 'I've got some Vaseline. You can use that too if you like. Always better than walking around with a lump of tissue on your face.'

'If you don't mind,' said Charlie, looking at the compact as she held it out. 'I'd rather not stand on Waterloo concourse looking at myself in a lady's vanity mirror. Perhaps you could put some Vaseline on my finger and help me get there?'

'Or … I can do it for you if you like?'

'Yes,' said Charlie with a nod. 'I think that's probably best.'

Eleanor pushed her sunglasses up over the top of her beret, reached back into her bag and pulled out a small, round tin of Vaseline. Opening it, she dabbed a little on her middle finger and reached up towards Charlie's face. 'It won't sting,' she said. It seemed odd to be doing this when minutes before she was filled with dread at seeing him again, but all the same, she touched her finger to his skin. 'There,' she said, leaving a tiny dot on top of the cut, 'all done. Oh. Wait. I've smeared a bit on your …' She swept her thumb over his jawline, cleaning away the grease. It felt intimate but the ease of it shocked her.

'Above and beyond,' he said, smiling. 'Thank you.'

'My pleasure,' she said, dropping the tin back into her bag.

'How's college?' he asked. 'You must have almost finished your first term, yes?'

'Almost,' she said, with a nod. 'It's been … interesting. Illuminating. I think I'm more confident. That happens, doesn't it? When you get away from your parents?' She smiled.

He smiled back. 'It can do, yes. You look like you're flourishing.' He paused and looked at her. 'And do you like the people?' He widened his stance and put his hands into his pockets. He looked like someone checking a cricket score.

'Yes. But I don't mix with many of them. I've made friends with a man in the year above. Jake. He and I have been rather inseparable.' She watched his face for a reaction.

Something flickered across Charlie's face. 'How exciting.'

Eleanor blinked. 'I think I might be in love with him.'

Charlie's eyebrows went up. There was something rather surprising about her openness. 'And is he in love with you?'

She paused. 'I don't know.' Her eyes drifted off, back to the clock. She had felt rather grown up dealing with a man's razor cut, but now, talking about Jake, she felt girlish. 'Maybe I'm not in love with him,' she added, looking back at Charlie. 'Maybe I just want to be in love. Oh dear. I suddenly feel rather silly. And there was I, impressing you with how mature I've become.'

'We all like to think we're in love with someone,' said Charlie, putting his hand again to where the rings were kept. 'Wouldn't the world be dull if we didn't?' He looked at her. There was something a little sad about how he said it.

He was being kind, not wanting her to feel embarrassed. She was grateful. Eleanor thought for a moment about what he'd said. 'Do you think you're in love with someone?' she said finally.

'Not yet,' he replied, casting an eye up at the departure board. 'I'm far too busy. And loving people from afar is rather pointless. Isn't it?'

'What a serious conversation we've ended up having,' said Eleanor, clasping her hands together. She paused and thought. 'Can I ask you your advice,' she said, screwing her eyebrows into knots. 'Do you mind?'

Charlie looked back at her. 'This is precisely why I was recruited by Agent Marjory.' He folded his arms to make himself look more serious. 'So no, I don't mind.'

Eleanor took a deep breath. 'There's a photographer,' she began. 'He's ... different, a little older. He has quite the reputation. A proper rogue, my father would call him. And he kissed me at a party. And it made me feel ... different. Alive somehow. And he wants me to go to his studio and be photographed. What do you think about that?'

'Goodness,' said Charlie, his eyebrows rising. 'I'm not sure I was expecting you to be quite so candid. Would your mother be happy with you going to see this man in his studio?'

'Absolutely not.'

'And, if you don't mind me asking, do you want to go to his studio to be photographed or to be kissed?'

Eleanor stared down at her shoes. 'I'm not sure. Photographed. No, kissed. Probably.'

'And what does the young man you're in love with think about it?'

'I haven't told him.'

'Would he be upset if he found out?'

Eleanor thought about Jake. She thought about the moment after the kiss in the kitchen and the moments since. 'I don't know. I'd like to think he might be jealous but actually, I'm not sure he'd care at all. Oh dear.' Tears sprang to her eyes.

'Here,' said Charlie, pulling a beautifully laundered handkerchief from his pocket. 'Take that. Look here, I don't know your chap, but if you were my girl I'd be bothered beyond belief. People treat you the way you let them.

And it strikes me that you wouldn't be considering going to this photographer's studio if you knew for certain that your chap loved you in return.'

Eleanor wiped at her nose. 'I'm sorry I'm blubbing. I'm mortified.'

'Don't be,' said Charlie. 'If you really want my advice, this photographer sounds a bit off. And if your mother would be appalled, then take note. Mothers have a terrible habit of being right.'

Eleanor gave a sniff.

'If I were you, I'd go and find your chap. Be honest. Tell him how you feel. The worst that can happen is you'll find out where you stand. And that's no bad thing.'

'I don't know if I want to know.' Eleanor twisted the corner of the handkerchief in her fingers.

'Of course you do. If you're trying to convince me you're a shrinking violet, I'm afraid I'm not buying it.'

Eleanor let out a laugh and looked up into Charlie's eyes. They were kind and compassionate and concerned. It was good to have a friend who was older. He seemed more sure of himself than anyone else she knew. She put her hand on his forearm. 'Thank you, Charlie. Sorry. It's all been a bit pent up. You won't report back to Marjory, will you?'

'No,' said Charlie, putting his hand on hers. 'I won't report back to Marjory.'

Eleanor glanced over at the platforms. Agnes had arrived. She gave a little wave.

'Hello, who are you?' Agnes said, looking straight at Charlie, her duffel coat done up to the top.

'This is my little sister, Agnes,' said Eleanor, putting the handkerchief into her pocket. 'Agnes, this is Charlie.'

Agnes's eyes widened. 'Oh no, the awful spy from your letters!'

Charlie gave out a laugh. 'The very same. Now I'm afraid I'm going to have to take down all your details ... how old are you?'

Agnes look worried. 'Thirteen.'

'Height?'

'I don't know!' She screwed her mouth into a grimace.

'And how much do you weigh?'

'How rude,' said Agnes. 'Everyone knows a gentleman should never ask a lady how much she weighs. You really are a terrible spy.'

Charlie and Eleanor both roared with laughter.

'It's fine, Ag,' said Eleanor, putting her arm around her sister's shoulder. 'He's teasing.'

Charlie glanced up again at the departure board. 'My train's on the platform. I should go.' He turned back to address Agnes. 'It was very nice to meet you, Agnes. And Eleanor, if you ever need a cup of tea ...' He gave her hand a squeeze and walked off, his tailcoat bobbing behind him.

'Thank you. And good luck with today!' called Eleanor as he strode away.

He stopped at the platform's end and waved back at them, and they both stood watching as he disappeared.

'He's very handsome,' said Agnes, looking up at her sister.

'Oh, come off it,' said Eleanor. 'Now where do you want to go?'

Chapter Twenty-two

Eleanor, her mind still swirling with Jake and John, had decided to take Agnes into Soho. They'd ended up in a café on the corner of Wardour Street and Agnes had sat, bacon sandwich in hand, agog at the troupe of dancing girls who'd traipsed in on their lunch break from the notorious nude revue next door. It was a cultural visit of sorts, Eleanor had argued, just not one their mother ever needed to know about.

It had felt strange, returning to an uncomplicated but deeply ingrained relationship. With Agnes, Eleanor had slotted straight back into her role of Girl from Brill, making polite enquiries about their parents, listening as Agnes rattled off pointless gossip about girls she was at school with.

Anxious that Agnes was going to return home and report all, Eleanor had taken her to the National Gallery next, and made sure to buy her a few postcards she could present to their mother.

'Can't I stay with you?' Agnes pleaded when they were back at Waterloo again. 'I could turn my knickers inside out and borrow your toothbrush.'

'No, Ag,' replied Eleanor, handing her a cheese roll, 'Mummy would have a fit. Show me your train ticket.'

Agnes scowled, reached into her duffel-coat pocket and pulled out a brown envelope. 'It's in there,' she said, with a pout.

Eleanor opened it and, having checked it, handed it back. 'Have you had a lovely time?'

'Not really,' said Agnes, staring off into the distance.

'Don't fib. And don't pretend you're livid.'

'I am livid,' said Agnes, her eyebrows knitted together. 'I can't believe you're sending me back.'

'I'm not sending you back. It's time for you to go home. There's a solid difference.' Eleanor looked up at the departure board. 'You can catch the quarter to. Platform four. Come on. I'll see you on.'

'But I haven't met any of your friends!'

'Quite right. Don't want you corrupting them. Now come here, and give me a hug.'

Eleanor felt a soft burn in the soles of her feet. She'd seen Agnes safely back on to the 5.45 train and, despite having walked all day, she decided to take Charlie's advice. Jake would be in Soho somewhere. She needed to track him down and find out where she stood.

She stopped at the midpoint across Waterloo Bridge and looked west. The sky was flushing pink behind the Houses of Parliament, long shards of thin clouds blazing in the dying sun, but her favourite view was the other way, towards St Paul's. There was something timeless about it, something that tethered her to the seams of the city. She was starting to feel as if she belonged.

She crossed the Strand and walked up past the Lyceum. The pavements outside the theatre were crowded with men in hats and coats waiting for a glimpse of Miss World contestants who were due to arrive. Their faces were blank and expectant and there was something about them that reminded Eleanor of her first days in the city: all wide-eyed and astonished. A large black saloon car pulled up and a flurry of shouts and cheers went up. Eleanor could just see the head of a woman but she was quickly enveloped by photographers and gawping men.

Eleanor walked on past the Royal Opera House, and turned left when she reached the junction with Endell Street. She walked past market traders, Covent Garden street entertainers on their way to work and theatre-goers standing wondering whether they had time to eat. She passed through Cambridge Circus, stopped to watch a busker, guitar in hands, drum strapped on his back and a harmonica on a frame around his neck. He was playing the latest Bob Dylan. He was good. She threw him a few pennies and crossed Shaftesbury Avenue to head into Soho. She liked that she knew where she was going. She felt as if she had a purpose.

He'd be in the French, a regular drinking spot on Dean Street. Recently, Jake had rather tired of the younger, faster crowd. Eleanor had put it down to the end of term and his incessant need for new faces. Instead, he was gravitating towards a more hardened set of artists, poets, authors and journalists, some of whom were wildly successful, others doomed to creative failure. It was a social scene where anything was endured except boredom.

Eleanor didn't care much for this new pack of acquaintances. She preferred it when it was just the two of them, together against the world. She was greedy. She wanted Jake all to herself. To her, this new set felt like a group of people terrified of not being relevant, but it was more than that: they seemed desperate not to feel lonely. They were trying too hard: too much booze, too many arguments, too much drama, but Jake was addicted to it. He loved the carelessness and the mischief. Perhaps he always had, she wondered. She cast her mind back to that first encounter: the black eye, the drunkenness, the reckless attitude to norms. It was the dangerousness of him she'd first been drawn to. Now, it was starting to feel like a sadness.

She pushed open the door of the French, the air thick with smoke and chatter, and immediately saw Hen sitting on a high stool by the bar, who, catching her eye, raised a hand. The pub was starting to fill with the usual mix of disparate people: a prop handler with a nose like a swollen strawberry, a faded beauty trying to cash a cheque with the barman, a stage doorman sneaking in for a swift pint before curtain up.

'What are you drinking?' asked Hen, reaching into her bag.

'Nothing, thanks,' said Eleanor, scanning the room. 'I'm looking for Jake.'

'Aren't we all?' said Hen, putting her handbag back up on the bar. 'He owes me five pounds.' She flicked her hair back and took a sip of the drink in front of her. 'Top tip if you're ever feeling queasy,' she explained, tipping the glass in Eleanor's direction. 'Port and lemon. Always seems to help. That or eating grated apple. But it must be grated. And it must turn completely brown before you eat it. Doesn't affect the flavour, but it works a treat on a poorly tum.'

'Are you ill?' Eleanor was still looking through the squash of people.

'No more than usual,' said Hen, sounding despondent. 'Anyway. No apple and no grater. So this will have to do. Bottoms up.'

'Here,' said Eleanor, handing her the sunglasses in her pocket. 'You should have these back.'

Hen eyed them with some enthusiasm. 'Oh, thank God,' she said, putting them on. 'Don't suppose you have a cigarette, do you?'

Eleanor shook her head. Hen always forgot she didn't smoke. She put one hand on the brass rail that ran around the edge of the bar, feeling anxious. 'I need to speak to Jake,' she replied. Her hand was trembling.

'Are you all right?' Hen tilted her head.

Eleanor pulled her hand away and clenched it. 'Yes. Bit tired, that's all. I've been looking after my little sister all day. Feet are killing me.'

Hen took another sip from her port and lemon. It was hard to read her, with the sunglasses on. 'Have you tried phoning him? Jake, I mean? At home?'

'No, I haven't.'

'If I was looking for someone,' she said, with a pout, 'I imagine that's where I'd start.' She pointed at the public telephone in the corner of the room. 'Darling,' she said, reaching across Eleanor to a man who had come in behind her. 'Can I have a cigarette?'

Eleanor turned and squeezed through the tangle of people between her and the telephone, snatches of conversation coming and going as she did so.

There was a stool by the telephone, and she sat and picked up the receiver. The room was noisy, and as she put the money into the slot, she faced the wall and covered her spare ear with her hand. 'Jake?'

'Where are you? You sound like you're at the bottom of the ocean.'

'I'm in the French,' Eleanor shouted to be heard over the din. 'I thought you'd be here.'

'Come here. We can go out later. I've got something I want to show you.'

'What?'

'Not telling. I'll show you when you get here. Hurry up.'

He hung up and Eleanor sat still for a moment, wondering how it was that she always found herself doing everything he asked. If he was addicted to gratification and indulgence, she was addicted to him.

She took the bus to Hampstead, listening to the quiet, idle chatter of two women who had spent the afternoon watching the latest Hitchcock. 'I hate birds as it is,' one was complaining. 'I'll have nightmares for months. I don't know why you suggested it. Why did you suggest it?'

Eleanor tuned out and stared from the window as the bus began the slow crawl up Haverstock Hill. As they passed her building, her mind wandered to Charlie and whether he'd managed to pull off his best-man duties. He seemed very, what was it exactly, capable, reliable? Her mind flitted back, as it always did these days, to Jake. Could she call him reliable? Not in the least.

It was dark by the time she arrived at Jake's house and, before knocking, she stood for a moment and tried to gather herself. She had to be clear about what she wanted. She wanted more than friendship, more than the light frivolities of their companionship. She wanted to feel the way she had that night in the kitchen, but this time with Jake's mouth on her neck. She wanted to feel his hands on her body, to be desired, but it went beyond that. She had found someone to whom she was devoted. He understood her. He gave her a sense of purpose. He inspired her. In him, she had found herself and now she wanted to make their connection complete. There was no turning back. She felt sick, excited, woozy. She had to tell him. She had to know.

She knocked.

The door opened and Jake stood there, his body splayed open in a grand hurrah. She felt the rush of adrenaline he always managed to induce. Every time she saw him it was the same: the electric shot of joy, all sense abandoned. She loved him. She was in love. Now she just had to tell him.

He was wearing a white cotton shirt, the sleeves rolled up, tucked into a pair of tight, sea-blue trousers that tapered at the ankle. He was sockless, his brown feet disappearing into a pair of faded deck shoes. On his head, at a rakish angle, sat a papier mâché crown. He looked delighted.

'Tah-dah!' he announced, with a grin. 'What do you think?' he added, putting one hand on his hip and tilting his head. 'I think I should wear this all the time, don't you? This or an outrageous bright red top hat. God,' he said, stopping to look at her, 'you look awful. Are you dying?'

'No,' said Eleanor, walking up the steps and into the hallway. 'Just tired. I've been giving my little sister a tour of London all day.'

'Have you eaten? There's some cold mashed potato in the kitchen. Hardly the Ritz, but I could fry it up for you. I think I've got some bacon.' As he walked ahead of her, there was a bounce to him. He was clearly pleased about something.

'I'm not hungry,' she replied.

'Good, I'm glad.' Jake stopped at the foot of the stairs and spun round, one hand up on the banister. 'Because I've got something to show you.'

'I know.'

'Can you guess what it is?'

'I don't know. A painting?'

Jake gave a small grin. 'Come on.' He took her hand and ran up the stairs, pulling her behind him. On the first landing, he stopped in front of a large door. 'It's something for my end-of-term show. But I've really made it for you. Do you remember me saying we must have a secret society? One that only you and I are members of?'

She nodded. She wasn't sure she was in the mood for this. She needed to be serious.

'Well. I have made you something entirely appropriate.' He swung the door open and swept his arm towards a tailor's dummy in the middle of the room. 'Behold!' he declared, 'the regal garments for Lady High of Everything Else!'

Eleanor walked into the room. It was surprisingly sparse: wood-panelled walls that gave the room the air of another century, no decorations other than some pencilled clothes patterns tacked to the wall with pins. In the centre of the room stood a dummy, and behind it a long, low wooden table covered with fragments of fabric, cotton and various pairs of scissors. A splendid frock coat was draped across the dummy's shoulders: royal blue with a gold trim, flared buttoned cuffs and a high stiff collar that had something of the Regency dandy about it. It was beautiful.

Eleanor stood and stared at it. 'You made that for me?'

'Who else would I make it for?'

'I didn't know you could tailor.'

'Did a summer at Savile Row. I should be doing fashion instead of painting, but my father sniffed at it. He can just about cope with an artist in the family. Tradesman? Absolutely not. Here,' he said, taking it gently by the shoulders, 'try it on.'

She slipped off her simple jacket, a dark navy wool blazer that was only one crest away from looking like an old school uniform, and turned her back to Jake, allowing him to place the sleeves on to her arms. She let the weight of the coat settle into her back and turned.

'Do up the buttons,' he said. 'I want to see if it fits.'

Eleanor did as she was told. She bent her head down and fastened the trio of large gold buttons at the front of the tunic. It fitted like a glove.

'It's beautiful, Jake,' she said, gazing down at it. 'I love it.'

'Look at the cuffs,' he said, standing back to look at her. 'I added something special.'

Eleanor lifted her right arm and twisted the side of the cuff upwards. Along the edge, there was a line of exquisite embroidery punctuated by two small hand-painted buttons. She peered at them. 'What's that?' she said, fingering one.

'Our royal crest,' he said, coming forward and standing close to her. 'I had to use a magnifying glass to paint those. Worth it though, don't you think?'

Eleanor looked up into his eyes and put her hand on his cheek. 'Thank you,' she said, then leaned towards him and kissed him on the lips. He stood there, passive, and Eleanor, feeling awkward, pulled away. She wanted to kiss him again, passionately, to wrap her arms about his neck, to feel his body pressing into hers. She ached with it, but she couldn't quite bring herself to force the moment. She wanted it to be like it had been with John.

'Look at the moon,' said Jake, folding his arms and wandering over to the window. 'It looks enormous.'

'That's an optical illusion,' said Eleanor, following him. 'It's all about the angles.'

Jake pulled a face. 'Nobody should ever be scientific when it comes to the moon. It's far too romantic. What was it Mark Twain said? "Everyone is a moon, and has a dark side which he never shows to anybody."' Jake's voice was now barely a whisper. 'I wonder what your dark side is.'

'I'm not sure I've got one.'

'I don't think I believe you.'

'Jake, I ...' She put her hand on his.

'I feel as if we're in danger of sliding into seriousness,' he said, cutting her off.

'Jake,' said Eleanor again, moving her hand to his chest. 'You don't need to do this.'

He smiled and gave a little shake of his head. 'Don't need to do what?'

'Keep up a front the whole time.' She watched as his face remained in a frozen grin.

'I'm not. I'm just happy, that's all,' he said, with a blink.

'No, Jake,' she said, taking his hand in hers. 'I don't think you are. You're spending all your time in the French with people you don't even like.'

'I do like them.'

'No, you don't. You spent every night last week in the French having arguments with people. I don't understand it. You're trying to turn yourself into something you're not. You don't need those people to be who you are. Remember who you are. I do. I miss you.'

He turned his head away from her and stared back out at the swollen moon.

'I've just made you a beautiful coat,' he said, his voice barely audible. 'I'm not sure why you would think such a thing. Or why you would say that to me. Perhaps you don't like me at all?'

He withdrew his hand from hers.

Eleanor felt a surge of panic. She had come to tell him that she loved him but she was getting it all wrong. She had to get this back on track.

'That's not true, Jake. Of course I like you. I more than like you. I love you.'

'But I love you too,' he whispered, still not looking her directly in the eye.

'No,' said Eleanor, pressing closer to him. 'I mean properly.'

He looked back down at her, his eyes filling with tears. 'I do love you properly.'

Eleanor knew there was no turning back. 'I mean like this.'

She grabbed his face and pressed her lips into his, kissing him the way John had kissed her. He didn't kiss her back. She stopped and looked into his eyes. They looked pained and uncomfortable. 'Why don't you want to? Why do you never try to kiss me? What's wrong with me?'

'There's nothing wrong with you. Don't,' he whispered, turning his face from her. 'Please.'

'I don't understand, Jake. If there's nothing wrong with me, then ...' She reached for his hand but he pulled away, his cheeks wet, his face contorted.

'Please don't,' he whispered, his forehead knitting into a pained knot. 'I can't.'

Eleanor watched him. He laid a hand across his eyes, shielding himself from her gaze. She'd never seen him so distressed.

'But why, Jake?' she began. 'What's wrong?'

Jake bit his lip, unable to look at her. 'There's nothing wrong.'

She changed tack. She needed a way in. 'I'm worried about you. Hanging out at the French, drinking too much, constantly getting into fights.'

'Everyone gets into fights.'

'No, Jake, they don't.'

'Maybe I want to be beaten. Maybe I deserve to feel pain. Maybe I like to feel ashamed.'

'What are you talking about?' She shook her head. 'Why would you want any of those things?'

He gave a shrug. 'Maybe it gives me a release. I don't know ...' His voice fell away.

'Release from what?'

He leaned back against the window, the moonlight falling on his shoulders, a delicate cape softening the shadows. He took a deep breath and lifted his head to look at her.

'I'm a queer.' He stared at her, his arms hanging loosely by his sides, his shoulders back, his chest out, his head slightly tilted.

Eleanor was unable to speak, her stomach plunging downwards, a dark weight descending. It wasn't true. She shook her head and gave an awkward laugh. 'Don't be silly. You can't be.'

'I am. I can't help who I am, Eleanor.'

'But,' her voice sank away, 'you can't be. I love you. You made that happen. You were romantic. I *believed* you.' She pulled at the coat. 'Why did you do that? If you didn't mean it? I don't understand ... I ...'

'I never kissed you, did I?' He turned to her, his voice flat and deadened.

Eleanor stared at him, not knowing what to do next. It was as if the air had been sucked from the room. She reached back for the window ledge and held herself up on it. 'Sorry,' she said, turning her face to the floor. 'I don't know what to ... Sorry. I think I'm going to faint.' Eleanor slumped backwards. She had come here full of hope, in search of the certainty of solid foundations, and here she was, the ground beneath her crumbling away. She had never known despair before and yet here it was, in the place she least expected to find it, dragging her down, the darkness enfolding her.

'Sit on the floor,' Jake said, taking her arm. 'Put your head between your knees.'

Eleanor shut her eyes and breathed deeply. Jake's hand was on her shoulder. She felt every contour of it.

'I'll be fine. I just need to sit here for a minute.'

'I'm sorry, Eleanor.' His voice was quiet and gentle.

She looked up at him, threw her head back against the wall and exhaled. Her chest felt heavy and leaden. Her hand went to her mouth. 'I don't know what to do,' she whispered. 'I don't know what to do. I love you so much.' Her bottom lip crumpled in on itself and she shut her eyes to hold back the tears. 'How could you have let this happen?'

'I don't know. I thought you understood. I needed you. I do love you, Eleanor. Just not how you want me to.'

Eleanor shook her head, tears falling on to her cheeks. 'No, Jake. No. You let me fall in love with you. You encouraged it. I don't know if I can forgive that.' Her heart was beating in her chest, her cheeks flushing, and she felt a pressure in her head that was almost unbearable.

'Please.' He reached down to take her hand. 'I can bear this sort of thing from other people but not from you.'

'I feel so stupid.' She pushed herself up. 'Stupid Eleanor. Stupid, green Eleanor from Brill. Falling in love with the first man who makes her feel worth something.' She shook her head.

'Eleanor, please . . .'

Reaching down, she fumbled at the buttons on the front of the tunic, but as she did, one button caught on the radiator behind her. She yanked at the sleeve and the button fell to the floor. 'You should have told me from the start, Jake.' She threw the coat down. 'But this . . .' She gestured towards him. 'This wasn't right. You've deliberately misled me.'

'Eleanor, I . . .'

'No,' she mumbled, walking towards the door. 'I can't. I can't do this.'

'We can carry on as we were. Best friends. We'll be fine. Please, Eleanor. You don't understand how hard it's been. I have to live a lie. With you I can be myself. I want to be honest. I want you to know me and like me. You're all I have.'

'No, Jake, I can't. I'm sorry.'

She could feel the shock turning to rage. She had one card she could play. He had hurt her and now she would hurt him. She looked at him and wiped a hand across her eyes. 'Don't follow me downstairs,' she said. She was gone before he could reply. She knew where she needed to be.

Chapter Twenty-three

John's studio was smaller than she had imagined. As she stood, taking it in, she could feel her chest beating but she wasn't sure if that was because of the climb up the four flights of stairs or because she knew precisely why she was there. She felt disorientated, shaky; her emotions were running riot. Her head was blurred from the desperate encounter with Jake. She felt broken, adrift and drowning.

She stood for a moment and took the room in, trying to calm herself, to adjust. She'd found John in the French. He'd been surprised to see her.

He threw down his keys and crouched down to open a cabinet. 'What do you want to drink?'

'I don't know. You choose.' Catching her breath, she walked over to the far wall, a chaotic mural of photographs, and looked at the rogue's gallery of men with gnarled faces, enigmatic beauties and other people who looked vaguely familiar. A length of string hung from one wall to its opposite, bedecked with the odd laundry of pictures yet to dry: a milkman delivering his first pints of the day, a boy with a bag of toffees, a woman applying lipstick in a café. The pictures were arresting and full of character. They were far better than she expected.

'Here,' said John, behind her. 'Scotch. I'm afraid I don't have any ice.'

She took the mug and stared down into it. 'I've never had Scotch before,' she said. 'It looks like tea.'

'Why do you think it's in a mug?' He took a sip.

'When did you take these?' She nodded over at the line of drying photographs. Her heart was pounding. This was not what she had expected to happen. This had not been her original intention. Yet here she was, catapulted to this darker, more visceral world.

'Yesterday,' he said, touching the corner of one delicately. 'I'm not sure I'm happy with them yet. I might re-develop the negatives. The tone is a bit off.'

Eleanor could smell the deep, peaty aroma of the Scotch as she lifted the mug to her lips. It felt hot in her mouth, a strange smoky taste, and then, as she swallowed, a sharp after-burn at the back of her throat that made her gasp. She wanted to forget. She wanted the pain to go away. She wanted to punish herself for being so stupid. She drank again. 'Goodness,' she said, her eyes watering a little. 'That's very strong.'

'That's the point,' said John. He stood looking at her, his eyes examining her face. 'You have a good profile,' he said, his thumb sweeping across her jawline. 'I can do something with that. You look tired though. And you've been crying. Can you sit over there?' He pointed towards a wooden stool in front of a black cloth backdrop. 'I'll get my camera.'

She sat and put the mug on the floor by her feet. She could feel her hands trembling. Her eyes felt hot and puffy. She had taken a cab from Jake's back into town and had cried all the way. She felt numb, in denial, betrayed. He had let her love him, knowing all the while he couldn't love her back, and yet, somehow, perhaps she had known, deep down. Perhaps she had but was too naive to recognise or vocalise it? Perhaps that was part of his allure, the unattainable Jake who was fabulous and fun. Well. She didn't want to be safe any more. She looked up.

'I think I want you to take a picture of me looking like this. Tired and having cried, I mean. I think that would be more honest.'

John was standing with his back to her, fixing a lens to his camera. He cast a look at her over his shoulder but said nothing. Instead, he curled his camera into one hand and put a record on with the other. 'Do you like jazz?' he asked, walking towards her.

'I don't know enough about it,' she said, gripping the edges of the stool with her hands.

'This is Ella Fitzgerald,' he said, gesturing to the record player. 'I find her sound rather sexy. What do you think?'

She stared up at him. 'Yes. I do too.'

He took a picture of her, stopped and rolled on the film. 'Lift your chin up.'

Another click of the camera.

'Why have you been crying?' He held the camera back to his eye and stared at her through it.

'I went to see Jake to ask him if he loved me.' Her honesty burned her. She could feel the wheels of her own self-destruction turning. She had offered herself up and lost everything.

'And what did he say?'

'That he can't love me.'

John let his camera drift to the side of his cheek. 'Oh,' he said. 'You didn't know. I rather assumed you did.'

Eleanor shook her head. 'Do you think I'm a fool?'

'No,' he answered, watching her carefully. 'If anything I find it rather endearing. Were you shocked?' He put his camera back to his eye.

'I suppose I was, yes.'

He took another picture and lowered his camera to look at her. 'I need to change the reel.'

He walked away and Eleanor watched him, the curve of his shoulders, his hands as they changed the film, his legs, his neck. There was a strange comfort to be found: the way he so calmly knew who he was, the fact he wasn't judging her for being so stupid. He was wearing that black leather jacket again, this time with a white T-shirt underneath. There was something of the film star about him, James Dean? Was that who she was thinking of? Something in her didn't care what she was thinking. She needed to forget the day, to forget Jake, and yet she couldn't. They had parted on such bad terms. Her sadness was deep and impenetrable.

'Will you kiss me again?' Eleanor said, her voice soft and quiet. It was almost a plea, a call for help. There was nothing romantic about the request, no sentimentality. She didn't want to feel foolish or naive. She knew what she needed.

'Would you like me to?' He walked towards her.

'Yes.'

'Chin up,' he said, lifting his camera to his eye.

She looked beyond him into the darker corner of the studio. There was a bed, unmade, just visible behind a screen. She wanted to be reckless.

'Look into the lens,' he asked. 'Do you trust me?'

'Not at all,' said Eleanor.

The camera clicked.

'Do you like me?'

The camera clicked again.

'I'm not sure I do. I think you're quite hard to like.'

'I think you might be right,' he said, the camera clicking again.

'I want to have sex with you,' she said. 'I need to forget everything. I need to feel desired. And I need it not to matter.'

He lowered the camera and looked at her. 'Why are you happy for it not to matter?'

'Because one day it will.'

John moved over to the large wooden table in the corner of the room and put his camera down. He drained the last of his Scotch and turned the record player down a little. Taking off his jacket, he draped it across the back of a chair. He went over to a socket in the wall, bent down and turned it off, plunging the room into darkness. Eleanor said nothing and waited for her eyes to adjust. She could just make him out, walking towards a covered window. He pushed the black cloth to one side and moonlight streamed in. He stood for a moment, his silhouette against the night sky, then came towards her. He took her hands, pulled her up to him and kissed her, slowly. She kissed him back.

'One day,' he said, moving down to her neck, 'it will matter.'

Her back arched as he kissed her again, just below her ear.

'But not today.'

PART THREE

*'To live in hearts we leave behind
is not to die.'*

Thomas Campbell

Chapter Twenty-four

Now

Rachel couldn't find a single photo of her mother.

Surely there was one of Eleanor somewhere? She looked around her mother's bedroom. There were pictures of Charlie with Johnny, pictures of Charlie with Johnny and Rachel, pictures of Johnny and Rachel, a picture of Johnny and Francesca on their wedding day, a picture of Agnes with Eleanor's parents, and that was it. There was even a picture of Charlie on her parents' wedding day, but Eleanor wasn't in it. It was as if Eleanor didn't exist. Rachel stared at the moments in time from her family's story and felt a pang of something deep and sad and unnerving.

'This can't be right,' Rachel murmured, and she turned, padding back down the corridor towards her room and the family albums. When Charlie died, she had found solace in the tapestry of their lives: summers, Christmases, Easter egg hunts, country walks, muddy adventures, cricket on the beach, holidays abroad, building dens, the arrival of new pets and the saying of goodbyes to dead ones. All of it was recorded, but Eleanor featured nowhere.

There was a simple explanation, of course: Eleanor was always the one holding the camera, but it struck Rachel that Eleanor had extracted herself from their memories. Whether that was intentional or not was another thing entirely, but Rachel sat and felt consumed with guilt. None of them had made Eleanor matter.

How had Rachel never noticed this before? She felt appalled with herself, even with Charlie, that it had always been Eleanor recording their lives. Her absence from these memories seemed more than an oversight: it felt cruel.

She pushed herself up from the bed, her face etched with the curious expression of someone who still can't quite believe something might be true. There was a glimpse of hope: up in the attic there were boxes she was yet to go through, things from Eleanor's past. Her search had intensified. She'd read everything of her mother's she'd managed to get her hands on: her diaries, some old letters, cards, odd scribbles in notebooks. She'd tasked Agnes with providing her with a list of people she might be able to speak to: old friends, acquaintances, agents, gallery owners, buyers. She was consumed with unlocking her mother's memories.

What had her mother wanted her to know? She could not move forward until the past had been released.

There was only one thing for it. Rachel had never liked heights and she stared at the attic door above her, the step-ladder extended. She wondered if this was sensible. 'This is how people die,' she said to herself. 'You fall from a ladder and break your neck and then you lie dead for days and someone finds you after two weeks and your face has been eaten by cats.' She stopped and screwed her mouth into a ball. She clasped the ladder with both hands.

She edged up slowly, gripping the sides so tight her knuckles looked like marbles. One step at a time, spreading her weight, making sure her feet were firmly planted. She felt a little silly being so nervous. This was the stuff she had always left to Claude or Johnny or her father, but now, with no man in her life, she was damned if she was going to give up before she'd started.

Three quarters of the way up the ladder and she was able to push open the door and look in. She had a small torch in her mouth, held sideways like a chicken leg, and, taking it in her hand, she switched it on. It cut dimly through the darkness. 'Oh lord,' she mumbled. 'Isn't there a light somewhere? There must be.'

As she shone the thin beam upwards, it caught a bare light bulb. A cord hung down from it, a knotted loop tied into the end of its length. It looked like a tiny noose.

Rachel rested the torch on the attic floor and pushed herself up and on to the inside ledge. Her legs were dangling down towards the hallway and, looking at them, she had a strange, vertiginous sense of dizziness. Unnerved, she scrabbled up and pulled at the cord.

The bulb threw a foggy light through the large space, across tea chests, old rolls of carpet, paintings that nobody wanted to look at any more but couldn't bear to throw away, boxes of Rachel's school exercise books, and an open suitcase filled with creepy toys, none of which Rachel recognised. There was an old typewriter, probably once Charlie's. Rachel let her fingers drift over the keys. She pressed down on the R, the sound of the thick clunk satisfying and reassuring. She picked it up and put it down near the top of the ladder. She'd keep that.

A large blue trunk was shoved hard up into the eaves. On its top, a thick leather strap was tied through a buckle, and Rachel, with some effort, set about undoing it. She paused before lifting the lid, half concerned this might be the moment some dread source of evil finally leaped out, hell bent on withering her soul, but, as she pushed upwards, she was relieved to see it was filled with nothing more than a heap of books, used art pads, bundles of letters, more old diaries and various papers. Her eyes widened. 'Brilliant,' she mumbled to herself. Every new thing she could find and read represented a small hope that she would find what she craved. She crouched down and pulled out a battered cardboard file.

Opening it, she found some rather arresting pencil sketches of a young man in various poses: sleeping on a chaise longue; reading a book in a striped deckchair; in profile, his face cupped in his hands. There was a larger one, his face straight on; he had a curious smile, as if he were in on a secret. Rachel stared at it and, placing it flat in front of her, she covered everything on the picture with her hands, leaving only the eyes still visible. Were they the same eyes as the ones in the unfinished portrait in her mother's studio? She wasn't sure. She gave a sigh. She had no idea what she was even looking for: a letter, a confessional, an ancient note to self? Rachel didn't know. It was incredibly frustrating.

Rachel set the sketches to one side and reached again into the trunk. She pulled out a bundle of letters tied up with a length of garden twine. Undoing the loose bow, she took the top envelope and removed the letter. It was written on thin, tissue-like blue paper, the handwriting juvenile and the borders dotted with crude cartoons of what looked like some sort of terribly sad rodent. She turned the letter over. It was signed at the bottom. *Agnes.* Rachel turned back to the beginning.

Dear Eleanor,
You must come home immediately. I have to insist. Mr Montfort has escaped. There has been no sign of him for

three days. Of course I immediately checked the back of the piano. The hole is still there from the last time, but Mr Montfort was nowhere to be seen. This is extremely important and calamitous and potentially life-destroying. Mr Montfort was supposed to be coming with me to school for a presentation. What shall I present now? Mother says I should try to catch something in the garden, but all I managed to find was a snail, a slug and a few ants on a stick. Who is going to be impressed with any of these? They haven't even got names. Not like Mr Montfort. What shall I do, Eleanor? Write by return of post. THIS IS URGENT.

Rachel smiled and pulled out another.
I am writing this while on the toilet, it began.
Goodness. Rachel frowned. Was this another Agnes letter? She turned it over. Of course it was.

I hope that's shocked you to your very core. In other news, I have decided my new hero is Charles Baudelaire. He wrote an entirely scandalous book of poetry called *Fleurs Du Mal*, which means *The Flowers of Evil*, and it's entirely unwholesome, which is entirely thrilling. Mother doesn't know I have it. But I have. And I've read it. I expect I am ruined now. What do you think of that?
Agnes
PS: You never write back. This is unacceptable.

Rachel gave a snort of laughter.
She opened another.

Dear Eleanor,
I am trying to imagine what life would be like if I had three arms. Think of all the extra things I could do.

Mother is always telling me I am very bad at time management, and I think this might be the solution to all my problems. Not only would I be able to write two letters at once (assuming my extra arm is another right arm) but I could make a small income by charging people money to see it. For this to work I would have to keep my third arm hidden. (I could have it tucked into an extra-large sleeve or a day sling.) People won't pay for something if they've seen it already. But if they haven't seen it they will be dying to see it. I think I could become quite rich. I have enclosed a picture of me with my third arm. The person with the loudhailer is you. Mummy is in the booth, to collect the takings. Daddy is hiding behind the booth because he is embarrassed that we're working in a fairground.

Are you well? You never write back. This is annoying. So write back.

Agnes.

PS: Do you know where I could get a third arm? This is important.

Absolutely bonkers, Rachel thought. She looked at the crude drawing Agnes had included. It was exactly as described.

There were heaps of them. Aware that she could get lost in Agnes's letters for the rest of the day, she set them to one side and reached back into the trunk. There was a velvet bag, about the size of a paperback book, deep purple with a faded yellow trim. It turned over at the top like an envelope and was tied shut by a small hoop attached to a pearl-like button. It felt heavy in her hand. There was something in it.

She reached in and pulled out a battered book, dark navy, almost black, with a gold circle at its centre, engraved with an extended hand holding a group of naked figures writhing in confusion. The book was *The Prophet* by Kahlil Gibran. Rachel ran her palm across its front, an old habit that seemed to run in the family (books were like pets, they should always be stroked), and opened it. It was a first edition. Scrawled on the inside cover, someone had written, *For Eleanor. Love knows not its own depth until the hour of separation.*

The handwriting was unfamiliar.

Rachel turned the pages, stopping to read a few passages, and then, as she went to flick through the rest, something fell from it into her lap. It was a photograph, black and white, of Eleanor. Rachel held it with both hands, hungry to look at her mother again. She was staring up, her expression a mixture of terrible disappointment and anticipation. She looked as if she had been crying, and there was something inevitable about her, as if she had resigned herself to some unknown fate. Her hair was tied back, gathered under a scarf headband. She wore no make-up. Rachel could just make out a few freckles across her cheeks. She looked tired.

Rachel felt a surge of excitement. She turned the photo over and read the inked stamp on the back: *John Farson. Frith Street Studio, Soho, 1964.* Something rattled in the back of her mind. Wasn't he a famous photographer? Had he given her this book? It was hard to tell, not possible to leap to conclusions. The presence of the photo in the book didn't mean it had come with it. Eleanor may have used it as a bookmark: odd, though, given her inbuilt resistance to ever seeing herself in photos, but still … Perhaps the photo belonged to someone who admired her and had included it with the gift? Was that Charlie's handwriting? It didn't look like it.

Something else was in the bag. An expensive-feeling envelope, the sort that might enclose a very smart invite.

There was a card inside. She read it. *Heard you were taking the plunge. Thought you might like something old. J.* Was the book the 'something old'? Rachel held the card next to the inscription in the book. It was the same handwriting. *J* must be John Farson. 1964: that was the year before Eleanor married Charlie, but the same year they met. Eleanor had never spoken about having any boyfriends before Charlie. Rachel felt conflicted, a proprietorial bristle on Charlie's behalf. She'd dig into this further. She set the contents of the velvet bag to one side.

She looked at the large pile of diaries in the trunk. She'd read all the ones downstairs and was thrilled there were now more to plunder. She picked the top one off the pile. 1979. Two years before Rachel was born. She opened the diary.

September 10th.
Argued again. Decided I wanted to go for a very long drive and ended up at Waxham beach in Norfolk. I had thought I might go to Cambridge for the day, but when I was there I had an overwhelming desire to see the sea. So I drove on until the road stopped and the dunes began. Walked for hours and sat and drew the seals. One lay no more than a few feet away. It was entirely unbothered. Wish I felt the same.

She flicked on a few pages.

October 23rd.
There is something about the Queen's Lane Coffee House that is so appealing. It does me good. To leave the house and the studio and Charlie. Things have become claustrophobic of late. We both know why but lack the courage to say anything out loud. I am certain the

'problem' isn't mine. It's making me resentful and I don't
know what to do.

Rachel frowned. She had never had the slightest hint
that Charlie and Eleanor had gone through a tricky patch.
In fact, she had no recollection of them ever arguing. She
had one memory, she must have been only three or four,
of a heated discussion at the bottom of the garden and
her mother stomping back up to the house, tears in her
eyes, but that was it. The thought of Eleanor troubled
made her more real, more human. Rachel flicked quickly
to the end.

December 31st.
The night before a new decade! A time to reflect on what
I have achieved in the last ten years and what I might
achieve in the next. I could rattle on about careers or
ambition or material things, but I suppose the one
gaping hole is the one Charlie and I have failed to fill. I
so desperately want a baby but fourteen years of trying
have taken their toll. So if resolutions are something to
be embraced, then I make mine this: that this year I shall
start to think about adopting.

Rachel stopped, frozen by the word that spun out from
the page, her heart thumping in her chest.
She flicked back again and read, hurriedly and anx-
iously: repeated references to the 'problem', the silent weight
that hung over them. She sat back, numb and hollow. Her
thoughts raced away. Eleanor had wanted to tell her something. Something important. Something she should have
told her years ago. That's what she had said. Rachel had replayed that moment over and over. It would not slip away.
This had to be it. Her mind slid and skittered. If she was

adopted, where had they got her from? Did she have biological parents still alive? She let the diary slip from her hand.

'Is that it, Eleanor?' she called out into the darkness. 'Is that what you wanted to tell me?'

There was nobody to answer her, and the only sound was her quickened breath and the dark creaking of the eaves.

Chapter Twenty-five

'Of course you're not adopted,' said Agnes, her eyebrows knitted into a look of disbelief. 'I remember Eleanor being pregnant. She was sick on my shoes. They were suede. I was furious.'

Rachel sat back, her face a mixture of confusion and relief. 'But Eleanor's diary is full of stuff about them having a problem and then there's the entry where she writes it plain and loud. She was going to seriously think about adoption.'

'But that doesn't mean they did adopt. Some people take ages to get pregnant. I wouldn't read too much into that.'

'Are you sure?'

'I'm certain,' said Agnes, opening the fridge door and peering in. 'Do you think I wouldn't have known if you'd been adopted? Don't be ridiculous. I had to come over and cook Charlie his supper. She couldn't bear the smell of food. Do you want me to go shopping for you?' She cast a look back at Rachel, sitting at the kitchen table. 'You've got nothing in.'

'I'll be fine. I think there are some fish fingers in the freezer.'

Agnes's face squeezed itself into an expression of guilty delight. 'Ooh, I love a fish finger: white bread, lots of butter, squeeze of mayonnaise and ketchup. Food of the gods. All the same, I think I'll do a shop. You haven't got any biscuits.'

'Part of me feels oddly disappointed. I thought I'd worked it out – what Eleanor wanted to tell me. I was steeling myself to start searching for my real parents.'

'Charlie and Eleanor were your real parents.' Agnes's tone was a little clipped.

'I need to find Eleanor's diary for 1980. The year before I was born. Can't find it anywhere. Not down here. Not up in the attic. Can't find her last one either. It's infuriating.'

'I've left that list you asked for,' said Agnes, pointing towards an envelope on the table. 'It's not very long, I'm afraid. It's everyone I could remember.'

Rachel let a small silence reset the mood.

'Your letters are hilarious, by the way,' she said, pushing back and resting the soles of her feet on the edge of the table. 'I found a whole pile of them. There was one about a plan to make money with a third arm. You were clearly off your rocker.'

Agnes turned and folded her arms, her mouth curling into a smile. 'Oh, I remember that,' she said, her eyes narrowing. 'My best wheeze was sending letters of complaint to sweet manufacturers. Used to get free packets straight back. I thought it was quite brilliant. Misshapen Smarties, not enough sugar on a Jelly Tot, anything untoward with a crisp – back it went, sellotaped to the paper – and, hey presto, I'd be sent a replacement packet. I was like a cottage industry.'

Rachel smiled. 'Nobody writes letters any more. It's a shame.'

'I know. Where's the joy in scrolling back through emails? We're all letting our memories slip away into the ether. Do you want a cup of tea?'

Rachel shook her head. She stared at her toes. She'd been walking barefoot again. They were filthy.

'I didn't know they'd had trouble getting pregnant,' she said, lowering her feet back to the floor. 'Eleanor never mentioned it. I feel a bit weird finding out, when I can't ask her about it.'

'Tread with caution when you read those diaries,' Agnes said, opening a cupboard above the kettle. 'People are the most unreliable narrators of their own lives. They write what they want to be true. Remember that.' She stopped and peered further into the back of the cupboard. 'You really haven't got any biscuits?'

'Sorry.'

A heavy clanking noise came from the garden and Agnes turned her head towards it. 'Is that Caspar?'

Rachel nodded.

'Rachel, you can't not have biscuits when you've got men in doing jobs.'

'All right!' she said, holding her hands up. 'I'll get biscuits!'

'Have you stopped being awful to him?'

Rachel's eyes widened. 'I wasn't awful. I was just a bit ... abrupt. Besides, I got him a drink last week. I put ice in it.'

'Hang on,' said Agnes, reaching for her phone. 'I need to phone the palace. I hope I haven't missed the cut-off for the honours list. Ice, you say? That's above and beyond.'

Rachel laughed at herself. 'I didn't mean it like that. I meant I wasn't being awful.' She glanced up at the clock above the sink. 'Six o'clock. Do you want a glass of wine? I think that's the only thing I've got in the fridge. There's loads left over from the wake. And someone's got to drink it.'

'I need to get back, so thank you but no.' Agnes picked up her bag and rifled through it for her car key. 'Take the bottle out to the garden. Share it with Caspar. You can make up for the lack of biscuits.' She leaned down and kissed Rachel on the cheek. 'And give your feet a wash,' she added, heading for the door. 'You look like a Victorian urchin.'

Rachel waited for the front door to close behind her aunt. She stared down again at her feet. They really were very dirty. Pushing herself up, she walked to the sink and turned the tap on. It was an old ceramic farmhouse sink and, resting one hand against its edge, she lifted her leg up and stuck her foot under the flowing water. It was quite difficult.

'There's a hose in the garden,' said Caspar, behind her. 'Might be easier.'

'You keep making me jump, Caspar,' she said, looking over her shoulder at him. 'You're like a garden ninja. I never hear you coming.'

'Sorry,' he said, smiling. 'But that does look a bit uncomfortable.'

'It is,' she said, lifting her leg back out. 'I don't know why I didn't go upstairs to the bathroom. Actually, I do know. I couldn't be bothered.'

'And now you've got one clean foot and one filthy foot.'

Rachel looked down at her odd feet. 'Yes. I have.'

Caspar paused, then: 'Do you want me to get the hose out?' He thumbed back towards the garden.

'Yes. I think that's probably best.' She nodded. 'Actually, would you like some wine? I'm going to have a glass.' She was surprised she'd said it, but was still feeling churned up from her moment of panic in the attic. She was glad of a friendly face. 'I haven't got any biscuits.'

'No biscuits?' Caspar pulled a face of mock disgust.

'I know. My aunt has chastised me to the full. To be honest I'd be glad of the company. So if you would like . . .'

'I'd be very happy to have a glass of wine, yes.'

'Good.'

Rachel stood, her foot held out, as the water from the hose cleaned the dirt from her skin. It was sharp and cold, a delicious refreshment at the end of another long, hot day, and she watched as the water bounced off her and on to the red clay tiles of the terrace. They didn't speak. Rachel couldn't decide whether she found this odd, but there was something comforting about the unexpected lack of awkwardness. She had a dirty foot and he was fixing that.

'Thank you,' she said, as her foot emerged pinker and fresher. 'That's better. Now I don't look as if I've been dipped in chocolate.'

Rachel walked towards the terrace table, her wet foot leaving an imprint as she went. The late afternoon sun was still burning down, and as she sat on the bench at the table she watched as her footprints evaporated away. The wine was sitting in the shade, two glass tumblers next to it. Somewhere inside, smart wine glasses were sitting at the back of a cupboard, but she'd grabbed the first things that came to hand. She wasn't in the mood for fancy. She was still unnerved, still feeling that moment of shock and disquiet she'd had in the attic when she'd discovered her mother had been thinking of adopting. She needed to soothe herself, to calm herself down.

'Small one for me, please. I'm driving.' Caspar turned the tap off at the wall and began to roll the hose in.

'What's that plant there? The one with the white flowers?' She pointed towards a shrub that edged the terrace.

Caspar rubbed his hands clean and walked towards her. 'Hibiscus. Pretty, isn't it? Flowers for months on end.'

'That's it. Hibiscus. I always get it confused with the other one. What's it called? The one that drops its flowers every day?'

'Cistus.'

'Yes, cistus.'

'Did you know that some cistus species can self-combust?'

'What? Seriously?' She handed him the filled tumbler.

Caspar nodded. 'They emit an oil. If it's too hot, up they go.'

'I'm surprised we're not all self-combusting in this heat. Cheers.' She raised her glass towards his.

'Cheers.' Caspar lifted his glass and drank.

As Rachel took a sip, she noted Caspar's wine was half gone with one gulp. Perhaps he wanted this over quickly?

'I went through a phase of being obsessed with spontaneous combustion,' she told him. 'I think I'd just read *Bleak House*. Find one picture of a pair of legs poking out from a pile of ash and down the rabbit hole you go.' Rachel mustered a thin smile. She took another sip.

Caspar pulled out a chair from the table and sat. He was very tanned, the hair on his forearms bleached blonde. He wore a pair of battered CAT boots and, as he stretched his legs out, he balanced the heel of one on the tip of the other. Rachel looked at the muscles in his legs. It had been a very long time since she had had sex.

'I planted a couple of lovely roses today. Paul's Scarlet Climber. They'll be stunning when they mature.' He put his glass down on the tabletop and picked at the side of his thumb.

'Where?' Rachel shaded her eyes with her hand to look out into the garden.

Caspar nodded over at an esplanade in the centre of the garden. 'Up the side trellises. Your mum ordered them. But they only arrived yesterday. She knew what she was doing. Knew her stuff. It's such a shame she won't see them.'

Rachel eyed him. His head was down, concentrating on whatever was bothering him in his thumb. She looked back out over the garden. She found some comfort in it still being Eleanor's work in progress. She may be gone, but her garden could be finished. Rachel felt her chest fill. It was another thing to regret: another thing she had paid little to no attention to when her mother had been alive.

'How long did you work for her?'

'Coming up a year.' He continued to pick.

'A year?' Rachel couldn't hide her surprise. She felt a short pang of guilt. She'd had no idea.

'I met you about six months ago, actually,' he said, not looking at her. 'You've forgotten.'

Rachel pursed her lips into a thick pout. She wasn't sure how to answer. 'I'm quite bad at that,' she said, deciding to be honest. 'It's one of my more regrettable traits. I'm not sure what it's down to. I'd like to think it's because I worked in a gallery. You meet so many people ...' Her voice tailed away. 'No excuse. I need to be better at that.'

A bird was singing in a crab-apple tree to the right of the terrace, its call loud and passionate. Rachel squinted towards it but the tree was in silhouette against the low evening sun.

'Do you forget people?' She was still looking towards the darkened tree.

'No. Never.'

Rachel turned back. 'I sometimes wonder whether always remembering is a gift or a curse. Forgetting some people would be a blessing.'

Caspar lifted his troubled thumb towards his mouth and bit at the side of it. 'Everyone is interesting,' he said, staring again at his thumb. 'You just have to be interested in them.'

Rachel scrunched her nose up. She wasn't sure if that was meant as a criticism, but it felt like one. They sat, the birdsong trilling through the warm air. Rachel cast a glance again in its direction. 'What is that?' she said. 'I can't see.'

'Robin,' said Caspar, not needing to look up. He reached out for his glass and took another gulp.

'Do you want some more?' Rachel lifted the bottle from the table and proffered it up.

'No. Driving. Robins are supposed to be dead loved ones saying hello. Did you know that?'

Rachel frowned. 'No, I didn't. Nice thought. I wish I believed it.'

'Your dad did. When Pip died, he swore blind she was in the garden.'

Rachel shifted in her chair. 'Was Pip your ...?' She couldn't quite finish the sentence. It felt like an intrusion, an unearned intimacy.

Caspar nodded his head. 'Your dad was amazing. He wrote the eulogy for me. I didn't ask him to. He just handed it to me in an envelope so I didn't have to worry about it. He couldn't make cakes, so he did that for me instead. That's what he told me. I'll never forget it. He was a good man, your dad.'

Rachel went to say something but nothing came. This was not what she had wanted. It felt like a rope pulling her back to sadness.

'Anyway,' Caspar continued, 'every time I hear a robin sing, I think of Pip.' He picked again at his thumb. 'Bloody thorn. It's driving me mad.'

Rachel put down her glass and pushed her chair back. 'Come on,' she said, standing. 'I'll get it out.'

She led him to the downstairs toilet where there was a medical kit of sorts, and they stood facing each other over the sink as Rachel rooted around for a pair of tweezers. As they stood in close proximity, she could smell the earth on him, the mint he'd been cutting back, the faint sweat of an honest day's work. Claude had never smelled like this. His scent came in expensive drifts: the gentle cologne, the fragrant soap. He smelled affluent, exclusive, ambitious. There was a window over Caspar's shoulder and, as Rachel found the tweezers, she glanced up at it. 'Step back a little, if you can,' she said, taking his hand in hers. 'I'll be able to see better.'

His hand was large, scarred with the endless nicks of a thousand brambles and stained with soil. It didn't feel rough, more used, like a much-loved satchel, and Rachel held it gently, turning his thumb towards the light. She could feel her heart beating a little faster and she was aware she was avoiding looking up at him.

'I can see it,' she said, her voice soft and low.

'Don't worry if you hurt me,' he said.

'It's already out,' she said, holding up the tweezers to present the offending thorn. 'I may be useless at many things, but getting splinters out is a speciality.'

Caspar grinned. 'I didn't feel a thing.'

'Now wash your hands,' she said, 'so it doesn't get infected.'

She turned back to the sink and turned on the hot tap. She ran the end of the tweezers under it, aware of Caspar behind her, and then turned towards the handrail and a small blue towel.

She heard the soft pump of the soap dispenser and the sound of water running through his hands. She dropped the tweezers back into the medical kit and waited for him to finish so she could place it back in the cabinet above his head. He glanced sideways at her. She was staring at him.

'Sorry,' she said, shaking her head. 'I'm not being weird. I'm just waiting to put this back up there.' She pointed at the cabinet.

'Hang on,' he said, moving towards the blue towel.

His arm touched hers and she felt the soft blonde hairs against her wrist. He stood back and held his hand out. 'Do you want to ...' He raised his eyebrows.

For a moment, Rachel panicked that he might be about to ask her if she'd like to kiss him, but she pulled herself together. Of course he wasn't. She didn't trust herself. Her imagination was running wild these days. She looked at him again, properly. He was staring at the medical kit.

'Thanks,' she said, handing it over.

He put it back up into the cabinet and, turning, opened the door into the hallway.

'Thanks for that,' he said, stepping out. 'Well. I'd better be off.' Rachel stood, her back to the sink, looking out at him.

'Actually, I think I need to pee,' she said, and put her hand on the doorknob.

'Oh,' said Caspar, and the air of awkwardness they had managed to avoid returned. 'OK. Well. Thanks for the wine. And the thumb.' He gave it a wiggle in her direction. 'See you next week.'

'Yes. See you next week.'

She closed the door and stared in horror at the back of it. Why had she said that? What was the matter with her?

She pulled down her shorts and sat down heavily on the loo. She knew exactly what was wrong with her. Reality was settling in: she may never discover what her mother wanted her to know and nothing was going to change. She was going to have to live with that moment in the hallway on the day her mother died for ever.

Chapter Twenty-six

Rachel stuck her tongue out and stared at it in the mirror. It looked swollen and sickly, the regretful aftermath of a late night in that, on reflection, hadn't been a good idea.

Why did I open that other bottle? she thought. Never drink alone, Rachel. Bad idea. She reached for the toothpaste and squeezed some on to her finger. That was the problem with long, warm evenings: they confused you into thinking you might be on holiday, but Rachel was not on holiday. She was on her own, trying to make sense of everything.

She was no nearer to finding out what Eleanor had wanted to talk to her about. Rachel had become fixated on a button; she had a book and a note from someone whose name began with J and who may, or may not, be nothing or everything; she knew her parents were considering adoption, but Agnes had put that concern to rest. Did any of these things matter? Was she looking for significance where there was none? Rachel heaved a sigh and pushed herself away from the bathroom sink. The hangover was making her maudlin. That wouldn't do.

She had so many questions. She knew the maths: she'd always known her parents had got married in 1965. They didn't have her until 1981. Why on earth hadn't she asked her parents about their life before her while she had the chance? Fifteen years was a long time to wait for something you want so badly. Were there miscarriages? Anguished trips to the doctors? How had Eleanor felt when she found out she was pregnant? Was she overjoyed, astonished, terrified? Had Rachel been worth the wait?

She sloughed herself into fresher clothes – a pair of turquoise cotton shorts and a white, short-sleeved blouse – and padded down to the kitchen to flick the kettle on. She felt stiff, and as she waited for the water to boil she stretched her arms above her head and pressed her palms towards the ceiling. The lifting from the previous day had taken its toll. She had carried as much down from the loft as she could manage, and the kitchen table was now covered with Eleanor's old diaries, notebooks and letters. She stared out of the window. It was yet another endless blue-sky day. Perhaps the best thing for her hangover would be to sit in the garden and read what she'd found?

The delicate velvet bag was also there, the photo of Eleanor lying on top of it. Rachel picked it up and gazed into her mother's sad eyes. She was reminded of a moment, a dinner party long ago, where Eleanor had been arguing that time was not linear. Eleanor believed time went upwards, like layers of rock, ages stacked on top of each other.

Rachel stared at the photo. She wanted to find her mother, looking up at her from a time below. What had her mother wanted to tell her? What song had the robin been trying to sing?

She turned the picture over and looked again at the stamp. *John Farson. Frith Street Studio, Soho, 1964.* Rachel's forehead furrowed as she tried to think. She was positive she'd heard of him before. Had her mother ever mentioned him?

The kettle behind her bubbled to a crescendo and Rachel, putting the photo down, reached up for a small cafetière on the shelf above the work surface, then opened the fridge and pulled out a bag of ground coffee. She breathed in the deep, roasted aroma. It was her favourite smell of the day. It meant she was alive.

Pouring the hot water over the coffee grounds, she eased the plunger into place and carried the cafetière to the table. She sat and opened her laptop.

John Farson. She typed his name into her search engine. Return.

9,890,000 results.

Oh. OK. He was famous.

She clicked on images and a mass of black-and-white portraits filled her screen: two drunks sleeping, a woman with an aquiline nose and a cigarette holder, an East End gangster type suited and booted and then, as Rachel clicked to the next page, she saw the picture of her mother, the sad eyes staring out. It featured in one of his anthologies. He'd given the picture a name. 'Virginem Expectatio'. Rachel frowned. What did that mean?

She clicked back to Results and opened his Wikipedia page. *John Farson (28 May 1940) is an English photographer, best known for his work on sixties Soho. He ...*

'Hang on,' said Rachel to herself, frowning. 'He's still alive.'

She went back to Images and scoured a little further. There he was, a shock of salt-and-pepper hair, side parting, a floppy fringe, his head slightly tilted, his eyes a little deadly, like a shark, his jawline strong and masculine. She looked at him. Not bad.

She sat back in her chair, her mind churning. Taking her phone from her pocket, she rang Agnes.

'Hello, darling!' Agnes's voice was bright and tinkling. 'Did you have that drink with Caspar?'

'Yes. Well, he had one then went home. I carried on. Rather wish I hadn't. I'm suffering a bit.'

'Oh, never mind that. Sometimes it's worth it.'

Rachel grimaced. She wouldn't tell Agnes the rest. 'Listen,' she said, 'odd question, and you might not know, but can you remember why Mum and Dad took so long to get pregnant? Did one of them have a problem?'

'Gosh,' said Agnes, her voice ending with an exhalation. 'It was so long ago. I know Eleanor went to the doctor. She was fine. But I don't know if Charlie went. I don't think Eleanor wanted to put him through it. Still, it all worked out in the end.'

'Yes, I suppose it did.'

There was a short silence.

'Rachel,' said Agnes, sounding thoughtful, 'I worry you're beating yourself up over nothing.'

'I probably am. But ... yes, I probably am.'

'If you've still got questions, you've got her diaries,' said Agnes. 'Why don't you look in the last one she wrote in? You might find something there.'

'I can't find it, remember?' said Rachel. 'Her last one and the 1980 one. Can't find either. I've only got the old ones. Perhaps she stopped keeping them?'

'Eleanor never stopped,' said Agnes. 'They'll be somewhere. I can come over and help you look if you want?'

'It's fine. You're right. I'm obsessing. I need something else to think about.'

'It's such a lovely day. Go for a walk. Or just enjoy the garden. Perhaps you need a break? A proper one. A holiday. You could visit Johnny?'

'Maybe,' said Rachel, picking at a thread in her shorts. 'Thanks for your list, by the way. I've googled everyone on it.'

'Darling, I hate to cut you short, but I've got a man up my oak tree. That's not a euphemism.'

Rachel laughed.

'I promised him a cup of coffee. Do you mind?'

'Of course not. Go look after the man in your tree.'

'I'll call later. Bye-bye, darling!'

'Bye.'

Rachel slipped the phone back into her pocket and stared again at the image in front of her.

Did she look like him? Was she imagining that?

It was like Charlie used to say: suggestion is a powerful impulse. Whether it was to be believed was another matter. She took Agnes's list and turned it over. Taking a pen, she wrote *TO DO* at its top.

Find John Farson, she wrote, then sat back.

The question was how.

Chapter Twenty-seven

Then

Eleanor picked the knife up from the kitchen work surface and ran it under the lip of the envelope. It still had butter on it, something she hadn't noticed, and as she pulled the letter out, she gave a small huff of annoyance. It was five days since she had slept with John Farson. She hadn't been back to college since. She had lain in bed, barely eating, crying over the hopelessness of her feelings for Jake and not wanting to see anyone.

Give into sadness. It was something her mother had told her, long ago. She needed the intensity she had felt to diminish. She was still bruised but she was ready to get up.

'Stupid,' she muttered, fingering the greasy line of butter at the top of the paper.

It was another letter from Agnes.

I've only gone and done it, she announced. *I have kissed Clement, the vicar's son. It wasn't a peck. There was nothing polite about it. I pushed him up against a clematis and clamped down, like a plunger.*

Eleanor gave a loud laugh for the first time in nearly a week. It felt like a relief. She glanced down from the kitchen window into the flats below. Charlie was setting up his typewriter. He had a cigarette in his mouth, not yet lit, and he was trying to straighten the piece of paper he'd inserted into the roller. He was clearly struggling. She hadn't seen him since Waterloo. She had to stop and remind herself of when that was. How strange. She had felt every hour, every minute of the days since she'd last seen Jake. All the same, she was in need of some kindness.

She rapped on the kitchen window to catch his attention. He didn't notice and Eleanor felt a surge of purpose. She rapped again and waved, and this time, the movement catching his eye, Charlie looked up at her.

Eleanor smiled and pointed at his typewriter. 'Take it out and start again,' she said, miming as she did so.

He looked up at her and shook his head. 'What?' he seemed to mouth.

She smiled and made her movements more exaggerated. 'Take it out,' she said, making a yanking movement with her arm. 'And start again.' She mimed picking up a fresh piece of paper and winding it into the typewriter.

Charlie, still staring up at her, ripped the paper from his machine, scrunched it into a ball and threw it over his shoulder. Eleanor grinned. He smiled back at her and then mimed a cup of tea. His eyes widened as he looked up and he gave a shrug. Eleanor laughed and shook her head. 'I have to go to college,' she shouted.

He shook his head and held his hands up. He didn't understand.

'College,' she shouted again.

Charlie held his finger up, signalling for her to wait a moment. He reached for a piece of paper, wrote on it, and held it up. *WHAT?*

Eleanor laughed again. She grabbed Agnes's letter and, taking a pen from her pocket, wrote *COLLEGE* on it. She held it up to the window and waited to see if he could read it.

Charlie, making a show of the whole thing, took his glasses off, cleaned them, put them back on, peered up and then wrote something on the back of his piece of paper. He held it up.

BOO HOO.

Eleanor laughed again. He put down the piece of paper and smiled up at her, a warm, genuine, heartfelt smile. Eleanor stared down, reluctant for this fun to end. She needed something else to write on. The back of the letter was already used and the envelope had butter on it. She held up a finger, telling him to hang on. She ran from the kitchen to the sitting room and opened a drawer that was filled with stationery. Pulling out a piece of writing paper, she bent over the table and quickly scribbled something on to it. She ran back to the kitchen window and held it up. *DRINK LATER?*

Charlie stared up, nodded and wrote again. He held his note to the window. *I'D LOVE A DRINK. 7 P.M.?*

Eleanor nodded. Charlie smiled and, still looking at her, put another piece of paper back into his typewriter. He rolled it and, turning to look at it, realised the paper was positioned worse than his original attempt. The pair of them, in their separate flats, fell about laughing.

Eleanor glanced up at the clock in the kitchen. She was going to have to go. She tapped her wrist and pointed away from the window towards her door. He nodded and gave her a wave. She waved back, picked up her bag from the kitchen work surface and left the flat.

The smile lasted until she got to Chelsea.

She hadn't seen Jake since that terrible day. She wasn't surprised. He was difficult to find at the best of times, but the fact he had made no attempt to seek her out pained her. Why she hadn't expected it, she didn't know.

She had thought of nothing else as she had lain in her flat over the last few days, curtains drawn, sad records on a loop. After the intensity of their weeks together, it felt strange not knowing what was he doing, thinking and feeling. Jake was incapable of being on his own. He needed other people's energy to live. After their confrontation he would have stared at the door she'd walked out of, pulled on a jacket and gone straight to Soho. She knew it. His life would be rattling on without her. It hurt. She still loved him and missed him. She longed to see him, but it was all done for now.

John, however, had been in touch. He'd sent a note – though Eleanor knew he wasn't interested in an emotional sense. It wasn't enough; she was well aware of precisely who he was. It felt scandalous to have given herself to him so freely. He was a fox of a man, wandering London at night, prowling for titbits. Eleanor seemed caught between two wild things: one who could satisfy a physical need but provide nothing else; the other who filled her heart with promises and possibilities but could deliver nothing. It was hopeless.

The sex had been painful, something she hadn't been expecting. John had assured her it got better with practice – then he had gone down on her and from that moment she knew she could never feel the same again. The fire he had ignited had almost frightened her. Nice girls aren't supposed to like sex. It was an unspeakable wickedness to think of it being something you could do for pleasure.

The weather had got a little warmer, but despite the brightness of the day there was still a crispness to the air. Eleanor was wearing trousers, a pair of dusty-blue corduroys, some Chelsea ankle boots, a short duffle coat and, as ever, Agnes's pink beret. It had become her calling card, a reminder of where she had come from. As she stepped off the bus, her thoughts turned again to Jake. The thought of never seeing him or spending time with him was too much to bear, ridiculous even. She was filled with regret: she wanted to return to how things had been before. She had been so happy, and now she'd broken the spell. There seemed to be no turning back.

She walked up the steps towards the college entrance and passed a few students chatting. She hadn't thrown herself into college life in the way she knew she ought to have done. She had allowed herself to be an island and with Jake that had been fine, but now, adrift, she was aware she should be making more of an effort. She made herself another promise: life was not all about Soho and the strange creatures who inhabited it. Everyone was interesting. You just had to show an interest in them.

'Hello,' she said, as she walked past a small group lounging on the stairs.

They looked at her and carried on with their conversation.

Eleanor bristled a little at the slight and walked on. It wasn't their fault. She had been aloof and dismissive. All the same, her head went down and she quickened her step, but as she did so she felt a hand on her arm.

'Hey.'

She stopped and turned round. It was a woman from her drawing class. Eleanor wasn't sure of her name.

'It's Eleanor, isn't it?' She had a kind, open face, brown hair cut into a bob and rather overdone eye make-up. She was wearing a red minidress, bold in this weather, white woollen tights and dark burgundy leather knee boots.

'Yes.'

'I'm Amy,' she said, holding out her hand. 'I don't know if we've spoken properly before.'

'No, I don't think we have. Are you doing Textiles?' Eleanor lied and nodded.

'Sculpture. Look,' she began, her face furrowing into a knot of concern, 'it's none of my business but you're friends with Jake Blair, aren't you?'

'Yes, I mean I ...' Eleanor shifted uncomfortably. 'Yes. Yes, I am.'

'Well, have you heard?' She stared at Eleanor.

Eleanor blinked. 'Heard what?'

'He was arrested. Last night. For gross indecency. They're going to throw him out of college. His father refused to stand bail so he got someone else to do it. He's probably going to jail.' She said the last bit in an excited hush. Eleanor found herself bristling, panic coursing through her. Her mouth felt dry.

'How do you know this?'

'He's here. He's come to get his stuff.'

With that, Eleanor turned and leaped up the stairs. She pushed open the doors into the entrance hall and ran through to the staircase beyond, sprinting up to the third-floor studios. She was out of breath, but she had to see him, she had to catch him before he disappeared for ever. She pressed through the tangle of students standing in the hallways, her bag banging against legs, backs, radiators, blood surging in her forehead.

'Excuse me,' she yelled out, trying to clear a pathway through to the dark wooden door behind which he might be.

'Please be here,' she whispered, as she pushed forward. 'Please.'

She opened the door and then stopped, her chest heaving. 'Jake. Thank God. I've just heard.'

Jake turned and looked at her. He was pulling things from a locker and putting them into a large suitcase. 'What have you come for?' he said, looking away. 'I thought you didn't want anything more to do with me.'

'No, Jake, I ...' She stepped forward, struggling to find the right words. He looked shattered and unwell. She wanted to run over to him, tell him it was all right, that she took back everything she had said, but deep down she knew that wouldn't be true. Her pain was still raw and tender. She swallowed. 'What happened? I was told you've been thrown out of college.' She tried to keep her voice quiet and even.

'Good news travels fast, I see.' He took a handful of brushes and threw them into his case.

He was angry with her, defiant. She needed to remain calm. 'What happened, Jake? Please.'

'Why do you want to know?' He turned on her. 'You don't care. Not really, Eleanor. If this is about you wanting to feel better, then I'm afraid I'm not interested.'

'It's not like that.' Eleanor shook her head. 'Really. It's not.

'Well, you know already, don't you? I was arrested. And now I'm being thrown out. And that's that.' His bottom lip buckled.

Eleanor stared at him. He looked broken, a shadow of himself. 'Jake ... I ... please. What's gone wrong?'

He gave a short laugh. 'What's gone wrong? I would have thought that was obvious. Really, Eleanor. You don't have to do this. I'm perfectly happy to creep away. I don't need you standing over me like a hawk.'

Eleanor just stood there, her bag dangling from her hand. She didn't know what to do or how to behave.

'Shall I tell you why I was arrested?' He threw another handful of brushes into the open case. 'I was rather tight.

I'd been at the French with Hen. I wanted to walk home. I don't know why. I just did. A man approached me, well-to-do type, the sort that know they're queer but get married anyway. He had a wedding ring on. I knew what he wanted and we went into Regent's Park. I let him touch me. He didn't want me to touch him. That would be cheating, he said. Cheating on his wife, he said, was not what he wanted. He was putting my cock in his mouth at the time.'

'Jake, I don't want to—'

'No, I don't expect you do,' said Jake, his eyes ablaze. 'Nobody ever wants to know the details. I'm not allowed to love anybody. I have to wait till it's dark and for embarrassed and ashamed men to tell me they find me attractive. Turns out someone saw us, from one of those terribly nice Regency apartments, and called the police. When they arrived, the man, who started crying, told them I had tricked him into going into the park. I called him an abject liar. The police didn't believe me. Turns out he's some politician's son. He was ushered away. They arrested me and took me to the police station in Camden. I was charged without an interview. I'm not entirely sure that's even allowed. I phoned my father in Italy. That created quite a stink in the police station, but I was past caring. But my father ...' Jake's voice caught in his throat and he raised his chin, his chest out, in an act of physical defiance. 'My father wanted nothing to do with me. So I called Hen and she came and bailed me out.'

'You could have called me,' Eleanor said, wiping her eyes.

'No,' said Jake, shaking his head. 'I couldn't.' His voice fell away, his shoulders falling too. He looked more vulnerable than she had ever seen him. He turned and pulled some sketch pads out from the locker.

'What are you going to do?'

'I'm going to run away,' he said. 'I've squared it with Hen. They'll go after her for my having jumped bail, but there it is. I've given her the money to cover it. Make sure she doesn't spend it all in the French before they get to her.'

Eleanor nodded. Her fingers were knotted together. She felt more desperate than she thought possible. She had spent days thinking of nothing other than him. She had thought about what she would say to him, she had had arguments with him, cried with him, laughed with him, all in her head, and now here she was, face-to-face with him, and the rug had been pulled out from underneath her, again. She didn't know what to do. She stood, hopeless and helpless, searching desperately for the right words that would not come.

'Don't feel sorry for me. I'm going to Morocco. I shall be quietly tolerated there.'

Eleanor shook her head. 'The thought of you being quietly tolerated is simply awful.'

Jake pulled out some packets of pencils and threw them into the case.

'Maybe I should have been boring,' Jake said, as he knelt down to close the suitcase. 'Boring and unremarkable and unafraid. Here,' he said, tearing a picture from a pad. 'You can have this.'

He held it out. It was a delicate pencil drawing of Eleanor. She was resting her head in her hand and she was reading. He had captured her completely.

Eleanor could barely speak. She shook her head, her eyes tight and ready to burst, her chest leaden and aching. 'I didn't mean what I said,' she managed to say. 'I didn't mean to hurt you.'

'I'm not sure that's true,' he said, tying the leather fastener at the top of the suitcase. 'But I don't blame you. You were right. I did want you to love me. And that was wrong of me. For what it's worth I did love you, Eleanor. As best as I was able. Perhaps I should have been like the man in Regent's Park and married you.' He stood and looked at her.

'I would have married you. I would.'

Jake shook his head. 'No,' he said, pulling the suitcase upright. 'You deserve far better.' His eyes softened. 'I want you to believe something about yourself, Eleanor. You are talented and fascinating and beautiful and wonderful and you must never settle for anyone who doesn't think so.'

Eleanor's eyes filled with tears again. 'I don't feel any of those things,' she whispered. 'I only feel that when I'm with you.'

'One day,' he said, going to pick up his case, 'you will understand that you don't need anyone to make you feel any of those things. Nobody can make you feel anything. It's all in you. Your choice. Choose to be Eleanor.'

He put a hand on her forearm.

Well,' he added, wiping his eyes, 'that's it. I have my things. I'm stealing my father's car. He'll be furious, but he's told me I'm cut off without a penny so I think it's the least he can give me. If I'm feeling very spiteful I shall take the Picasso in the front room. I'm catching the two o'clock ferry from Dover, then I shall drive to Marseilles. Think of me occasionally, won't you?'

He began to walk towards the door and Eleanor threw herself at him. She was sobbing. 'Please forgive me. Please.'

Jake looked down at her and gently removed her hands from his. 'Look on the bright side,' he said, smiling, 'you'll never have to see me grow old.'

'But I want to see you grow old.' She couldn't stop the flow of tears now.

He wiped her cheek with his thumb. 'And I won't have to see you grow old either. All those wrinkles. Moustache. Hairy chin ...' His voice petered out. He was trying to put a brave face on things, but neither of them was in the mood for being funny.

'Please don't go,' Eleanor whispered.

He looked down at her for one last time. 'This won't do,' he said, wiping his eyes again. 'It's bad enough everyone knowing I'm indecent. Quite another to have me weeping as I leave. I don't want to give them the satisfaction.' He took a deep breath. 'I love you.' Leaning down, he kissed her. 'Goodbye, Eleanor.' He didn't wait to hear her answer.

Eleanor, frozen with sorrow, watched him leave, her heart ripped from her chest once more.

Chapter Twenty-eight

Now

Rachel turned and looked at the table. Over the past week she'd managed to read a lot more of Agnes's letters, all of which were screamers, but she was yet to return to Eleanor's diaries. She was almost afraid of them. As to what would have been Eleanor's most recent one, she still hadn't managed to find it. Unless her mother had a secret hiding place, Rachel was beginning to wonder if Agnes might be wrong. Perhaps Eleanor had stopped writing? Perhaps she simply had nothing more to say?

Rachel had returned again and again to the pages on the internet featuring John Farson. He had never married: often the sign of a closet homosexual or a profligate rogue, and seeing as there was no evidence of him having been gay, she had to assume he was very much the latter. It came as no surprise.

Photographers in the sixties were notorious, weren't they? Rachel felt a pang of regret that she had never sat down with Eleanor and asked her about being there, in the thick of it. Rachel hadn't been interested. That was the horrible truth.

She sat at her mother's drawing desk, her fingertips resting on the wooden surface. It was covered in a multitude of tiny scars and spattered with a constellation of coloured dots, caused by small acts of clumsiness by the artist over decades. Rachel liked this desk. It had character. It told a story. Her laptop sat in front of her and Rachel was thinking, her lips pressed together. John Farson was still alive. Why didn't she just go and meet him? She'd found the address of a studio, no longer in Soho, but in east London, and googled it. It was in a converted warehouse along the riverbank, east of Tower Bridge. Given John's age, Rachel was surprised he still had a studio, but then, like her mother, artists never really retired, did they? There was a phone number. Did she dare?

She picked up her phone and stared down at it, weighing up whether she had the courage. This was all on a hunch, a whim, the say-so of a button, a photograph and a mysterious inscription. Rachel felt vaguely amused by the whole thing. Of all the things she saw herself turning into, amateur sleuth wasn't one of them.

'To hell with it,' she muttered, and tapped out the number on the screen. She held her phone to her ear.

'Hey,' said a woman's voice. She sounded young.

'Hi. I'm calling to … this is a little odd. Is John Farson there?' Rachel's heart was beating.

'No, he's not. Who's calling? If it's about the *Tatler* thing, he's not interested.'

Rachel blinked. 'Sorry, I don't know what the *Tatler* thing is. It's not about that. I think John used to know my mother. She's in one of his portraits.'

'Do you want a copy of it?'

'No, I've already got one. I was wondering if I could meet him. My mother …' Rachel cleared her throat. 'My mother died recently and I've got lots of unanswered questions.'

'Are you a journalist?'

'No, I used to work in a gallery. Although I'm not doing anything at the moment. I'm just trying to ... get to the bottom of something.' Her voice petered out, and she waited for a response.

'I can ask him,' said the woman, 'but he might not remember. He's photographed an awful lot of people.'

'I think they were friends in the sixties.'

The woman gave a dismissive snort. 'Then he really might not remember. Look, I'm happy to ask for you. What was her name?'

'Eleanor Ledbury.'

'Oh. The artist?'

'Yes.'

There was a noise of paper rustling and somewhere, in the background, a dog began to bark. Rachel ran her fingers through her ponytail and wound a thick strand around her forefinger.

'Would it be possible,' Rachel asked again, 'to meet him?'

'I'm not sure. Look, I don't want to get your hopes up. There's nothing in his diary, but he never remembers to put anything in it, so that's sort of meaningless. I'm not sure it's worth making an appointment. He's terrible at keeping them. If he wants to meet you, he'll turn up. If he doesn't, well ... If you really want to talk to him, your best bet is to find him in Soho. He goes there most evenings.'

'Do you know where?'

'Usual haunts. Ivy. Soho House. Groucho. Are you a member?'

'No.'

'Do you know anyone who is?'

'No, I don't think I do.'

'You could try the French. He likes it there. Look, if you want I can ask him whether he'll meet you. He might say yes.'

Rachel sat back in her chair and looked down at the unfinished painting of the young man that was leaning against the wall. There was something appealing about trying to find John Farson in Soho.

'No, it's OK,' she said. 'I won't make an appointment.'

'Do you want me to give him your number?'

'Not yet. I'll try Soho first.'

'He's a lazy bastard at the best of times. I don't see him from one week to the next. He hasn't got a phone. He hasn't got email. He's a bloody nightmare.'

Rachel smiled. She needed a challenge. She looked at her watch. She had all day to think up a plan. 'It's fine, I'm happy to go looking for him. And thank you.'

Rachel put down her phone and tapped her fingers on the desk. 'Well,' she said to herself. 'This is exciting.' She pushed herself up and went to walk back through the studio. The button she had found all those weeks ago was still sitting on the plinth next to the canvas that remained untouched. She stopped and picked it up. Maybe she should take it with her? Perhaps he might recognise it. She wrapped it back in the piece of embroidered cotton and tucked it into the pocket of her shorts.

She really was feeling a little better. She had a purpose, she had a project and she was feeling more connected to her parents than she ever had. There was no point in feeling sad about that. She could regret her lack of interest in her mother while she'd been alive or she could embrace everything she was feeling now. She wanted to choose the latter.

She walked into the kitchen and picked up a cornflake packet standing on the sideboard. It was empty. With a sigh, she tossed it into a large plastic box that sat next to the bin. It was full and she watched as the cornflake packet hit a plastic milk container and skittered sideways across the kitchen floor. She'd pick it up later. There was a chocolate cake sitting in the middle of the kitchen table, another offering from Agnes. She'd left it on her way to the airport. She was flying out to Italy to visit Johnny for a long weekend. She stared at it. She couldn't eat cake for breakfast, could she?

Hang on. Was it Thursday? Rachel frowned and reached for her phone. Oh. No, it wasn't. It was Friday. 'Don't know where the days go,' she muttered, then stopped and looked up, her face caught in thought.

It was Friday. That meant ... she glanced up to the clock on the wall. Ten o'clock.

Throwing her phone on to the kitchen table, Rachel ran from the kitchen and leaped up the stairs, two at a time. Grabbing the banister at the top, she pushed herself on to the landing and skidded into her mother's bedroom. She threw off her tatty bed shorts and crumpled T-shirt and quickly pulled on a bra. A bra! When was the last time she'd worn one of those? She heard the crunch of tyres on the gravel. Opening the wardrobe, she pulled out a pair of figure-hugging Capri trousers and a light, airy sleeveless blouse, and put them on. She looked at herself in her mother's full-length mirror. She looked dressed. It would do.

Outside, she heard footsteps walking down the side of the house. She paused, frozen, listening to whether the side door into her mother's studio opened. It didn't. He had gone to the shed. Perhaps she'd make him a cup of coffee and take it out to him? Yes. She'd do that. Quickly, she trotted back to the kitchen.

A watched kettle never boils. It was a favourite saying of Charlie's and as Rachel stood, arms folded, she felt every second of it.

'I mean, it's not as if I *like him* like him,' she said, muttering to herself. 'I'd do this if anyone came to the house.'

Turning away from the still-boiling kettle, she found the largest mug in the cupboard and pulled one down for herself too. They could stand in the garden, having their coffee in the morning sun. That would be a pleasant thing to do. She placed the mugs down and let her hands rest, palms down, on the tabletop. She looked at the cake. There was a spoon next to it. Without thinking, she picked up the spoon, took a great hunk of cake and stuffed it into her mouth.

'Cake? For breakfast?'

'Jesus!' Rachel's hand went to her mouth and she stood upright, her other hand clutching her chest. She swallowed. 'Caspar, seriously. You have got to stop doing that. You're going to give me a heart attack.'

He smiled. 'Sorry. I was just wondering if I could ...' Behind him the kettle had boiled. He pointed to it. 'Make myself a coffee?'

'No, no,' said Rachel, holding her hand up in protest. 'I'll make it. I was about to anyway.' She held up the two mugs. 'And as for the cake. I need to eat it for breakfast. And lunch. And supper.' She walked to the kettle and put the mugs next to it. 'I'm skin and bone. I used to have a bum. And a tummy. And ...' She ran a hand over her flat chest. She looked up and smiled at him.

Caspar's eyes were a little too wide for Rachel's liking. He held his hands up. 'Please don't expect me to reply to that,' he said. 'If there's one thing I know for a fact, it's never to pass comment when a woman is talking about her weight.'

Rachel laughed. 'You're right. You're absolutely right. If you'd said anything, I would have hated you for the rest of my life. Do you want milk?'

She turned and opened a pot of instant coffee. She wouldn't do a cafetière for Caspar. He didn't seem the sort.

'Yes, please. And one sugar.'

Rachel tutted.

'I know. I know,' Caspar protested. 'But it used to be three. So I'll take all the applause, thank you.'

Rachel lifted the kettle and poured water into the mugs. 'I used to have sugar in my coffee. Couldn't bear it now. It's funny, isn't it? How something you can't be without becomes genuinely revolting. It's like when you split up with someone and at the start you're all "woe is me" and listening to sad songs and crying and staring into the middle distance and then without noticing you're suddenly "how in the name of hell did I ever ..." Well,' she said, handing Caspar his coffee – 'we don't need to go into that. But you feel lighter. Less burdened.'

Caspar made a small noise that Rachel couldn't quite interpret. She picked her mug up. 'Was that a snort of recognition or are you choking on your coffee?' She took a sip and stared at him.

Caspar swallowed and stared back. She could tell she was putting him on the spot, and as she watched his face she could see him trying to work out how to reply.

'Umm,' he said, widening his stance a little.

'Sorry, I'm being a bit full-on. This is what happens when you don't really see anyone all week. I never used to be this intense. Honest.'

'Do you ...' Caspar began. 'Do you feel less burdened?'

'I'm not sure,' Rachel replied, thinking about that. 'I feel less ... decimated. So I suppose that must mean yes.

Almost. Maybe. Let's say maybe. There's always room for improvement.'

Caspar nodded. 'Great. That's great.' He took a sip. 'Well, I'd best get on.' He held his mug up. 'Thanks for this.'

He didn't want to chat. Rachel couldn't help but sound disappointed. 'No problem. Let me know when you need another.'

Caspar nodded again and moved towards the studio. As he stepped down, he stopped and looked back. 'You look great, by the way. You should eat as much cake as you like. And you'd still look great.'

Rachel stared at him as he smiled, turned and walked off through the studio. Gripping her mug, she felt the first shoots of something fluttering somewhere in the depths of her chest. It was a feeling she hadn't had in a very long time.

Before she could go anywhere she needed to wash her hair, so she stood in the bathroom, fixed the plug into place and turned on the taps. She thought about asking Caspar if he wanted to go with her to London. No. Not this time. Besides, asking someone if they want to come and help you stalk a man in his late seventies isn't up there on the best first-dates list. Rachel smiled to herself. 'Look at you,' she mumbled. 'Thinking about a first date.' She raised an eyebrow.

Going over to the bathroom window, she gave it a shove. She looked out over the garden and saw Caspar. He was sawing a long length of wood. 'This is because I haven't had sex,' she told herself. 'That's all this is. It's just raging hormones and pheromones and green shorts and muscles and ... oh God.' He carried the wood over to the beginnings of some kind of structure and nailed it into place. Rachel narrowed her eyes. 'What's he doing? Is he making a pergola? From scratch?'

She turned away and reached for some shampoo and conditioner. Putting them on the corner of the bath, she started to undress.

Her phone rang.

Stopping what she was doing, she reached into the pocket of her trousers and pulled it out. Unknown number. Perhaps it was the woman from the studio. She leaned back towards the window and peered out. Caspar was banging more nails into wood. She lifted the phone to her ear.

'Hello?'

'Rachel,' came the voice. 'I'm outside. Can I see you?'

Rachel froze. It was Claude.

Chapter Twenty-nine

Rachel stared out from the front door, her face a picture of disbelief.

Claude was standing there, a large bunch of flowers in one hand. He looked contrite, his eyes pleading. He was wearing a crisp white shirt, the sleeves rolled up to the elbows, some light tan trousers and a pair of just-bought desert boots. He looked smart but not too smart.

'Can I talk to you?' he asked. 'I need to.'

'I needed to speak to you, Claude. For hours, days, weeks. I don't remember you being particularly interested in helping me out. And showing up uninvited to my mother's funeral after you left me high and dry at the altar? Was that really necessary?'

'Please, Rachel.'

'Wait here. Let me turn the bath off.'

She shut the door in his face and stood for a moment, her hands on her hips, thinking. This was the last thing she had expected. She turned and walked slowly up the stairs. Make the bastard sweat it out. She had half a mind to leave him there, waiting, and not go back. She'd keep the water in the bath. She was damned if she was going to give him more than ten minutes. She needed to stay calm and measured. 'People treat you how you let them,' she said to herself as she turned the tap off. It was something Charlie always used to say. 'People treat you how you let them.'

She walked back down and stood before the front door. She had no idea why he was there or what he wanted. She would find out and send him packing. One deep breath and she opened it.

'Thank you,' he said, offering up the flowers. 'I got these for you.' It was a beautiful bouquet of red and white roses. He'd spent a lot of money. She didn't take them.

'You can put them in the kitchen sink. I'll find a vase later.' Her voice was terse. She turned and walked back down the hallway. Behind her, Claude stepped into the house and shut the door. Rachel steeled herself. She felt irritated, which made her anxious. She didn't want to lose control.

'The house looks lovely,' said Claude, following her. 'The lavender in the front garden is glorious. And the holly-hocks. I've always loved hollyhocks, though some people swear they're weeds.'

Rachel walked into the kitchen and, turning to face him, leaned against the Aga, her arms folded. 'Let's just get on with this, shall we?'

Claude looked at her, then went over to the sink and picked up the large old-fashioned plug from behind the taps. It wasn't attached to anything, a constant source of annoyance to everybody, but nobody had the heart to fix it. It was part of its charm. Claude pressed it into place, put the flowers into the deep basin and ran the cold tap.

Rachel watched him do it. It felt like an intimate act, aggressively so. It was like he'd walked in and everything was back to normal. Well, it wasn't.

'That should be enough,' he said. He turned and smiled. 'It's really good to see you, Rachel.'

'What is this about, Claude?' Rachel tilted her head.

He looked her straight in the eyes. 'I want to get married.'

Rachel let out an explosive laugh. 'I'm sorry? You want to get married? Who to?'

'To you.'

Rachel shook her head, incredulous. 'Have you lost your mind?'

'No,' he said, his voice quiet and measured, 'I want to marry you. I always wanted to marry you. And I still do.'

'Claude.' Rachel's arms drifted out sideways as she gripped the bar at the front of the Aga. She looked as if she were hanging on to a ship. 'I'm not sure if you remember what we were supposed to do two months ago. But you had a chance to marry me and you didn't take it. You humiliated me. You left me thinking I never wanted to fall in love again.'

'I know, I ...'

'No,' Rachel held up a finger to stop him, 'I'm talking. I won't bore you with how I had to deal with the aftermath of what you did, but if we're in any doubt as to whether I'm prepared to put myself through that again, let's scotch that rumour from the off, shall we? I'm not. And I never will be. Is that it? Are we done? You want to get married.' She narrowed her eyes and stared at him as if he might be insane. 'I don't know how you have the cheek to turn up here. If Eleanor was still here she'd be kicking you out the door. *I* should be kicking you out the door.'

'Rachel,' he edged towards her, 'what I did was despicable, but there was a reason and I'm sorry it's taken me this long to tell you. I wasn't in a position to—'

'I'm not sure if I care any more, Claude,' Rachel interjected. 'I've only just started to feel all right. You're not the only upset I've had to deal with, remember? The brass of you is quite something.'

'I expect you to be angry with me, that's fine.'

'Oh, that's good of you,' said Rachel, unable to hide the sarcasm.

'Please,' he said, moving his hand to the back of a chair under the kitchen table, 'I'd like a chance to explain. I think you deserve that.'

Rachel's mouth dropped open. She shook her head in astonishment. He had floored her entirely. 'OK, Claude,' she said, throwing her right arm into the air. 'OK. Knock yourself out.'

'Do you mind if I sit?' He pulled the chair out from under the table.

Rachel gave an indiscriminate shrug. Two months ago, this moment had been all she longed for; now it felt like an intrusion into her well-being, a violent drag back to a pit she had only just started hauling herself out from. He sat down and, resting his elbows on the table, knitted his fingers together in front of him. He looked like he was about to explain how osmosis worked or discuss the merits or otherwise of the Norman Conquest. That was not what he was about to explain. He was about to explain why he had broken her heart.

'The morning of the wedding, I woke up and realised I hadn't been honest with you. I never had. I had kept something hidden.'

'Are you about to tell me you're already married and you've got a wife called Deborah and three children in Devon?' Rachel's tone was dismissive.

'Please, Rachel, I know this is difficult but if you can let me get it out in one go ...' He looked up towards her.

Rachel rolled her eyes. She exhaled and leaned back against the Aga, folding her arms again. She felt hostile, but she needed to protect herself and she gripped her opposite elbows as he began to speak.

'There's no way of softening this so I'm just going to tell you straight out. Do you remember my shoulder operation?'

Rachel cast her mind back. About a month into their relationship he'd had a minor operation. 'The rotator cuff thing? Yes. What's that got to do with anything?'

'Do you remember I was on tramadol, for the pain?'

'Yes ...'

'I never stopped taking them.'

'Sorry? What?'

'I was addicted to them. I was an addict. And the night before we got married, I ran out. And I panicked. And I drove to London and got some from my dealer—'

'Dealer?' Rachel's mouth fell open.

'And, because I hadn't had any in forty-eight hours, I went mad. I overdosed.'

'What are you talking about?' Rachel stared at him. She was taken aback. 'I would have been contacted by the hospital, or by the police. This is rubbish.'

'No.' Claude shook his head. 'It's not. I didn't have any ID on me. And, besides, I didn't want you to know. I was too ashamed. The hospital pumped my stomach, and on the morning of our wedding I signed myself into a rehab unit. I sent one text to Tom saying I wasn't coming and then they took my phone away from me.' He paused and looked into Rachel's eyes. 'And that's why I wasn't there. And that's why you didn't hear from me. And I am so sorry. I was in a dark, dark place. I don't expect you to forgive me, but you deserve an explanation and I'm sorry it's taken me so long to give it to you. I want to make it up to you.'

Rachel felt her defences crumbling. This was not what she had been expecting, but she was racked with an overwhelming feeling that it was bullshit. He was making this up. He was manipulating her. He had chosen the one excuse that any decent human being would accept. She blinked.

'I was with you for five years. I was never aware of you having a drug problem.' She kept her voice low and calm. 'Ever.'

He unclasped his fingers and turned his palms upwards. 'No, I hid it very well.'

'I'm going to be honest with you, Claude,' she said, her hands still gripping her elbows. 'I'm not sure I believe you. I finally got out of the house and went to Oxford after weeks of hibernating and wanting to die and I saw you, in the gallery. You looked so happy I wanted to kill you. So you weren't in rehab then, were you?'

'No, I wasn't. After four weeks I was back in the gallery. I didn't want to lose the business. I've still got difficulties with that. I won't bore you ... but I was going back, one day a week. Perhaps I should have contacted you sooner. But I didn't feel strong enough.'

She fixed him with a penetrating stare. 'Let's be honest, shall we? Is this bullshit? What do you really want?'

Claude shook his head. 'It's not bullshit. I'm sorry. I should have told you. And I wish I had. But I didn't.'

Rachel's hands went to the side of her face. 'Claude, I can't even begin to believe you.'

'I've got the number of the rehab unit.' He reached for his phone. 'Do you want it? You can call them.' He held his mobile out towards her.

Rachel stared at it. Her mind was in turmoil. 'I can't,' she said, shaking her head. 'My God, Claude, you really know how to stick the knife in.'

She turned away from him and gripped the work surface with her hands. Behind her, Claude stood up from the table and came over to her. She felt his hands on her upper arms. 'Please don't,' she said.

He turned her round and leaned towards her. Rachel put a hand on the middle of his chest. 'No, Claude. No. I'd rather kiss raw sewage. Please don't,' she said again.

'You're angry with me,' he said, still holding her. 'I understand. I just want us to get through this. We can get through this.'

Rachel stared up at him, her face contorted with confusion. Claude leaned in again and Rachel twisted her head away from his.

There was a noise to their left, and as Claude looked towards the door Rachel pushed herself away from him.

'Hi,' said Claude, putting his hands on his hips.

Caspar stood looking at them both, in his hand some just-picked sweet peas. 'Sorry, I didn't mean to—'

'Do you mind giving us a moment,' said Claude, blocking Rachel from Caspar's view. 'I just need to speak with my fiancée.'

Caspar stepped towards him, his jaw tightening. Rachel, still reeling from what had happened, was incapable of speech. She looked at Caspar, her eyes wide and shell-shocked. Caspar looked at her, then back at Claude, and placed the sweet peas down on the table. 'Sure,' he said, and with that he turned and left.

Rachel sat down heavily in the chair at the end of the table, her head in her hands.

'You still love me, Rachel,' said Claude, turning back to her. 'I know you do.'

Rachel didn't answer. Every scrap of resilience she had shored up was starting to drift away, the tender little shoots of optimism she had nurtured withering back. She felt powerless again, plunged back into the nadir she had tried so hard to escape. She didn't have the strength for this. She didn't have the strength for any of it.

Upstairs, the bathwater sat in the tub. It was stone cold by the time it was emptied.

Chapter Thirty

Rachel stared out over the garden. Claude had finally left. She sat in a deckchair, her arms hanging down, her legs splayed out in front of her. It was if she had been dropped from a height and left where she'd landed. She'd wanted to call Agnes but knew she would have turned her phone off. She always did when she was in Italy.

The garden was carrying on with its usual business: some plants thriving, others clinging on for dear life in the heat, bees busy among the lavender, butterflies, chaffinches, gold-finches, the odd jackdaw, a thrush singing loudly from the top of a shrub. Somewhere to her left, a fat bumblebee was humming. Away in the distance, she could hear children playing. There was life all around her and here she was, im-mobilised again by doubt and fear.

Was Claude lying? What if it was true? Would he hurt her again? Round and round the endless thoughts went, detritus in a dark tornado. She was tied between two hard rocks: did she trust him or her own instincts?

She lifted her arm and glanced at her watch. This wouldn't do. She needed to distract herself for a while, give herself a bit of respite. She needed to get back to her search for the truth. She had been making good progress with tracking down John Farson and yet now here she was, the wind knocked out of her. She didn't feel strong enough to chase after him. Perhaps she would write, before going to meet him? Yes, she would do that.

She pushed herself up from the deckchair. It was hard not to feel furious. Here she was again: chest heavy, mind crammed to bursting, incapacitated in fog. She resented it, and yet there was another small voice, pernicious, damaging, rattling at the back of her mind: You did love him, you want children, do you really want to start again? She pushed the thought away and walked towards the studio doors.

Her mother's bureau was a stylish walnut affair. She'd bought it at a car-boot sale and had been rather proud of it. She had loved sitting there, gently fingering all the headed letter paper, the embossed cards, the envelopes with their bright red lining. Eleanor did posh stationery. It was a luxury she adored.

Rachel poured herself a glass of water and sat. She pulled down the drop-front writing slope and instinctively ran her palm across the green leather insert. The fitted interior was all business: pigeonholes that ran across the back, with two small drawers at either side. The pigeonholes were rammed with old letters, Christmas and birthday cards, the odd bill, leaflets for local walks, village round robins and takeaway menus for restaurants that were too far away to deliver. Rachel looked around for a wastepaper basket. She could chuck all this stuff away. Start at the left and work her way across. Clean start. Write the letter.

There were a lot of beautiful invitations: weddings, christenings, gallery opening nights, summer exhibitions, book launches, milestone birthday parties. Her mother had been in demand. Rachel had no memory of her ever going to anything.

There were bundles of old tickets too: trips to the RSC at Stratford, the occasional West End musical, BFI films including Q and As with the directors, concerts at the Barbican, gigs to see Bowie, Dylan, the Rolling Stones, Led Zeppelin. Memories, relegated, suddenly came flooding back: Rachel, sitting on her mother's lap, watching *The Threepenny Opera*; sitting huddled in the back of a Land Rover, wrapped in a blanket, driving home in a snowstorm from *The Merry Wives of Windsor*; the sandwiches Eleanor made when they went to the Open Air Theatre in Regent's Park; the homemade lollies on hot summer days; the little boxes of paints, the brushes, the constant encouragement – all of it had been forgotten.

Had she got her mother all wrong? She had chosen to remember her as someone distant, inaccessible, and yet here was evidence to the contrary. Eleanor had devoted herself to giving Rachel special memories. It wasn't her fault Rachel had chosen to forget them. Was she making the same mistake with Claude? Did she have him wrong? Was the hurt and embarrassment of that day clouding her judgement? What did it say about her – that he didn't contact her to tell her what he was going through? Was she as much to blame?

She picked out a pile of letters and leafed through them. There were a lot of bland thank-yous, guests who had stayed for the weekend, grateful brides who'd only just sat down to open their presents. Then there were the fan letters, the admirers of Eleanor's professional life, the collectors, the people who could only afford the poster of their favourite painting. Eleanor, it would seem, had taken the time to write to all of them. She had included little pencil drawings. Not for everyone, just for the people who couldn't afford her work. Their gratitude leaped off the page. Her mother had been kind.

Rachel let her eyes drift up and out of the window. The sky was blue again, as it had been all summer. A few vapour trails had made a saltire and she stared up at it. Her heart was filled with regret: she had chosen to remember only the arguments, the differences, the complicated edges. What a waste.

She set the letters to one side, unable to throw them away, and sat back. She pulled open the drawer to her right and picked out one of Eleanor's envelopes, thick, creamy, expensive. She let it sit in the middle of the green leather. What else had she forgotten?

Her eyes lighted on the small panel at the back of the bureau. Rachel had spent hours playing at this desk when she was little – and, as she stared at it, another memory began to surface.

'Wait,' she murmured, and sat forward. The bureau had a secret compartment. Eleanor used to leave messages there for Rachel to find. It was all coming back to her now. The puzzles, pertinent quotes, riddles, requests, surprises Eleanor would leave there for her. How had she forgotten?

Her index finger reached out towards the panel and she pressed into the bottom right-hand corner. There was a tiny click and Rachel slid the panel to one side. Something was inside, a piece of paper folded in half. Rachel could feel her heart beating. She leaned forward and pulled it out.

She took a sharp intake of breath. It was dated the day Eleanor had died.

Rachel,

Agnes always says that when you have something difficult to say, it's sometimes better to write it down in a letter. It helps, she says, to clarify the mind. She's right.

You have left for the day and we aren't getting on. I can't remember when that started or why. Not really. Can you? When you come back I am going to talk to you. Properly. We need to clear the air, find a way to move forward. This rancour has to end.

Our distance hasn't the first thing to do with Charlie. We both loved him. You know that. I don't think it has anything to do with Claude either. It's about you and me.

My success has been your undoing. I think you feel that you have failed, that I have had some hand in that. It feels odd to feel the need to apologise for my own success. I don't want to. I can't do that for you. I doubt you'd want it in any event.

I hate it. Does that shock you? The endless requests for portraits. The phone calls from galleries, the greed, the buyers for whom paintings are investments, the bankers, the trust fund layabouts, the people with their expensive cars and their expensive shoes and their expensive hair to whom I have to be polite and smile and hope they want to pay me money so they can make more money than I could ever dream of. That's what I do. I'm not an artist. I'm a facilitator for the wealthy.

But this isn't why I wanted to write you this letter. I'm not being entirely honest with you.

I have something to tell you. I'm not sure how to do it. It's a secret I've kept ever since the day I knew you were coming. It's been a terrible burden. I've tried not to resent it. I'm not sure I succeeded.

I was going to tell you after you got back from honeymoon, but that didn't happen. I should have told you, but I couldn't. And the reason I couldn't tell you was because I loved your father very much. You were the greatest gift of his life. His sun rose and set with you.

But Charlie is not your father, Rachel. And today, when you get back, I am going to sit down and I am going to tell you why Charlie never knew, and who your father really is.

Rachel stared down at her mother's handwriting as the world stopped. She turned the piece of paper over, but there was nothing more. She shook her head. 'You're leaving me with this?' she yelled. She put her fingers back into the panelled compartment but there was nothing else in there.

'No, no, no,' she cried, staring down at the words she couldn't bear. 'This can't be true. It's not true.'

Memories of Charlie flooded back: him stitching her name into the back of her school shirts, teaching her to swim, letting her lick the spoon when he made fruit cakes, showing her how to use a catapult and making sure she knew how to bowl overarm. She thought about the day he'd driven her to university and cried all the way there. She thought about the times she'd sobbed into his chest because yet another boy had let her down. She thought about the twenty-pound notes he used to slip into her hand, with a wink, when Eleanor wasn't looking. She thought about the books he sat writing, the jumpers with the holes in, his old brown brogues, his lovely soft hands, his kind eyes, how he always smelled of wood. He was so familiar, so much a part of her. The thought of not having been his child was too much to bear.

She ran to the kitchen. Picking up her phone from the charger in the wall, she rang Agnes.

'*There's a jolly good reason I can't answer the phone right now ...*'

'No, no!' Rachel yelled. Agnes's phone would be off for days. She'd been stung once on a previous trip for not turning off her data roaming, and that was that. Never again. Rachel felt frantic. She had to speak to someone who would understand.

She couldn't deal with this on her own. She felt desperate, hollowed out.

She stared down at her phone, pressed Favourites and looked at the four names listed: Dad, Mum, Agnes, Claude. Two of them were dead, one was unavailable and the other ...

She shook her head. 'I can't, I can't ...' Her voice was strained, choking almost. She slid down to the floor, her back against the Aga, holding her phone with both hands. A strange, guttural wail filled the room. She clutched at her chest.

She had discovered what her mother wanted to tell her. Her head fell into the crook of her elbow; her knees were pushed up against her chest. She wanted to make herself as small as she could. She wanted to disappear, for the hurt to vanish; she needed someone to tell her it was all right.

Her thumb moved back to her phone. She was out of other options.

She pressed Call. He answered.

'I'm so glad you rang,' said the voice. 'I've been worrying about how we left things.'

'Can you come here?' Rachel managed to get the words out. Her voice was no more than a whisper. 'Come to Brill? Now?'

'What's wrong? Has something happened?'

'Please, Claude,' she whispered. 'I need you to come.'

She leaned forward, her forehead resting on her knees. She felt ashamed, humiliated, beaten. Rachel let the phone slip from her hand. The letter was clutched in her other.

PART FOUR

'Make the most of your regrets ...
To regret deeply is to live afresh.'

Henry David Thoreau

Chapter Thirty-one

Then

Eleanor had never seen anything like it.

There was a group of nuns sliding down Primrose Hill on tea trays.

'It's like that old joke,' said Charlie, blowing on his hands. 'What's black and white, black and white, black and white?'

Eleanor looked at him quizzically.

'A nun rolling down a hill.' He grinned. 'Do you want the first go?' He'd brought a sled, an old wooden thing with some thick rope tied between the front runners.

'No, you go first. I'll wait here.'

It had been snowing for days and London had ground to a standstill. The air, normally acrid and metallic, had a crispness you could feel in your lungs. Everyone was smiling. There was something so joyous about snow: the crunch underfoot, the way the air became so still and quiet. It was as if everything you didn't want to look at disappeared for a while; it felt like a relief.

Charlie had come to get her, sled in hand, and they had walked from Belsize Park to Primrose Hill. Eleanor walked everywhere of late. If the journey was less than eight miles, she'd do it by foot. It gave her thinking time and a sense of peace. She could observe, stop and look at places and people and imagine what Jake was doing at that precise moment.

She hadn't heard from him and had no idea whether he'd made it to Morocco. He had vanished from her life entirely, and without him she felt diminished, like the shorter days. Since he had gone, she had withdrawn into herself and found a more respectable version of Eleanor, one who could turn up and make polite conversation. Was this who she really was? Jake had been her fairground ride, a white-knuckled adventure, but he had seen something in her that nobody else ever had: she was fun, she was interesting, she had things to say.

Her friendship with Charlie was softer, uncomplicated. She was so fond of him, grateful for him even, but whether he could ever instil in her the same ferocious passion was another matter. She sat on the bench at the top of the hill and watched as Charlie set his sled down. The hill was alive with joy: children making snowmen, parents holding toddlers' hands as they walked in snow for the first time, lovers walking arm in arm, wrapped together against the cold. The nuns were having a snowball fight. Eleanor watched them, her eyes smiling.

She stared up into the sky – low, yellowish cloud that meant more snow was on the way. Everything was already a carpet of thick endless white. It was like Narnia.

'Eleanor!' She looked downslope. Charlie was waving at her to catch her attention. He was sitting astride his sled. He wanted her to watch him. She smiled and gave him a little wave of encouragement. He was so sweet, innocent even. This must be what mothers feel like, she thought: protective, nurturing, indulgent.

He pushed himself off and she watched as he zoomed off towards the bottom of the hill. His scarf was trailing behind him, a striped marker that made him look like a classic Christmas card. Below him, she could see a large St Bernard bounding heavily across the lower pathway. 'Oh no,' she muttered. She stood up, straining to see. Charlie, noticing the enormous dog, steered the sled sideways, but the sled flipped and Charlie tumbled sharply. Eleanor stood. Charlie was lying face down in the snow. He wasn't moving and Eleanor, feeling a short, sharp pang of anxiety, instinctively went to run down the hill but, as she did, Charlie sat up and shook his head. She waved at him. He waved back. He was fine.

A little embarrassed she had panicked, Eleanor returned to the bench. Charlie, dusting snow from himself, retrieved his overturned sled and began the long trudge back up the hill. Strangers were asking him if he was all right and Eleanor watched as he laughed it off, assuring people he was fine.

Eleanor shifted her focus back to the nuns. They'd finished throwing snowballs and were making a snowman. 'They should make a snow Jesus,' she murmured.

Charlie sat down heavily next to her and rubbed his knee. 'Well,' he said, smiling, 'that didn't go according to plan.'

'Are you all right?' Eleanor turned and smiled at him.

'I'm fine. Only thing that's bruised is my pride,' he replied. 'Some snow's gone down my trousers though. I'll have to jump up and down a bit to stay warm.'

Eleanor lifted her hand to his face and brushed some snow from his fringe. 'You should have worn a hat. You'll catch your death.'

Charlie gestured over his shoulder towards a portable booth. 'They're selling hot chocolates over there. Would you like one?'

Eleanor nodded. 'Yes, please.'

He handed her the sled. 'Do you want a go?'

Eleanor scrunched her nose up. 'I don't think I do. Not while that big dog's on the loose.'

The St Bernard was continuing to cause chaos: chasing after people on sleds, jumping after snowballs, leaping into drifts. It was being pursued by a tiny slip of a woman in a fur hat brandishing a lead.

'I wouldn't have minded if it was carrying brandy,' said Charlie, standing up. 'But it wasn't. I'll get the drinks.'

Eleanor looked out over Primrose Hill towards the city beyond. She could just make out the edges of London Zoo and, further in the distance, the still-unfinished Post Office Tower. Everything was shrouded in a white fog. Where would Jake be now if he were still in London? she wondered. Holed up in a corner of the French, a just-drained Dirty Dog – beer with a shot of vodka – on the counter, half-lit cigarette hanging from his lower lip, chest out, glint in his eye and holding forth on who, in the pub, they should eat first in order to ensure their survival. She let out an involuntary laugh. The thought of Jake being up here in the freezing wind chasing wholesome pursuits was ridiculous. What would he make of her now? Her smile faded.

'Here,' said Charlie, holding out a large ceramic mug. 'You'll enjoy that. It's delicious.'

Eleanor took the mug between her mittens and cradled the warmth in towards her chest. 'Oh, that's lovely,' she said, looking up at Charlie. She took a sip. He was right. It was delicious.

A boy and his little sister ran by. He was carrying a sled and she, no more than five, was desperate to keep up. She slipped and fell in front of Charlie, who, seeing her face down, rested his mug on the bench and bent to pick her up.

'You all right?' he asked, his eyes warm and smiling.

The little girl nodded and Charlie nodded back. 'Off you go then.'

He watched her scamper off. 'I can't wait to have children.' He turned and looked at Eleanor.

'You'll be an amazing father, Charlie,' she said. 'What will you do if you have a boy?'

'I shall teach him how to swim, how to use a catapult and how to bowl overarm.'

'And what if you have a girl?'

'I shall teach her how to swim, how to use a catapult and how to bowl overarm. They're the only life skills anyone ever needs.'

'I don't know how to use a catapult or bowl overarm.'

'Then you have been very badly let down by the men in your life. I shall have to teach you.'

'I'll hold you to that.'

Balancing the mug between her knees, Eleanor reached into her leather satchel and pulled out a sketchbook. 'I should do some drawing,' she said. 'So I can remember.'

'Do you keep a diary?' Charlie's cheeks were reddening in the wind.

'Yes, I always have. Do you?' Eleanor pulled out a pencil from her pocket.

'No. Never have. Odd, don't you think? Considering I'm a writer.'

'Perhaps that's why you don't. It's no release. Where's the fun in doing what you do all day?'

'Maybe.' Charlie looked down the slope. 'Ha! Look!' he said, pointing. 'That woman's roped in the group of nuns. They're all chasing that wretched hound.'

Eleanor followed his finger and made a few quick strokes on the paper in front of her. She enjoyed sketching: quick informal marks that served as mnemonics – the odd hat, how the man with the round belly sat comfortably, nuns running after a dog, a woman sitting on her bike, the boy with the trailing scarf . . .

'Is that me?' Charlie tilted his head.

'Might be.' Eleanor closed her book and looked up at him.

He sat again, this time nearer to her. 'Don't,' he said, fingering the top of the pad. 'Let me see.'

'I'm not sure if that's allowed,' said Eleanor, suddenly self-conscious. 'Artists have to maintain a certain air of mystery ...'

'Show me.'

Something about his face was so open, so kind, Eleanor found herself handing the book to him. 'All right,' she said. 'Help yourself. I don't mind. But they're only sketches, remember.'

'Are you sure?'

Eleanor nodded.

Charlie took the book and opened it to the page Eleanor had just drawn on. 'It's very impressive,' he said, 'the way you can capture someone so completely so quickly.' He smiled at her. 'It's a real gift.'

'I'm not terribly good at taking compliments,' she said, stuffing her hands into the pockets of her coat. 'Don't give me any more.'

'I'm not sure if I can promise to keep to that.' Charlie turned his attention back to the book and flipped the pages the other way towards the front. As she watched him, Eleanor realised the book was filled with sketch after sketch of Jake.

'Who's this?' Charlie pointed to a rather arresting picture of Jake, his lips slightly pouting. He looked like a beautiful flower.

'Jake,' said Eleanor, her voice quiet. 'That's Jake.'

'The chap that ran off? Have you heard from him yet?'

Eleanor shook her head. Charlie let the book rest in his lap. 'I'm sure he's all right, you know,' he said, putting his hand on her arm. 'You'd have heard if anything terrible had happened.'

'Perhaps,' she said, looking away, over towards where Soho would be if she could see it. She hadn't been there since he had left. She hadn't been able to bring herself to. 'Mind you,' she added, 'I haven't really seen anyone who knows him.'

'You should. Go and see them. If nothing else it'll put your mind at ease.'

Eleanor turned back and looked into Charlie's eyes. She pulled her hand from her pocket and took his. 'You're a very good man, Charlie Allen.'

Charlie smiled and opened his mouth to say something but stopped. He looked away momentarily, as if trying to work something out, then turned back and gripped her hand a little tighter.

'I can feel how cold your fingers are through my mittens,' said Eleanor. 'Here, give me your other hand.'

Charlie put down his mug and let Eleanor take his hands in hers. Pressing them between her own, she rubbed them together. 'How have you not got mittens? I shall have to ask Agnes to knit you some.'

'Eleanor,' said Charlie, his voice calm and steady, his face filled with nothing but hope. 'Would you like to be my girlfriend?'

She was surprised at the question and hesitated but, looking at him, Eleanor realised how easy and natural it would be to say yes. Somewhere, deep inside, she knew. 'Yes,' she said, with a nod. 'I think I would.'

He leaned in to kiss her. His lips were cold but somehow, between them, they managed to feel nothing but warmth.

Chapter Thirty-two

'Champagne?' Eleanor couldn't hide her surprise. 'For me? Really?'

'Well, it's not every day your girlfriend is offered a gallery exhibition before she's even left college. I rather think you've deserved it.'

He gripped the cork and twisted the base of the bottle. Eleanor took off her coat and let her bag slip to the floor. She wasn't used to being spoiled, not since Jake. She sat, her hands falling on to her knees, and smiled up at Charlie. They'd been official for a few weeks and had settled into a calm routine. She'd go out, walking and drawing, he'd spend the day writing, she'd come home and they'd eat together. It was quiet and domestic and straightforward.

She was a little tired. The past few weeks had been rather overwhelming. Her end-of-term show had been received with an intensity that had taken her by surprise. She was being hailed as the Next New Thing, the artist that collectors should buy now while they still can. Three gallery owners had offered her exhibitions. She had thanked them and pressed their cards into her pocket and then stood, not knowing quite what to say or do. Nothing in her life to date had prepared her for success.

'Here,' said Charlie, handing her a glass. 'I'm so proud of you. Cheers.'

She took a sip and smiled again. 'Don't get too excited. People say things they don't mean all the time. It'll probably fizzle to nothing.'

Charlie took her hand in his. 'You need to have more self-belief. You're extraordinarily talented, Eleanor.'

Eleanor made a small involuntary noise. She didn't believe him. The only person she'd ever really believed was Jake, but he wasn't here and her safety net was gone. She was standing on her own, facing the world, and she wasn't quite ready for it. She put her glass down on the table. 'I should eat something,' she said, her voice a little weary. 'Haven't had anything since breakfast. I'll keel over if I don't.'

'I've made supper,' Charlie said, 'I roasted a chicken earlier. Shall I get it out now?'

'Yes, please,' said Eleanor with a nod. 'Might buck me up. Sorry. I'm being rather dull.'

'You're just tired,' said Charlie, walking towards the kitchen. 'Kick your shoes off, relax.'

Eleanor listened as he busied himself, and slowly slipped her feet out from her sandals. She wasn't sure how she felt: incredulous, surreal, lucky, but also strangely sad. She wished Jake had been there to see it. She missed him terribly.

She stared out of Charlie's sitting-room window and up to her own on the floor above. Her mind flitted back to the first time she'd seen him, how she had felt embarrassed and reluctant, and now here she was, sitting on his sofa, her shoes abandoned on the floor. She felt comfortable with him, untroubled. Was it enough?

'I locked myself out again today,' Charlie called from the kitchen. 'Caretaker wasn't too pleased.' He reappeared, holding a platter of cold chicken and a tomato salad.

'He'll start to think you've got a crush on him,' said Eleanor, running a hand through her hair. 'How many times is that now?'

'Actually, I've lost count,' said Charlie, putting the plate down on the table. 'Here,' he said, handing her a fork. 'Do you want a separate plate or shall we go medieval?'

'Fork's fine.' She pushed herself up and stood over the table, digging her fork into a large piece of chicken breast. 'I'm starving.'

Charlie followed suit and they both stood side by side, silently digging in. Eleanor, her fork pronging a tomato, picked up a drumstick with her spare hand. 'Honestly,' she said, her mouth already full, 'I can't eat this quick enough.'

Charlie looked at her and put his fork down. 'I've got something to give you.' He smiled softly.

Eleanor's eyes widened. 'As well as the champagne?' She swallowed. 'Charlie! I'm not sure I deserve all this fuss.'

He wiped his mouth with his fingers. 'Eleanor,' he began, 'I've loved the last few weeks. You've made me happier than I can remember.'

She stopped what she was doing and stared at him. He looked rather serious, suddenly. His hand moved to the pocket of his trousers. Her eyes followed his hand and she felt a surge of anxiety.

'And so I got you this,' he said, pulling out a tiny blue box. He held it out.

Eleanor's anxiety intensified. This wasn't what she thought it was, was it? She was still holding the half-eaten drumstick. Should she put it down? What was she going to say?

Charlie stood there, his jaw firm and resolute, and she felt a rush of adrenaline, dizziness almost, that she wasn't sure was excitement or fear.

'Eleanor,' Charlie began. He went down on one knee and looked up. 'Will you do me the honour of being ...'

Eleanor felt horrified. She had no idea what she was going to say.

'My spare key holder?' He opened the box with a flourish and there, sitting inside it, was a brand-new Yale key.

Eleanor let out a gasp. 'Oh! Charlie! You absolute terror!'

He burst out laughing and stood up. 'Your face was a picture! I mean, honestly, I won't make that bad a husband.' He handed her the key and gave her a kiss on the cheek.

'I didn't mean ...' Eleanor began, shaking her head, 'Sorry. I'm not terribly good at surprises.' She gave him a playful punch and grinned up at him.

Charlie nodded down at the key in Eleanor's hand. 'This is, of course, a great responsibility. Think you can handle it?'

'I'm not sure. Perhaps I'll wait till you're out and invite all the ne'er-do-wells of Soho round ...' she said, but then her face fell enough for Charlie to notice.

'Have you still heard nothing?'

She shook her head and put down the drumstick.

'Go to Soho,' he said, taking her in his arms. 'Find your friends. Someone will know something.'

Eleanor rested her head on Charlie's chest. She had put off returning to Soho, but Charlie was right. It was the only place there might be answers.

'It's going to snow again, tomorrow,' said Charlie, kissing the top of her head. 'Wrap up warm, won't you?'

She nodded. Soho was calling. It was time to go back into the wood.

Chapter Thirty-three

'My God,' said Hen the next day, clutching Eleanor's cheeks. 'Where have you been? I wondered if you'd chased off after Jake. Gone to live in the souk like an exotic princess.'

Eleanor shook her head. 'No chance. I wouldn't be able to bear the heat,' she said, unwrapping the scarf from her neck. 'I've always preferred the cold.'

'You rather than me. I am absolutely loathing this ghastly weather. Weeks, it's gone on. I hate snow. Everyone's supposed to be so cheerful. It's an affront. Snow is not wonderful. It stops you going where you're supposed to go. It looks pretty for five minutes and then it's eternal grey slush and freezing misery and disgusting white lines on your shoes you can never get rid of. No, thank you.' She tilted her head. 'Don't suppose you've got a cigarette?'

Eleanor suppressed a small smile. Of course she would never remember. 'No, sorry. I don't smoke.'

Hen screwed her mouth sideways, as if this was the most monstrous inconvenience. She scanned the length of the bar. They were sitting in the French, and it was rammed with the usual lunchtime ragtag of boozers, and writers on deadlines, and people trying to make a name for themselves. Eleanor looked towards the door. Hen had told her she was expecting John.

'Muriel! Darling!' Hen called out to a woman with an extraordinary aquiline nose who was leaning on the counter, talking to a craggy-faced man in a trench coat. 'Would you lend me a cigarette?'

The woman raised an eyebrow and held out a cigarette packet. 'You only lend what you want back,' she said archly. 'I don't want it back. Here, take it.'

Hen widened her eyes into a picture of obsequious gratitude. 'Thank you, darling. Thank you.'

She reached into her handbag for a box of matches. 'Of course I have news,' she said, striking a match and holding it to the end of her cigarette. She took a drag and shook the match out, a thin swirl of phosphorus drifting through the air. 'I'm seeing a poet. In the carnal sense. It's awful.' She gave a shrug. 'Not because I'm not fearfully mad on him. I am. But he keeps insisting on writing poems about my breasts.'

Eleanor laughed.

'I'm flattered, of course,' Hen took another drag, 'but I find myself hoping he never becomes famous. Imagine having a poem about your breasts being dissected in some stuffy classroom two hundred years from now? Poets don't know what they're doing. They're damning you for all eternity as a slut.' She paused. 'I mean, I *am* a slut. But that's neither here nor there.'

Eleanor laughed again. She had missed this, the energy of misfits.

'I've got a job too.' Hen gave a scowl. 'Can you imagine? A job! I'm working in a bookshop on Old Compton Street. It's owned by the loveliest old man. Only problem is, he never wants to sell any of his books. It's ridiculous. Customers come in asking for the latest this or the latest that and he pretends we haven't got it. Packs them off to Foyles. He's quite mad.'

'I think I understand that,' said Eleanor, tilting her head. 'I can't give books away. I've never understood people who can hand books on. You spend so much time with one. They're like friends.'

'Oh, I can think of plenty of friends I'd happily hand on. John!' She glanced over Eleanor's shoulder and waved. 'Look who's turned up like a bad penny!'

Eleanor turned towards the door and saw him. He was still wearing that battered leather jacket, zipped up this time, a heavy college scarf and a pair of rather tight trousers that seemed to be far too short in the leg. She could see his socks. They were red.

Hen frowned. 'What in the name of hell are those trousers, John? You look most peculiar.'

John came between them, and Eleanor felt his hand settle in the centre of her back. He ignored Hen and leaned down to kiss Eleanor on the cheek. 'Where have you been?' he asked, looking at her, his dark eyes staring into her. She hadn't seen him since that night at his studio over a month ago.

'Here and there,' said Eleanor, mustering a smile. She looked away from him. She felt unnerved by him. This was no surprise.

John turned back to Hen. 'Do you want a drink?'

'God, I thought you'd never ask,' she replied, quickly downing the three-quarters-full glass of white wine in front of her. 'Same again, please.'

'You?' He turned back to Eleanor.

'I'm fine, thank you,' she said, pointing to her own unfinished glass.

He nodded and waved towards the barman.

'Seriously, John,' said Hen, peering down at the red socks. 'What has happened here? Are you on a dare? I don't think I've ever seen you look more like an accountant from Penge.'

'I jumped over a brick wall and split my trousers,' he replied, waving again to get the attention of the barman. 'And I've lost my house key. So I borrowed these from Michael.' He pulled at the trousers.

'Michael Babbington?' Hen pulled a face of incredulity. 'John, he's smaller than I am. No wonder you look like you're in shorts.' She let out a hoot of laughter. 'Oh, that's too precious. Really.' She took another drag of her cigarette. 'What were you doing that you had to jump over a wall?'

John raised an eyebrow and gave a knowing smirk. 'Nothing terribly serious.'

Hen grabbed Eleanor's forearm. 'Of course he's being entirely disingenuous. We can imagine what you were up to quite easily, can't we, Eleanor?'

Eleanor said nothing.

'A Dirty Dog and a glass of white wine,' said John, as the barman approached. 'Actually, make that two glasses of wine.'

'No, I . . .' Eleanor began to protest.

John pressed his fingers into the small of her back. 'I insist. We haven't seen you in ages. It calls for a celebration, don't you think?'

'Absolutely,' said Hen, grinning. 'Like Persephone back from the Underworld, our muse has returned.'

'Have you got a cigarette?' John asked Hen.

'Don't be ridiculous.'

She had forgotten how jolly they all were, the lively conversation, the intense interest in everything and everyone. It was refreshing to be back in the thick if it, the wild, heady swirl of Soho society. You could never be bored. You could be despondent, you could be jealous, you could feel wretched, ecstatic, inflamed, but bored? Never.

'Oh God,' said Hen, with a dark scowl. 'It's bloody snowing again. When is it ever going to end? It's too much. It's the end of days, it really is. What next? Penguins in Piccadilly Circus?'

'I'm rather fond of snow,' said John. 'We should make the most of it. Make a snowman in Soho Square. Challenge anyone drinking in the Coach to a snowball fight.'

'Where would the fun be in that?' said Hen, her eyes wide. 'Everyone in the Coach is close to death.' She leaned forward and put her hand on Eleanor's arm. 'Coach and Horses, darling. Always rammed with actors who haven't worked in years. The moaning is incessant. You can practically taste the bitterness. I've always thought acting was *the* most pointless profession for a grown-up. Unless you're very beautiful and very stupid, in which case it's your only hope.'

'Didn't you want to be an actress?' John took a drag on a cigarette he'd managed to bum from a waif-like artist in the corner of the bar.

Hen let out a short, sharp scream. 'Take that back! That's a monstrous libel! No, I certainly did not want to be an actress.'

'Hen,' said John, laughing, 'you're in that film with John Mills. You had lines.'

'That doesn't count. The director cornered me in the Gargoyle and he'd bought me a bottle of champagne. Don't mistake manners for ambition.'

John rolled his eyes.

'Eleanor, you're as quiet as a mouse!' said Hen, as the drinks arrived. 'You're as enigmatic as ever. You've been sitting here for an hour and you've managed to tell me nothing. I need to know everything, in gory detail, immediately.'

'I'm not sure there's much to tell ...' Eleanor shifted on her feet. She was yet to bring up the matter of Jake. Hen's conversation was always like a wild horse chasing skittishly across a field. It was hard to keep up and she hadn't yet had an opportunity to pick the right moment.

'There's always plenty to tell,' insisted Hen, leaning in. 'Who are you sleeping with? You must be sleeping with someone.'

'I've got a boyfriend ...' Eleanor stared down at the counter. She didn't want to catch John's eye

Hen let out a louder scream. 'Since when? Who is it? I demand to know!'

'He's called Charlie. We've been going out for a couple of weeks now. He's writing a book.'

'Of course he is,' said Hen, sitting back on her stool and sucking on her cigarette. 'Aren't they all?'

'No, he really is. He works for *The Times* too. He's rather ... respectable.'

'Oh God,' said Hen. 'I'm so sorry.'

John stared down at her and Eleanor looked away. She was immediately aware of that old, visceral sexuality that so unnerved her. It was something she didn't have with Charlie. That relationship was different. It was based on trust and respect and laughter. Sex hadn't come into it yet. Eleanor wasn't sure she even minded, but here, with John standing next to her, she was reminded of what she was capable of.

'How's the sex?' Hen asked, taking a sip from her wine.

Eleanor felt a little hot. It was as if Hen had read her mind.

Hen leaned forward. 'Wait. You *are* having sex, aren't you?' She looked incredulous.

'No, not yet.'

'What a waste,' said John, his eyes boring into her.

'I hope this isn't a repeat of Jake,' said Hen, raising an eyebrow.

'No ...' Eleanor shook her head.

'Then what's wrong with him? What's wrong with you?'

'Nothing.' Eleanor stood firm. 'We're just ... waiting.'

'What on earth for? If you want to buy a car, bloody drive it.' Hen gave a small guffaw. 'My poet and I are forever at it. In fact I think I've broken his gearbox.'

She shot John a wink then turned to the barman, who was within shouting distance. 'Another round, please! We're dying of thirst!'

'Have you heard from Jake?' John said, staring down at her. He had a way of unnerving her, of making her aware of herself.

Eleanor shook her head. 'No. It's one of the reasons I wanted to see you, Hen,' she added, looking towards her. 'I've heard nothing. Have you?'

'Not a peep. Not a telegram. Not a letter. Not a phone call. I actually feel quite abandoned. I like to think he's on a grand adventure in some dusty mountain, panama hat, white linen trousers, finding treasure and sources of rivers and tombs and things. God, John, I don't know if I can look at you in those ridiculous trousers for a second longer. Eleanor, you're a better person than I am. I'm begging you. Take him up to Regent Street and help him find some trousers.'

The streets were unusually empty. There were very few cars, even fewer buses, and the only people braving the weather seemed to be heading back to their offices after a lunchtime in the pub: heads down, collars up, hands in pockets, backs bent into the wind. The snow was coming down in thick flakes, the ones you can catch in your hand

and marvel at. As John and Eleanor walked together down Shaftesbury Avenue it was hard not to feel romantic. Eleanor didn't want to feel romantic – but then, she noted with some alarm, romantic was not what she was feeling at all. She was feeling something very different. She was feeling dangerous.

She had no emotional attachment to John, not like with Charlie. Yet here she was, overwhelmed with the inevitable. John was the temptation she was unable to resist, the quick and easy gratification for a need that burned within her. She knew full well where this was all heading and it was hard not to feel a little thrill.

'I should leave you to it,' she said, coming to a stop in front of Eros. 'I'm sure you don't want to be lumbered with me while you shop.' She stood and tried to focus her thoughts on Charlie. She needed to come to her senses. She should try to be a better person for him.

John stared up at the black statue in front of them. It was covered in a thick layer of snow but was still identifiable. 'Everyone makes the mistake of thinking Eros was the God of Love.' He stuck his hands into his jacket pockets. 'But he wasn't. There were lots of gods, all different kinds of love. Anteros – he was mutual love. Pothos, longing. Himeros, desire. Aphrodite, sexual love and beauty. But Eros was all about passion. Blind passion.' He looked at her. 'I don't want you to leave. I want to be lumbered with you for the rest of the day.'

Eleanor could feel her heartbeat quickening.

'Shall we sack off the trousers?' he asked. 'Bit cold, isn't it?'

'I'd rather be in the warm, yes.' She sounded nervous. She couldn't help it.

'Do you want to come to my flat?' His fingers brushed some snow away from her fringe.

'You haven't got your key.' She tried to collect herself, to resist.

'I can climb up the drainpipe.' He stood looking at her. She watched his eyes move slowly over her face. She looked at his lips. 'I think we'll be a lot warmer there.'

She knew what he meant. She knew what he wanted. She wanted it too.

'Shall we?' He moved his body towards hers and slipped his hand under her jacket and into the small of her back. His thumb pressed against her skin. She wanted him to kiss her.

'Yes,' she said. 'Let's go.'

Chapter Thirty-four

Eleanor lay on her side and stared at the soft, white layer of snow piling up on the window ledge outside. She'd never seen snow like it, not in central London. It must be, what? Eight, ten inches?

Behind her, John was getting dressed. This had felt rather wonderful earlier. Now all Eleanor could feel was ... what, exactly? She wasn't sure yet if it was regret. Would she be happy if Charlie knew? Absolutely not. Was this a terrible betrayal? Of course it was, but this was 1964, she tried to reason. Free love was all the rage. This was the life that Jake had showed her in Soho. But she didn't belong here really. She was a migratory bird, flying in when the wind turned cold. Soon, she would have to return home.

She turned on to her back and watched him. 'Do you think we'll do this again?'

He glanced over at her. 'I don't know. Would you like to?'

'I probably shouldn't.'

He started to do up the buttons of his shirt. 'I like having sex with you,' he said.

'How many other women do you sleep with?'

He paused and looked down at his buttons. Fastening the last, he lifted his head, his arms falling to his side. 'Enough.'

Eleanor blinked. 'Do you ever wish you had one person? Someone special?'

He thought about that. 'No.'

He moved towards a chair with a jumper draped over its back. Taking hold of the sleeve, he flipped it towards himself and pulled it on.

'Does that upset you,' he asked, turning down the neck of the jumper so the tops of his shirt poked through.

'Not at all. I imagine if I thought I was your girlfriend it would be terrible.'

He shot her a wry smile. 'I can't disagree with you.'

'I admire your aloofness.' She sat up, the blankets falling down to her waist. She leaned back against the headboard, naked and confident. 'But I'm not sure it's something to aspire to. You're the only man I've ever had sex with. I have nothing to compare you to. Are all men like you?'

'Yes,' said John, reaching for a silver kettle. 'They'll pretend they're not. But they are.' He turned and smiled.

'I'm not sure I believe you,' she said.

She swung her feet to the floor and reached for the knickers she had discarded earlier. They were lying half inside one of her shoes. She paused before plucking them out. She stood, pulling them over her bottom, and looked around for her sweater. It had been abandoned somewhere over by the sofa in the studio.

Eleanor found it and threw it over her head, pulling at the sleeves as she pushed her arms through. Behind her, the kettle boiled.

'Do you want a cup of tea?' John lifted the whistling kettle up from the flaming gas ring.

'No,' she said, 'I don't think I do. Have you seen my tights?'

John pointed to a soft grey heap on the floor. She picked them up, sat on the edge of the bed and began to scrunch one leg up into her hands. She dipped her toe into the end and pulled upwards.

'Do you sleep with Hen?' She scrunched the other leg up into her hands.

'Occasionally.' John spooned some tea leaves into a metal strainer.

Eleanor paused, then dipped her foot into the other leg of her tights. She stood and pulled them up and over her knickers, then she picked up her short corduroy skirt and stepped into it.

'What is it like? With Hen?' She didn't look at him as she asked.

'Very loud,' said John, pouring water into the strainer. He stopped and waited until the water had gone through. He poured again.

'Do you love her?' She attached the clasp at the back of her skirt and pulled up the zip.

'Not in the way you mean,' he said, taking the spent tea leaves and chucking them into the bin. 'If I ever married someone, it would probably be her. But only because we understand each other. We're very good friends. Sometimes that's enough, isn't it?'

'I don't know.'

He turned and reached for a half-full bottle of milk and splashed a little into his cup. He turned and looked at her. 'Do you love your boyfriend enough?'

Eleanor stood, now fully dressed bar her shoes. The little electric heater had given the room a balmy, heady feel.

Outside it was still snowing. The sky was darkening and the street lights were being lit, the fat flakes of snow moving languidly through dark yellow pools of light. She felt marooned here in this room. Everything outside had come to a dead stop. There were no sounds of traffic, no sirens, no people shouting or laughing. It was so quiet you could hear the snow landing. She thought about Charlie. The snow would melt.

'Yes,' she said. 'I think I do.'

'Will you tell him about this?' He took a sip from his cup.

'No,' she said. 'He wouldn't understand at all.'

'It's easy to forget there's a world beyond Soho.'

Eleanor blinked and reached down for her shoes. She put one hand on the end of the bed and used the other to pull her shoes on. She was starting to feel a sense of dread: she could feel the real world, where responsibilities and consequences existed, churning in her chest, slowly strangling every moment of pleasure she had indulged in. Hen had been right. She was Persephone. She had failed the test. She had eaten the pomegranate seeds and now there would be consequences. She didn't belong here.

'I don't think we should do this again,' she said, reaching for her coat.

She shut the door and left.

Chapter Thirty-five

There were no buses.

Eleanor stood on Regent Street and, covering her eyes to shield them from the falling snow, looked both ways. It was late. No sign of a single bus, a single cab, nothing. She stared up, the Christmas lights blurred in the storm: two prancing reindeer, back to back, their antlers splendid candelabras, above them a suspended stage curtain of illuminated balls topped with brilliant stars. Eleanor had always loved the Christmas lights on Regent Street: the trip to see them had been a yearly feature of her childhood. They would travel up on the train, see the lights and, if her mother was in a very good mood, they'd be allowed to spend their pocket money in Hamleys.

Ahead of her, she could just make out the spire of All Souls, the prominent circular vestibule that sat like an exclamation mark at the end of the street: the Bath stone, with its soft honey colours, blended perfectly with the snow-filled sky. Eleanor began to walk towards it. She wished she'd thought to wear boots but she hadn't, and as she crunched her way through the deepening snow she felt the wet cold seeping over the tops of her shoes.

There was a strange, other-worldly atmosphere to the deserted streets. The wind whistled out from the side roads and she pulled her scarf up, covering her ears, nose and mouth. She thought about cutting sideways and making her way back to Soho. John had headed off to find Hen at the Gargoyle or the Colony, niche little member's bars that let the party carry on till dawn. Her heart wasn't in it. She didn't need to see John again and she certainly didn't need the inevitable grilling that would follow from Hen. She felt a pang of worry. Would John tell her what they had done? Of course he would.

Her heart plunged downwards, not because she worried about what Hen would think, but because Charlie didn't deserve to be thought of as a fool. Suddenly, Eleanor felt terrible.

She knew it was late, but Eleanor was consumed with a need to see him. She had tried going down to the Underground at Piccadilly Circus, but the grille was up and a handwritten sign had been attached to the padlock. *Closed due to weather.* Eleanor peered at it and turned back, not quite sure what to do. With no sign of a bus or cab, she was faced with a rather grim certainty. She was going to have to walk to Belsize Park.

The gates into Outer Circle, the road that cradled Regent's Park, had been locked to traffic, and as Eleanor walked past them she knew that any chance of seeing a cab was gone. It really was peculiar. She felt like the last person alive. The air was still, the only noise the soft muffled notes of snow falling through the air. She wasn't wearing a watch, but the fact the gates were locked told her it was past midnight. The temperature was dropping, she could feel it, and her thighs, only protected by woollen tights, were beginning to sting. She began to follow her own breath.

Her thoughts turned to how she would tell Charlie what she had done. She had told John she wouldn't, but she wasn't sure she could bear the burden of keeping it from him. She knew she may never feel the same burning desire for Charlie as she had for other men, but she could trust him, he would never let her down, and she loved him for it. She wanted to be with him and she didn't want this liaison to ruin that. Her mother had taught her it was always better to pour iodine into an open wound, however much it hurt. It was difficult, not because she knew she had betrayed Charlie but because she knew she had enjoyed sleeping with John.

Eleanor wasn't clear yet as to how to tell him. She should not be defiant. She should not be blasé. She knew that, for Charlie, it would matter. She had to prepare for the worst. She hoped the bitter cold of the storm would give her clarity.

She wondered what Jake would have told her to do if he were here. He'd be dismissive, of course. Why shouldn't she do what she liked? He was a hedonist, a purveyor of pleasure. He would have shrugged and failed to understand the problem. He had been a safety net to catch all bad behaviour, but now the safety net was gone and here she was, walking alone with nothing but her thoughts.

It took another hour to get to Haverstock Hill. As Eleanor let herself into the hall, she looked up at the clock that hung on the wall. Ten past two. Outside, the wind had picked up again and eddies of snow were swirling against the glass of the door. There was a small radiator next to the postboxes, and before taking the stairs (she didn't want to use the lift this late at night), Eleanor leaned into it and pulled her wet mittens off. Her fingers were red. Her legs felt frozen, burned almost, and she turned round, pressing her bottom into the warmth of the radiator. She felt sad, burdened, anxious. Letting her hands rest on the top of the radiator behind her, she pressed her head down into her chest and prepared herself.

She would tell him, tonight. That would be best. If she waited till tomorrow it would never be done.

The cold had given her courage.

She took the spare key to Charlie's flat from her pocket.

She let herself in and stood for a moment in his hallway to allow her eyes to adjust to the dark. The layout for each flat was identical, and she knew to go left to his bedroom. She trod softly and, pressing her palm against the bedroom door, she pushed it open and peered in. Charlie was fast asleep. He hadn't heard her.

It was the first time she had seen Charlie in bed. His head was lolling to one side, facing her, and his left hand was resting against his cheek. Slipping off her jacket, she went towards him and sat carefully on the edge of the bed. She laid her hand on his arm, the sleeve of his pyjamas soft to the touch.

'Charlie,' she said, her voice soft so as not to startle him. 'Charlie, wake up.'

He gave an indiscriminate murmur and his hand moved up from his cheek to cover his eye.

'Charlie,' she said again.

She took his hand and put it into hers. It was warm and comforting and Eleanor stared down, waiting for him to look at her.

'Charlie.'

He stirred and, with a confused frown, opened his eyes. His immediate reaction was to smile. 'What are you doing here?' he said, his voice slow and sleepy. 'Your hand is so cold.'

'There's a blizzard, Charlie,' she said, 'I had to walk home from Soho.'

Blinking, he pushed himself up against the backboard of the bed and ran his spare hand through his hair. He looked puzzled but not alarmed. 'Are you all right? What's happened?'

He looked at her, then reached over to his bedside light. 'What time is it?'

Eleanor caught his hand before he switched it on. 'No,' she said, 'don't put that on. I can see you perfectly well. It's about half past two.'

'Half past two?' he said, leaning back. 'What's wrong, Eleanor? Why have you come here now?'

'I wanted to see you.'

'You feel frozen,' he said, feeling her hand with both of his. 'Here,' he said, moving over and holding up his eiderdown, 'come under. I'll warm you up.'

Eleanor pushed off her shoes. They were quite ruined and the feet of her tights were wet through. 'I've got soggy toes,' she said, warning him. 'Do you mind?'

'I can cope with soggy toes,' said Charlie, pulling her into him. 'God, Eleanor, you're like ice. You should have called me. I'd have walked out to meet you.'

Eleanor clamped her eyes shut. It was so typical of him to think of her first.

'Why did you have to walk home?'

'The Underground was closed. Everything has ground to a halt.'

He put his head against the back of hers and wrapped his arm around her waist. 'You smell of snow and winter,' he murmured. He was going back to sleep.

'Charlie,' she said, 'I need to talk to you about something.'

'We'll go out for breakfast,' he mumbled. 'We can talk at breakfast.'

Eleanor turned on to her back and twisted her face so she was facing his. 'I can't wait for breakfast. I need to talk to you now.'

Charlie opened his eyes again and looked at her. He seemed puzzled but not cross. 'Why are you so out of sorts?' His voice was gentle, calm.

'I've done something terrible.'

Charlie pulled back to look at her better. 'Do I need to put my glasses on?'

'No, I don't want you to see me properly.'

'Pass me my glasses,' he said, sitting up again. 'They're on top of the book next to you.'

Eleanor reached across and passed them to him. She turned away and curled herself into the eiderdown. She wasn't sure she could look at him any more, not now he could see her.

'What have you done? What is all this about? Are you in trouble? Eleanor?'

'I went to see Hen at the French.'

'Are you drunk? Is that it?'

'No. I went to see Hen at the French. And John came. Jake's Soho friends. I might have mentioned them. And John had split his trousers. Hen sent me with him to help him buy a new pair.'

'Wait,' said Charlie, rubbing his temple, 'who is John?'

'He's the photographer I told you about when we bumped into each other at Waterloo. Ages ago. Weeks ago.'

Charlie tried to reach back into the corners of his memory.

'And the snow had started. And it was cold. And I went back to his studio.'

'Hang on,' said Charlie, trying to remember, 'is he the one who wanted to sleep with you?'

Eleanor swallowed. 'Yes.'

There was a pause and Eleanor sensed Charlie's body stiffening.

'What have you done, Eleanor?' He sounded low and serious.

'I've been with him. I didn't want to keep it secret from you.'

Charlie sat up further. 'What does that mean? Been with him all evening? What does that mean?' There was an air of panic in his voice.

'I slept with him,' she said, her voice almost at a whisper. 'We had sex.'

Charlie's hand, resting on her arm, withdrew and he shifted over towards the wall so he wasn't touching her. His arm reached over her head and a bright, rather harsh light filled the room. Eleanor covered her face with her hands and she felt him push himself to the bottom of the bed and on to the floor. As she heard his footsteps leave the room, she lowered her hands from her eyes and clasped them into fists over her mouth. Beyond the room, she heard a door being pushed open and then, rather suddenly, she heard Charlie vomit. She felt rigid, unable to say or do anything. A heavy silence followed.

Charlie reappeared in the doorway of the bedroom.

He said nothing but instead opened the door of a rather shabby-looking wardrobe in the corner of the room. Turning his back to her, he pulled off his pyjama top and pulled a shirt from a wooden hanger. He put it on.

'Charlie, I—'

'No, thank you, Eleanor,' he said, his back still turned. 'Not yet. I don't want to have this conversation in my pyjamas.'

He undid the thick cotton cord at the front of his pyjama bottoms and let them fall to the floor. Picking them up, he folded them neatly and placed them on a chair next to the wardrobe. Eleanor couldn't see his face. She couldn't read what was going to come next. A pair of dark corduroy trousers were draped over the back of the chair and, taking them, Charlie pulled them on and tucked in his shirt. He turned and opened a drawer, taking out a jumper and a pair of socks. He put on the jumper, arranged his shirt collar and then sat on top of the folded pyjama bottoms as he pulled on the socks. Underneath the chair was a pair of brown brogues. He placed his feet into them and tied up the laces. He stood and turned towards the bed.

'Can you get up, please?' he said, not looking directly at her. 'If you're cold, bring the eiderdown with you. I'd like to talk to you in the sitting room.'

Eleanor pushed herself up and, wrapping the eiderdown about her shoulders, followed him, silently, from the room.

In the sitting room, Charlie turned on a side lamp and went towards a small cabinet, opened it and poured himself a Scotch. Eleanor looked around the room. She could sit at the dining table or on the sofa. The dining table felt too formal so she sat on the sofa and, lifting her knees to her chest, folded herself into a protective ball. 'Would you like a drink?' he asked, his back still to her.

'Yes, please,' she said. 'Not Scotch.'

'Sherry or brandy?'

'Sherry, please.'

He poured and, without looking at her, handed her the glass.

'Charlie,' she said, trying to catch his eye, 'can you look at me?'

'I'm not sure I can. Not at the moment.'

He stood by the window, staring out at the snow.

'I'm sorry. I'm so sorry,' Eleanor began. 'I don't love him in the least. It was just … a moment. And I'm telling you because you mean too much to me to lie to you.'

'Have you slept with him before?'

'Yes. Once. Before Jake left.'

'Have you had sex with anyone else?'

'No!' Eleanor sounded affronted at the suggestion. 'Just him. Sorry. I don't know if that makes it better or worse?'

'I don't think anything makes it better. I don't think anything could be worse.'

'I don't love him, Charlie.'

'That's not the point,' said Charlie, still looking out into the night. 'What matters is that you don't think enough of me not to have done it.'

'But, I do—'

'No, Eleanor. You don't.'

'Charlie, I've walked through a blizzard and all I could think about was you and how I needed to be honest with you. If I didn't think enough of you, I wouldn't be here.'

'This has nothing to do with your respect for me. You're here because you want me to tell you it's all right. That I don't mind. But I mind a lot.'

'I'm glad you mind a lot. I would mind a lot. And I do respect you, Charlie. It's why I've told you.'

'I remember now, that conversation, at Waterloo. I remember it clearly. I remember the look in your eyes. I remember thinking you were reckless and young. I remember thinking you were beautiful and intriguing. And I remember thinking that I rather wished I was the man you were hoping to have sex with in a dark studio in Soho. But I wasn't. People treat you how you let them. It's the single most important lesson in life. Respect is earned. And if I let you treat me like this I can't respect myself and you won't respect me either. It's impossible.' He stopped and looked down into his Scotch. 'I don't know why I've poured this. I don't even want it.'

He placed it down on the table to his left.

'But, Charlie—'

He interrupted her. 'There's nothing you can say that's going to fix this. What's done is done. I'm not even angry with you. That's not what I feel.'

'Please be angry with me. It might help.'

'No. I can't. I just feel … sad.' He turned away, his hands deep in his pockets.

Eleanor pushed herself up from the sofa, letting the eiderdown fall from her shoulders. She walked towards Charlie and put her arms around him, her face flat against his back. 'I'm so sorry, Charlie,' she whispered.

'I know you are,' he replied, his voice soft and weary. 'And so am I. Perhaps when you go, you might leave my spare key?'

Eleanor felt tears pricking at her eyes. 'Is that what you'd like?'

'Yes, I think it's best.'

Eleanor stood back, reached into her pocket and placed the key on the dining table. She turned and walked back to the bedroom, where she picked up her jacket and shoes. They were too cold and wet to wear. She let herself out and stood in the dimly lit corridor; she could see the snow still falling through the window. The winter had become bleak. She thought of Jake, somewhere in North Africa. The air would be warm where he was, it always was. As she trudged up to her flat, she had never felt more lost.

Chapter Thirty-six

Now

Rachel focused on the fennel on the chopping board and brought down the cleaver with a smash. As the faint smell of aniseed filled the air, she dropped the cleaver from her hand. She hadn't needed to use it, she could have used a knife, but she felt like she wanted to break something, throw a vase against a wall, tip clothes out of a bedroom window, get into a fight. She was in a stinking mood and she knew why.

You can't call off a wedding twice, can you?

Rachel had only herself to blame for her swirling thoughts. In the months since finding Eleanor's letter, she had found herself completely reliant on Claude again. Agnes had turned her long weekend into a month in Italy and, with her aunt gone, he had been her only hope. With no one else to turn to, she had quickly, albeit hesitantly, slipped back into the life she had known. So here she was, in the flat above the gallery, making Claude a light salad. Beside the chopping board, lying on the marble counter, was a list of canapés sent by the chef from a reception venue picked by Claude two weeks after he had persuaded her to marry him again. The revelation about Charlie had hit her harder than she had expected. It had felt like losing him all over again and her anger with Eleanor had not only returned but intensified. Who was her biological father? Agnes didn't know either. Rachel had had to wait for weeks to tell her. She'd been as shocked as Rachel had been. She was back to square one and in an impossible position.

Despite her better judgement, Rachel needed continuity, an anchor to hold her down. Claude, for all that he had done to her, had stepped in to fill the void. Nature abhors a vacuum. He was her shoreline defence, stopping her from crumbling away. It was ugly, but necessary.

She hadn't expected Claude to be so organised about the wedding re-do. She'd thought she could agree to it and they could muddle along for a bit, test the waters, but Claude seemed hell-bent on getting it done as quickly as possible. He was like a man trying to close a business deal.

She still wasn't sure whether he'd told her the truth. And yet who would lie about something so terrible? She had to believe him. This was all she had.

Here she was, on another treadmill to disaster – or so it felt. The invites had gone out last weekend. She'd had a few phone calls from friends and family. They couldn't believe it. Neither could she.

Rachel looked down again at the fennel and reached for the mandoline. She would slice the fennel, chop an apple, a Pink Lady, into matchsticks, add coriander, chilli oil, lemon juice and salt, and toss it all together. Perhaps she would flatten a chicken breast and pan-fry it? Perhaps she'd chuck all this in the bin and eat a box of doughnuts?

With everything going on, she still hadn't even started on her plan to track down John Farson. All that had come to a halt. Uncovering the truth had caused nothing but pain so far. She was done with it. She needed to stop looking back and start looking forward. Her future was with Claude again.

'Hello, hello!' A voice came up the stairs. It was Agnes. Rachel hadn't seen her much of late. She said she avoided coming into Oxford if she could help it – 'The parking is terrible' – but Rachel rather suspected it was more to do with not wanting to see her fiancé.

'I'm in the kitchen,' Rachel called back.

Agnes appeared, large Tupperware box in hand. She was wearing a battered blue Barbour, undone, a bright pink jumper that was almost certainly a home knit, and a thick tweed skirt. She would have looked uncharacteristically school-ma'am-ish if it hadn't been for the enormous furry deerstalker she was sporting.

'Hello, darling, hello,' she said, as she breezed in. 'What do you think of this hat? I just bought it on a whim.' She put down the Tupperware and stood there quite still, her eyes wide, waiting to be assessed.

'I think it looks very toasty,' said Rachel.

'Yes. It is,' said Agnes with a nod. 'Getting ready for autumn and all that. Good. Mission accomplished.' She took it off and threw it on to a table. 'Now then,' she added, pressing on, 'I have brought a cake.'

'Thank God.' Rachel abandoned the fennel.

'You know I've been doing that buttercream course?'

'No.'

'Yes, you do. The decorative buttercream course, where you make flowers and all sorts. It's art. It really is. There are about a hundred piping nozzles. I'm supposed to make a floral wreath cake. Well,' she said, 'here it is.'

She pulled the lid off the Tupperware and pushed it towards Rachel. 'What do you think of that?'

'Goodness,' said Rachel, peering in. 'That's … a lot of buttercream.'

'I know. I'm not entirely sure it's edible. I think it's one part cake to five parts buttercream. The roses are quite good though, aren't they? Not as fiddly as you'd think. Next time I'll stick to two colours. I think I went a bit mad, but I wanted to try out all my food colourings. Do you want a bit?'

'I'm not sure I want to ruin it.'

'Oh, to hell with that. It's a vanilla sponge underneath. Come on. Get some plates.'

Rachel took two side plates from a shelf underneath the counter. 'I haven't got a cake slice,' she said, placing them next to the chopping board. 'What's best? Bread knife? Carving knife?'

'No need,' said Agnes, reaching into her pocket, 'I carry one with me wherever I go these days.' She pulled out a shining stainless-steel cake slice. 'Honestly, since I've been doing this course I've gone cake mad. I shall be twice the size by the end of it.'

Agnes pressed the cake slice down into the heaped mass of multi-coloured buttercream roses. She cut again and, with some difficulty, removed a slice. 'Oh, good grief,' she said, laughing, 'don't look at the sponge. I've lost my glasses and used plain instead of self-raising.' She laid it on the plate and Rachel opened a drawer to find two forks. 'Here,' Agnes added, picking up the list of canapés lying on the marble counter, 'where shall I put this? Don't want it to get dirty.'

'Wherever you want,' said Rachel, dismissively.

Agnes glanced at it and realised what she was holding. 'Ah,' she said, her voice flattening. 'All that again.'

'Yes. All that again.' Rachel handed Agnes a fork.

'Canapés? Really? Why don't you scale it all down? Keep it simple. Elope. Just the two of you. Go to Vegas, have fun, get married by Elvis?'

Rachel stared at her aunt. Agnes clearly lacked any genuine enthusiasm for this wedding. She was going through the motions, trying to be the stalwart brick wall Rachel could collapse against.

'You don't think I should be doing this, do you?'

Agnes paused, aware that her response needed to be careful. She glanced down at the floor, then back up again. 'I worry that you might be doing it for the wrong reasons. I know why you've got back with him. I understand it, I do. Finding out about Charlie has knocked you for six. It's knocked us all for six.' She shook her head. 'I still can't quite believe it. And the thought of Eleanor keeping it secret for all those years ...' Her voice faded away. It had hurt her as much as it had hurt Rachel: the lies, the secret never told. Neither of them had a clue who Rachel's biological father was.

Agnes shifted. 'I think when people are hurting they want safe corners, and sometimes the corner that looks the safest isn't. If you can look me in the eye and tell me you think Claude is the very best you can do, then I shan't say another word.' She stopped and waited.

'I can't.'

'No,' said Agnes, her voice filled with regret. 'I know you can't.'

'I don't know what to do.' Rachel stared into Agnes's eyes, waiting for guidance. In moments like this, Rachel felt the loss of her parents most keenly. They were no longer there to answer that call, to listen quietly, to offer up a kind word.

'Darling, I know what I want you to do but I can't make that call for you. I just can't. You're going to have to dig deep, Rachel. Work out what you really want. Do you know what you want? Here,' she said, pushing a plate towards her. 'Try that.'

Rachel dug her fork into the sharp end of the cake and shovelled out a large mouthful. Agnes was right. It was almost entirely buttercream. She thrust it into her mouth, looked startled, shook her head, grabbed a piece of kitchen paper and spat everything into it.

'Oh no,' said Agnes. 'That bad?'

'You've used salt. You've mixed up sugar with salt.'

Agnes slammed her fork down on to the counter. 'Not again. I keep doing this. Damn my blasted glasses. The pots are identical. What a disaster.'

'The roses look good though,' said Rachel, filling a glass with water. She glugged down a mouthful, then swilled and spat into the sink. 'But it tastes disgusting. Sorry.'

Agnes gave a short, irritated sigh and pressed the lid back on to the box. 'I don't know where my brain has gone. Truly. I couldn't remember my own postcode last week. Away with the fairies. Oh well. No cake for us.'

'You can have some salad if you like? There'll be plenty.' Rachel gestured towards the mandoline.

Agnes shook her head. 'I'm fine. I had a late breakfast. And don't think I've forgotten you haven't answered me ...'

Rachel rubbed at her mouth with a kitchen towel. 'No, I haven't, have I?'

'I know you, Rachel.' Agnes waggled the list of canapés and put it down on the counter. 'Perhaps better than you know yourself. Is this what you want? Really?'

Rachel exhaled and folded her arms. 'I don't know. That's the honest answer. I simply don't know. And it's making me ... furious. It all feels so impossible. Here I am, feeling lost again. No answers. Except that the man who I thought was my father wasn't. Eleanor left a note for me that only raised more questions. I need to let the past go for now. It's too dangerous. Claude is the future I've chosen. I have to start looking forwards.'

'She wouldn't have intended this to be the way you found out, Rachel.'

'I don't care. I just need to stand very still and root myself somewhere new, and if marrying a man who lost his mind but is trying to make it up to me is the person who can provide me with that stability, then I guess I'm taking it. What other option do I have?'

'Do you love him?'

Rachel gave a shrug. 'I suppose so. I said yes, didn't I? That must mean something. God, when did everything get so complicated? I lie in bed every night and I think about what Eleanor did and the secrets she kept. What does that do to a person? The burden of it leaves me breathless. And she was right. About my painting, and my resenting her success. The idea that she thought I hated being creative when actually it was all I ever wanted to do kills me. And then I think about where I am now and the fact that I'm getting married again because Claude feels guilty. Because I feel guilty for not believing him. It all goes back to guilt.'

'If it's any consolation, I don't believe him either. Do you know what I think? I think he was embarrassed. Embarrassed and ashamed, and this was all he could come up with to cover his tracks.'

'But then that makes him a terrible person,' Rachel said, with a sigh. 'Ugh. It's all so dark and joyless.'

'You should come back to Brill. Everything becomes clearer in Brill.'

'I can't. Claude doesn't want to live there. He doesn't like the drive.' She pulled a face.

Agnes frowned. 'You're not going to sell?'

Rachel shrugged. 'I think we'll have to. I won't be living there. Johnny won't be living there. Claude is pushing for us to put it on the market. He says the month in rehab put the gallery in financial trouble. It would mean the debts here are paid off.'

'He wants you to pay off his debts?' Agnes gave a dismissive tut. 'Rachel, that house has been in our family for a hundred years. It's who we are.'

'I know, I know but ... I'm not sure I can afford the luxury. And Brill is so full of the past. I'm not sure I can go back.'

Agnes narrowed her eyes. 'You should go back. Go to Brill. Remind yourself of how much you love it. What it means to you. Caspar's finished the rose garden. It's looking wonderful.'

Rachel felt a pang at the mention of his name. 'How is Caspar?'

'Very well. I popped up there two days ago. Wanted to get some cuttings. He was there. Anyway, he handed in his notice. Should have told you but it slipped my mind. Like everything else these days.' She rolled her eyes.

'What? He's leaving?'

'Wants to go travelling. Good for him. End of the month, I think. You should see him before he goes. He'll be there tomorrow. He likes you. He'd appreciate it.' Agnes took off her Barbour and draped it across the back of a chair. 'Well. I'm here now. Shall I make some tea? Do you fancy one?'

'I'll have one.' Claude appeared in the doorway behind them and they both turned to look at him. He looked smart but rather overdone: a three-piece suit, a bow tie, red shoes.

'Goodness, Claude,' said Agnes, 'you look like a children's entertainer.' She walked over to the kettle and carried it to the sink.

'I think I look rather dapper,' Claude said, pushing his chest out. 'I think it helps to have an image. When you run a gallery.'

'I hear you're trying to persuade Rachel to sell Brill,' said Agnes, giving him a hard stare. 'I disapprove entirely.' She turned the tap on and held the kettle under it.

'I'm not surprised,' said Claude, 'it's a big decision.' He picked at a piece of fennel and popped it into his mouth. 'But it makes no sense to keep it.'

'No sense to you,' said Agnes, turning the tap off. 'But then it's not yours.'

'Yet.'

'Is that why you've come back to marry my niece? So you can take it?'

Claude paused before answering. 'No, of course not.' He went to take another piece of fennel but there was nothing to pick at. The bulb was still sitting on the mandoline. 'Shall I do the rest of that?' he asked Rachel, pointing towards it.

'If you like,' she answered. 'But be careful of your fingers.'

He moved across and stood next to her. He was still looking at Agnes, who now had her back to him, slotting the kettle into place. She turned and, as she looked back at him, he leaned towards Rachel and kissed her on the cheek. 'This looks like it's going to be delicious,' he said, and smiled.

That was not for her benefit, Rachel thought. That was a show of something, not affection, something else, and it was entirely aimed at Agnes. A small power play, perhaps. Whatever, it irritated her and she moved away to lean against the cooker.

'Are you well, Agnes?' Claude went into charm mode. 'You're looking well. Have you managed to avoid this terrible chest infection that's doing the rounds? I've only just shaken it off. Thought it would never leave.' He took the fennel and began to slice.

'I'm perfectly well, thank you,' said Agnes, a little tight-lipped. 'I never get colds. Never have. I am immune to them. I put it down to having grown up in a house with no central heating. Stiffens the sinews. Makes you robust. Besides, I've always rather enjoyed getting into a cold bed. There's something rather delicious about it.'

'Hot water bottle,' added Rachel, nodding.

'Exactly,' agreed Agnes, punching the air with her finger. 'Freezing sheets, leaping in, finding the bottle, pulling the blankets up to cover your nose. Bliss. And mark my words, when your bedroom is like ice in the morning, you leap out of bed. Nowadays everything is so … pampered.'

'I can't bear being cold,' said Claude, sliding the fennel up and down.

'No,' said Agnes, 'I don't imagine you can.'

Behind her the kettle boiled and she pulled down a blue teapot from a shelf above her.

Rachel watched Claude closely. He was going to cut himself. She was sure of it. She should stop him before it happened. She really should.

'What sort of roses has Caspar put in?' She turned her attention back to Agnes.

'Oh!' Agnes beamed. 'They're glorious. A red climber. So romantic. He did tell me. It's on the tip of my … no, no, it's gone.' She shook her head and sighed.

Rachel glanced back at Claude. He was trying to give Agnes his full attention while slicing the fennel. She folded her arms.

'Earl Grey or builder's breakfast?' Agnes held up two packets of teabags.

'Earl— oh!' Claude let out a small yelp. 'Oh lord. I've cut myself, Rachel,' he said, holding his hand up, 'it's quite bad. I think it's quite bad.'

'I did tell you to be careful.'

'No, Rachel, I'm serious, it's quite bad. You're going to have to help me. I'm wearing an Armani suit.'

Rachel and Agnes caught each other's eye. Agnes, pursing her lips together, turned back to the teapot.

'Rachel,' Claude pleaded again.

'All right. Don't panic. Hold your finger up and I'll get the medical kit. Where is it?'

'In the bathroom.'

Rachel pushed herself away from the cooker. She was in no rush. There was no sense of urgency. 'Go and stand over the sink in the bathroom. I'm not going to do it over food. I'll find the plasters.'

'Yes. You're right,' he said, walking through the doorway. 'Oh God. It's dripping down my arm, Rachel.'

Agnes watched him go. She clamped her eyes tight shut for a moment then opened them. Rachel pulled out a packet of plasters from a drawer and went to follow him. Agnes gripped her by the arm and stopped her. 'You need to work out what you want, Rachel,' she whispered.

Rachel stared down at her aunt, her head full of Charlie and Eleanor once more. They wouldn't want this for her. She deserved better. 'I know.'

Chapter Thirty-seven

Then

Eleanor stared down into Charlie's flat. She hadn't seen him for two weeks now. His curtains hadn't moved and no lights had been on. The typewriter had sat on the table, no paper in it, his chair tucked tightly under. There had been no signs of life at all, but today, as she looked down, she saw a book on the table. He must be back.

Eleanor pressed her forehead against the window. She felt awful. It was painful how much she missed him. The weight of his absence surprised her. She hadn't been able to bring herself to tell anyone what had happened between them. It would mean explaining herself, and she didn't have the strength for it. She had opened a bottle of wine, a rare extravagance, and was painfully aware that she was drinking it to feel worse.

She drained the last of it and drew the back of her hand across her mouth. He was punishing her, she thought. Well, she'd taken her medicine. It was one thing to teach someone a lesson, another thing entirely to be cruel. Why hadn't he forgiven her? She hadn't thought once about going back to Soho. She wanted nothing to do with anyone there.

A pocket of anger bubbled in her chest. She was young, she'd made a mistake, she reasoned. If he could just see past it, they would be fine. She had to do something, anything. She'd write him a note, stick it under his door. That would do it.

Animated by her plan, she stumbled into the sitting room and pulled open the stationery drawer. Marjory had some rather smart monogrammed writing paper, and she took out a few sheets and sat down, then scrawled through the florid initials at the top with a pen and replaced them with her own.

Charlie, she wrote, *I want to see you. I need to see you. I miss you. I love you. I love you. I love you. I've been punished enough. Please stop. I love you. Eleanor.*

She stared down at it. Short and to the point.

I'm sorry, she added. *Please. I'm so sorry.*

She folded it in two. She would deliver it immediately.

Leaving her door on the latch, she went to the staircase and walked down to the floor below. It had been painted, the long-awaited decorations having begun, and the landing smelled of new carpet. Eleanor padded along the corridor, barefoot, her steps quickening. Looking over her shoulder to make sure nobody was watching, she crouched down and slipped the folded note under his door. Now she had to wait.

She slept fitfully. The wine was keeping her awake and she had a headache, deep and thumping, behind her eyes. Eleanor sat up and reached for the glass of water beside her bed. She felt wretched, her tongue swollen and purple, her eyes hooded. Pulling back the curtain, she looked down towards Charlie's apartment. It wasn't quite dawn, but there was enough light to see his curtains weren't drawn.

Where was he? Eleanor leaned back into her pillow and stared ahead. Where was he sleeping? Was he with someone else? The thought stabbed at her. She clamped her eyes shut, her bottom lip crumpling.

She woke again, an hour later. The blanket was wet through, the glass beside her on its side. Eleanor sat up and ran a hand through her hair. She was amazed she hadn't been sick. She removed the glass from the bed covers and peered out again from behind the curtain. There was still no sign of movement from Charlie's flat and she was consumed by the same empty anguish of a few hours before. Pushing herself up, she removed the wet blanket from the bed and carried it to the sitting room. She pulled out a chair from the dining table, hung the blanket over the back and glanced down at the table. There was a piece of paper and a pen.

'Oh God,' she mumbled to herself. 'The note.'

What had she been thinking? If Charlie was with someone else, she had to get it back. Picking up a ruler from the bureau and pulling on a jumper, she went to her front door and peeked out. At the far end of the corridor, one of her neighbours was standing, waiting for the lift. She stood, door ajar, and listened until he was gone, then walked out. A breezy conversation wafted up from the ground floor: something about the weather and whether the postman was arriving later these days.

She trotted down the stairs and turned on to Charlie's corridor, the voices below bleeding away as the outer door opened and shut. Behind her, she heard the latch of a door sliding open. She ran towards a right-hand turn that put her out of sight and leaned against the wall. She wasn't sure why she felt so panicked. Most people in the building knew who she was and yet there was something furtive about her, something that might induce someone to ask her what she was up to.

She crept towards Charlie's front door and got down on her hands and knees. There was a small gap, enough for her to see through, and, placing her cheek flat to the carpeted floor, she could see the note. She slid her ruler through the gap, scooped it into the middle of the folded paper, and pulled it back out. Grabbing the note, she pushed herself up and ran back to her flat.

She stood, panting slightly, and stared down at the note in her hand. What was the point? Charlie wasn't going to forgive her. It was hopeless. She walked to the bathroom, scrunched it into a ball and flushed it down the toilet. She would forget about it and head straight to work.

College had broken up for Christmas weeks ago and, rather than return to Brill, Eleanor had taken a job at Hamleys. She'd seen an advert in the *Evening Standard*. Artists wanted. She was required to dress as an elf and demonstrate Etch A Sketch, a mechanical drawing toy that was currently all the rage.

'You're late,' said a fleshy man holding a clipboard. He was dressed in a dark green Santa outfit, the middle management of Christmas.

'I'm sorry, Mr Machin,' she said, pulling off her hat and coat. 'The bus broke down. We had to wait for a replacement.' It wasn't true, but it would keep him off her back.

He tapped at his wristwatch. 'You've got five minutes to get to your floor. Look sharp and don't let it happen again.'

She changed quickly, pulling on a pair of bright yellow tights and a green tunic with a jagged trim. Next she had to buckle a large black belt around her waist and put on red ballet pumps with slip-on felt covers that curled up at the tip into a point. She also had a hat to wear, a red felt triangle with a tiny bell at its peak. The costumes had come out of storage. Hers smelled like rain on a hot pavement.

The Etch A Sketch display was on the ground floor, such was its popularity. It meant Eleanor was constantly in demand, but had the disadvantage of being rather cold. To draw people in, the doors were wedged open, the shop workers performing tricks with yo-yos to entice in any children. Hamleys hardly needed the footfall: schools had broken up and the store was rammed to bursting.

'How does it work?' A woman in a tight floral headscarf was holding one of the display models behind Eleanor.

'You use the knobs to draw pictures. This one moves the stylus vertically.' She pointed to the dial on the left. 'And this one ...' she added, pointing to the right, 'moves it horizontally. If you move them together you make a diagonal line. Have a go. They're terribly popular.'

'Are you really an elf?' asked the little boy with the woman. He had soft blond hair and was in a beige wool jacket that was far too big for him. It had enormous pockets and was fastened with two large brown buttons. He was in shorts and socks, one of which was up to his knee, and a pair of brown buckled shoes that looked as if they'd had a polish for their grand day out.

'Yes,' Eleanor replied earnestly, 'I really am an elf.'

'Do you know Father Christmas?' He looked terribly serious.

Eleanor nodded. 'Quite well, actually.'

The boy's mother, who was struggling with the Etch A Sketch, suppressed a smile.

'What's he like?' the boy asked.

'Very greedy, but lots of fun.'

'And is it true you live in Lapland?'

'Quite true.'

The boy pursed his lips and thought. 'Which Underground line is it on?'

Eleanor laughed out loud. 'Well,' she began, wondering how she was going to pull this off, 'it's on an invisible line that's somewhere between the Northern and the Metropolitan. It has to be kept hush-hush or everyone would get on it. If you look very hard at a Tube map, you can just make it out.'

'Is that true?'

'Elves aren't allowed to lie. It's one of the conditions of the job.'

'Oh,' said the boy, who looked a little disappointed. 'I told a lie once. Does that mean I can never be an elf?'

'I'm sure Father Christmas could overlook a past mistake. But if you really want to be an elf, don't tell any more lies.'

'I can't get the hang of this,' said the boy's mother, shaking her head. 'Are you really supposed to be able to draw pictures?'

'Yes,' said Eleanor, turning her attention back to the woman. She held up an Etch A Sketch where she'd made a picture of a rather intricate flower. 'It just takes practice.'

'Goodness,' said the woman, peering at it. 'That's impressive. And they are frightfully popular.'

'Very. Everyone seems to want one for Christmas.'

'All right,' said the woman, 'I'll take one.'

Eleanor smiled and handed her a boxed Etch A Sketch. 'You can pay over there by the counter.' She pointed in the direction of a long queue.

Eleanor watched as they made their way towards the counter. She was still feeling the effects of that bottle of wine. She wondered if she could sneak off for a cup of tea. She looked for Mr Machin. He wasn't on the floor.

'Hello, Eleanor.' She knew the voice instantly.

She looked round. 'Charlie,' she said, her heart leaping. 'I ... what are you doing here?'

He held up a boxed Action Man. 'Christmas present for the nephew. I'd be run out of town if I didn't get him one. I'm getting the right thing, aren't I?'

He looked well. His hair had grown out a little which made him look younger and he was wearing a pale blue cashmere scarf, tied into a rough knot, the ends tucked into the top of his navy duffel coat. He looked as safe and uncomplicated as he'd ever done. Eleanor longed to hug him.

'Yes. You're lucky to get one. There've been queues.'

'How are you?' His tone was polite. 'Actually, I knew you were working here ...' His voice trailed off.

Her heart leaped a little. Had he come to find her? 'Currently desperate for a cup of tea,' she said, mustering a smile. She was trying to see if he might warm to her, whether there was any sign of his usual playfulness, but he stood and gave a short nod, the way a police officer might, or a man taking you for a driving test.

'So you haven't gone home?' He glanced down at her elf outfit.

'No. I didn't want to go back to Brill just yet.' She smoothed down her tunic. 'And it's good money. And fun.' She tried another smile.

There was a short pause.

'I haven't seen you,' she offered. She didn't want him to walk away.

'No,' he said, shifting, 'I've been in Henley. Friend's place. I've finished my book.'

Her eyes widened. 'Charlie!' she said, her smile broadening, 'I'm so pleased. Are you happy with it?'

'I think so.' He looked thoughtful. 'I've managed to persuade a literary agent to take me on. He's hopeful it'll find a publisher.'

'That's wonderful.'

'Long way to go yet. Still. It's done.'

Eleanor glanced over Charlie's shoulder and saw Mr Machin staring at her. She picked up an Etch A Sketch and handed it to Charlie. 'Here,' she said, 'hold that. Then I won't get told off. If a man with a big belly comes over, pretend you're thinking of buying it.'

'I should go really,' he said, not taking it from her. 'I only popped in to get this.'

Eleanor felt a surge of panic.

'I've missed you terribly,' she said, staring up at him, her voice urgent. 'I've looked for you every day.'

Charlie said nothing.

'I pushed a note under your door last night.'

He frowned. 'Did you?'

'And I scooped it out this morning with a ruler. I've gone quite mad.'

Charlie's face softened a little. 'Look, Eleanor, I—'

'Is everything all right here?' Mr Machin loomed into view.

'Yes, Mr Machin,' said Eleanor, aware that she was on the verge of tears. 'I was just ...'

Charlie took the Etch A Sketch in her hands and turned to Mr Machin. 'Am I allowed to try it out? Is that all right?'

Mr Machin blinked. 'Yes, of course.' He glanced at his watch. 'I might need you to help out on Meccano this afternoon, Eleanor. I'll let you know.'

Eleanor nodded without speaking.

Charlie watched Mr Machin as he marched off towards a rack of bears. He looked back at Eleanor. Her chin was resting on her chest and her fingers were knitted tightly together. 'Would you like supper tonight, Eleanor? At my flat?'

Eleanor looked up at him, her eyes watery. 'Yes,' she said, her voice little more than a whisper. 'I'd like that more than anything.'

Charlie nodded. 'Shall we say seven? I'll cook.'

She nodded again and wiped at her eyes.

'Don't be sad,' he said, putting a hand on hers.

'I'm not,' she said. 'I'm happy to see you, that's all.'

Charlie glanced over her head and watched as Mr Machin walked off through a large door. He reached into his pocket and pulled out a handkerchief. 'Here,' he said, 'have that. I seem doomed to be forever bumping into you and lending you handkerchiefs.' He smiled down at her and she gave a small laugh.

'It's probably a sign,' she said, taking it from his hand.

He nodded slowly. 'Maybe it is.'

Outside, the elves with their yo-yos called out to people to come in, a Christmas carol was playing through the store, and off to their left a metal monkey was banging a drum.

Suddenly, it felt like Christmas.

Chapter Thirty-eight

Now

There had been a sharp November frost that morning and everything was tinged with silver. She had returned to Brill with the justification that she needed to keep on top of bills and boring bits of post. It was probably no coincidence she'd be doing it on the day she knew Caspar would be there, but whether she was capable of admitting that to herself or not was another matter.

Rachel loved this time of year: waking up and seeing the spiders' webs stitched through the hedgerows. Frost sharpened the eye, highlighted the contours, gave every leaf a moment to shine. Tall thistles, of no consequence as winter set in, now stood proud, ornamental grasses, past their best, were stiff with one last hurrah. Everything had a texture, a shape, a noble relief.

He wasn't with her yet. She had arrived early, got up before Claude was awake, and driven out to beat the morning rush hour. The traffic in Oxford was a nightmare at the best of times, but during the school run it ground to a halt. She stood and looked out at the view. There wasn't a cloud to be seen and the sky had a watery, pale blue hue. Everything looked fresh, as if the slate had been wiped clean.

Rachel wandered up on to the terrace. Agnes was right: the roses looked magnificent, the deep blood red popping out from the frost-covered backdrop. Rachel was amazed they were still going. It must have been the long summer.

Rachel tucked her hands into the sleeves of her jumper. It was colder than she had thought, though not unpleasant: she always enjoyed the sharp crispness of a late autumn day but she should have worn a coat. She stared up, hoping to see some clouds on the horizon, but there were none.

The key was where it always was: hidden inside a false stone near the front door, under an upturned flowerpot that was shoved against the wall, behind a cistus. She never took the key with her. There was something about always leaving it there that felt right. Despite having lived in it all her life, it still didn't feel like her house. It was Eleanor's. It always had been.

She crouched down and tapped the key out. She remembered Eleanor buying the fake stone from a slightly dodgy-looking website. She was thrilled with it. 'Look at that,' she had said, placing it on the kitchen table like a lost artefact. 'Would you ever know that wasn't a stone?'

Rachel had rather sourly pointed out that burglars probably spent most of their time looking for stones that looked precisely like stones. 'They're not idiots,' she had said, feet up on the table, nose in a Sunday paper, 'they've got the internet too.'

It had been Charlie's idea to put it inside a flowerpot, and the three of them had all stood round, trying out different ones to see which was less conspicuous. Plastic looked wrong and the aluminium seemed far too showy, so they chose a chipped terracotta thing that seemed to disappear wherever you put it. 'It does look abandoned,' Charlie had said. 'All the same, let's hide it behind a shrub.' It was simple yet complicated. A security system that still clung to a yesteryear hope that people were inherently honest and good.

Rachel let herself in. The house was cold and carried that unwelcome odour of somewhere forgotten. On that awful day when she'd sat at her mother's bureau, she had wanted to run away, to never come back. The house felt different now, heavy with the absence of her parents. Caspar or no Caspar, she was here reluctantly. She wasn't sure she could change that.

She picked up the heap of bills and letters from the doormat and, walking through to the kitchen, separated out the catalogues for plants, fashion and gadgets and the leaflets for pizzas, window cleaners and taxi services and dropped them all immediately into the empty recycling bin.

Sliding the letters on to the kitchen table, she went through to the sitting room beyond the studio and began getting a fire going. It was a ritual she always enjoyed: cleaning the grate, carrying out the ash, setting a handful of natural firelighters made from wood shavings, then stacking up a three-layered tier of kindling and finally finding the perfect log to sit on top. Charlie had taught her how to do it. She would never do it any differently. He had taught her so many things, she thought. She wondered if he would have bothered if he'd known she wasn't his.

The log basket was empty, so she pushed herself up from her knees and opened the door out from the studio into the garden. The log pile was behind the shed and as she walked towards it she could hear a bird singing. It was the same call she'd heard when she had sat in the garden with Caspar. It must be the robin. She stopped and looked for where it might be. The low sun was bright, and she raised a hand to her forehead in order to see better. 'Where are you?' she muttered. She walked on, towards the shed, the sound getting louder. She stopped, her hand resting on the door, and listened. She frowned. The noise was coming from inside.

Rachel released the latch and slowly and carefully opened the door. She looked in. She couldn't remember the last time she'd been inside it. When she was little? The inside of the shed had a sense of ramshackle splendour: tools were hung neatly on hooks on the walls; shelves towards the back were dotted with gloves, weedkillers, pond cleaner, slug pellets. An old battered chest of drawers sat to the right. It was rammed with bulbs and seed packets. From the ceiling hung a length of wound rope, some upturned bunches of cut lavender, and the cord for the lawnmower, which sat in the far corner, its front covered in a moss-like mess of old grass cuttings. There was a smell of wood and peat and a faint suggestion of something oily. It was an honest, straightforward no-nonsense shed, and at the very back, sitting on top of a large bucket of birdseed, was the robin.

'Hello,' said Rachel.

The bird let out a shrill chirrup and flew up into the corner of the shed, where it perched.

'How long have you been in here?' It stared down at her. 'Come on, come out. You don't live in here. Come out, out you come.' She stood back and opened the door wide and the bird, seeing its opportunity, flew past her and settled on a post a few feet away.

Rachel stared at the robin, which was showing no signs of flying off, and thought about Caspar's appealing fable that these birds were the dead come back to keep an eye on us. She found herself longing for it to be true. Which of her parents might this robin be? Which did she want it to be?

'Eleanor?' she said, holding her hand out. 'Is that you?'

The robin flew off and Rachel stood there, her arm still extended, and watched it fly away over the trees. Her hand fell to her side. She felt sad suddenly, a little foolish. She closed the shed door and went to the woodpile. There was an upturned wheelbarrow next to it and, pulling it upright, she tugged her sleeves over her hands so as not to get splinters and threw logs into it.

Rachel pushed the logs up to the house and carried them in. There were some long matchsticks in a miniature coal scuttle at the side of the hearth and, taking one, she struck it and held it to the tightly rolled wood shavings. A thin plume of smoke began to swirl and Rachel sat back and watched. She loved the smell, the sound of the wood as it burned. It felt comforting and calming.

She hadn't had breakfast. She'd leave the fire to take hold and walk to the village bakery to pick up some bread. She pushed herself up and went back to the hallway and, passing the coat rack, reached up and grasped a blue gilet from one of the hooks. It had been Eleanor's, and as she pulled it on she noticed the faint smell of her mother's hand cream. It caught her unawares. The coats in the hall were always intended to be communal: big, functional, waterproof, warm. They were still here – Charlie and Eleanor – hanging on hooks, waiting to be useful. She stared up at Charlie's old Barbour and reached out to take the sleeve, as if there might be an echo of him to hold on to, too. At least he had never known. It was her only comfort.

She still wasn't sure whether she wanted to revisit her search for the truth. As to whether she could forget about working out who her biological father might be, that was another matter.

She walked out from the house and turned her mind to her other predicament. Claude was getting on her nerves.

She tried to remember if he'd got on her nerves before, but her memories were clouded. Besides, she wasn't sure she had been capable of being honest with herself back then. There is an energy to a wedding: once you've declared it's happening, the race is on. It's like an enormous whirlpool: round and round you go, in ever-decreasing circles. Everyone expects.

Eleanor would not approve, Rachel knew that. She'd have packed Claude off with a flea in his ear, whatever his story. She was not an abrupt woman generally, far from it. If anything she was too restrained, too mindful of other people's feelings, but in certain situations she had a capacity for brutal honesty that Rachel had never been able to embrace. What would Charlie have said to her? Nothing, directly. It had never been his style. He'd have taken her for a drive, walked her around a museum, avoided the subject and then, at the very end, asked her if she was happy.

She knew she wasn't.

The bakery was busy, but to Rachel's relief they had croissants. She bought four. Two for her and two for Caspar. She felt nervous about seeing him and, as she walked back to the house, she hoped she'd see his battered green van sitting on the driveway. It wasn't there. She looked at her watch. It was still early.

Back in the kitchen, she turned on the radio and pulled a plate out from a cupboard. The croissants were still warm, and after making herself a coffee she sat and devoured one. A programme was on about people who think they're in the wrong jobs and she sat, idly listening, one eye on the clock, picking at the second croissant thoughtlessly.

Restless, she stood up and walked through to the studio. It was exactly as she had left it all those months ago, she thought, staring at the blank canvas she had set up. The button, the mysterious one she hadn't been able to place, still sat on the plinth. She picked it up and rolled it in her palm, wiping away the dust with her finger. She felt a pang of regret that she'd given up on getting to the bottom of it. She never did go looking for John Farson. Was he her father? She picked up the small piece of embroidered cotton and wrapped the button back up. She'd return it to her mother's box.

Rachel wandered through to the sitting room, threw another log on the fire and, kicking off her shoes, curled herself into the sofa opposite. She needed something: clarity, certainty, the absence of doubt. Had she given up on ever finding it? She didn't know.

The warmth from the fire began to fill the room. Rachel yawned and turned her face into the cushion behind her. She reached up and pulled down the blanket that was folded across the top of the sofa, wrapped herself into it and shut her eyes.

'Hello.'

Rachel sat up with a start. Caspar was standing there, hands on hips, in the doorway. He was wearing a dark blue sailor's roll-neck, a hole worn at the elbow. Underneath she could just see the cream colour of an old T-shirt. His trousers were a workman's navy cotton, a little baggy, tied at the waist with a brown leather belt. He'd taken his boots off. His feet were large, his socks tinged with mud. He walked into the room and threw a couple of logs on to the fire. 'I wouldn't have woken you but I could see the fire was going out. You all right?'

'Yes.' Rachel ran a hand through her hair and looked at her watch. 'God,' she said. 'I just dozed off. How long have you been here?'

'About an hour.'

'I bought croissants.' Rachel pushed the blanket to one side and swung her legs to the floor. 'There are two for you. If you want them?'

'I brought bacon butties with me. But thanks.'

'You don't have to eat them. The croissants, I mean. I just thought I'd . . .' Her voice petered out. Caspar unnerved her. She wished he didn't.

Caspar took the poker and shoved one of the logs into the glowing embers. 'There you go,' he said, hanging the poker back in place. 'That should do it.' He turned and glanced down at his socks. 'I took my boots off. Didn't think you'd want mud all through the sitting room.'

'I don't mind.'

'But I do.'

Rachel looked up at him. She was so happy to see him. She wanted to tell him, to leap up and hug him, but she couldn't.

'I saw Agnes,' Caspar added, his hands slipping into his trouser pockets.

'She told me.'

'Did she tell you I'm leaving?'

'Yes,' Rachel said, watching his face, 'she did. We'll be very sorry to see you go.' She corrected herself. '*I'll* be very sorry to you go. You've done such a fantastic job.'

Caspar gave a small nod. 'I think I've got the garden to where your mum and dad wanted it. It's just maintenance now. It won't be difficult.'

'I don't know anything about gardening,' said Rachel, 'I'm hopeless.'

'No, you're not.'

'Agnes said you're going travelling.'

'That's the plan,' he said. 'Not sure where yet. Don't fancy India or Thailand. I'll feel like a granddad. I think I might go to Scandinavia. See the Northern Lights. I've always wanted to do that.'

'Oh, wow.'

'There are some amazing rail journeys there, up into Lapland. Huskies. The lot.'

'I'm jealous.'

'Or go to New Zealand. I've never been.'

'Apparently it's beautiful. You might not come back.'

'No, I might not.'

Rachel felt a tightness in her chest.

'I'm glad I've seen you,' he began.

Rachel's heart leaped a little. 'I'm glad I've seen you too.' Her voice was soft, hopeful. 'I haven't been here in a while. I think I needed a rest from all the clearing out. It was getting a bit much. I was becoming obsessive ...' Her voice trailed off.

'Ah,' said Caspar, holding up a finger. 'The thing is, I found something. Something that was your mum's.'

Her heart sank. He didn't mean it the way she meant it.

'It was in the shed, in one of the bulb drawers. She must have been in there on the day she died. I only found it a few days back. Hang on. I'll get my boots on.'

As he walked to the studio, Rachel pushed herself up from the sofa. She slipped her feet into her shoes and followed him out. He was standing by the door into the garden, one hand resting on the door frame, the other pulling on a boot. She stood just behind him, waiting. He didn't bother doing up the laces. He looked at her over his shoulder. 'It's still in the shed. I don't like to let myself into the house when no one's here or I'd have left it on a table.' He moved off and she followed him, neither of them speaking.

'I found a robin in there earlier,' she said, walking just behind him. 'It was trapped in the shed.'

'He's always in there. And don't worry,' said Caspar, his boots crunching white footsteps across the grass, 'he's not trapped. I cut a hole out above the door.' He pointed to it as they approached the shed. 'Now he can come and go. It's his shed really. I'm only borrowing it.'

Rachel stood and looked up at the little square hole. She hadn't noticed it before.

Caspar opened the door and reached into an old oak box. 'Here it is,' he said. 'I haven't read it or anything. That wouldn't have been right.' He pulled out a leather-bound book, about the size of a paperback, and held it out.

Rachel took it and opened it randomly. 'Oh my goodness,' she said, staring down at the pages. 'It's her last diary. I've looked everywhere for this.' She flicked through it until she found empty pages, then flicked back to the last day Eleanor had written in it.

I shall talk to Rachel. Tell her everything. Now that Charlie's gone, it's time.

There was more below it. Perhaps this was it. The answer to Rachel's final question. Her hands began to shake. She couldn't do this now, not in front of Caspar.

Rachel closed it and looked up at Caspar. 'I'll read it properly later,' she said, her voice trembling.

'I thought you should have it,' Caspar said, 'you're her daughter.'

'Yes,' Rachel replied. 'I am.'

I shall talk to Rachel. Tell her everything.

Rachel stared down at the last diary of her mother.

She had to face her demons. It was time to find out the truth.

PART FIVE

*'It takes courage to grow up and become
who you really are.'*

E. E. Cummings

Chapter Thirty-nine

Then

1965

Eleanor's wedding dress hung from the top of the wardrobe door. On the bed was a large pile of post. Agnes pounced on it.

'There's so many of them!' Agnes's face was alight with excitement. 'Cards, letters, even telegrams. Can I open them? Please, Eleanor? Can I open them all?'

Eleanor sat at the dressing table, leaning in towards the mirror as she attached a false eyelash. She was in a thin silk dressing gown and her hair was up, arranged into a complex plaited knot held together with a floral pin.

'All right,' she said, not blinking, 'do the cards first. You can read them out to me.'

'Oh, super,' said Agnes, throwing herself on to the bed. She pursed her lips as her finger hovered over the cards. 'This one,' she said, picking a cream embossed envelope. 'Let's start with this one.' She opened it. 'Lovely stationery,' she offered. 'Super expensive, I imagine. I do like it when someone has proper envelopes, don't you?'

Eleanor glanced at her sister in the mirror. 'You're such a peculiar child, Agnes. Most teenage girls are into film stars or screaming at pop stars. You like envelopes.'

'And trombones,' said Agnes, sliding her finger under the lip of the envelope. 'I really like trombones. I wish Mummy would let me have one.'

'I imagine Daddy doesn't want the infernal racket. Trombone? What's wrong with learning to play the piano?'

'I think my skills lie in blowing,' she replied idly. 'Oh, this one's from that lady who lent you her flat.'

'Marjory?'

'Yes. "Darling Eleanor, I can't tell you how thrilled I am to be able to congratulate you on your wedding day. And to think I may have had some tiny hand in it! I am sure you will have a lifetime of happiness together. So sorry we can't be there. Please give my best love to your mother. And, of course, love to Charlie." That's nice, isn't it? Super card too. Look at that. Isn't it pretty?' She wafted the front of the card into the air so Eleanor could look at its reflection. 'Just think, you'd have never met Charlie if it hadn't been for Marjory. That's mad, isn't it?'

'No, I don't suppose I would.' Eleanor twisted round. 'Can you find me a box of tissues? I've used too much lash glue.'

Agnes threw herself off the bed and ran out from Eleanor's bedroom.

'Are you ready, Agnes?' Her mother's voice called up the stairs.

'Yes!' Agnes shouted down. 'I'm just getting tissues for Eleanor.'

'You are not ready, Agnes, because your shoes are down here and you are up there.'

'I don't need them yet. I'll put them on when we come down.'

'Tell Eleanor she's got ten minutes. And the car is here.'

Agnes ran into the bathroom, opened a cabinet, pulled out a box of tissues and ran back. She stopped at the top of the banisters and leaned over. Her mother was standing in the hallway, hat and gloves on, checking she had her essentials in her handbag. 'Can I go in the car with Eleanor and Daddy?'

Her mother looked up at her. 'No, Agnes, you absolutely cannot.'

Agnes curled her lip and went back into Eleanor's room. 'Here,' she said, putting the tissues on the dressing table. 'Mummy says the car's here. You've got ten minutes.'

'I heard.' Eleanor pulled a tissue from the box and dabbed at her eyelid.

Agnes threw herself back on the bed. 'Shall I read another letter?'

'Yes. Why not?'

Agnes fingered through the small pile. There was a blue envelope with an exotic stamp. 'This one's from abroad,' she said. 'Who can that be from?'

'Which country?' said Eleanor, standing up.

'How can I tell?'

'What does the stamp say?' She walked over towards her dress, hanging from the top of the wardrobe.

'Not sure,' said Agnes, peering at it. 'Are you putting your dress on?'

'Yes, do you want to help me?'

Agnes threw down the envelope and pushed herself off the bed again. Eleanor slipped out of her dressing gown to reveal a brand-new lingerie set.

'Blimey,' said Agnes. 'You look top-notch.'

'Rigby and Peller,' said Eleanor. 'Cost an arm and a leg. Worth it though. Can you do me up at the back?'

Taking the dress carefully from its hanger, Eleanor stepped into it. It had an ivory empire-line bodice and angel-bell sleeves. Her mother had made it using a *Vogue* dress pattern and had assured Eleanor that the new figure-skimming skirt was all the rage.

Agnes did up the zip at the back. 'Do you need help with the veil?'

'No,' said Eleanor, picking it up. 'It just pins in. It's on a hairband. Read me that letter. I'm starting to feel nervous. It'll calm me down.'

'Are you?' Agnes's eyes widened. 'Are you rigid with nerves? Are you terrified about tonight?'

'What do you mean, "tonight"?' Eleanor frowned.

'You know!' said Agnes. 'Wedding night!'

'Oh, Agnes,' said Eleanor, leaning back towards the mirror and pinning in the veil. 'We've done it lots of times. I certainly don't feel nervous about that.'

'I'm shocked to my core,' said Agnes flatly, throwing herself back on the bed. 'Ooh! When the vicar says the "does anyone know" bit, I really ought to stand up and shout "Yes! I know! I'm afraid they cannot get married because they've done it. Loads of times. Like rabbits!"'

'You most certainly will not.'

'I think it might be my religious duty, Eleanor.' She picked up the blue envelope.

'Agnes, you haven't got a religious bone in your body.'

'That's not true. If we were Catholic, I could probably be a nun. Morocco,' she said, peering at the postmark. 'The stamp's a man who looks terribly dull and the postmark says Morocco.'

Eleanor stopped what she was doing and turned to stare at her little sister.

'Who do you know in Morocco? It's got something in it too.' Agnes gave the envelope a squeeze.

'Give it to me.' Eleanor held out her hand.

'You said I could read them.' Agnes gave a pout.

'Agnes!' A call came from downstairs.

'To me, please.'

Agnes held it up and Eleanor took it in both hands. She stared down at it, her heart racing. It was his handwriting. She hadn't heard from him in nearly a year, not since he had left. She ran her fingers over the writing – confident, bright blue ink – then turned the envelope over. 'No return address,' she murmured.

'Who's it from?' asked Agnes, getting on to her knees. 'Come on, open it!'

'Agnes!' The voice was more insistent.

'Ugh,' said Agnes with a huff. 'Don't open anything unless I'm in the room.' She ran towards the hallway. 'COMING!'

Eleanor slid her finger into the corner of the envelope. Inside there was a card, a little larger than a calling card, and a tiny parcel. She looked at the card.

> Heard you were taking the plunge. Thought you might like something old. *J.*

Eleanor dropped the card on to the bed and turned her attention to the tiny parcel. It was wrapped in exquisite paper and tied with a little red ribbon. She undid it. Her heart was beating faster.

Eleanor stared down at the piece of beautifully embroidered cotton in her hand. *'My love, my love,'* she whispered. There was something inside it: a gorgeous, hand-painted button. For a moment, Eleanor couldn't place it, and then she remembered.

'Oh my,' she said, sitting down on the edge of the bed, her eyes filling with tears. 'He's alive.'

Chapter Forty

Now

'I heard you're getting married again,' Caspar said, gathering his things. The sun was starting to go down. 'Offer still stands.'

'What offer?'

'To make your bouquet.' He looked directly at her.

Rachel, momentarily disarmed, gathered herself and shook her head. 'No. Thank you, but no. I don't think it's going to be a bells-and-whistles wedding, to be honest. Not after last time.' She leaned against the old Victorian radiator on the wall, her hands behind her, and tilted her head. 'Can you believe I'm even doing this?'

'I'm not sure how to answer that.'

'Answer it honestly. Would you? Please?'

'Then no. I'm not sure I can believe it. You must be a very special person to be able to forgive him.'

'I'm not sure I have, in all honesty.'

Caspar stood, coat in hand. 'If I knew you better I'd have a lot to say.' His voice was quiet and calm. 'And if I knew him better, I'd have even more to say. But I don't. And it wouldn't be right of me to stick my oar in. It wouldn't be right. Not all opinions are helpful.'

'I don't know.' Rachel's head fell down. 'Maybe I'm looking for excuses. I've made my choice. And there it is.'

'You're allowed to be happy, Rachel.' Caspar pulled his coat on.

'Ignore me,' she said, trying to be breezy. 'I'll be fine. And I'm keeping you from the rest of your day.'

She held out her hand. 'Thank you. Thank you for everything you've done. My parents adored you.'

Caspar took her hand in his, leaned towards her and kissed her on the cheek. He smelled of grass and wood and smoke.

'I adored them too.' He smiled down at her.

Rachel nodded. She wasn't sure what else to say. She wanted to tell him about Charlie, about what she'd found out, but something prevented her.

'Well. That's that.' He stood back and pulled some battered gloves from his pocket. 'I've still got a few bits and bobs to sort out before I'm done, but I might not see you again. I hope, whatever you choose to do, you're happy.'

Caspar turned and Rachel stood there, the darkness deepening behind her, unable to say or do anything to stop him.

She'd poured herself a large glass of red wine and put a record on. Charlie had been a great fan of vinyl, his taste widespread and eclectic, his collection a library of riches to satisfy any mood. She'd chosen a classic – *Dusty in Memphis* – and she sat staring into the fire, the glorious understatement of Dusty's vocals the perfect mix of vulnerability and desire. Her mother's diary, the one Caspar had found in the shed, was on the coffee table, staring up at her. She wasn't happy. She had to admit it. People who are about to get married don't ask acquaintances they barely know whether or not they're doing the right thing. You only ask for other people's advice when you know the answer you want to hear. She needed permission to not marry Claude and she knew it.

'What a mess,' she muttered.

She took a large gulp from her glass and picked up the diary. She took a deep breath and turned to the final page.

> I shall talk to Rachel. Tell her everything. Now that Charlie's gone, it's time.

She read on.

> As for J, I haven't seen him in so long. It feels like a lifetime ago. Another thing I gave up. Was it worth it?

Then, infuriatingly, a short shopping list, a phone number and that was it. Her last entry.

Rachel lingered on the final clues.

J, again.

Rachel stopped and stared up at the painting above the fireplace. It was of Eleanor, a sweetly drawn pencil portrait that Charlie had always adored. She was reading a book, head tilted to one side. As she looked up at it, it suddenly occurred to her she had no idea who had drawn it. She frowned. Putting down the diary, she pushed herself up from the sofa and pulled a leather pouffe in front of the fire. Standing on it, she reached up and carefully took it down. She peered at the canvas corners. There was no signature, so she turned it over.

'Oh my God.'

On the back of the painting, drawn on to a piece of brown paper, was the exact same crest that was on the button she'd found, along with an inscription.

For Eleanor. With all my love. J.

Rachel flipped the painting back and looked at it again. 'Is this your doing, John Farson? Did you commission this? Did you draw it?'

Whoever had drawn it had clearly loved her.

Her phone rang. She leaned the picture against the side of the sofa and reached into her pocket. It was Claude.

'Great news,' he began. 'I've got a buyer for Brill.'

'It's not on the market.'

'No, I know, but trust me, it's perfect. Cash buyer too. No chain.'

'Claude,' said Rachel, 'it's not on the market. Why are you trying to sell my family home?'

'I'm not,' Claude protested, 'I'm having supper in Summertown. Couple of buyers. One of them is looking for somewhere near Oxford. I just happened to mention it.'

'Just happened to mention it?'

'Sure,' said Claude. 'It's not a big deal. It came up in conversation, that's all.'

'Right.'

'I said I'd ask if she could come and have a look.'

'You did what?'

'Rachel, I'm not trying to be difficult. I'm just telling you about a conversation. That's all it was. A conversation. I said it might be a while before it came on. That's it. I thought you'd be pleased.'

'I'd be pleased or you'd be pleased?'

There was a short pause.

'What's wrong? Have I done something wrong?' His tone was conciliatory. Claude was brilliant at arguing. Always had been. Rachel knew she was terrible at it: nought to a hundred in under ten seconds, shouting, crying, the works, but Claude was a master at it. He knew how to throw the bomb then retreat, arms aloft, *what did I do, this is all on you, I'm trying to be reasonable here.* She resented it. He did it every single time.

'Actually, Claude,' she began, bristling, 'yes, you have done something wrong. Brill is nothing to do with you. It belongs to me. I'll decide what we do with it.'

'I know that. Sorry. I thought I was being helpful. It's fine. I'll tell her she can't see it.' He paused again. 'It's going to be pretty embarrassing. She's a good client. But OK.'

Rachel chewed at her cheek. How dare he accuse her of embarrassing him. She tried to keep her cool. 'Don't do this again, Claude.'

'OK, OK. I'm sorry.'

'Who is she?'

'A client. From the gallery.'

'Who?'

'I'm not sure you've met her. She bought a few pieces when you and I weren't . . .' He moved on. 'She was a venture capitalist. Retired when she was thirty-five.'

'Lucky for some. What's her name?'

Claude hesitated. 'Does it matter?'

'What's her name?'

'Kate. Kate Monroe.'

'Well, she can't come to Brill.'

'I know. I heard you. Look, I shouldn't have mentioned it. I'm sorry. I have to go back. The starters have arrived. I'll call you later.'

Rachel stared down at her phone and opened Safari. *Kate Monroe. Venture capitalist*, she typed in and pressed Return. Images. She was attractive, sleek, had expensive hair, clothes, she knew how to stand, arms folded, powerful. She knows she can have whatever she wants. Relaxed in her own skin. Filthy rich.

'No,' said Rachel, expanding the picture of her with two fingers. She looked exactly like the sort of person who would knock the cottage to the ground and replace it with a glass-and-burnished-metal box on stilts. 'No. You don't get to live here.'

She tucked her phone back into her pocket and looked again at the picture. This was John Farson's work, she was sure of it. She reached back through the tangle of weeds in her mind. There had been another note in a pile of letters she'd gone through, months ago, way before she had started to piece things together. They were all in a box in the studio.

She ran in, adrenaline suddenly pumping, and, grabbing the box, brought it back to the sitting room and threw the contents on to the floor. She had a vague idea of what she was looking for. A rather smart envelope, fancy writing. Back then, it had seemed nothing, just another invite, but now ...

'Got you.'

She turned the envelope over in her hand and lifted the back lip. It was lined with a deep red tissue. There was a notelet inside, thick, heavy, and she pulled it out and read.

> I find myself back in London. Don't ask. Might you care
> to meet me for supper? A last AGM, if you will? It would
> be delicious to see you. And I have news. Of course I do.
> You won't come unless I tempt you. Next Wednesday? 8
> p.m.? Find me at the usual spot. J.

She turned the envelope back to its front and looked at the postmark.

4 June 1980. Nine months before she was born.

'Well, that settles it,' she said, pulling her phone back out from her pocket. 'I think it's time I met Mr John Farson.'

Chapter Forty-one

Then

11 June 1980, 12.35 p.m.

Eleanor stared down at her watch.

She'd fobbed Charlie off with some tale about an old girls' reunion. She wasn't sure why she'd lied to him. All the same, she had. They had not been getting on: Eleanor wanted a baby. So did Charlie, but fifteen years of trying was taking its toll, the gap in their lives sinking deeper and wider. Some couples are able to survive the lack of children. Eleanor was not entirely sure she could. She was thirty-four. She still had a chance. If she was going to jump, the cliff edge was approaching and she had a plan. She knew exactly where he'd be.

Soho was changing. It had gone through something of an identity crisis in the seventies: the secret enclave of artists and writers had been turned, with the help of a corrupt police force, into a proliferation of sex shops, peep shows and massage parlours, but the backlash had begun. Eleanor walked down Berwick Street, past the red-light striptease joints and girls leaning in doorways.

The French, despite the commercialisation of the streets around it, had managed, against all the odds, to retain its reputation as a sanctuary for the interesting. Eleanor couldn't remember the last time she'd been in.

But needs must, and she was here again.

It was unseasonably hot and Eleanor was dressed accordingly: billowing white cotton shirt gathered into a knot just over her midriff, a pair of bright blue Bermuda shorts and a pair of navy deck-shoes. She looked at ease, confident in her own skin, ready. She walked across Wardour Street and took the thin side street towards Dean Street. She didn't feel nervous. She knew what she wanted.

It was lunchtime and, given the weather, the doors of the French were wide open, people spilling on to the pavement, pints in hand. Eleanor pushed her way past a knot of animated young men discussing politics. She looked over at the bar. He was at the far end, leaning against the wall, an early edition of the *Evening Standard* sitting on the counter in front of him, a glass of Scotch in hand. She had been right to assume he'd be here. He was in the same spot as he always had been. Nothing had changed. She walked towards him.

'Hello, John.'

He looked up, expecting nothing, but, on seeing her, his face broadened into a wicked smile. He was ageing well: he looked a little leaner, his jaw more chiselled. 'Well, well,' he said, taking her in. 'Persephone is back from the Underworld. Took your time, didn't you? What's it been? Five years? More?'

'Longer, I think,' she leaned in to kiss him on the cheek. 'How are you?'

He tapped out a cigarette and threw it on to his bottom lip. 'Not too shabby,' he said. 'Can I get you a drink?'

'Please. White wine.'

He gestured towards the barman, then turned back to take her in. 'You're looking good. Very good.'

'Country air,' she said, leaning against the counter. 'Turns out it's disgustingly healthy.'

'Sounds awful,' then, seeing the barman approach, 'Large white wine, please. And I'll have another one of those.' He stabbed towards his own glass. 'I heard you had a rather successful exhibition. Congratulations.'

'Thank you. Right gallery. Right buyers. Right time. I'm very lucky. Sorry. I should have let you know. Should have invited you along.'

'Not my scene,' said John, lighting his cigarette. 'The booze is always awful. And then I get trapped in corners with bored housewives from Mayfair who pretend they need advice on how to spend their husband's money.' He raised an eyebrow.

'It's not like you to turn down a damsel in distress.'

'Who said I turned them down?'

Eleanor gave him a wry smile. 'How are you, John? Really?'

He gave a shrug and narrowed his eyes at her. 'You haven't got a drink in your hand yet. Steady on.' He took one of her hands and held it out, his eyes scanning her body. 'Seriously. You look fantastic.'

'Want me to put it on the tab?' The barman placed two glasses on the counter between them.

John nodded. 'Please. Thanks, mate.' He looked back at Eleanor, a small frown dancing across his face. 'Are you hungry? Do you want some crisps?'

Eleanor laughed. 'I didn't know they did crisps in the French.'

His mouth curled up at one side, his eyes light and mischievous. 'They didn't. About six months ago, Francis

Bacon was in, went absolutely mental and demanded salty snacks. We had a show of hands. Everyone thought peanuts were beyond the pale. Pork scratchings were too much like hard work. So they got crisps. And do you know what? I've never seen a single fucker buy a packet.'

Eleanor laughed and shot him a suspicious look. 'Wait. Is this an ongoing thing? See if you can get someone to buy a packet of crisps?'

John took a long drag and blew a thin length of smoke out from the corner of his mouth.

'Yeah, all right,' he said, putting his hands up. 'There's a sweepstake behind the bar. Don't get excited. It's only twenty quid.'

'I'll have a bag of ready salted.'

John shook his head. 'Too late. You are now in possession of dark and terrible knowledge. Crisps are off the table.' He took a deep sip of his Scotch.

She looked at him. He still had that roguish charm she'd always found so appealing. He was wearing a white T-shirt, his arms brown and muscular, his long legs in tight black jeans. He looked in shape, relaxed, sexy.

'Still married, then?' he said, his eyes flitting to her wedding ring.

She held her hand up, turning the back of it towards him. 'Fifteen years. Where do the years go?'

'Kids?'

'No. Not yet.' She shook her head and reached for her glass.

'Want them?'

'Yes, I do. Very much.'

He gave a sniff. 'I'm not certain I ever did. Mind you,' he added, 'I'm not entirely sure I haven't already got some.' He looked up at the ceiling, wondering about that. 'Someone would have told me. Or maybe they wouldn't?' He turned and gave Eleanor a warm smile. 'I'm really pleased to see you. It's been too long.'

'I'm pleased to see you too.' It felt strange, being back in a world that seemed to have stood still. Her life was so different now, so removed from the intricate ins and outs of the Soho scene. She had escaped it, before it did her harm, and now here she was, back for nourishment.

They looked at each other, a moment of quiet and mutual acknowledgement.

'You haven't answered my question,' Eleanor said, breaking the silence. 'I want to know how you are.'

He flicked some ash into an empty can in front of him and cleared his throat. 'Same old game. Hand-to-mouth commissions. Drifting through life. 'Twas ever thus.' He sucked on the end of his cigarette, the smoke swirling over his ear. 'Know the problem with me, Eleanor? I've never had ambition. I think we have to conclude that I'm a bit of a lazy bastard.'

'I don't think that's true,' said Eleanor, watching him. 'I think you are ambitious. Artists who say they're not ambitious are simply afraid they won't be successful.'

'Hmm,' said John, smiling knowingly. 'And there it is. You have an uncanny knack of nailing things on the head. Have you heard about Hen?' He wanted to change the subject.

Eleanor shook her head. 'No. Nothing bad, I hope?'

'Hen doesn't do bad. Hen does catastrophes she can turn into anecdotes.'

Eleanor smiled. 'True.'

'She's bought a caravan and has gone off to live on a farm somewhere. But it's not like a caravan your gran would have taken on holiday to Hastings. It's pulled by a bloody horse.'

'What?'

'I know. She rang me three weeks ago. She was having to wash in a bucket.' He took another drag of his cigarette. 'It can't last. I think she's picked up some romantic notion that she might be a nomad, wandering about like a fucking medieval *Shepherd's Play*. I mean, come on. Unless she can find a brook that's flowing with champagne, I can't see her lasting. She'll be back. Soho is the oasis to which she must always return.' He gave the statement some gravitas.

'Like us all.'

'Well,' said John, with a smile, 'we've all got to drink.'

'Shame. I was rather hoping to see her,' said Eleanor. 'I've missed her ... energy.'

'Energy? How diplomatic of you.'

'You two should have got married. I don't understand why you never did?'

'Really?' John sounded surprised. 'You want one woman to have to endure me for the rest of her life? I thought you liked Hen? Did you hear about her old man?'

'Yes. Awful.' Hen had been married, very briefly, to a theatre producer thirty years her senior. She'd sent Eleanor a card after the event. He'd died of a heart attack, dropped dead at the tail end of a press night. It had been in all the papers.

John shook his head. 'Terrible. I'm so glad I wasn't there. What do you do? Give them a chest pump? Kiss of life? Let them go, I say. I've never known a man come back who wasn't diminished. Live life to the full. No fun being a shadow of your former self.'

'If I didn't know you better, I'd say you've become rather fatalistic, John.'

'Always was. You really are looking exceptionally fine, Eleanor.' He leaned back and looked at her. 'I hope you don't mind me telling you.'

'I don't mind at all.'

'I always think marriage takes a woman's sparkle away. Not you. Looks like you're on top.' His eyes danced over her again and Eleanor watched him as he did it. He wanted to flirt with her. She could feel it.

'What are you doing in town?' He picked up the dropped conversation.

Eleanor straightened. 'I've come to see Jake.'

'Jake's in London?' John leaned back. He looked a little hurt. 'How long's he been back?'

'I don't know. I'm seeing him later.'

'Can I tag along?'

'No, you can't.'

John let a small smile play on his lips. 'Fair enough. I shall have to be happy with my role as the warm-up act.' He placed a hand over his heart and pulled a face of mock pain.

'I came to find you, too. You're exactly where I thought you might be. Do you know, in all the years I've known you, I've never had your telephone number?'

'No point. I haven't got one. I'm touched. You can carry on trying to make me feel better if you like. I won't mind a bit.' He raised an eyebrow.

Eleanor moved a little closer. She could just smell the soap on his hands, a hint of something carbolic drifting through the thick scent of the cigarette. It was hard not to be cast back to that night in the snow, all those years ago.

'I got into terrible trouble because of you, many, many years ago.' Eleanor let her fingers edge towards his. 'I made a mistake.'

John eyed Eleanor's fingers then stared at her. 'I remember it.'

'So do I.'

Their eyes locked and a moment of understanding passed between them.

Oh,' he said, penny dropping. 'Is this going where I hope it's going?'

Eleanor stood a little taller. She felt confident, undeterred, determined. 'Yes,' she said, her eyes not flinching. 'It is.'

'Are you sure?'

'Yes,' replied Eleanor, her voice clear and certain. 'I am.'

John drained his drink and pulled his wallet from his back pocket. He took out a ten-pound note and slipped it under his empty glass.

'Come on then,' he said, nodding towards the door. 'You'll remember the way.'

Chapter Forty-two

11 June 1980, 7.55 p.m.

Eleanor stared up at the blue plaque on the wall. She had such memories of the house in Hampstead: the wild parties, the laughter, the giddy, heady love she didn't know what to do with. Jake's parents had moved to Italy permanently but Jake had kept the house on, a base in London for whenever he might need it. She felt overwhelmed, fizzing with excitement. It would be the first time she had seen him since that awful encounter in Chelsea sixteen years ago.

She had left John in bed, the afternoon of uncomplicated sex a throwback to a different time, a different Eleanor. Back then, Eleanor had been young, hungry to shake off her inexperience. Now she was in control, the balance between them had shifted. It had given her energy but, more than that, it had given her hope. She had made a terrible mistake all those years ago. She wouldn't make it again. This time, she wouldn't tell Charlie.

The front door opened. They both stood there for a moment, beaming at each other. Was this really happening? After all this time?

'I saw you coming up the road,' Jake said, standing in the doorway, legs slightly apart, one arm holding the door away from him. 'I stood upstairs and watched for you. Not that I'm over-excited or anything.'

Eleanor felt her smile broaden.

'Spit spot,' he added, gesturing inside with his head. 'Or *all* the neighbours will be gossiping.'

She climbed the steps towards him. 'I feel like the Cheshire Cat,' she said.

'No disappearing, thank you. What *are* you wearing?' he said, looking at her shorts.

'Bermuda shorts,' she replied, casting a look down. 'They're very fashionable, Jake.'

'Are you sure? You look as if you might be delivering mail.' His tone was light and playful, and just like that they were whisked back across the years.

He stepped to one side and she walked past him into the hallway, then turned and looked at him properly. He was still impossibly handsome, a little gaunt but not enough to dull his edge. He was wearing a white linen shirt, fashionably louche, and a pair of cream cotton trousers. He looked like an Englishman abroad, an eternal traveller of hot lands, as dazzling as ever. She felt overjoyed, bursting with love.

'Well, come here then,' he said, opening his arms. 'I've waited sixteen years for this.'

She threw herself into him, her cheek against his, and he cradled her into him, pulling her tighter in. He was pleased to see her. She felt delighted.

'I was worried you weren't really that keen to see me,' she murmured, not wanting the hug to end.

'Don't be ridiculous,' he said, not wanting to let her go. 'You're still my favourite person in the world. You always will be.'

They leaned back and looked at each other, their eyes sparkling, their smiles wide and unfettered.

'Do you think we should feel a little embarrassed?' he asked, with a small, probing tease. 'About our last encounter?'

'Well,' said Eleanor, raising an eyebrow, 'you were a filthy gay on the run. I should have made a citizen's arrest ...'

They both laughed.

'Come on. Let's go in. You're here. At last. Let's have a drink to celebrate. Gin and tonic? Martini?'

'Whatever you're making.' She looked around the hallway. The walls were covered with different paintings: a Hockney, an Andy Warhol. He'd redecorated. It felt modern, relevant. 'So is this yours now? Your parents are still alive, right?'

'Yes. Clinging on like barnacles. They're still in Italy. Never come here. I'm mostly based in California but it's been nice to have a base back in the old country.' He smiled. He seemed relaxed, happy. 'And now it's not illegal to be gay, my father relented, let me have the place. I rather think he enjoys having a poof for a son. It makes him infinitely more interesting. I even visit them occasionally. We pretend to get on for a week and then we go back to our own little lives. It's not that intolerable.'

She followed him to the sitting room. He bounced to a drinks cabinet and pulled out a silver cocktail shaker. 'Seeing as we're celebrating, I'll make martinis.' He opened an ice bucket and scooped a handful of cubes into the shaker.

'Are we? Celebrating?' Eleanor pulled the strap of her handbag over her head and let it fall to the floor.

'But of course. All reunions should be celebrated and I have news, remember?' He picked up a bottle.

'What is it?'

'We'll get to that. I'm making them with gin. I am against vodka martinis on moral grounds. How dry do you like it?' He stood, bottle of vermouth hovering over the measure.

'As dry as you like.'

She sat and looked around the room. It felt minimal and masculine; a pair of cow-print chairs sat on an oriental rug, staring out the window towards Hampstead Heath. She looked up. To the left there was now a mezzanine gallery. He had knocked through the ceiling into the room above. The effect was dramatic and gave the space an abundance of light.

'This room is amazing,' she said, sitting down on a purple sofa.

'Took for ever,' he replied, dropping olives into two glasses. 'I had an affair with an architect. He was a nightmare. Still, I suppose this room was worth it. I rather like the enormous windows. Don't you?' He shook the shaker.

'They're wonderful.'

'Almost there,' he said, pouring the martinis. 'Twist of lemon zest ... and we're ready.' He handed Eleanor a glass and held up his own. 'Well, then. Cheers.' He took a sip. 'Mmm. Perfection. Do you need more vermouth?'

'No, thank you.'

He placed his glass on a side table and sat opposite her, crossing his legs and looking at her as if he might be about to conduct an interview. 'Now then.' He grinned and his eyes widened. 'Where do we even start?'

'I know!' Eleanor laughed. 'We need slides and graphs and pictures and string!'

'Let's do the basics. I am single. *What* a waste!' He clutched at his chest and closed his eyes to feign despair. 'Are you still married?'

Eleanor nodded. 'Yes, to Charlie. You should meet him.'

'Do you think he'd like me?'

'Yes, I do. I think he'd like you very much.'

'Hmm,' Jake pondered. 'I find straight men either want to beat me up or are terrified they'll end up in bed with me. Unless they're terribly confident.'

'He is confident. He's a quietly confident man.'

'How long has it been? Fourteen, fifteen years? An eternity! Are you still in love? Is that even possible?' Jake stared at her.

Eleanor paused. 'I think I'll always love him. He's the kindest man I know.'

'Kindness is quite underrated, don't you think? Costs people nothing, yet so few are capable of it.'

'I had sex with John Farson this afternoon.' Eleanor put her glass down on the table in front of her and knitted her fingers together. 'Goodness,' she said, as if she'd surprised herself. 'I'm not sure I expected to blurt that out.'

Jake shook his head. 'I'm sorry? John Farson? Why on earth would you do that? He's so ... disappointing.'

'Is he? I've always known where I am with him.'

'Are you sure that's true?'

Eleanor paused. 'Yes.'

'Well, I didn't expect our catch-up to get off to quite such an explosive start.' Jake narrowed his eyes. 'Are you having an affair with him?'

'No, not at all. It's a one-off. I don't intend to do it again.'

Jake frowned. 'You make having sex with someone who's not your husband sound like a disappointing afternoon tea at Fortnum and Mason. What's going on, Eleanor?

There's more to this than meets the eye.' He leaned forward and stared at her.

Eleanor cleared her throat. She felt awkward, on the spot, and yet, back here, with Jake, she felt capable of being more honest than she had in years. 'I think I wanted to remind myself of what I am capable of.'

'And you thought having sex with John Farson would help?'

'It might.' She fell silent.

'Is your husband relaxed about you sleeping with other men?'

She shook her head. 'Not at all. I won't tell him.'

'Can you keep secrets?'

'To the grave.'

Jake sat back in his chair, thinking, then leaned towards the side table and picked his martini up. He took another sip. 'I think I need a little more lemon zest.' He stood and returned to the drinks cabinet.

Eleanor placed her hands on her knees. She was startled she had told him but it made her feel unburdened and light.

'It feels odd,' he said, carving a long strip of zest from a lemon. 'Not knowing who you're married to.'

'You'd like him. He can be very funny,' she said immediately. 'And he's dependable, a proper best friend. Uncomplicated. If he was a dog, he'd be a Labrador.'

'Leading around the blind?'

'Yes,' said Eleanor, smiling. 'Leading around the blind.' She smoothed down her top.

Jake turned and looked at her. 'I'm puzzled. If you're so fond of him, why are you having sex in the afternoon with John Farson?'

Eleanor shrugged. 'Everyone who loves dogs longs to run with wolves, don't they?'

Jake watched her as he took a delicate sip from his glass. 'Sorry. I don't buy it. You're not telling me something. That or you wanted to impress me. Did you want to shock the unshockable?'

'Are you shocked?'

Jake laughed. 'Do you know, I think I *am*.'

'Don't read too much into it, Jake. I love Charlie,' Eleanor said, thoughtful and considered. 'Very much.'

'So why sleep with another man? Even *I* know that's a bit odd, Eleanor. There's something else going on. I can smell it.' He sat back down and leaned towards her, his face shimmering with anticipation. 'Will you tell me?'

Eleanor looked at him and smiled, the deep fondness for him flooding back. 'Maybe later,' she said. 'I want your news first.'

'Ah,' he said, sitting back. 'I want no drama. I'm only telling you because you deserve to know and despite everything' – he flapped a hand into the air – 'you're still my favourite person on earth.' He stopped and stared at her. He wasn't smiling. He was reading her face. 'The fact is, I'm leaving Britain. For good.'

'What?' Eleanor stared at him.

'I'm emigrating. To California. I'm hardly here as it is. But now I'm making it official. So there it is. We're back together again and now I'm leaving.' He lifted his glass in salute.

All the joy she had experienced on seeing him again was sucked away and her heart plunged downwards. She sat there without saying anything, her mouth slightly open. She had felt so euphoric to see him again and now she was tongue-tied and at a loss. 'I suppose I should say congratulations.' She shook her head, unable to stem the tears that were coming. 'But I'm not sure I can.'

He reached across and took her hand, a silent, tender moment.

Eleanor wiped at her eyes. 'Sorry,' she said, 'I don't mean to cry. Actually, no. I take that back. I do mean to cry. I lost you. And now you're going away again. Oh, Jake,' Eleanor said, moving towards him. 'I've missed you so much. It's so good to see you again.'

She encircled him with her arms and let her head fall on his shoulder.

'I hope you're wearing waterproof mascara,' he said, stroking her back. 'This shirt is handmade.'

'No,' said Eleanor, 'I'm not. And stuff your handmade shirt.'

Jake reached into his pocket and pulled out an unused tissue. 'Here,' he said, handing it to her. 'Blow your nose on that.'

She blew into it and held the tissue tight in her fist. She leaned into him, closing her eyes.

'I've still got the button you sent me,' she whispered.

'Quite right,' he said, his cheek dropping on to the top of her head.

'I'm still sorry.'

'Don't be.'

'And I still love you.'

'I still love you too.'

Eleanor leaned back and they looked into each other's eyes. 'I hate that you're emigrating. They don't deserve you.'

'I know,' said Jake. 'But think of it this way, I shall die with a beautiful tan and you will never have to deal with hair growing out of my ears.'

'Or your nose.'

'The only tragedy is that I have lived long enough to see hair growing out of yours.'

Eleanor laughed and gave him a soft punch in his belly. He reeled backwards, pretending it had hurt, and fell on to the sofa on his back. 'I die! Adieu!' He opened one eye. 'Why haven't you got children?' He sat up. 'If you had children they could all be named after me.'

Eleanor's face fell. 'We haven't quite managed it.'

'Quite managed it?' Jake frowned. 'It's not like mastering royal icing.' He paused and watched her expression, a thought dawning on him. 'Oh,' he said, pointing at her. 'Eleanor, did you sleep with John Farson to try and get pregnant?'

'No, I ...' She shook her head.

'I don't believe you.'

'Honestly, Jake,' she said, her hand on her heart. 'I didn't.' He stared at her, his eyes wide. She turned her face towards the window. 'I mean, I don't think I even can get pregnant.' Her voice fell away. 'I don't know. Maybe I did. Maybe I just want to know. Am I a terrible person?' Her head fell towards her chest.

'Did you tell John?'

She shook her head.

'I can't lie, Eleanor, it is a bit terrible. But I suppose I understand why you've done it. What on earth will you do if it's worked?'

Eleanor's face crumpled. 'I don't know.'

Jake stood and went to hold her. 'I've made you cry again,' he said, his voice soft. 'This hasn't been a very merry reunion, has it?'

Eleanor shook her head. 'No, don't say that.' She gripped his hand. 'It's so wonderful to see you.'

'Come on,' he said, wiping her cheek with his thumb. 'Let's go lie on the roof. We can put the world to rights.'

There was no moon and, with a cloudless sky, the stars were in abundance. Jake had made her a light supper but Eleanor had little appetite. They were lying on their backs on a dark blue futon, pillows under their heads, plates discarded to one side.

'Have you ever been in love, Jake? Properly, I mean.'

Jake turned on to his side to face her. 'Once. I think. When I was in Morocco I went to work as a studio assistant to a photographer. Basic stuff. People's children. Family portraits. Pictures of dogs. Don't ask. Needs must. I had zero money. Anyway, the photographer was Danish and had the most beautiful cheekbones I've ever seen. I was completely obsessed with him.'

'What went wrong?'

'His wife.'

'He was married?'

Jake nodded. 'I went to live with them. It was probably the closest I've ever come to domestic bliss. I adored them both, really. It was my fault. I got rather jealous and told him he had to choose between me or his wife.'

'Oh dear.'

'He chose his wife.'

'Poor Jake.' She put her hand on his. 'I don't like to think of you being on your own.'

'I'm never on my own. You don't need to worry. Besides, I'll be fine in California. They seem to like me there.'

She let her fingers entwine with his. 'You could stay here. Come and live with me instead. I make excellent lasagne.'

'Now there's an offer. Thank you but I couldn't possibly,' said Jake, his cheek flat against the pillow. 'I'd try and steal your husband. Honestly. I can't help myself. It's like a tic.'

'Well, good luck with that. Charlie's not remotely gay.'

'Of course he's not. He hasn't met me yet.' Jake gave a small, wry smile.

Eleanor smiled back at him.

They both turned on to their backs and looked up into the night sky. A sharp and painful thought stabbed into

Eleanor's mind: was this going to be the last time she saw him? She couldn't bear it. 'Is there anything I can do for you, Jake? Before you go?' Eleanor asked. 'Something you've always wanted?'

Jake lay thinking. 'I'm not sure. I've been to the zoo ...'

'I'm serious. I want you to think of something you have always wanted. However ridiculous. However huge. I want you to tell me what it is.'

Jake let out a deep sigh and stared upwards. Below them, the noise of an occasional car, the distant chatter of people walking. Above them there was no noise, nothing to drown out any given thought.

'I've always wanted to be a father.' Jake's voice was serious. 'It's my only regret. So there it is. Turns out you and I have always been alike.'

She looked at him, her chest full of love and empathy and kindness. She lay her hand on his chest, leaned in and kissed him.

'Thank you, Eleanor,' he said. 'Thank you for coming. It means so much to see you. I've thought so many times about the last time we were together. It haunted me, actually.'

'Me too. I thought I would never recover. Sometimes I wonder if I ever did.'

His thumb caressed the top of her hand. 'I'm sorry I couldn't love you in the way you wanted. But I did truly love you. Do you believe me?'

Eleanor nodded. 'Yes. I do. You're the person who gave me everything.'

'I wish I *could* give you everything.' He looked back up at the sky, his face wistful.

Eleanor stared at him. There was a way he might. She turned the words over in her head for a moment before saying them out loud. 'I want to sleep with you,' she said, her hand squeezing his.

'What do you mean? Sleep with?' He frowned.

'I mean I want to have sex with you. Do you think you can manage it?'

'I'm not sure. I've never slept with a woman.' He sat up. 'I think I feel slightly startled.'

'Think of it as a once-in-a-lifetime experience.' She smiled.

'Eleanor, to sleep with one man who isn't your husband might be considered careless, to sleep with two, on the same day is … bold.'

'Do you think I'm awful suggesting it?' She looked away. 'It's strange. I feel as if I'm hovering up there.' She pointed up at the sky. 'Looking down on myself. Does that make sense? I want a child. I want a child more than I love Charlie. I think I would rather do this, and see if I can get pregnant, than leave him and try to start again. I love him very much. And I'm not sure I could leave him. It would destroy him.'

'And yet you can do this.'

She turned back and gripped Jake's hand. 'But I'm doing it to save my marriage. And if I did have a child, I'd rather have yours than John Farson's.'

'Might be too late for that.' He smiled, gently.

Somewhere across the rooftops a window was open, and as Jake took her in his arms they could hear the soft refrains of Ella Fitzgerald. 'I feel suddenly embarrassed,' he said, his voice tender. 'I'm not sure quite what to do.'

'Just kiss me, Jake. Properly,' she said. 'Let's start with that. Don't worry. I'm not trying to turn you straight.'

'Darling, there's absolutely zero chance of that.' He leaned back and looked at her, his face screwed into an expression of mischievous bemusement. 'Are we actually going to do this?'

Eleanor put her hand on his chest. 'I've always wanted to. Did you know that?'

Jake's face softened. 'No. I didn't.' He paused. 'Maybe I did. Sorry. I could never be what you wanted me to be.'

Eleanor shook her head 'You were everything I needed you to be, Jake. You brought me to life. And you made me feel safe.'

He gave a small, curious smile. 'I felt safe with you too. I still do.'

Eleanor ran her fingers through his fringe. 'And thank you,' she said. 'I never said thank you.'

'What for?'

'For being interested in me, for making me confident, for showing me the way.'

'I did nothing,' he said. 'The loudest person in the room is always the one with the least amount of talent. You were always the star. You still are. Look at you now. You're a proper famous artist. Thank God I'm going to be in California. I'd be behaving appallingly, sitting in Soho, shouting about how I *know* you.'

'Silly,' she said, softly. She looked up at him.

He leaned in and kissed her gently on the lips. It felt soft and sweet and wonderful. 'That wasn't so terrible,' he said. 'Shall we?'

'Yes, let's,' she murmured, and arched her neck back as he kissed her again, just below the ear.

'You might have to tell me what to do,' he whispered.

'You're doing fine,' she whispered back. 'Now stop talking. And let's get on with it.'

Chapter Forty-three

July 1980

Eleanor ran into the toilet and threw up. It was the second time that morning. Beyond the door, she could hear her client, a gossipy columnist who infuriated everyone but was good for sales. Eleanor had been commissioned to paint her, a well-paid job with a guarantee of a spot in the National Portrait Gallery. Eleanor was struggling: she didn't like the woman and now here she was, staring down a toilet bowl.

She flushed and turned to look at herself in the mirror. She was pale. Eleanor turned the cold tap and cupped her hands into the flow, leaning down towards it and splashing it up into her face. She pulled a paper towel from a neat pile then stood, her hands over her face, as the nausea settled down. She breathed out and looked at herself again. It was hard to tell whether this was what she hoped it was or a bout of food poisoning. She'd had leftover Chinese food for lunch. It was entirely possible it was that.

She threw the paper towel into the bin by the door and walked back out into the room. She was painting at the client's warehouse apartment, one of the new developments that were springing up along the Thames, converted wharfs in Southwark that were now all the rage. The client was staring out of the window, one hand on her hip. She looked irritated.

'Sorry,' said Eleanor, walking back towards her easel. 'I feel a bit better now. Hopefully that's the last of it.'

The woman made a show of looking at her watch. 'I'm not sure you appreciate quite how busy I am. You've been in there for the best part of half an hour. What do you want me to do? Paint myself?'

'If you want we can rearrange. I don't mind.'

'I bet you don't.'

Eleanor ignored the snipe and picked up her palette. She always felt uneasy with sitters like this: entitled, arrogant, rude. Columnists who became famous in their own right were an odd breed: poachers turned gamekeepers, more interested in themselves than the celebrities they wrote about. Besides, Eleanor wasn't in the mood. She wanted to get to a chemist before closing time.

The woman took up position. Against Eleanor's advice she had chosen to stand like Botticelli's Venus. There was nothing to be done. That's how she wanted it: she was to be an eternal beauty, a hint of the divine, absolutely full of herself. They had attempted conversation early on but had no common ground. Every name the woman dropped, Eleanor (who didn't own a television) had never heard of. Eleanor was not interested in whose party the woman had been to, whose book launch she was trying to get out of, or what pair of shoes an admirer had sent her as a gift. It was all so unimportant, so insignificant. It was astonishing to Eleanor that anyone could aspire to such a thin life.

The telephone in the corner of the room rang. The woman, heaving another exasperated sigh, stepped out of pose and went to answer it.

'Hello?' She picked up the receiver and walked with it towards one of the enormous floor-to-ceiling windows. 'Of course I know who Sofie Chappelle is. Everyone knows who Sofie Chappelle is.'

She twisted the telephone cord around her forefinger.

Eleanor watched her blankly. She didn't know who Sofie Chappelle was.

'Sorry, no can do. I'm having my portrait painted.' She made it sound as if it was wonderful.

Eleanor thought it was anything but.

'I know. So grand and fabulous. The painter's Eleanor Ledbury. I know, I know. It'll probably be selling for a small fortune. You never know. I might be the new Mona Lisa.'

Eleanor rolled her eyes.

'She's got me posing like Venus.'

Liar.

'No, not the statue with no arms. The Botticelli. No, I'm not naked. She's imagining that bit. I'm rather glad. Means I don't have to be on a wretched diet.'

Eleanor made a mental note to make her look cherubic.

'It's all rather draining. Not allowed to move a muscle. I've been at it for hours.'

Forty-five minutes, actually. And thirty of those involved the artist in the toilet throwing up.

'Look, I can't promise anything, but if they're insisting it's me then I suppose I shall have to try and fit them in. They'll send a car? And back again? Wait. Let me ask.' She turned to Eleanor and held the receiver to her chest. 'What time will we be done? Sofie Chappelle has specifically asked that I interview her and she can only do today.'

'We can stop whenever you want.'

The woman lifted the receiver back to her ear. 'Yes, it's going to be tricky. Look. Perhaps we could do it over supper?'

Eleanor put down her palette. There was clearly going to be no more painting today.

'Great. Tell them to send a car to me for seven.' She walked back to the telephone and dropped the receiver on to it. She looked at Eleanor and tossed her hair. 'Sorry. We're going to have to wrap up. Can you liaise with my PA? She'll arrange another afternoon for this.' She wafted her finger around.

'I don't think we'll need one,' said Eleanor, packing up her things. 'I know precisely what I'm going to paint.'

'Oh,' said the woman, taken by surprise. 'So you don't need me?'

'No,' said Eleanor, looking straight at her, 'I don't need you at all.'

There was a pharmacy on Borough High Street, squeezed between a sandwich bar and a balti restaurant. The smell of curry leaves and coriander was drifting out from a vent and Eleanor was overwhelmed with another urge to be sick. Fighting it, she pushed open the door into the chemist. The bright tinkle of a bell sounded above her and Eleanor was relieved to discover the shop smelled clean and antiseptic.

She'd never bought a pregnancy kit before. Fifteen years of marriage and she'd never missed a period. All the same, she didn't want to tempt fate, so she headed first to the dark blue bottles of milk of magnesia and picked one off the shelf. There was nobody else in the shop.

Eleanor approached the counter. The chemist was a rather short, thin man, balding with a wispy comb-over. His face was pinched, and he was wearing a pair of round tortoiseshell spectacles, a white coat, a blue checked shirt and a brown woollen tie. His name was Mr Colin Sneddon. 'Can I get that, please?' Eleanor pushed the bottle towards him.

He took it from her and rang up the item on the till. 'That'll be one pound twenty, please.' His voice was whispery, his hands soft. 'Will there be anything else?'

Eleanor paused. She wasn't quite sure why she felt embarrassed, but she did. 'And do you have one of those kits? To see if you're pregnant?'

His eyes darted to her wedding finger. 'We have the Prepurex. Would you like that?'

Eleanor nodded. She glanced over her shoulder. She really didn't want anyone else to come in.

Mr Colin Sneddon reached up to a shelf behind the counter, pulled a box down and placed it on the counter. 'Do you know how to use it?'

Eleanor shook her head.

'Don't worry. All the instructions are inside. Very easy. Follow it to the letter. It's quite straightforward.' He stopped and noticed her discomfort. 'Would you like me to put that in a bag?'

Eleanor nodded. 'Yes, please.'

Two hours later, back in Brill, Eleanor sat on the bathroom floor and stared at the picture in her hands. It had six panels with captions: 1. URINE; 2. ANTISERUM; 3. MIX; 4. LATEX; 5. MIX; 6. ROCK 2 MINS.

She dropped the thin piece of paper to the ground next to her and looked at the pipettes, sampling tubes and mixing plate. It all felt very complicated. What if she got it wrong? Eleanor opened the door of the bathroom and stood there, listening. Charlie was downstairs, working. For now, she wanted to keep this to herself. Satisfied she couldn't hear him, she walked briskly towards the stairs, trotted down and made a beeline for the crockery cupboard in the kitchen. Opening the door, she stood up on tiptoes and looked in.

'Where is it?' she mumbled.

'Where's what?' Charlie came in behind her and reached into the fruit bowl for a banana.

Eleanor didn't turn round. 'The little gravy jug. I need it. For a still life.'

Charlie frowned. 'Still life? You haven't done one of those in ages.'

'No, I don't mean a still life. I mean for background dressing. The portrait I'm doing. I thought it might be fun to have a roast chicken in the background. Behind you know who. And a gravy jug.'

Charlie let out a generous laugh. 'Oh, that is good. She'll *hate* that. If she understands it, that is. Here,' he walked towards her, 'let me have a look.'

He stood behind her, one hand on her shoulder, the other holding the banana. 'I can see it.' He reached up and pulled it down. 'There you go,' he said, handing it to her. He took another bite of the banana. 'Shall we have lamb shanks for supper?'

'Yes, OK.' She turned to walk out of the kitchen.

'With colcannon? And carrots?'

'Yes. Lovely.'

'Have we got any carrots?' He continued to call from the kitchen. She heard the door of the fridge open. 'Oh. We've got no carrots.'

'There's plenty of peas,' she called back, walking up the stairs. 'And beans. We've got all those beans in the garden. Go and pick some.'

'Will do.'

That would bide her some time. She slipped back into the bathroom and clicked the door shut behind her.

'Right then,' she said, looking at the gravy jug. 'Let's get this done.'

She had hidden the testing kit in the airing cupboard. She would check it before supper. Charlie had opened a bottle of red wine and was standing in the kitchen, shelling some broad beans. Behind him, a large stainless-steel pot was covered with a tinfoil lid. The radio was on. *The Archers.*

'Want a glass?' Charlie said, seeing her walk in.

She paused. 'Actually, no, not tonight. I fancy some sparkling water.'

'Really? It's a nice one. Rioja.' He nodded towards the bottle.

'Mmm,' she said, hunching her shoulders up. 'I don't know if I ever really like red wine on a hot day.'

Charlie paused, half-shelled broad bean in his hand. 'This is news to me. There's white in the fridge if you'd prefer it?'

'No,' she said, walking to the fridge, 'I think I just fancy some water.'

Charlie smiled and went back to his shelling. He would be happy enough: cooking and listening to the radio. She poured herself a glass of water, then walked through to her studio and out to the terrace beyond.

It had been an unsettled July. Days had begun cool and dull with only the occasional outbreak of sunshine. There had been a lot of rain. Good for gardeners, they said. Eleanor looked out at the garden. There was so much to do. They'd taken on the house but her mother had never been interested in gardening and had let it run wild. Summers were always an explosion of buttercups and ox-eye daisies, heaped corncockles fighting with bellflowers for anyone's attention. It had its charm but left the garden feeling a little ragged and unloved during winter. She would have to do something about it.

Eleanor felt unsettled, excited, terrified. She wanted to be pregnant so very much. If she was, there was no chance it was Charlie's. They'd had a fallow period in the lead-up to that afternoon in London, but not enough so it would be suspicious. She wished she hadn't felt the need to do it at all. She had to cling to what she had told Jake. She was saving her marriage. She believed that with every bone in her body. She clamped her eyes shut. God. She wouldn't even know which one of them was the father. What a mess.

Charlie appeared in the doorway to the studio. 'Almost ready. Do you want to eat out here?' He peered up at the sky. 'Or do you think it might rain?'

Eleanor squinted at the evening sun. 'I think it'll be fine. It's warm enough. Let's eat out here.'

Charlie nodded. 'I'll plate up.'

Eleanor glanced at her wristwatch. The waiting time was over. Placing her glass on the table, she walked back through the house, passing Charlie in the kitchen.

'Just going to pee,' she murmured as she passed him.

She walked slowly up the stairs, aware of every atom in her body: her breathing, the feel of the wooden stairs beneath her feet, the way she gripped the banister, the steady beating of her heart.

The airing cupboard was at the end of the landing, and as she walked towards it she could feel herself already wanting to cry. Was she prepared for disappointment or trouble? She didn't know. She put her hand on the cupboard knob, took a deep breath and opened the door.

She stood there, staring.

At the bottom of the test tube there was a dark red circle, a promise, a declaration, a person not yet known. She was pregnant.

Eleanor's hands instinctively went to her mouth and she clamped them hard against her lips to hold in every last feeling that was screaming to escape.

She was pregnant.

She had to make a choice. There and then. She couldn't go back on it. She couldn't betray it. It was a choice that would be lasting and would bind her for ever. The child would be Charlie's. He would never know.

She wiped at the tears that were coming. She turned round and walked back to the garden.

'Charlie,' she said, stepping back on to the terrace. He was sitting at the table, his mouth full of lamb shank. In front of him was the gravy jug. God, she hoped he'd washed it.

He looked up at her.

'Charlie,' she said again. 'We're pregnant.'

Eleanor knew, in that moment, that she would never see a man more happy.

The choice had been made. It was a burden she was ready to bear.

Chapter Forty-four

Now

Rachel turned on to Old Compton Street and stared down at the scribbled note she'd made earlier. Her hand was shaking. She was nervous.

Coach and Horses. Groucho. The French.

She had rung John Farson's gallery for a second time, this time determined to meet up with him. The message had been the same as before. They had no idea when he might make an appearance and her best bet was to head to Soho and scour the drinking holes.

She'd been to the Coach and Horses and had no luck. She'd asked for him at the bar, but the landlord, an ex-military type with a nose like a pumice stone, had been rather abrasive.

'He's never in the Coach before six,' a woman at the bar had said. She was in her seventies, a relic of a bygone era. 'Try the French.' She was applying a violently red shade of lipstick and staring into a handheld compact. She turned and looked at Rachel. 'Do you know him?'

'Umm, no. Not really. He knew my mother.'

The woman raised an eyebrow. 'I suspect he knew a lot of mothers. Darling,' she said, to the man next to her, 'have you got a cigarette?'

Rachel had pushed her way out on to Greek Street. It was bitterly cold, a weather front coming in from the east. She'd glanced up at the sky and wondered if it might snow. If he wasn't in the French, she'd decided, she'd sit and wait. It was too cold to be wandering about.

She turned on to Dean Street, walked in to the French and stood for a moment to drink it in. It was one of a dying breed: a pub with a personality.

She pulled off her red woolly hat and mittens and ran a hand through her hair. Her nose and cheeks were burning from the cold. She looked around. There were very few people in there, none of whom, on a quick assessment, was the man she was looking for. It was only just past midday. She'd timed it perfectly.

Rachel walked to the bar and pushed herself up on to a tall wooden stool against the wall. Above her were a host of black-and-white photographs, famous patrons, staring out, drinks in hand, cigarettes on lips, wearing suits and ties and an air of world-weariness. She undid her coat. She wouldn't take it off quite yet. It really was very cold.

'Half a Guinness, please,' she said to the barman.

She glanced towards the other people sitting at the bar: two men, both reading the *Evening Standard*, heads down, fingers resting around glasses like parrots on a perch. There was a couple sitting in the far corner. One of them had a map out and was staring at it intently: tourists or out-of-towners, it was hard to tell.

'Cash or tab?' The barman threw down a little cardboard coaster and placed her Guinness carefully on it.

'Cash,' she replied, and reached into her pocket for her purse.

'Two pounds.' The door into the saloon swung open and a blast of cold air blew through. 'Make sure that door's shut, will you, mate?' The barman called across the room.

Rachel looked towards the door. It was a man in his mid thirties, clean-shaven, dark suit. Not who she was looking for.

She gave the barman her money and folded her purse back into her pocket. Her fingers were still cold from walking, despite the mittens, and she cupped them to her mouth and blew on them.

She took a sip of her Guinness and opened the book she'd brought with her. She had nowhere else to go, nothing else to do. She would sit and wait.

He came in, holding a cumbersome roll of carpet. 'Derrick,' he called to the barman, 'can I stick this behind the bar?'

The barman, who was pouring a Ricard, casually glanced in John's direction. 'No, you fucking can't.'

There was no further discussion on the matter. Instead, John leaned the thick carpet up against the bar and waited to be served. He sniffed and scanned the room with the radar-like precision of a man who needs to know if there are any outstanding rounds he needs to honour. Satisfied there were none, he rested his chin into the crook of his thumb and forefinger and waited.

Rachel stared at him. He was very attractive: short salt-and-pepper hair (he still had it all), echoed by a closely cropped soft white beard. He was muscular, tall, with an interesting prominent nose. His eyebrows were still dark, a thick frame for his eyes, which glowered with a dark intensity. He was wearing a tight brown leather jacket and a pale blue scarf knotted about his neck. He exuded sexual confidence. Rachel immediately understood why Eleanor might have been drawn to him. Was this her father?

She closed her book. If she didn't do this straight away, she would lose her nerve. She dropped down from her stool and, picking up her bag, walked to his side of the counter. He narrowed his eyes and glanced at her as she came and took the stool next to him.

'That side not to your liking?'

'Hello,' she said, holding out her hand. 'I'm Rachel.'

Bemused, he took her hand and shook it. 'John.'

'Yes, I know.'

He gave her a puzzled look. 'You're not a photography student, are you?'

'No, I'm not really doing anything at the moment. I used to work in a gallery in Oxford.'

'I've already got a gallery.'

'I know.'

'Hang on,' he said, looking towards the barman. 'Usual please, Derrick.' He looked back at Rachel, who was still staring at him. 'Are you staying?'

'Yes, I am.'

'Do you want a drink?'

'Yes please. Half a Guinness.'

'You've been played like a kipper there, John,' said one of the men glued to the front of the bar, with a lazy smile.

John raised an eyebrow and looked at Rachel again. 'Well, then. Here we are.'

'That's a very large piece of carpet,' said Rachel, nodding towards it.

'I know. I'm not sure what I'm going to do with it.'

'Have you just bought it?'

'No,' said John, with the same bemused look, 'bloke owed me some money. Gave me that instead. Apparently, it's been in his family for years – worth a few bob.'

'You took someone's family heirloom?'

'Well,' said John, rubbing his beard with his hand. 'He did owe me rather a lot of money.'

'Cash or tab?' asked the barman, placing their drinks in front of them.

'Tab,' said John. He took his glass and raised it in Rachel's direction. 'Cheers.' He took a glug. 'Bloody freezing out.'

He licked his lips and turned and looked at her again. 'How old are you?'

'I'm not sure that's a polite question.'

'No, I'm trying to work out how inappropriate it would be to flirt with you. You can't be too careful these days.'

'I'm Eleanor's daughter. Eleanor Ledbury.'

His eyes widened and he leaned back to look at her properly. 'I'll be damned,' he said, his voice lowering to a murmur. 'I'll be damned.'

Rachel watched his face carefully.

'You look just like her.'

'Funny you say that,' she said, 'I never thought I did.'

John looked surprised. 'Hey,' he said, his face growing more serious, 'I'm really sorry. About what happened. About her death, I mean. Read it in the paper. I felt a bit bad, not going to the funeral and that. Wasn't sure if it was right to go. So I didn't.' He took another sip of his drink.

Rachel nodded. She was weighing up when might be the right moment to get to what she actually wanted to talk about. She didn't want to bludgeon him with questions. It wasn't an interrogation.

He smiled at her. 'It's very nice to meet you. I really liked your mum.'

'I know. I've read some of your letters.'

'Letters?' John frowned. 'I don't think I wrote her any letters.'

'Really?' Rachel reached into her pocket and produced the note she'd found inviting Eleanor to supper. 'How about this one?' She held it out. '"I find myself back in London,"' she read.

John narrowed his eyes. 'Fuck, I need glasses. I refuse to get them. It's a slippery slope.' He took the letter and held it at arm's length. He shook his head. 'Can't read it. But it's not my handwriting. Besides, I never write letters. Sorry.'

Rachel frowned. If this letter wasn't from John, then he wasn't J, and if he wasn't J, then she was back at square one again. She reached into her pocket and pulled out the little blue button. 'Did you give her this?'

'What's that? A button?' He gave a small laugh. 'No. I never gave her a button.'

'Or a copy of *The Prophet*?'

'What's that? A newspaper?'

'No,' said Rachel, her heart sinking. 'It's a book.'

John shook his head.

She looked up at him. 'Did you have an affair with my mother?'

He paused and raised his eyebrows. 'Blimey,' he said, leaning into the bar. 'This escalated quickly. I'm not sure how to answer that.'

He looked down at her. There was something pleading in her eyes. Not in a needy, unattractive way, but a raw honesty. He cleared his throat. 'I wouldn't call it an affair,' he said, 'not exactly.'

'But you dated her?'

John squinted up at the ceiling. 'No,' he said, 'I wouldn't say I did.'

'So what happened?' Rachel's heart was pounding.

John paused. 'We just ... liked each other. You know? We just did that thing that grown-ups do. We moved in the same circles.' He shrugged.

'So you did sleep with her?'

John opened his mouth but said nothing, then, 'You know,' he began, 'I'm not sure how to tell this story without it sounding wrong. Because it wasn't.'

'Did you love her?'

John's eyes were fixed on hers. 'No, not in the way I think you mean,' he said.

Rachel blinked and stared down into her Guinness. 'My mother tried to tell me something on the day she died. Something she should have told me a long time ago. That's what she said. I found out what it was and I wondered if it was about you.'

John frowned. 'Found out something?'

'God, it's absolutely *freezing* outside. I can't believe I came out without gloves. John, have you got gloves? You must give them to me immediately.' It was the woman from the Coach and Horses. She wedged herself up against the bar and placed her handbag ceremoniously on the counter. 'Are you buying?'

'Derrick,' said John to the barman, 'glass of wine for Hen.'

Hen licked her top teeth with her tongue, then, noticing Rachel, 'I see you found him. What is this? Why is there a roll of carpet at the bar?'

'You don't want it, do you? It's worth a few bob.'

'I have zero interest in purchasing a carpet from a man I have never trusted in a public house that serves as nothing more than a depository for the desperate, no. Thank you, John, but no.'

'Do you know who this is?' John nodded towards Rachel.

'We met at the Coaches,' said Hen, keeping an eye on the barman. 'Don't be stingy, Derrick. You've got very stingy of late.' She turned back. 'But we haven't been formally introduced.'

'This is Rachel. She's Eleanor Ledbury's daughter.'

Hen's eyes immediately widened and she leaned forward and grabbed Rachel by the hand. 'My darling. My dear darling. Oh! I so adored your mother. The only reason I look forward to dying is the thought I'll see her again. Oh! Come here. Let me hug you.'

Rachel allowed herself to be enveloped. Hen was wearing a rather chunky woollen overcoat, and as Rachel put her arms round her she realised Hen was tiny inside it. 'Let me look at you,' she said, holding Rachel away from her. 'Doesn't she look like Eleanor, John? Doesn't she?'

John nodded.

'I was devastated when I heard. Took to my bed and stared at the ceiling for days. Weeks. Couldn't bear it. We couldn't bear it, could we, John?' Hen let out a deep sigh. 'So horribly unfair. She didn't even smoke. She was the good one who got away.'

Hen let go of Rachel's hand. 'You don't happen to have a cigarette, do you?'

Rachel shook her head. 'No, I gave up.'

'Sensible. Sensible.'

'Here you go, Hen,' said Derrick, passing her the glass of wine.

She took a sip. 'So,' she said, turning her attention back to Rachel. 'What brings you here? Why did you want to see John?'

There was an awkward silence. Hen's eyes flitted between the two of them. 'Ah,' she said, reading the situation. 'I see there has been an exchange to which I cannot be party. How very tantalising.'

'I don't mind you knowing,' said Rachel, undeterred. 'Eleanor had something she wanted to tell me. On the day she died. I've spent months trying to find out what it was. I was consumed with it. Bits and pieces, little clues. It drove me mad, actually. Made me feel ill, and then I found a note she'd written. She wrote that my father ...' Her voice caught in her throat. 'My father wasn't my father.'

'Ahhh.' Hen took a small, measured sip from her glass. 'And you think she wanted to tell you about John?' Her voice was steady, as if she was testing the water.

'I'm not sure. I'm not sure of anything. I found lots of things she'd been given ...'

Hen looked at John and then at Rachel. 'I think I know what Eleanor wanted to tell you,' she said, her face deadly serious. 'But it's not about John. I'm not sure it's right that I tell you.'

Rachel's heart was racing. 'Please.' She gripped Hen's arm. 'Please tell me. I need to know everything. It's the only chance I have. Even if it turns out to be wrong. I know she was in love with someone. Someone whose name began with J. I thought ... I assumed ... it was you.' She looked at John.

'She did love someone else,' Hen said, her voice low and quiet. 'But not in the way you might think.'

'And it certainly wasn't me. She didn't love me at all. You know, Rachel, she loved Charlie very much.' John's voice was kind. 'You mustn't ever think she didn't.'

'But you slept with her? In the summer of 1980?'

John frowned, reaching back into the corners of his memory. 'I might have done.'

'It was nine months before I was born.' She looked up at him.

John took her hand. 'I'm not the guy you want. I had mumps when I was little. I can't have kids.'

'But you slept with her? That summer?'

'There was a last time. It was the day she saw Jake. I remember that.'

'Jake? Who's Jake?'

'Oh my God,' said Hen, staring at her. 'You don't know, do you? You really don't know. Darling. You've met him.'

Chapter Forty-five

Then

May 1984

In the words of Mark Twain: 'Rumours of my death have been greatly exaggerated.' Have I got a story for you. I'll wait to see you to explain all. I shall be in London for the rest of this week. It would be lovely to see you. My tenants in Hampstead are refusing to move out so I'm staying at the Langham. The staff here seem to be under the misapprehension that I am an obscure member of the royal household. In a fit of boredom, I fibbed to the bartender and told him I was Prince William's godfather. It seems to have gone round the hotel like wildfire. Staff keep saying 'Hello, Lord Blair' and smiling at me. It's most disconcerting. I'm too embarrassed to put them straight and, besides, they seem to be getting such pleasure from it. Anyway, you shall have to keep up the pretence and ask for Lord Blair.

Perhaps we should go to the zoo after all? Tomorrow? Midday?

J.

Eleanor closed her eyes and held the letter tight to her chest. It was the first she'd heard from him in years. He'd always been terrible at keeping in touch. He was like a rare bird, appearing when you least expected it. She exhaled with relief. He had always been capable of taking her breath away, pulling the tablecloth out from under her with a flourish. She felt overwhelmed with happiness.

She walked from the hallway into the kitchen, tucking the letter into her smock pocket. Rachel was sitting in the high chair Charlie had made her, elbow on table, crayon in hand. She was forever drawing. Behind her, Charlie was scooping an egg from a pan of hot water. He dropped it into a little eggcup and sliced the top off, buttered a thick piece of white toast and, cutting it into five tall soldiers, placed them on the plate. Picking it up, he sat down at the table.

'Shall I eat these?' he said, picking up a soldier and pretending to eat it.

'No, Daddy,' said Rachel, frowning.

'Are you sure? They're so delicious, nom, nom, nom.'

'No, Daddy!' Rachel put down her crayon and reached for the buttered toast in Charlie's fingers. He let her take it and sat watching as she sucked at the end of it.

'Is that nice?'

Rachel nodded.

'I've had a letter from Jake,' said Eleanor, standing in the doorway. 'He's in London for a week. He's asked if I want to meet him tomorrow.'

'He's back?' Charlie's eyes widened.

Eleanor nodded and smiled. 'Yes, he is. Only for a week.'

'You know, I'd love to meet him one day.' He picked up a small plastic teaspoon and dipped it into the egg.

Eleanor hesitated, but knew she'd have to invite him. 'You can come if you like?'

'I can't. Not if it's tomorrow. I've got an editorial meeting. All day, too.' He pulled a face at Rachel. 'Poor Daddy.'

'Poor Daddy.'

'You'll have to take Rachel,' he added. 'Or we could ask Agnes to pop over?'

Eleanor's chest lightened. 'It's fine. I'll take her with me. We can make a day of it. Go to the zoo.'

'The zoo!' said Charlie, giving Rachel a playful poke. 'Would you like that, little bean? A trip to the zoo?'

Rachel nodded and rammed her soldier into her egg. Charlie smiled and looked up at Eleanor. 'That's the plan, then.' He turned his attention back to Rachel. 'You're getting that yolk everywhere. Where's it supposed to go?'

Rachel pointed to her lips. 'In my mouth.'

He laughed and gave her a kiss on the forehead.

Eleanor watched. He was devoted to her, the best father a little girl could want. Tomorrow, she would meet her real one.

It was a glorious, sunny day. They'd got the train and treated themselves to a ride in a taxi to Portland Place. Rachel sat high on Eleanor's knee, staring out of the window, wide-eyed, pointing at the big buildings, the crowds, the department stores; the imprints of her little index finger dotted the glass, a constellation of wonder.

Eleanor was not nervous. She felt light, the way you might feel if you were walking through a meadow, or staring down at your toes in warm sand. He had no idea what she was about to tell him. It would be wonderful.

The cab pulled up by the Langham and a man in a smart frock coat and peaked cap stepped forward to open the door. Eleanor let Rachel slip down from her lap and, after paying the fare, they both got out and walked up the stairs to the revolving doors in front of them. The hotel lobby was plush, with floor-to-ceiling marble columns, an art-deco-inspired floor and, beyond, an enormous dining room from which the sounds of a string quartet were emanating. It all felt rather grand.

Jake was sitting, his legs crossed, in an armchair to their left. He was reading a book and was dressed in a cream linen suit. He looked well. She hadn't seen him since that night four years ago. From the moment she had made her decision, Eleanor had focused on Charlie, on the family she was making. Jake had been the most important person in her life. Now, that person was Rachel. Eleanor smiled.

'Lord Blair, I presume?' She tilted her head in his direction.

Jake looked up. 'Have you read this?' He waved the cover at her. 'Don't. It's just AWFUL.' He threw it on to the round side table next to him and leaped up out of his chair. 'You look stunning, as ever.' He leaned in and kissed her on the cheek, then turned his attentions downwards. 'Now then,' he said, looking at Rachel. 'Who on earth are you?'

'Tell him,' said Eleanor, encouraging her.

'I'm Rachel,' she said, staring up at him. 'Who are you?'

'I,' said Jake with a flourish, 'am Lord Blair.' He shot a wink towards Eleanor.

Rachel screwed her nose up. 'Silly.'

'Oh no,' Jake said, 'she's on to me already. This won't do. Quick, we must vacate immediately before my cover is blown. Would you like to go to the zoo, Rachel?'

She nodded.

'It's such a beautiful day,' said Jake. 'Shall we walk? We can go through Regent's Park.'

'Yes,' said Eleanor, linking her arm through his. 'That would be lovely.'

***

The park was at its best: flowers were in bloom and the soft scent of just-cut grass made the air delicious and woozy. They'd decided to stop on the way and buy ice creams, tall swirls with chocolate Flakes thrust in at an angle. They sat on a bench watching Rachel as she ran after a puppy, ice cream in hand.

'How long before that falls on the floor?' Jake asked, nodding towards Rachel as she ran back and forth.

'Five minutes, tops,' said Eleanor with a smile. 'Prepare for tears.'

'Well,' said Jake, pulling the Flake from the side of his ice cream. 'Shall I tell you why I'm in London? Now don't panic. This story has a fabulous ending.'

'All your stories do.' Eleanor leaned back. She loved how they slotted straight back, the years evaporating. It was as if she'd only been with him yesterday. She'd missed this.

'So three months ago I was feeling terrible. Not just ill or poorly. TERRIBLE. And my mother – my parents are living in Pasadena – did I tell you?'

Eleanor shook her head.

'They live on a golf course. I can't even. So my mother insists I go and see her doctor. I swear to God he's so old he probably knew people from the Bible.'

Eleanor laughed.

'And he takes a blood sample. Honestly, you should have seen him. It was like watching a hypodermic needle at a rave.' He lifted his hand and shook it theatrically. 'And he calls me two days later and says, "Oh, hello, Jake. I'm afraid you've got cancer."'

'What?' Eleanor's hand went to his, her face etched with concern.

'Wait.' Jake held a finger up. 'Remember there's a big ending. So I go to see him. He says, "Yes, cancer, it's termi-nal." TERMINAL. I go into hysterics. Can you imagine? I then tell around fifty people I am about to die. Everyone's crying. It's appalling.'

'Why didn't you tell me? I could have ...'

'Wait!' Jake stopped her again.

'But did you have treatment? Please tell me you're better. Please.'

'Did I have treatment? No. Eleanor, it's far worse. I never even had cancer.'

'What?'

'So my mother's doddery doctor mixed up my blood sample with another of his patients. Put the wrong label on it. Sent it off to the lab. Results come back. I'm told I'm dying and there's no hope. Other chap is told he's got glandular fever. In a way, I think I'm glad. I got to find out how popular I am. Turns out, I'm *very* popular.' He grinned.

'Hang on. Stop,' said Eleanor, shaking her head. 'So you didn't have cancer. And everyone thought you were dying?'

'Yes. I couldn't bring myself to tell them straight away,' he said with a shrug, 'I was terribly embarrassed.'

'That's the absolute worst excuse I've ever heard.' Eleanor looked away again at Rachel. A puppy was running around her, trying to lick her ice cream. Eleanor turned back. 'Hang on. If you weren't ill, how did nobody else notice? You must have seen another doctor?'

'No! I hadn't. He'd told me I was terminal, remember? So I'd rather melodramatically turned down all treatment. And I had glandular fever. So I was exhausted all the time. It was completely plausible I was at death's door, but then I kept thinking, Why am I not feeling worse? I'm supposed to be dying. If anything, I'm feeling better. So there I am in San Francisco and my parents turn up. My mother has brought everything bar the kitchen sink, thinking she's come to nurse me to my last breath, and months and months go by, and one morning, she looks at me – bear in mind the doddery old fool has told me I've got weeks to live – and says, "Do you think we should get a second opinion?" Off we go. No cancer. Then, wait for it ... turns out he's done it before!'

'Stop it.'

'True. He was almost struck off.'

Eleanor let out a gasp. 'I'm not sure whether I'm ecstatic or appalled.'

'I know. Think of the other chap. He really was dying. Still, I wonder if it was a blessing not to know? Win-win. I didn't die. He died happy. So here I am. Let's call it my Lazarus Tour.'

'Rachel!' called Eleanor, glancing back over at her. 'Don't let the puppy lick your ice cream. No. Not for sharing.'

Rachel turned and looked at her mother but, as she did so, she lowered her arm and the ice cream fell with a fateful thud on to the grass.

'And that's that,' said Jake, watching as the puppy leaped on to it. 'Shall I get her another one?'

'No,' said Eleanor, going over to Rachel. 'I'll give her the rest of mine.'

Jake sat watching as Eleanor wiped the tears from Rachel's cheeks and put her own cone into the little girl's hand. Placated by the new ice cream and reassured the puppy was now busy eating her old one, Rachel carried on running around.

Eleanor returned to the bench.

'You managed it then,' he said, nodding towards Rachel. 'Of course, I'm dying to ask ...' He raised his eyebrows.

Eleanor looked at him and gave a soft smile but said nothing. She needed to do this properly.

'How old is she?' he asked, still looking at her. 'I can never tell with children.'

'She's three.' Eleanor sat down gently next to him.

'Three?' Jake lifted his head and frowned. 'Wait, so she was born ...'

'Three years ago,' said Eleanor, indulging him. 'It's not a trick.'

Jake smiled and gave a small shrug. 'Do you like being a mother? I imagine you're wonderful at it.'

'I like it very much. Charlie and I are very happy.' She paused. 'She's been a blessing.' Eleanor turned and looked at him and took his hand in hers, her eyes springing with tears.

He looked back at her, a little puzzled. 'What's the matter, why are you crying?'

Eleanor took a deep breath. She was trying not to completely lose it. 'I've waited a long time to tell you this,' she managed to say.

'Tell me what?'

She enveloped his hand with both of hers. 'She's yours, Jake,' she whispered. 'You're her father.'

Jake gave a half laugh, as if he couldn't believe what she was telling him. 'Don't tell me that night actually worked?'

'It's true. She's your daughter. I wasn't sleeping with Charlie and the only other person it could have been was John.' Eleanor wiped at her eyes.

'Then how do you know she's not his?'

Eleanor put a hand on his again. 'I saw Hen. You know they're together now?'

'At last.'

'She was trying to get pregnant. Wanted my advice. Turns out John had mumps as a child. Didn't realise it had left him infertile. So that leaves ...'

'Me.' Jake's eyes filled. He gripped Eleanor's hand. 'You're not making it up?'

Eleanor shook her head. 'No. I'm not making it up. You're Rachel's father.'

'Does Charlie know?'

'No. It would break his heart. He's devoted to her.'

Jake held a hand to his mouth. 'I never thought ... God ... this is ... too much. Sorry. Thank you,' he said, his eyes fixed on the little girl and her ice cream. 'Thank you.'

'No, thank *you*,' said Eleanor.

He looked over at Rachel, his face a vision of wonder. Eleanor let her hands slip from his and, as he pushed himself off the bench, Eleanor sat and watched. He walked over to Rachel and took her hand. He was smiling at her, full of joy. Rachel looked up at him; she was laughing, happy, the moment of the lost ice cream instantly forgotten. Jake crouched down and, without asking, Rachel folded herself into him, leaning against his chest as she finished the last of her ice cream. His arm went around her to steady her. Eleanor sat, watching them chatting as if they were old pals. She closed her eyes. Now she had to deal with the hard part.

Another mother had come into the park and was lifting her own three-year-old from a buggy. He was a boy, blond pudding-bowl haircut, red T-shirt and blue shorts, and as soon as his feet touched the ground he was running, punching fists like pistons. Rachel noticed him and gently pulled herself away from Jake to watch him. He had a ball. She looked back at Jake and then ran off to join him.

Jake stood watching her and then looked over at Eleanor on the bench. He was smiling, as if amazed. Eleanor braced herself.

'I don't know what to say,' he said, his voice low and gentle. 'I'm entirely astonished. She's beautiful. Perfect. You must never see me again, Eleanor. I will try and steal her from you.' He sat down, his eyes still fixed on Rachel.

Eleanor put her hand on his forearm. 'I don't think I will be able to see you again,' she began. Her voice was filled with regret.

Jake turned to look at her. 'What? Why?'

'She'll start to wonder who you are.' Eleanor watched him. She wanted to be as kind as possible. She threaded her fingers into his.

'Can't we pretend I'm some uncle or godfather or —'

'We can't, Jake. You know we can't. Charlie can never know.'

Jake stared at her, his mouth slightly open. It was the first time she'd ever seen him lost for words.

'You must never tell,' she said, squeezing his hand. 'Promise me, Jake. I'll never tell her while Charlie is alive.'

He lowered his eyes and looked down at their entwined hands. She had seen him angry, defiant, broken. She had seen him triumphant, dazzling and ablaze. But she had never seen him small and defeated.

'But can't we . . .' he tried again.

Eleanor shook her head. 'We can't.'

'I want things all to myself,' he said, quietly, 'I know that. I'm fun and I'm stubborn but I'm greedy.'

'I know.'

'It's funny,' he said, wiping his eye. 'I've always thought of you as my family. And here we are. A family. She's half of me and half of you. She's both of us.' His voice faded away.

'I mean it, Jake, I won't be able to see you again.'

'I understand.'

They sat in silence, letting the sadness settle. Eleanor knew she was doing the right thing. Choices have consequences and, as much as she loved Jake, she had to protect the relationship Rachel had with Charlie.

'I've got a camera,' he said, reaching into his jacket pocket. 'Would you let me? A picture I can keep?'

'Of course,' said Eleanor.

Jake's enthusiasm rallied. He was putting on a brave face. 'We must have a picture. All of us. Together.'

He stood and approached the mother of the little boy. He showed her the camera and pointed back towards the bench. Eleanor sat and watched as Jake walked over to Rachel. He stood talking to her for a few moments and then took her hand and walked back to the bench. She was glad she had told him. It was done.

'You sit here,' said Jake to Rachel, lifting her on to the bench. 'In the middle. Ready?'

The three of them smiled towards the woman holding the camera, a happy family, on a sunny day in the park.

On the ground, by Jake's foot, his ice cream sat, upturned and abandoned. Eleanor thought about Charlie. She was looking forward to seeing him later, but for now she was happy to be with the two people she loved most fiercely.

Chapter Forty-six

Now

Rachel stared out from the train window. She wished she could dredge up the memory from her past but it was lost to her. She had met her father and she couldn't remember.

Her feelings towards Eleanor were so conflicted she could barely pin them down. On the one hand, she had cheated on Charlie, but, on the other, Rachel understood why. Eleanor had wanted a child more than anything. Didn't the outcome justify the infidelity? It was a secret she had steadfastly kept while Charlie was alive. He never knew. So where was the harm?

If there was no harm, why did it feel so raw, so painful?

She'd rung Agnes, crying, and had arranged to pop in to see her before going on to Brill. She didn't know what to do with this. There was a part of her that felt excited. But the sharp thrill was counterbalanced by a deadening guilt.

When she arrived at Agnes's she found her aunt standing at the window, waiting, her face etched with concern. Rachel fell into her arms, weeping, and allowed herself to be steered into Agnes's sitting room, where a plate of lemon and pistachio biscuits was waiting.

'Have one,' Agnes said, gesturing towards them. 'They're fresh from the oven. I'll make some tea.'

Rachel sat down, sniffling, and glanced around the room. Family photographs were everywhere, the history of their lives played out in silver frames: old school photos of Johnny, front teeth missing; Johnny and Rachel together, spades aloft on a beach; Rachel in a nativity play; graduation photos; shared family holidays, Agnes and Eleanor entwined; Johnny and Francesca on their wedding day; and a new addition – a little picture of a scan, the new baby who was due any day now, tucked behind a silver pot on the mantelpiece. This was who they had been, this was who they were. Families, Rachel thought, are the accumulation of memories. That is what you hold on to.

Agnes came back in, a tray in her hands. 'I'm still in shock,' she said, sitting down. 'So I can't imagine how you feel. Are you absolutely sure?'

Rachel nodded. 'No doubt. There was a part of me that wondered if Eleanor had got it wrong, that it wasn't true. But it is. I'm so glad Charlie never knew.'

Agnes placed the tray down and reached for Rachel's hand. 'It doesn't matter, not really. You know that, don't you? He was the person who looked after you, who never stopped being proud of you. He talked about you all the time, you know?'

'Did he?'

Agnes nodded. 'Any excuse and he'd be Rachel this, Rachel that. Eleanor was the same. Sometimes I used to think the only thing they were interested in was you. You were the great gift of their lives. Everything changed after you arrived. They were happy again.'

Rachel's face screwed itself into a tight knot. 'Crying again,' she sniffed. 'When is this ever going to end? I feel as if I've been crying for months. I don't know. Please tell me she loved him. It's made me doubt even that. Thinking she might not have is killing me.'

'Of course she did,' said Agnes. 'She loved him very much. And if what you've told me is true, that Charlie couldn't get her pregnant, then she would have done it for the pair of them. What would have been the point of telling him? She wanted him to be happy. Is there even an atom of you that thinks Charlie wasn't happy?'

Rachel shook her head.

'A father isn't the act of conception. A father is the person who puts you to bed, teaches you to read, shows you how to make daisy chains, holds your hand in department stores, picks you up when you fall, mends you when you're broken. A father is care and attention and unconditional love. That was Charlie. You had the right father. Never be in any doubt about that.'

'It's so hard,' said Rachel, wiping her eyes. 'I've had such a tough year.' She stared down into her lap. She'd tried so hard to clamber back: an adored father lost to a cruel illness, the emotional turmoil of what should have been her wedding day, finding Eleanor in the lupins, and now this. It was too much.

'I know you have.'

'I miss them so much.'

'So do I.' Agnes pulled Rachel towards her and held her tight. 'Grief is painful, so jarring, but let it come, Rachel. Give into it. Allow yourself to feel it and be kind to yourself while you do. It's the little moments that catch you unawares – something happens and you think, Oh, I must tell Mum – and then you remember.'

Rachel looked over her aunt's shoulder. There was a soft breeze blowing in through the sitting-room window. 'Parents are like trees. You stare at them every day and can never imagine them gone. And then, when they are, it's so odd how you can forget. You can't remember the tree ever being there. But, in a way, they're never gone. They're all here ...' Rachel touched her chest. 'And here ...' She lifted a finger to the side of her head.

'And nobody can take that away. I still talk to my parents all the time. You will too.'

Rachel pulled herself away and, reaching for a tissue, wiped her nose. 'I think it's time I stopped waiting for my past to fix my present,' she said. 'Agnes,' she said, looking straight at her aunt, 'do you think it would be all right if I didn't marry Claude?'

'Oh, thank God.' Agnes threw herself into the back of the sofa and clamped her eyes shut. 'THANK GOD.' She opened an eye. 'I never liked him. Ever. Although this isn't going to be one of those awful situations where I tell you exactly what I think and you change your mind and then we have to silently remember this moment every Boxing Day over cold turkey?'

Rachel laughed. 'No, Agnes. It won't be. Sometimes you have to see what you need in order to work out what you don't. If there's one thing I've realised through all this it's that I will never have with Claude what Eleanor and Charlie had. I don't need him.'

'I will say one thing. Think about Charlie. Think of the man he was, the father he was.' Agnes gripped Rachel's knee. 'Now think about Claude. There's no comparison, is there?'

Rachel shook her head. 'No,' she replied, her voice resigned, 'none at all. I don't know. Oh God. What if what he told me about rehab was true?'

Agnes raised an eyebrow. 'If that turns out to be true, I'll eat my own leg.'

'I know, but ... I need to do this properly. I want to be able to look myself in the mirror. Treat people how you want to be treated and all that.'

Agnes smiled. 'You're your father's daughter, Rachel. He'd be proud of you.'

Rachel stared down into her lap.

'Do you know who the chap is? Your biological father?'

Rachel looked up. 'I know his name. Jake Blair. Did you know him? Have you met him?'

Agnes shook her head. 'Jake Blair ... the name rings a bell. But your mother must have known him so long ago. I'm sorry.'

'Apparently I met him. I don't remember it. But Hen, Eleanor's friend, told me Jake had said he'd met me.'

'What? When?'

'When I was little. Eleanor told him she wouldn't see him again. She never wanted Charlie to know. But he's still alive.'

'Goodness,' Agnes said. 'Are you going to try and find him?'

'I'm not sure. I need to think about that.'

'Well,' said Agnes, patting Rachel's knee, 'let's have some tea. And those biscuits aren't going to eat themselves. Come on, get stuck in.' She leaned forward, picked up a biscuit and took a bite. 'Oh,' she said, her eyes smiling, 'they've turned out very well. Very well indeed.'

Rachel felt exhausted but calm. She'd got a taxi back to Brill – she didn't want to go back to the flat and to Claude – but as it pulled up she saw Claude's car sitting on the driveway. What was he doing there? It was dark and, asking the cab driver to drop her off on the road, Rachel got out and walked to the garden gate. She'd go in at the back. She released the latch, pushed the gate open and walked along the garden path, past the lupin patch where she had found her mother all those months ago. She stood for a moment, remembering the cold chill that had gone through her. Eleanor had wanted to tell her that day. She had to remember that. Perhaps it was better she had found out the way she had? There would have been a row, accusations and the onset of an arctic froideur. At least they didn't have to live with that.

Rachel walked up to the back door and stopped. There was a light on in the sitting room and a soft golden glow was bleeding on to the lawn. Rachel put her hand on the door handle. She stared down at her fingers. She pulled back and quietly walked across the terrace towards the light. The curtains weren't drawn. She stood, hidden in the darkness, and looked in through the window.

Claude was standing in the centre of the room. He was not alone.

Rachel couldn't quite believe what she was seeing. Claude had his arms around another woman and they were kissing. It was Kate Monroe.

She let out a small laugh. She blinked. Now then, she thought, how to deal with this?

Turning around, she walked back the way she had come and decided to go in through the front door instead. She walked heavily across the gravel. She wanted them to know she was coming. She took the key from under the flowerpot and let herself in.

'Hello!' she called out. 'Hello! Claude! Are you here?'

Dropping her bag on to the floor, she removed her coat, listening out for any movement. In the distance, she could just hear muffled voices. 'I hope they're panicking,' she muttered to herself.

She hung her coat on the rail by the door, briefly touching Charlie's and Eleanor's old coats as she did so. 'Come on,' she whispered, 'let's get this done.'

Strengthened, she walked down the hall and through the kitchen, then stepped down into the studio and towards the sitting room.

She pushed the door open. Claude was standing by the fireplace. He looked flustered. Sitting in her father's armchair was Kate Monroe. She looked put out.

'Hello,' Rachel said. She stood and looked at the pair of them.

'I thought you were in London,' said Claude, going towards her to kiss her on the cheek.

'Well, I'm not,' said Rachel. 'What are you doing here?' Her eyes flitted back to the woman. She looked agitated.

'I ... umm,' began Claude, glancing at the woman, 'I was showing Kate round the house.'

'Right,' said Rachel, with a nod. 'What for?' She folded her arms.

'Sorry,' said Claude, shaking his head as if he'd forgotten something, 'I haven't introduced you ...' He ran a hand through his hair.

'No need, I saw everything I needed to see in the garden. I'm glad you were both enjoying yourselves.' She stared at Claude.

'Look, Rachel, I ...' he began.

The woman narrowed her eyes. 'What do you expect?' she started. 'You won't leave. It's monstrous. I don't know why Claude doesn't have you evicted.'

'No, Kate—' Claude tried to stop her.

Rachel frowned. 'Sorry? Have me evicted?' She turned and threw a quizzical look in Claude's direction.

'Rachel, I can explain ...' He grabbed her by the upper arm. 'I think we should talk about this on our own.' He tried to walk her out of the room.

Rachel pulled her arm away and stood her ground. 'No, I think I'm fine discussing it here, with Kate, thanks.' She was like the photo Rachel had seen: smart, wealthy-looking, attractive. 'Have me evicted?'

'Don't pretend you don't know what I'm talking about,' said Kate. 'You are refusing to leave. This is Claude's parents' house.'

Rachel's eyes widened. 'So this is your parents' house, is it, Claude?'

Claude was backing away. 'I can explain ...'

'Can you?' said Rachel, almost enjoying herself. 'I'm not sure you can.' She turned towards Kate. 'I hate to be the bringer of terrible news, Kate, but I'm afraid you've been grossly misinformed. This is not Claude's parents' house. It's my parents' house. It's my house. Wait.' She held a finger in the air. 'Did you know our current status is "about to get married"?'

'What?' Kate shot a look towards Claude. 'What's she talking about?'

'Kate, I ...' began Claude.

'Oh, I get it now,' said Rachel, the penny dropping. 'You've been so keen for me to sell this house, haven't you, Claude? Wanted me to put it in your name for tax purposes. What was the plan? Get me to agree to that and then turf me out? Pay off your debts?'

'No, Rachel, don't.' Claude was frantic.

'His debts? How you have the brass, I don't know.' Kate stood up. 'You got him into terrible financial trouble. You need to take responsibility for that.'

'Wow, Claude.' Rachel turned and looked at him. 'You really are an epic piece of shit. OK.' She walked over to Claude and pushed him towards the door. 'Out you go. That's it. We're done.'

She turned back to Kate. 'And you can get out too. Come on. Out you both go. I'll leave you two to sort your mess out.'

'Rachel, I ...' Claude pleaded.

'No, thank you,' she said, marching them both towards the open door. 'Not interested.'

'What's she talking about, Claude?' squealed Kate, grabbing her bag. 'Why aren't you stopping her?'

Rachel shook her head at them as they stood on the front doorstep, looking in. It was like the clouds had parted and she had perfect clarity. 'I'm so embarrassed for you. Now fuck off, then fuck off again and then, when you've fucked off, fuck off a bit more. Goodbye.'

Rachel slammed the door in their faces and stood there, a smile breaking out on her face. She looked up at her parents' coats. 'What did you think of that? Good, right?'

She bent down, opened her bag and pulled out the Tupperware box Agnes had given her. 'OK,' she said, tucking it under her arm and walking towards the kitchen. 'Glass of wine. I think I've deserved one.'

As she stood, pouring herself a glass, Rachel felt her shoulders lift. She took a deep breath. Finally, she knew – and truly knew – who she was. She was a daughter of a kind man, she was the daughter of a brilliant woman, but more than these things, she was Rachel.

Chapter Forty-seven

Then

Last May, a Sunday

Rachel laid her head on Charlie's shoulder. His breathing was laboured. He'd caught a cold from Eleanor and they were worried he wouldn't be able to shake it off. He was on the daybed in the studio, the doors open into the garden.

Eleanor was out on the terrace, clearing away the lunch things. She looked tired, preoccupied, consumed.

'You'll look after her, won't you,' Charlie whispered.

Rachel looked up at him. 'Mum? She's never needed looking after. Besides, can you imagine me trying? She'd have none of it. She'll be a terrible patient.'

Charlie smiled. 'Yes, she will. But you'll try? For me?'

Rachel put a hand on his chest. 'Of course I will. Not that I'll need to, because you're going to get better.' She sat up and smiled down at him. His eyes were sunken and his skin looked sallow and grey. 'Do you want anything? Cup of tea? Glass of champagne? Dancing girls?'

He shook his head. 'Just.you,' he said, gazing up at her. 'Just you.' He raised his arm and ran his hand through the front of her hair. She leaned her cheek into the palm of his hand. It was soft and warm and comforting.

He gave a small smile and patted her on the arm. 'I think I might have a sleep now. Do you mind?'

Rachel shook her head and looked at her watch. 'I have to go anyway,' she said. 'I've got to meet Claude and pick the canapés.'

He gave a nod.

'And you need to get better. So you can walk me up that aisle. Do you hear?'

Charlie laid his head back into the pillow behind his head. 'I love you, little bean.'

'Love you too.' Rachel leaned in and kissed his cheek. She pushed herself off the daybed and padded out to the terrace. Her shoes were by the table and she sat to put them on.

'Sorry,' she said, as Eleanor piled some plates into the crook of her elbow. 'I should be helping.'

'It's done now,' she replied, not looking up.

Rachel tied her shoelaces and stared out across the garden to the view beyond. The sun was just starting its descent; soft, pink clouds stretched across the horizon. 'Look at that sky,' she said, sitting back. She had a thought. 'It's so beautiful. I sometimes think we should have our reception here.'

Eleanor frowned. 'Please, no. I don't think I can cope with it at the moment.'

Rachel hesitated. 'I didn't mean for you to do it all ... it's just so lovely here. Anyway. It was just a thought.'

'I'm run ragged, Rachel.' Eleanor's voice was weary and defeated. She'd had a lot on her plate: she was caring for Charlie while trying to prepare for another exhibition. 'You don't know the half of it. I know you're getting married, but the occasional thought for someone other than yourself wouldn't go amiss.'

Rachel glanced back at Charlie in the studio. 'Sorry, I ...' Her voice petered out.

Eleanor picked up the condiments in one hand and walked into the house. Rachel watched her go, then pushed herself up and stood at the studio door, looking in at Charlie. He was so weak, it was painful to see.

He opened his eyes. 'Before you go,' he said, lifting his hand. 'I found something.'

She went towards him and took his hand in hers. 'What?'

'It's in the top drawer, over there ...' He looked over at a wooden cabinet. 'Open it.'

Rachel did as he asked and, as she pulled the drawer open, let out a joyful laugh. 'Oh my God, you found it!' She lifted the catapult into the air.

'Go on, go on.' His voice was thin, no more than a whisper.

Rachel smiled at him and turned to look around the room. There was a bowl filled with old corks, a collection from long afternoons, late nights and the occasional random celebration. Taking an empty brush tin, she set it on top of one of Eleanor's easels. 'Right,' she said, coming back to perch on the edge of the daybed, 'let's see if I've still got it.'

She placed a cork in the sling of the catapult and, with a wink to Charlie, she shut one eye, hooked her top teeth over her bottom lip, aimed and fired. The cork flew through the air and hit the tin square on, sending it skittering across the studio floor.

'Yay!' Rachel cried out, and looked over her shoulder to see Charlie grinning.

Eleanor reappeared in the doorway. 'What was that?' She was wiping her hands on a tea towel.

'Dad wanted me to have a go on the catapult.' She waved it in the air.

'I'd rather you didn't do it in here. I've got wet canvases.' She turned and went back into the kitchen.

Rachel pulled a face at Charlie. 'Now see,' she whispered, 'you've got me into trouble.'

Charlie put his hand on her arm. 'It was worth it.'

'Yes,' said Rachel, 'it was.' She looked again at her watch. 'I'm going to be late. I've really got to get going. I'll come and see you next Sunday, OK?'

In the kitchen, something smashed. 'Damn it.'

Rachel stood and went through the doorway to see Eleanor on her knees, picking up pieces of broken glass. 'You've got shoes on, haven't you?' she said, without turning round.

'Yes.'

Rachel looked back at Charlie. His head had drifted to one side.

'Do you need me to ...?' She checked the time.

'No,' said Eleanor, noticing her glance at the clock on the wall, 'you get off. It's fine.'

'I'm sorry if I ...' said Rachel, sensing a certain coldness.

'It's fine.' She dropped bits of glass into a bowl. 'Do what you need to do.'

Rachel picked up her bag from the kitchen table and reached inside for her car key. There was no point saying anything further. Eleanor was tired and overwrought and when this wedding was out of the way, Rachel thought, she could be of more help.

Eleanor tipped the broken glass into the bin and stood still for a moment, arms hanging at her sides. She walked back into the studio, stopping to check on Charlie. There was a breeze drifting in from the garden and, not wanting him to be cold, she took a blanket and placed it over him. She ran her hand across his hair.

'I think I'm going to plant out the lupins,' she said, quietly.

He gave a small murmur. 'Thank you for looking after me,' he whispered.

Eleanor walked away into the garden and, behind her, Charlie quietly drifted to another place.

It would be the last thing he ever said to her. That was the thing about Charlie: he always knew when to leave.

Chapter Forty-eight

Now

'It's a girl!' Agnes was beside herself. 'Can you believe it? I'm a grandmother.'

'Oh that's wonderful news!' Rachel stared down at her phone screen. 'And is Francesca well?'

'Yes! All good! Wait. Here's Johnny. Johnny! I'm FaceTiming with Rachel!'

Johnny appeared. 'Hello, Squirt.'

'Congratulations! How does it feel? To be a dad?'

Johnny grinned. 'Amazing. Wonderful. Terrifying. Little girl too. Guess I'm going to have to step up to the plate. We're going to call her Eleanor. Didn't want to tell you before we knew.'

'Oh, Johnny,' said Rachel. 'She'd have loved that.'

'Eleanor Mark 2. Let's hope she's just as awesome.'

'Yes,' said Rachel, nodding. 'Let's.' It was a second chance, thought Rachel, an opportunity to appreciate her mother for who she was. Not the ill-remembered version Rachel had clung on to, the real one.

Agnes came back into frame. 'We have to go, they're bringing the baby in. I'll call you later! Ciao! Ciao!'

'Bye! Enjoy it! Enjoy every minute.'

Rachel stared down at the blank screen and felt her heart fill. There was something so rejuvenating about a new member of the family, someone she would come to know and love and do anything for. She slipped her phone back into her pocket and picked up the paintbrush.

She'd almost finished the painting. It had turned out rather well: a portrait of her mother, her back to the viewer, surrounded by lupins and lavender, one hand outstretched, the other in her pocket. She was wearing the thin cashmere cardigan she used to wear on summer evenings, and Rachel had painted it so that the bottom corner was caught upwards in a breeze. You could just see the last button. It was the button Rachel had found, all those months ago, the link to Jake Blair, the man who was her father. She touched a small dab of white on to one edge, leaned back and looked at it. That would do. Dropping the paintbrush into a jam jar of dark water, she stood and wiped her hands on the bottom of her smock.

Rachel had wasted so much time on Claude. All that emotional energy burned up on a pyre that wasn't worth it. He had stolen her time to grieve: for Charlie and now for Eleanor. Rachel stood, hands on hips, staring at the painting. It was a full stop to the past. She had been living in the shadow of someone else's life. She had her own skills, her own things to say, her own path to tread. 'Goodbye, Eleanor,' she said. 'Thank you for trying so hard, for protecting me, for looking after Charlie, for giving a damn.'

Rachel had found peace, at last, with who she was, with who her mother was and how her past supported her future. There was one more thing she needed to do and then her recovery would be complete.

She took her phone out from her pocket and wrote a text. 'I got your email. Yes. I can meet you tomorrow. Midday?' She pressed Send.

Behind her, the door into the studio opened. Caspar had been back a few weeks and had rung Rachel to see if she still needed a gardener. She'd invited him back without hesitation. 'All done,' he said. 'I've pruned back all the roses. Don't worry if it looks a bit drastic. They needed it.'

'It's pitch black outside. I didn't realise you were still here. Caspar,' she said, smiling. 'Would you like a glass of wine?'

He smiled back at her. 'Why not? Yes,' he said, 'I would. You been painting?' He wandered in and peered at the canvas.

'There's a story to that,' said Rachel, slipping her paint-smeared smock over her head. 'Perhaps I'll tell it to you later. Shall we open one of Dad's special bottles? I feel like we should. The crates are in the garage. Grab that torch from the shelf. We'll need it.'

'It's freezing out, by the way,' said Caspar, pulling down the torch. 'You'll need a jumper or something.'

They walked through to the hallway and Rachel reached up and pulled down Eleanor's old coat. 'This was Mum's,' she said, smoothing it down. 'I love putting it on now. Still smells of her, too. Just. Any excuse. Old and battered and warm. And not remotely flattering.'

'You don't need anything flattering,' said Caspar, tapping at the torch to check the batteries were working.

Wrapping herself into her mother's coat, they went out through the front door and walked across the gravel to the garage. Caspar stepped ahead of her and pulled open the side door. 'Be careful,' said Caspar, 'you can't see a thing in here.' He turned the torch on. 'Where's the wine?'

'Over there.' Rachel pointed towards a tall shelving unit.

Caspar shone the torch towards the far corner of the garage. The floor was covered in all manner of mechanical flotsam: an old motorbike that Charlie never finished doing up, bits of engine, ancient lawnmowers and crates of nails and screws and hooks and all the other detritus of a do-it-yourself life. 'Here,' he said, holding out his hand, 'follow me.'

Rachel slipped her hand into his. She could feel the dirt between his fingers.

'Watch that,' he said, shining the torch down at the floor and a rather lethal-looking rake. 'I should come in here at some point and sort this all out.'

They stopped by the stacked wine boxes and Caspar shone the torch across them. 'Which one do you fancy?'

'Let's have the Rioja.'

Caspar took his hand from hers and pulled down the wooden box above him. 'How many do you want out? If you carry one and I carry one then I can still hold your hand.'

He stood and looked down at her.

'I've missed you, Caspar,' she said.

'I've missed you too.'

She had been looking forward to seeing him, and now he was here in front of her she felt tongue-tied and hopeless. She wished she had the courage to tell him she'd been thinking of him. Not just casually, or whenever he'd been mentioned, but all the time. She thought of him in the morning. She thought of him when she lay in bed at night. As she stared up at him now, this beautiful, masculine man whose socks were dirty and who didn't care if he got a splinter, she wished that she was brave.

She wanted to sit next to him, in front of the fire on a Sunday, radio on in the background, bellies full from a roast and a few glasses of wine. She wanted to wash his socks and mend the hole in his jumper. She wanted to run her hand across his jawline. She wanted to kiss him. She wanted to stand, mug in hand, on a cold day and watch him fix a fence. It was time to be brave.

'Let's take one each,' she said, her voice confident and calm. 'Then you can still hold my hand.'

They trod carefully back through the relics of her parents' past and back out on to the gravel driveway. The air was biting cold and the sky clear, and Rachel stopped for a moment to look up. 'I love it when you can see the stars. I always look for the Plough and the Seven Sisters and the Crab and Orion's Belt. That's it. I don't know any other constellations.' She gave a small laugh. 'You'd think I'd try to learn a few more. Nope. Just them. Family in the sky.'

Caspar followed her lead and stared upwards. 'Maddest thing I've ever been told: water came here on a meteorite. Did you know that?'

'Really? You mean, here, to earth? It wasn't here already?'

'No. Came from somewhere out there.'

'Hang on. All life on the planet came from water ...'

'I know. We're all aliens.'

Rachel turned and looked at him. 'Is that true?'

Caspar nodded. 'Would I lie to you?'

'No,' she said, smiling, 'you never would.'

'Rachel,' he began, looking down at her, 'I'm not sure I want to wait another week to see you. Can I come and fix the garage up for you? I'm free tomorrow.'

'Tomorrow sounds lovely. I don't think I want to pay you for coming to see me any more. What do you think about that?'

'I feel all right about it.'

'Well, then. Here we are.'

She smiled up at him and Caspar, still holding her hand, leaned down and kissed her. He smelled of bonfires and leaves and crisp winter days, and she felt his stubble on her lips, and nothing felt more straightforward or easy. She squeezed her fingers into his. 'I'm very glad you did that,' she said.

'Can I do it again?'

'Yes,' said Rachel. 'You can.'

In her pocket, her phone vibrated. She'd had a text. She smiled up at Caspar. She'd look at it later.

Epilogue

It was three days before Christmas and Rachel had spent a pleasant afternoon at the Langham with cakes and finger sandwiches and Hen. She made an effort to see her every time she was in London. It was important now. Rachel had found a portal back to her mother's own story. She wanted to maintain the connections, listen to the anecdotes, remember the myths.

Hen was great fun – eccentric and skittish – and Rachel had laughed and sat and listened as if she were a child again, open-eyed and incredulous, to tales of a different time with different people, a magic carpet ride to a world that no longer existed. Afterwards they had hugged and wished each other a merry Christmas and Rachel had stood and watched Hen as she wandered off, a little unsteady, into a sea of last-minute shoppers. She had never done this with Eleanor. She wished she had.

Rachel had come so far. She had found a sense of peace, an acceptance of who she was and where she had come from. It was her life to live and she felt comfortable, but she had one last thing to do.

She pulled up the collar of her coat, walked past All Souls and cut left into Fitzrovia. She was heading to Soho, choosing the back route to avoid the crush. Christmas songs bled out from cafés, and shop workers were wearing Santa hats. She still had a few gifts to get: Johnny and Francesca were coming over to spend Christmas with her at Brill. It would be the first time she'd meet little Eleanor. She wanted to give her something she could love for ever.

She meandered slowly, stopping at the Scandinavian Café for a mulled wine. She was in no rush and sat for a while, staring out at the passers-by, and let her mind settle. She thought about Charlie and how much she had loved him. She must teach Eleanor how to use a catapult.

She glanced at her watch. It was almost six. She pulled out the purse from her pocket and left a generous tip. Office workers were gathering in pubs, the smokers huddled around outdoor heaters. Some were wearing Christmas jumpers, the jolly results of Secret Santa. Everyone was smiling, the holidays were coming and there was an air of goodwill that felt infectious.

She walked down past the Sanderson Hotel and crossed Oxford Street. The crush of people was intense, and Rachel dived right down Dean Street to make her way into Soho. There was a large building site at its end, and she found herself regretful that so many of the places Eleanor and Hen had frequented were now gone. The character of the place was being stripped away, sterilised, the gnarly corners that were once havens for the odd were now chain stores filled with out-of-towners.

Thankfully, a few of the old places were still standing. He'd asked her to meet him for supper at the Soho Diner in Old Compton Street. It was a stylish refurbishment, tables and banquettes around the edges, with a long wooden bar to one side. There was the warm hum of chat and laughter coming from within.

Rachel smiled, took a deep breath and reached into her pocket to hold something tight in her hand. Opening the door, she looked over at the bar. He was there, white hair slicked back, still handsome after all these years. He was dressed immaculately, as if he might be off to the theatre. He was reading a book and, as she looked at him, her mind flashed back to the hotel lobby, all those years ago.

She walked towards him. 'Hello, Jake,' she said, pulling her hat from her head.

He looked up at her, his eyes instantly sparkling. 'Are you who I think you are?'

'I'm Rachel. Eleanor Ledbury's daughter,' she said. 'And I've got your button.' She opened her closed fist to reveal it.

Jake looked down at it, then looked back at her. His eyes were deep and blue and alive.

'Well, now,' he said, with a twinkle, 'what's the longest word you know?'

Acknowledgements

Throughout the book, there are references and quotes to other works of fiction and non-fiction. If you would like to delve further, then here is all you need.

I make reference to an excerpt from a poem that's been sent to Rachel. The poem is 'Going Without Saying' by Bernard O'Donoghue. It's a lovely poem and has been a comfort to me many times.

Jake quotes the late great Samuel Taylor Coleridge as they enter the Ad Lib. It comes, of course, from 'Kubla Khan', a poem Coleridge wrote, aptly, after a crazed night on opium. That poem also mentions Xanadu, which, as anyone knows, is the happiest song to dance around your kitchen to. Go and find it and put it on now. You will thank me.

At the funeral, they sing my favourite hymn, 'Dear Lord and Father of Mankind', written by John Greenleaf Whittier. He was an American Quaker who, by all accounts, disapproved of singing in church. The verses in the hymn are taken from a longer poem by Whittier called 'The Brewing of Soma', which is about the Hindu habit of consuming hallucinogenic drinks to whip up religious fervour.

Agnes finds the book *Brief Lives*, by John Aubrey. It is a work of pure eccentricity and if you haven't read it, you should.

'Bye Bye Love', which appears on the Ray Charles album *Modern Sounds in Country and Western Music*, was written by Felice and Boudleaux Bryant. Its best-known version is by the Everly Brothers. It's also the first song Paul McCartney ever performed on stage and was covered by the Beatles during the *Let It Be* sessions. I chose the Ray Charles version because *Modern Sounds* was enormously popular at the time Eleanor is trying to paint Jake.

The second song from the same album is 'You Don't Know Me'. It was written by Cindy Walker and the first version of the song to chart was by Jerry Vale. The bestselling version of the song was by Ray Charles. It charted at Number 2 in the American Billboard Hot 100 in 1962.

The book Jake gives Eleanor is *The Prophet* by Kahlil Gibran. It's a series of prose-poetry fables and is a beautiful journey through the human condition. If you have never read it, it's an inspiration.

The Mark Twain quote 'Everyone is a moon, and has a dark side which he never shows to anybody' is from his 1935 *Notebook*.

In a letter, Agnes writes about a volume of poetry by Charles Baudelaire, *Fleurs du Mal*. It caused such a scandal when it was first published in 1857 that Baudelaire was prosecuted for insulting public decency and fined 300 francs. Of course, the prosecution made it wildly popular, and Baudelaire included another thirty-five poems in the second edition, published in 1861. Take that.

The title John Farson gives his portrait of Eleanor is 'Virginem Expectatio'. It means Expectant Virgin, of course.

The second Mark Twain quote, 'Rumours of my death have been greatly exaggerated' – or a version of it – was made by Mark Twain in 1897. He was on a speaking tour he had been forced to go on to cover some debts. While he was in London, a rumour picked up speed that he had died. There's some suggestion that an American paper posted his obituary. Twain was asked about it by a London reporter and the famous quote was his response.

I did a lot of research for the sections of the book set in the sixties and I found the following books invaluable:

Never a Normal Man by Daniel Farson
Fear and Loathing in Fitzrovia by Paul Willetts
Dog Days in Soho by Nigel Richardson
Soho in the Fifties and Sixties by Jonathan Fryer
Sacred Monsters by Daniel Farson
Soho in the Fifties by Daniel Farson
The Gilded Gutter Life of Francis Bacon by Daniel Farson

As you'll have gathered, I owe a great debt to Daniel Farson, who meticulously detailed life in Soho when it was still interesting. I have named the character John Farson in his honour.

The other person I have named a character after is Henrietta Moraes. Hen is named after her. She was the muse of the Soho artists of the time, and if you would like to learn about the real Hen, she wrote a wonderful autobiography, simply called *Henrietta*. I have used a few moments from her life in this book.

As for thanks, I would like to thank my extraordinary editor, Emily Griffin, whose laser-beam notes take everything to the next level. It's been a joy working with her. I'd also like to smother my agent, Sheila Crowley, with a confetti cloud of gratitude. She is trustworthy, wise and wonderful. I am very lucky to have her.

And thank you to Georgie, who puts up with me disappearing into my office and not washing my hair and sitting typing with yoghurt down my front. I don't know what I'd do without you.